What Readers Are Saying About *Dark Star*:

"An unvarnished look at sin and redemption, confidently written. *Dark Star* is an impressive debut."—JAMES SCOTT BELL, author of *Sins of the Fathers*

"*Dark Star* is chock-full of suspense, excitement, and intrigue, with a spark of grace. Creston's creative writing artistry weaves together a novel that is cutting-edge evangelism and speaks to our postmodern world today."—GARY LAFERLA, author of *Finding Your Way* and pastor of Calvary Chapel Ministries

"From the very first line of *Dark Star*, I was gripped by the story of Everett Lester. Creston has captured on paper the struggle that lies deep within each of us—a dark longing for power, fame, fortune, and even escape from the past. While many of us may never go to the extremes that Everett does, we certainly are tempted to seek our own way apart from God. *Dark Star* offers not only a wonderful read; it's also a resource that can be passed on to others who are searching for the living Truth."—ANGELA

"Creston Mapes is an exciting up-and-coming novelist, and *Dark Star* is destined to touch the lives of many people—especially those involved with the rock 'n' roll scene. This book has the potential to lead many to a saving knowledge of the Lord Jesus Christ!"—DENNIS

"Exciting. Enthralling. Moving. This novel brings fresh new enjoyment to Christian fiction. *Dark Star* is a thriller you won't want to put down!"—ABIGAIL

A NOVEL

CRESTON MAPES

Multnomah® Publishers *Sisters, Oregon*

DARK STAR
published by Multnomah Publishers, Inc.

Published in association with the literary agency of Mark Sweeney & Associates, 641 Old Hickory Blvd., Suite 416, Brentwood, Tennessee 37027

© 2005 by Creston Mapes, Inc.
International Standard Book Number: 1-59052-472-1

Cover image by Willie Maldonado/Getty Images

Scripture quotations are from:
New American Standard Bible® (NASB) © 1960, 1977, 1995
by the Lockman Foundation. Used by permission.
Holy Bible, New Living Translation (NLT)
© 1996. Used by permission of Tyndale House Publishers, Inc.
All rights reserved.
The Holy Bible, New King James Version (NKJV)
© 1984 by Thomas Nelson, Inc.
The Holy Bible, New International Version (NIV) © 1973, 1984 by International Bible Society,
used by permission of Zondervan Publishing House
The Holy Bible, King James Version (KJV)

Multnomah is a trademark of Multnomah Publishers, Inc.,
and is registered in the U.S. Patent and Trademark Office.
The colophon is a trademark of Multnomah Publishers, Inc.

Printed in the United States of America

For information:
MULTNOMAH PUBLISHERS, INC.
POST OFFICE BOX 1720
SISTERS, OREGON 97759

05 06 07 08 09 10—10 9 8 7 6 5 4 3 2 1 0

For Mom and Dad,
A lifetime of thanks for your patience, generosity, and
unconditional love—and for encouraging me to dream big.

Deepest gratitude to my agent, Mark Sweeney; his wife, Janet; and my editor at Multnomah, Julee Schwarzburg. You three believed in this manuscript early, and for that, I will always be grateful. I'm honored to work with you.

Special thanks to Multnomah's Don Jacobson and family, and Doug Gabbert and family—for reading, enjoying, and getting behind *Dark Star.*

To Kristina Coulter, Sharon Znachko, Chad Hicks, Chris Sundquist, Lesley Warr, and the whole team at Multnomah—thanks so much for your great work.

I am indebted to Joseph Cheeley III for your time and legal expertise.

Thanks to Bern, Min, Vibe, Frank, and Phil for your prayers and support. For your encouragement, I'm grateful to Gary LaFerla, Robyn and Thom Holmes, Richard Brown, Bob Westfall, Ken Malone, Angie Ramage, Calvin Edwards, Paula Kirk, Cecil Murphy, and Dennis Relova.

Finally…thank you, Patty (the steady one). I hope you enjoy the book; you can finally read it now! Abigail, sincerest thanks for your creative input. Hannah, Esther, and Creston—thanks for your patience and prayers while Daddy concentrated on "the book"!

But in a great house there are not only vessels of gold and silver, but also of wood and clay, some for honor and some for dishonor.

2 TIMOTHY 2:20, NKJV

1

It was a glorious blaze, the fire we set. A wicked, glorious blaze. Its flames leapt as tall as we were at fifteen years of age, however tall that was. Dibbs was short, so the flames even went above his head.

We stood like some kind of untouchable demons with our backs to the fire, legs locked apart, and forearms crossed above our heads with fists clenched. Our white-, black-, and red-painted faces were lowered, our eyes staring at the wet, almost freezing Ohio street beneath our booted feet.

As cars approached our black, soldierlike silhouettes and the burning wall of fire behind us, they slowed and turned around to find another way to their part of the neighborhood.

Ah, the power. Adrenaline pumping. Hearts pounding. Fear mixed with fascination.

We felt like gods.

Then we heard the sirens, a bunch of them, coming it seemed from every direction.

We took off, sprinting down the middle of the street in the direction of my house, malt liquor coursing through our bloodstreams, frantically looking for the first sign of headlights or flashing red lights in the blackness.

There. Red lights. Painting the trees in the distance.

Dibbs dove headlong into a pack of thornbushes at the side of the road. I laughed when I saw him stuck in midair, arms stretched out in front of him like he was diving into a pool. He screamed from the pain of the prickers.

I lit down a side road near the city park and did a ten-foot baseball slide through the wet grass up to the base of a big willow tree. Lou Brock couldn't have done it better.

After the first fire truck and squad car passed, Dibbs came thumping down the dark street, his breath pumping steam into the frigid night. "Where are you, man?"

I darted to meet him, and we ran toward my house again, smack-dab down the middle of the street.

Out of nowhere, headlights catapulted toward us.

Next, the screeching of tires as a Dodge Charger's rear skidded toward us. In unison with the stop, the Charger's passenger door banged open and the dome light came on, illuminating my older brother Eddie who was—that night—our savior.

My name is Everett Lester. I've been asked by a New York publishing house to pen these memoirs. The experiences and encounters you're about to read are true, I can assure you of that because I was there for all of it. And the story isn't finished yet.

I am presently seated in a rather sterile courtroom in Miami-Dade County, Florida, at a long-awaited murder trial, portions of which are being shown on major network television.

It's a media circus.

As I write this, mobs of press people with phones, recorders, shoulder bags, and bulky equipment flood court-room B-3. Presiding judge Henry Sprockett, who resembles Dick Van Dyke, has had to settle the movement along the perimeter of the wood-paneled courtroom several times already. The hype is nothing unusual for me—I only wish it came under different circumstances.

Late that night, after our little experiment lighting the road on fire, I distinctly remembered staring at the white sink in my basement bathroom as the black, white, and red makeup swirled down the drain. I simply stared.

Eddie had shown up at just the right moment, as he would many more times during the days of my youth.

What if the cops had nailed you? What would Mom have said? What would my father have done?

The cold fact was, it just didn't matter.

As far back as I could remember, I was going to be somebody. I realized at a young age that I would have one pass at life—and I was going to make it a showstopper. A raging youth, I was brimming with emotion: everything from fear and anger to pride and insecurity. I felt like a big, bad, bodacious thunderhead ready to send out my lightning across the universe. A whole world awaited me out there, and my desire was to take it by storm.

Ever since my older brother, Eddie, sold me his worn-out KISS *Alive!* album for two dollars, I was hooked on rock 'n' roll. My friends—Dibbs, Scoogs, Crazee, and me—had a band called Siren. We played clubs throughout northeast Ohio, from Akron and Cleveland to Canton and Youngstown. We did numbers from bands like Queen, Rush, Bowie, KISS, and Springsteen, plus a bunch of our own tunes.

Early on, promoters came out to see us at bars like the Agora Ballroom, Backstreets, The Big Apple, and The Bank. We were one of the few amateur bands back then to use pyrotechnics in our shows. After several years, we changed our name to DeathStroke. By the time the band was five years old, I was twenty, and we had landed our first record deal with Omega Records.

Blastoff.

Before we knew it we were warming up for stars like John Cougar Mellencamp, Joan Jett, AC/DC, and Pat Benatar. The first record, *DeathWish*, sold 500,000 copies within six months of its release, and we were playing concerts on the road 260 days a year.

It's all a blur to me now. Like a dream. Large bits and pieces— even years—are simply missing, probably never to be recalled.

That was for the better, I was sure.

Miami-Dade prosecutors were having a field day with former DeathStroke drummer David Dibbs, who had occupied the witness stand for the past fifty minutes and was nervous as a cat.

Dibbs looked old now. White beard stubble showed distinctly on his tan face. He wore a light blue, cotton-silk shirt with a pointy collar, no tabs, unbuttoned to his chest; its long cuffs were unbuttoned also. Dibbs repeatedly threw his stringy brown hair off his face, back behind his right ear. He fidgeted with his hard hands and bit at the cuticles of his stubby, calloused fingers. Looked like he could use a smoke.

No wonder Dibbs was antsy. The bulldog, county prosecutor Frank Dooley, had led witnesses to reveal incriminating evidence from the past about Dibbs himself. The drummer had been forced to confess that all of us in the band, except Ricky, used drugs in excess during the heyday of DeathStroke— including marijuana, Valium, hash, cocaine, and heroin.

In reality, however, Dibbs had nothing to worry about. After all, he wasn't the one on trial here.

I was.

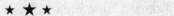

Scores of DeathStroke groupies camped out at record stores coast to coast, awaiting the release of our second heavy metal album, *Our Own Religion*. Needless to say, sales figures went ballistic, with the title track making it to the top of the charts within two weeks. Here are the words to that hit, which I penned, sang, and shared guitar duty on alongside John Scoogs:

> *Ain't no god above,*
> *Ain't no god below,*
> *Ain't no god in the afterlife,*
> *Ain't no god gonna keep me in tow.*
>
> *We got ourselves a new religion,*
> *One we call our own,*
> *It's about taking life by storm, my pilgrims,*
> *It's about livin' in the danger zone.*
>
> *If you want a little taste of heaven,*
> *Come with me after the show,*
> *I'll take you to kingdoms above and beyond,*
> *Anything you have ever known…*

Dibbs, Crazee, Scoogs, and I were gods. Fans worshiped us. We were on a pedestal so high, none of us knew how we got there or how to get back down to reality, even if we wanted to. Any drug, any girl, any meal, any instrument, any car—*anything*—was ours for the asking. Our manager, Gray Harris, saw to that as he took DeathStroke to breathtaking new heights.

By the time I was twenty-three, I was so strung out on booze, pot, uppers, and coke that I often got confused about what city we were playing. More than once I would grab the mike in, say, Baltimore, and yell to the crowd, "How ya doin', Pittsburgh? Are you ready to *rock?*"

I was ugly, all right, spitting into the crowd one night, stomping offstage another. I was drugged out and utterly insensitive. And I made no attempt to hide the fact that I was making time with as many women as possible while we rode the crest of this fame-driven wave.

Dibbs, our drummer and my best friend since childhood, was the first to approach me about my unbridled antics—and my growing dependency on drugs, which was beginning to vex even the regular users in the band.

"Dude!" Dibbs cornered me one night in Vegas between sets. "Clean it up, man. You're a zombie! You're ticking these people off. They're not gonna take this kind of abuse forever."

"Dibbs, chill, man! These groupies would follow us straight to *hell* if that's where we were playing. *Now get out of my face!*"

"Do you hear 'em?" he screamed above the roar. "I'm hearin' boos out there! They made us who we are, Lester. You need to clean up your act. I mean it!"

Clueless was I to the fact that Gray and the boys in the band had been putting out feelers to see if there were any other lead singers who might be able to take my place—a thought I would have both cursed and laughed at, had I known.

It was during this period that I started getting the letters from Karen. Don't get me wrong, we got thousands of letters each day from fans, not to mention hundreds of flowers, gifts, clothing, hotel room keys, and other strange paraphernalia. We also received death threats from angry parents, suicide notes from strung-out teens, and hate-filled letters from so-called Christian community leaders.

Amidst it all, Karen's notes stood out. Part of me passed them off as the fanatic obligation of some wigged-out cultist. But another part of me—a very tiny, unreachable part buried beneath layers of steel and stone—wanted to cling to the words like a suffocating person clings to oxygen, as if they were life itself.

Dear Mr. Lester,

  Unlike most of the mail you receive, this is not a fan letter. I am not a fan of yours, but I would like to be your friend.
My name is Karen Bayliss. I am sixteen years old and live in
Topeka, Kansas. Most important, I am praying for your salvation. I will not stop praying for you. It is my desire for you to
surrender your life to Jesus Christ and for you to lead your
following of fans to Him.

  You will hear from me often. Until next time, may the
Holy Spirit begin to draw you to Himself.

  Sincerely,

  Karen Bayliss

No return address, no phone number, nothing. Just a crooked
gray postal stamp on the envelope confirming that it came from
Topeka.

**Prosecutor Frank Dooley was a piece of work. Thick, dark
brown hair, not one out of place. Dark blue suit with a white
hankie sticking up out of the breast pocket. Long face. Always
tugging at his sleeves out in front of him, making sure about
three inches of white cuff could be seen, as well as two big
gold cuff links. His Southern drawl was as thick as Coca-Cola
syrup; every word had at least two syllables.**

**"Your Honor," he said in response to an objection from
my attorney. "It is my intention to make it crystal clear to you
what kind of individual we are dealing with here. Everett
Lester has been a troubled soul since the day he was born, and
I am simply asking the witness, who has been a lifelong
friend, to answer some specific questions about Mr. Lester's
youth."**

Judge Sprockett pinched at his protruding Adam's apple and overruled the objection.

"So then, Mr. Dibbs, is it true that the defendant, Everett Lester, was excessively violent as a boy?"

"I don't know if you would call it *excessive*. Boys are—"

"Mr. Dibbs," Dooley interrupted, "is it true that Everett Lester had three large pet piranhas when he was a teenager?"

"Objection Your Honor," said my attorney, Brian Boone, almost laughing. "What could having a few pet fish possibly have to do with—"

"Overruled. I'm going to humor you, Mr. Dooley, but let's make this quick."

"Mr. Dibbs," Dooley zeroed in on the witness, "is it true that Everett Lester had three large pet piranhas when he was a teenager, and that friends would pile into his basement bedroom to watch these flesh-eating creatures devour live fish and mice, and even rats?"

"Yes..."

"And is it true that Everett smashed mailboxes, shot guns at street signs and picture windows, set roads on fire, and tipped over cars with the help of friends?"

"Pellet guns. He used pellet guns, not real ones."

"That is not the question, Mr. Dibbs. The question is, did Everett Lester destroy mailboxes, shoot at homes, set fires, and roll automobiles?"

"Well…yes."

"And is it true that when you and Everett Lester were boys, he was known to sell drugs?"

"At times, yes, but his family—"

"Steal cars?"

"Yes, but you need to—"

"Sleep around?"

"Yes."

"And beat the living tar out of other boys for even looking at him wrong?"

Shaking his head and looking down, as if he were being disciplined, my old best friend managed one more yes, and Dooley was done with him.

2

As it turned out, the band members in DeathStroke did not kick me out of the group. It wasn't that I quit the drugs or alcohol, but over the years I built up such a tolerance that I was able to perform while flat-out stoned.

Besides, my compatriots were not about to get rid of their cash cow. They realized my popularity was the major factor in the success of DeathStroke. I was not only the group's charisma, but also the musician who had written the lion's share of our top hits. For their own good, my "buddies" chose to dance with who brung 'em, even though they were watching me disintegrate in the process.

Our third album, *Deceiver,* sold more than the previous two albums combined, going platinum in one year. At that stage of my life, I had everything anyone in the world could want. Between the income from concerts, records, gift sales, and endorsements, all four DeathStroke band members were millionaires. Imagine it—I was only twenty-four.

I was bewildered to find that, although powerful, those seven figures did not bring contentment. I always needed more; I *yearned* for more. More drugs, more booze, more women, and especially more power and recognition.

Coincidentally, it was during the *Deceiver* era that I started interacting with a popular West Coast psychic named Madam Endora Crystal, whose profound insights were said to have helped Hollywood celebrities, politicians, pro athletes, and Fortune 500 executives. Oddly enough, Endora resembled the mother-in-law witch by the same name from the old TV show *Bewitched*—red hair and all.

Endora lived in LA. I met her at a party thrown in Burbank by friend and actor Robert DeBron. During the bash, Endora performed ten- to twenty-minute psychic readings with any partygoer who chose to do so in a private study. I didn't participate simply because I didn't think it would have looked cool; I never wanted to appear like I needed anything from anyone.

It was well known in celebrity circles that Endora stunned people with her remarkable insights and accuracy. She was said to have uncanny psychic, medium, and channeling powers to explore the past, communicate with the dead and higher powers, and accurately predict the future.

At the party, Endora told me she was intrigued by me and would love the opportunity to do a reading. As the days went by following the party, I couldn't get her off my mind. So when we played LA several months later, I arranged for a limousine to pick her up and bring her to the Ritz-Carlton, where we were staying.

Our first private meeting blew me away. The woman knew details from the past that I never would have recalled, and she exhibited knowledge about personal matters that would have gotten anyone's attention.

She spoke of an older brother who loved me very much, yet while cloaking himself with a mask of happiness and success, was dreadfully troubled and dejected.

Obviously, she referred to Eddie, who had a high-pressure job in New York City, a tempestuous marriage, and three teenagers who regularly cursed him to his face. My heart felt dark and heavy, my stomach almost sick, when she told me Eddie would be wishing for his current problems in the years to come when he'd face what she termed a "long run of bad luck."

The oldest brother, Endora said, was the loyal one in the family, the model child. That would be Howard, still residing in northeast Ohio with a wonderful wife and three delightful children—and still taking care of my mother, Doris, who now lived with Howard's family.

Next, Endora spoke insightfully about my only sister. "This one has chosen to travel a different path," she said. "I'm feeling you are bothered by this new direction she has taken." After a moment of silence, she smiled. "But do not worry. It's going to be okay. Good things lie ahead for her."

Mary was four years older than me. After raising two boys and steering through an ugly divorce, she had become, in her words, a "born-again Christian." And yes, I was concerned. Every time I talked to her, she quoted the Bible to me. She wrote letters loaded with Bible verses. We argued about religion. She insisted Jesus Christ was the *only* way to heaven. I thought she had joined a cult.

"I've traveled the world, Mary!" I would yell into the phone. "I've seen more religions than you've seen movies. You can't tell me that the people I've seen worshiping their gods are going to hell! It's too small, Mary. If there is a God, He's got to be bigger than the one you're describing."

"Let's not argue, Everett," she would say. "We have such little time to talk." I was always traveling, and she had a new life in a small city in southwest Ohio. It was good to hear Endora tell me things would work out well for Mary. She was a kind person, and I hoped the best for her.

When we neared the end of that first session, Endora's countenance became disturbed as she tapped her long, black fingernails on the table between us.

"There is a dark cloud that, unfortunately, still hovers over you, Everett," she said with her eyes closed. "I sense something…missing in your life. I feel a heart, beating fast—very fast. Hoping. Wishing. Trying… There is warm water; it is dark and perilous. You are fighting to get through, to find what's missing…"

A tear actually slipped out the far corner of Endora's purple-shaded eye. And with that, *BAM*, it was over. She raised her head quickly and opened her eyes, as if to draw a line to stop what was happening. To separate herself from the emotion of it.

"That's enough," she said coldly, shaking slightly, and beginning to rise up as she spoke. "We'll cover more next time."

From that moment on, the forty-eight-year-old redhead named Endora Crystal became my personal psychic. I started her out on a retainer of twenty thousand dollars a month, plus expenses, to be at my beck and call. She traveled with us as often as possible, and when she wasn't touring with our entourage, she was within reach by phone.

The combination of my secret insecurity, constant drug abuse, and Endora's profound knowledge about me, my background, and my behavior led me to lean on her daily for encouragement. I trusted Endora, and soon she became kind of a spirit figure to whom I could run with all my problems.

If I was uptight after a show, drunk, empty inside, mad at the world, or bitter about the past, I would call her, no matter what time of day or night. Often, I would wake up in the morning with an aching feeling in the core of my stomach, and I'd phone her before my feet even hit the floor.

Endora had a way of drilling into my head that I was more than a rock star. She believed I had been sent "from the gods" to lead millions of people to the truth about life itself.

"The fact is, dear Everett," she said to me on many occasions, "there are *many* gods. I believe you have been chosen to reveal to society that *all* gods are good. It's obvious you yourself are a god. And people must be free to choose whatever god they want to serve: Apollo, Zeus, Buddha, Athena, Everett Lester—or even themselves!

"This truth will allow people to live freely. Do you see, Everett? No more guilt. No more condemnation. No more fear of judgment or damnation! And Everett, they must know that when they die, they will immediately live again on the Other Side—and possibly even be born into the world as a new baby or even an animal, a new personality. It's an unending cycle. Do you see? And it can be glorious, if you can just convince people. And you have the power, Everett Lester. You have the following…"

My attorney, Brian Boone, was small, quiet, and smart. A Harvard Law School graduate, he knew how to listen; and when he did speak, it counted. Brian was not intimidating in stature. Well under six feet tall, he had sandy brown hair, a friendly face, and a calm demeanor. He was one of those people some would describe as "comfortable in his own skin." I liked that about him.

Ever since I named Brian as my lead attorney, speculation ran rampant, not so much about his capability, but about the fact that he was a complete unknown. Naturally, because of my celebrity, everyone assumed I would be buying and building another Hollywood "dream team" of millionaire attorneys who would—legally or some other way—find a way to win.

But I didn't want the hype or the overkill. Instead, I wanted Brian Boone. This sure-footed, no-name Ivy Leaguer had served as legal counsel for DeathStroke well before the Endora Crystal case reared its ugly head.

Brian was a true gentleman and one of the coolest customers I'd met. Working with him briefly in the past, I admired how he used his informal, subtle style as a courtroom tactic, which made him uniquely effective. At times he would appear innocent and almost gullible, somewhat clueless to what was going on around him. But then suddenly, he would strike like a blood-sniffing shark with some brilliant revelation.

As my trial approached, I had told him to surround himself with all the legal assistants he needed to present my case with honesty and clarity. He did so by hiring four of his closest Harvard buddies. And we were on our way.

Today, Boone wore a dark gray suit. His jacket rested on the back of the chair beside me, as he stood in front of the witness stand, shirtsleeves rolled up.

"A great deal has been said about Everett Lester's character during this trial, and over the years in the media," Boone explained in his cross-examination. "Mr. Dibbs, you have known Everett since the two of you were children, growing up in the shadows of the smokestacks and refineries in Cleveland, Ohio. How would you describe him as a youth?"

Dibbs straightened his slight posture and rolled his hard hands. "Everett was the best friend anyone could have. I...I was a nobody growing up. Unpopular. Unnoticed. But Everett didn't care what other people thought. He was real. He would do anything for me, back then and now. Deep inside, there's always been a big heart."

"What was his home life like?" Boone strolled in front of the jury box with his hand on the wood rail and his back to Dibbs.

"Tough." Dibbs shook his head, looking down and holding in the emotion. "Everett's old man, Vince, was a maniac. Heavy drinker. Hardly ever around. Disappeared for weeks, staying with other women. And he was strict. He would...hurt Everett. But his mother, Doris, worshiped his father. She didn't put a lot into the four kids, just lived for

Vince. We always thought, if Vince died or left or something happened to him, Doris would just curl up and die."

"You used the word *maniac* to describe Vince Lester," Brian said. "That's a pretty strong word. What exactly do you mean by that? What made him a maniac, in your eyes?"

My head lowered slowly, the strength rushed out of me, and the backlog of string-tight emotions crept up to my eyes. The voices in the courtroom faded as I remembered…

Summertime. I was learning to drive. Mom had gone with me once in the station wagon, but she worked the pedals, and it was still all brand-new to me.

This humid July evening, I pleaded with Mom to take me again. Dad had been home from work on the line at the rubber plant for several hours. He entered without a word, pulled the shades in the family room, and began hitting the sauce. As he sat staring at the square, wooden TV, its glow bathed his hard, sweaty face in blue, and I didn't think he heard a word of the pleas I was making to my mom…until he stood up.

"Let's go," he said, tossing me the keys from his black work pants and gliding through the swinging screen door, drink in hand.

I looked at my mom, she shrugged, and I darted for the Ford.

But my joy was short-lived.

Dad insisted I do everything while he observed from the passenger seat. Nervous, I started the car—twice, resulting in a horrible grinding noise and a slap to the back of the head; not a drop of Dad's drink spilled.

Pressing the brake pedal hard to the floor, I tentatively shifted into reverse to back out onto McGill Avenue. With no help from the old man, I hit the gas—too hard. The Ford cata-pulted backward, bouncing straight across McGill and into the Salingers' front yard.

I panicked, literally feeling the heat of my father's wrath as he cursed a string of expletives, fumbled his drink, and scrambled to reach across for the brake with his booted left foot. But I was determined to make things right.

Having temporarily taken my foot off the gas to stop the madness, I reapplied it to what I thought was the brake. But it wasn't the brake. And we did not stop.

Instead, the Ford roared to life again, lurching backward, turfing the Salingers' front lawn, and barreling smack-dab into the front porch of their two-story Colonial.

Then we stopped.

Without missing a beat, my father turned the car off, got out, circled to make sure no one was hurt, and made a beeline for the driver's door. With rage in his eyes and his face dripping with perspiration, he reached through my open window and, his hands shaking violently, fumbled for my seatbelt, flicked it open, and extracted me through the window. As kids on bikes and neighbors on porches watched, I was kicked and beaten all the way back across McGill, up our driveway, and into my house.

By the time DeathStroke finally made the cover of *Rolling Stone*, I was twenty-seven. As usual, I was the centerpiece of the photo, wearing tight black leather pants, no shirt, and a brown, full-length mink coat. At the time, my head was completely shaved, I wore a silver hoop in my nose, and readers could clearly see the many dragons, serpents, and other dark tattoos that marched across my chest and arms and crept up the back of my neck.

Writing this memoir, my editor asked that I give more details about my personal appearance at this stage of the book. To answer that, all I can say is that my look fluctuated a great deal during that era.

The *Rolling Stone* cover caught me at a muscular stage when I had been working out regularly with a personal fitness trainer. At other times, however, when I was too doped up to do anything but perform, I guess you could call me just plain skinny. As for attractiveness, women used to say my dark eyebrows and solid jaw gave me a rugged, handsome look. But now I realize, people will say—and do—anything to get close to a rock star.

Scoogs, Crazee, and Dibbs surrounded me in the *Rolling Stone* shot but were dressed tamely compared with me. It was always that way. Our publicist, Pamela McCracken, knew it was my flamboyant personality that sold, so she showcased me whenever and wherever she had the chance.

By this time, the relationships between us band members were strained, to say the least. We practiced, recorded, and performed together but virtually never socialized anymore. Things became so tense and fragmented that, in many instances, only one or two of us would take the official DeathStroke jet to various tour cities while the others hopped their own private planes at the last minute. To be honest, I was most often the one left to travel alone.

Naturally, a lot of our problems centered around selfishness. We each wanted the spotlight and credit for the band's success. That problem grew in magnitude over the years.

Lead guitarist John Scoogs's guitar specials got longer and longer, as did Dibbs's drum solos. This bothered me immensely, because I didn't think their talent warranted such lengthy exhibitions, and I didn't like how it dragged things out. Plus, I believed the fans lost interest during those long stretches. Even Ricky Crazee, our bassist, wanted to write and sing more songs, but in my mind, the skill just wasn't there.

As for me, I just wanted to stay in the fast lane, party, meet women, and build my life as a megastar. The attention validated me. The approval of people met a need deep inside me, or so I thought. Because I wrote and sang all of our top hits, I just knew *I* was the reason DeathStroke continued to skyrocket in popularity.

Of course, we all knew that if we wanted to keep the coin flowing in, it was our job to make it look as if everything was peachy between us; Gray Harris made that clear.

Our fans wanted to see us jamming in unison onstage, hamming it up in photo sessions, working together in the studio, and complimenting one another in press interviews. So, come hell or high water, that's what we did, because each of us needed to keep the dream alive.

DeathStroke was why we existed, and there was no way we would allow it to be some faddy, flash-in-the-pan rock group. So, I guess you could say we became very good actors.

How did I get off on this tangent? Back to the *Rolling Stone* piece. Here's the interview I did with *RS* feature reporter Steve Meek. Remember, it was 1991, and I was twenty-seven at the time:

Steve Meek (*Rolling Stone*): This is a new look for you, the shaved head…

Everett Lester (DeathStroke): Yeah, how do you like it? We were in Atlanta last week, and Elton John's hairstylist got hold of me.

SM: Tell us, many people assume you are the very backbone and essence of DeathStroke. Would this group fall apart if you departed?

EL: *(laughing)* We're a team. We work well together. My style has contributed, I won't deny that. But DeathStroke wouldn't be DeathStroke without us four original guys.

SM: Your music and lyrics can be somewhat heavy at times, even depressing. Do you agree?

EL: Yeah, sure.

SM: Are the songs designed that way?

EL: The songs reflect who we are and what we're feeling. Some are depressing, some are upbeat and fun… Hey, that's life, isn't it? A roller coaster.

SM: It's been said that you had quite a tough childhood.

EL: I'm not making any excuses for our music, if that's what you're getting at. I mean, our popularity speaks for itself.

SM: Indeed, your popularity has soared. In fact, I don't think I've ever seen a band take off as DeathStroke has. Did you ever imagine you'd be such a universal star? Is this something you knew you wanted to do, as a kid?

EL: When I was young, I knew I couldn't live an average life. In many ways, I was frustrated. I knew that I had to either do something radical or I wouldn't be around long. I had to break out. Music was the escape.

SM: Some of your albums and lyrics have carried an almost outspoken, anti-religious theme. Why is that? Have you had bad experiences with religion in the past?

EL: I believe way too much emphasis has been placed on God in our country. Who has seen God? What has He done for me lately? What has He done for you? Jets fall out of the sky. People starve. Children are kidnapped. Earthquakes, floods, and disasters waste millions of lives. Where is God? I mean, get real. People talk about our show being a sham, a circus…but the biggest sham of the ages is the one about a supposedly loving God.

SM: Wow, that's heavy. You sound bitter.

EL: Call it what you want. I've just had it with this *(expletive deleted)* about God. If He was really in charge, things would be different…

SM: How so?

EL: What is this, *CHURCH?* Haven't you got any other questions?

SM: Okay… *(pause and shuffling of notes)* Let's talk about the *Armageddon* album. On this project, from start to finish, it seems that you are making a plea for people to follow you. You're making a statement that you have the answers to life's problems, almost as if you were kind of a chosen leader. Comment on that.

EL: Don't look too deeply. The bottom line is, there's freedom in our music. People who are hurting find release in our records, because they reveal truth. There's a part of each of us that just needs to cut loose. Our records let you cut loose and be who you are.

SM: All of your records have parental advisories. They advocate adultery, drugs, sex, and violence. Does it ever concern you that—?

EL: You don't get it, do you? There ARE no rules! My rules are as good as anyone's. Look at our following. DeathStroke has *millions* of fans around the world. We're millionaires. If we're so bad and so anti-religious, why hasn't this big bad God struck us down by now? Why are we so popular?

SM: I can't answer that.

EL: There is no God. *That's* the answer… *We* are the gods.

· · ·

SM: You and drummer David Dibbs grew up together and were best friends, is that right?

EL: Yep. Really all the guys in DeathStroke grew up in the same neck of the woods, the rock 'n' roll capital of the world—Cleveland, Ohio.

SM: What was your childhood like?

EL: My family lived in a tough neighborhood on the east side. My dad was gone, working or drinking, most of the time. My mom raised us four kids.

SM: You were the youngest?

EL: Yeah, with two older brothers and a sister.

SM: Are they happy memories?

EL: *(long pause)* No.

SM: What would you change about your childhood, if you could go back in time?

EL: I would have had one! I would have gone on a picnic. I would have heard my mother or father say, "You did well."

SM: That's touching. Well, you have certainly done well, monetarily. Tell our readers, when did you and David Dibbs start the band and how did it happen?

EL: One day we were all together at David's house—me, him, Ricky, and John. We sat around, talking about life and school and how we were all kind of outcasts. We weren't jocks; we weren't brains; we were nobodies. And we decided to start a band, right then and there. I guess we associated that with becoming popular.

So, Dibbs borrowed his mom's station wagon, and we all piled in and drove to our favorite music store in downtown Cleveland. It was a blizzard outside and pitch dark by four in the afternoon. We barely made it there. Together we went in on a Les Paul, a few drums, and a mike. The owner, a good friend to this day, let us put the stuff on lay-away. We built our own amps in Scoogs's garage, and that's when the magic started. The band was originally called Siren.

SM: Rumor has it that you and Dibbs are not close anymore, what can you say about that?

EL: Don't believe everything you hear. Hey, no doubt, we've been through a lot together. Let's face it. When you hit it big like we have, it's hard to keep your sanity. I think our success has made us all a bit crazy and scattered.

SM: Are you happy?

EL: *(pause)* No.

SM: But you're a world-renowned star!

EL: *(long pause)* A dark star.

SM: What would make you happy?

EL: I don't know. *(pause)* Maybe death.

. . .

SM: Word has it that you have your own personal psychic. What is that all about?

EL: What do you mean, "What is all that about?" You wouldn't understand until you had to wear my boots for a while.

SM: I'm not saying there's anything wrong with it. Even Nancy Reagan was said to have had some kind of astrologist…

EL: When you're in the limelight twenty-four hours a day, when you're on the road all year, you don't know who your friends are anymore, and you can't tell the difference between reality and fantasy some days. So, ya know, you like to think you can turn to someone who can provide stability.

SM: A lot of people would respond to that by saying, "Stability? In a psychic?"

EL: My response to them would be, "Take a flyin' leap." You try bein' Everett Lester for a day.

SM: Several years back you were engaged to actress Liza Moon. Then suddenly the wedding plans shut down. What happened?

EL: Man, you've really been through my garbage. *(pause and a long groan)* Liza and I decided we were both too busy to get hitched. She went her way and I went mine—which is what I'm about to do right now. *(He gets up and exits. Interview over.)*

Dear Liza. What did we have? Was it just a relationship built on drug highs and glitz, designed to arouse public attention? Or was it a forever friendship that I threw away? It all seems like just another bad trip.

Were we really together? You backstage while I played the Pontiac Silverdome and Madison Square Garden? Me in the wings as you accepted your Oscar? It's all a cloud of smoke. A mirage.

I dated the brown-eyed brunette Liza Moon on and off for three years. During that time, I was in another world. I lived for Liza. She was funny, upbeat, sophisticated, and *gorgeous*. Always smiling. Never taking anything too seriously. Constantly accepting me and my rowdy shenanigans.

After the Oscar for her lead role in the hit film *Bed of Mourning*, she changed. How could she not? Stardom throws your ego into overdrive and takes over your system. Stardom ruins people. Your head fills with helium, and your pride carries you away.

Liza, who formerly never touched drugs or alcohol, became a freebasing cocaine queen. Everyone in the industry, including me, watched her fall. Her appearance and personality were never the same once she started the habit. The whites of her shining eyes turned to red, and her beautiful personality shriveled. She began using tons of makeup to cover the dark circles beneath her eyes. She became sickeningly skinny due to anorexia. The light that used to beam from Liza Moon had been snuffed out—and so I left her, just like every other woman I had ever met.

3

The only constant in my life, besides Madam Endora and the endless number of shows we played, were the notes and letters that showed up every now and then from Karen Bayliss, the young lady from Topeka, Kansas.

She continued to write, just as she promised. It had been years now. And for some reason, I wanted to read what she sent. Don't get me wrong, I wasn't interested in her God, and she was not about to "convert" me to religion. I was interested in *her*. I mean, she wasn't even a DeathStroke fan. She hated our music and everything we stood for. Yet she kept writing and sending little gifts. I was curious. What made Karen Bayliss tick?

I instructed Jeff Hall, our fan club guru, to forward Karen's mail to me.

I still have the note she wrote after she read the *Rolling Stone* interview…

Greetings again, Mr. Lester,

Do you realize you are loved today? No, I'm not talking about the temporary love your fans give you. It will be gone in a few years. I'm talking about God's love. Christ's love for you. He willingly was beaten, spit upon, and nailed to a tree to forgive your sins—and mine.

You see, I'm just like you, a sinner. I may not have committed the sins you commit, but I've committed others that you probably haven't. We're all in the same boat, the whole sorry world. We all need to know and realize and believe that Christ took our sins to the cross with Him and we carry them around no more! We're free, because He paid the penalty for us and rose again to give us new life.

I read the interview you did in *Rolling Stone* recently. Your outbursts against God don't worry or bother me. Instead, they show that your insides are stirring. You are searching for something. What is it, Mr. Lester? You have everything this world has to offer. I guess it just proves that the Beatles song is true—money can't buy you love. Can it?

God is love, Mr. Lester. That is truth. And the truth shall one day set you free, along with millions of your fans. I pray for you many times each day.

Sincerely,

Karen Bayliss

P.S. Take care and remember, there's a love awaiting you that's more powerful than any drug you've ever tried!

The courtroom was completely hushed when the testimony of David Dibbs continued, and I felt every piercing eye.

"Everett's dad played head games," Dibbs said. "That's the best way I can describe it."

"What do you mean by that?" asked Boone.

"Everett could never measure up. Never. Every once in a while he would do something good, maybe score well on a test or help out around the house. Like he was reaching out to his parents, testing them to see what their response would be. I believe he tried to love his dad. But Vince would just tear him up."

"Can you give an example?"

"Yeah, for one, Vince would actually slap Everett, kind of jokingly. He would just slap his face again and again real quickly, laughing, egging him on. In his own demented way, I really believe he meant to hurt Everett—physically and mentally. It would humiliate Everett, because Vince didn't care who was watching. In fact, sometimes I think he did stuff like that on purpose when others were watching, just to embarrass him. I know it frustrated Everett."

"How do you know?"

"He would turn red and hold back the tears. Sometimes it would outrage him, and he would be on the verge of striking his dad, but I never saw him do that. I think Vince would have killed him."

"To your knowledge," pressed Boone, "did Everett's father abuse him physically, beyond what you've told the court today?"

"Objection, Your Honor." Dooley groaned, standing up. "Does this really have relevance in the case we are here to deliberate?"

"I think it does. Overruled. Answer the question, Mr. Dibbs."

"I saw the type of things I just described, the slapping sessions, quite often. And Everett would show up with bruises on his face and arms all the time. We all just assumed Vince was beating him, but I never discussed it with Everett. That's something I regret. He kept it all inside."

Dibbs was right. I felt like I was hemorrhaging inside back then. There was no such thing as love in my world, and I began to hate its concept. So I covered my bruised heart with a ready-to-fight exterior, and I covered the bruises on my arms with my first tattoos.

The years that followed after the *Rolling Stone* cover were like a dream. Unlike other fad groups that flash like a nova for a few years and fade away, the popularity of DeathStroke continued to soar.

We had become a group with longevity, a dynasty. With gold and platinum albums, TV appearances, a movie, and our own line of DeathStroke action toys and clothing, I couldn't keep up with all of the income, taxes, or business interests. I hadn't tried for a long time. Gray Harris handled all that, using a financial firm in New York to manage my personal holdings.

By the mid-nineties I was in my early thirties and getting tired and impatient doing the same old shows night after night, year after year. I kept trying to get the guys to speed up the tempo of the songs to finish the sets quicker, and that would throw off the lyrics, which came across slurred. But the DeathStroke fans kept coming, their numbers kept growing, and the cash registers kept ch-chinging.

My head was no longer shaved. Instead, my curly, dark brown hair now hung past my shoulders. I had remained quite trim for my six-foot-two-inch frame, simply because I was more interested in drugs and alcohol than food. The dozens of tattoos and body piercings—which snaked and curled their way from my ankles up to my neck—had made me look dirty and scarred.

Yes, drugs triggered my bad behavior, but it was more.

I was not only scarred on the outside; I was scarred within. I had not pleased my parents. My life brought them no joy. I really never felt accepted. The close family ties some of my childhood friends enjoyed were only fiction to me, and as I got older, I began to view such fairy tales with disdain and resentment.

But fame and fortune would heal my wounds, I was sure. Popularity and power were the pinnacle of life itself. If the whole world knew me and I had more money than I could spend, those would be the keys to life. Strike it rich and the contest would be over, right? The game of life would be won.

Not so fast.

I had everything—*everything*—the world craved. I didn't deny myself one tangible thing or any pleasure. If I was on the road in New Mexico and had a craving for spaghetti with brown sauce from the New York Spaghetti House in Cleveland, I would have it flown in. If I was lonely and wanted a female companion or two, groupies were lined up everywhere; I simply took my pick.

Yet, it all turned out to be futility—like chasing the wind.

Where was the real contentment and lasting joy?

I was mad!

I had worked hard to get where I was. I *deserved* peace and happiness…so where were they?

I couldn't buy them.

My frustration reared its ugly head in my music and lyrics. My apathy was reflected in the coldness I showed toward our fans. I vented my lack of fulfillment onstage by smashing microphones, guitars, and amplifiers—and by stirring fans into furious frenzies.

One afternoon in San Antonio, Texas, after our sound check, I was describing my discontentment to Madam Endora Crystal in a cold, concrete-block dressing room backstage. Endora, wearing a leopard-skin top and black skirt, sat amid a cloud of her own cigarette smoke on a white leather couch. Having taken off my T-shirt, I plopped down on the folding chair next to her, wiping the sweat from my face and neck with a large white towel.

"I've had it, Endora. I'm sick of the road; I'm *sick* of the band—I'm ready to bail. This is not cutting it for me anymore."

"Everett, let me ask you a question," Endora said patiently as she sat up to pour me a shot of whiskey from the makeshift bar on the coffee table in front of her. "What *would* make you happy?"

"I don't know." I swore, throwing back the drink, which barely burned my throat. "Maybe I need to go out on my own, cut a solo album...start a new band. I don't know, but *something's* got to change."

"Why don't *you* change, Everett?" said the intriguing redhead whose dark brown, almost-black eyes seemed to penetrate my mind like laser beams. "You want to be happy, right?" Endora filled my glass again. "Accept the praise of the people. They are blessing you every night. They are here to worship you. Receive it. Bask in it. This will give you the renewal you long for."

Without a word I hoisted another shot of Jack Daniels and helped myself to one of her long menthol cigarettes.

"Your popularity was planned by the gods," she said soberly, looking deep into me. "Your fans are crying out to you with adoration. Realize that you are accepted and loved—and enjoy it! Monumental things await you down the road, my dear. I know, because—"

"But you know the fans, Endora. They just want—"

"I've told you before, Everett, you are here, *you exist*, to help people—potentially millions of people—overcome their discontentment with life and their skepticism about death."

"How am I supposed to do that? I'm no preacher; I'm a musician."

"Oh, but you're wrong, young man. In a way, you *are* a preacher. You are on a mission from the gods."

I smirked, continued to wipe my sweat off, and pretended I wasn't interested.

"People *will* listen to you; they'll do whatever you say. I see it every night from behind the curtains in the wings backstage. The gods have given you the charisma to—"

"Endora! Don't brownnose me like everyone else. I hired you to be straight with me, to cut through the lies, to be the one clear voice. All the others just want my money or to be able to say they've been with me..."

Endora leaned forward, rubbed her cigarette out in the silver ashtray, and put her hand on my knee.

"Everett," she said quietly, "you have the power—the supernatural power—to send people home from your concerts *different people*, literally, different people. Do you realize that?"

I didn't say a word but instead tapped a small amount of marijuana into the thumb-sized bowl of the small silver pipe I found amid the junk on the table in front of me. Lifting the lifeline to my mouth and lighting the bowl with Endora's red lighter, the small nest of weed lit up hot orange, a few seeds crackling and popping as I took the smoke deep into my chest.

"If you don't believe me, test it. During a show. Test the waters. I dare you. See how much power you really have."

"Endora, you're weird, you know that? You're always talkin' so spiritual."

She tidied up the coffee table a bit, contemplating before she spoke. "The father and mother gods are loving beings who want *all* people to have joy—and the afterlife. I don't believe in hell and damnation. It's not true. I've communicated with too many people on the Other Side. I've *heard* from those who were supposed to have gone to hell. They've assured their families, by speaking through me, that they are okay. Everett, the dead are still involved in our lives!"

"How do you *know* that for a fact?"

"I've talked with them! Just like you and I are talking." She pointed a long finger at me. "I believe *all* people can reach the father and mother gods, simply by growing in knowledge. Look at yourself, for instance. If you would begin to get a grip on the fact that you *will* live another glorious life after you die, you would set yourself free. You would have a whole different view of life."

"You're saying I'm not going to hell?"

"Of course not!" she said with a smoker's laugh.

"You don't know what I've done."

"Yes I do," she insisted, almost joyfully. "Everett, there *is* no hell.

Only good awaits us. Don't you see? When we understand that there is life on the Other Side for all of us, it frees us up to have liberty in the here and now. *That* is the message you have been chosen to deliver. This is real. Why else do you think we've been brought together?"

The mixture of pot and booze was creeping up on me.

"Something's going to happen at tonight's show," she said suddenly, shifting in her seat and not making eye contact for a moment. "That is how the spirits will prove to you that they are moving with power in your life and prompting you to do as I say."

And she was right.

Late in the concert that night in San Antonio, I treated our fans like slaves, just pushing them to see how far I could get them to go. The next day's *San Antonio Gazette* quoted me as yelling these words to the crowd that night: "Hey, San Antonio, it's gettin' hot in here. And you know, if we're not careful—ha, ha—we're gonna burn this place to the ground! C'mon. Light it up…"

And they did.

The fire started slowly in about the thirtieth row on the floor as we ripped into our newest hit, "InSINerator." We had seen small fires before, but as fans began to throw chairs, clothing, and alcohol into the flames, it flared and spread rapidly. The panic that ensued caused a stampede to the exits. Thirteen people were hospitalized in the mayhem, one girl almost suffocated to death, and I'm certain many more went home injured and frightened.

Drugs helped me completely block out the fire in San Antonio along with all the other bad press. I didn't check on any of the fans who were hurt, and I didn't worry about getting into trouble with the law over what happened. We *were* the law. And we never had to look back, because the money and power behind DeathStroke got us out of every jam.

You've got to understand, the band members in DeathStroke were so drugged up and busy rushing from city to city, we didn't have the time or memory to care. We were separated—purposefully isolated—

from the results of things like fires, destroyed hotel rooms, skirmishes with the law, and relationships with fans that turned into lawsuits.

An aging Gray Harris served as our gauntlet, handling all the bad press, defusing the accusations, and settling the lawsuits out of court, behind the scenes so we didn't have to get involved. That's why he was paid seven figures.

When former lead guitarist John Scoogs was called to the witness stand, Miami-Dade prosecutor Frank Dooley tugged at his cuffs and licked his chops.

Scoogs looked good. His black hair was still long and in a ponytail, and he was clean-shaven. He had put on a much-needed few pounds since I last saw him and wore black jeans, a white mock turtleneck, a khaki sport jacket, and dark sunglasses. Hmm. Someone else must be dressing him these days.

Dooley's questions covered much of the same ground he'd already been over with other key witnesses. Scoogs confirmed that, yes, I had my own "personal psychic." Yes, I did a lot of drugs. Yes, I was known to become violent at times, both onstage and off.

But the next series of questions Dooley pursued began to hit a nerve with me, Scoogs, and, I was sure, the jury.

"Mr. Scoogs," Dooley said, taking his time, scanning his notes. "How well did you know Edith Rosenbaum, also known as Madam Endora Crystal—Everett Lester's personal psychic?"

"Fairly well," Scoogs said quietly. "She often traveled with the band, so she became a friend."

"And where exactly would Madam Endora stay when she accompanied DeathStroke on the road?"

"She had her own hotel room, just like each of us did. Our traveling show got so big, we eventually needed thirty or

forty rooms at each stop to accommodate band members, tour managers, publicists, staff, and people like Endora."

"I see." Dooley approached the witness stand. "Specifically, Mr. Scoogs, do you recall a stay at the Four Seasons Hotel in Charleston, West Virginia, in 1995 when a discussion ensued between Madam Endora and Everett Lester that centered around the topic of Mr. Lester's father, Vince?"

Closing his eyes as if searching the past, Scoogs said, "I remember several conversations like that."

"Yes, but do you recall specifically the time I'm referring to in Charleston when Endora attempted to convince Mr. Lester that she was hearing from his dead father?"

"I…may recall something like that."

"Well, Mr. Scoogs, why don't you stretch your mind a bit and tell the court what you *can* recall, precisely, about that conversation." Dooley tugged at his sleeves.

After staring down at his hands for what seemed like minutes, Scoogs cleared his throat and looked squarely at the prosecutor. "When Endora caught up with us at our hotel in Charleston, I remember her saying to Everett something like, 'I've been walking around all week long with this energy.' After jockeying around for a long time, she finally got around to telling Everett that the spirit of his dead father had been trying to communicate with her."

Instead of a loud uproar, I heard a great deal of movement all at once in courtroom B-3. People shifting positions in their seats. Papers ruffling. Equipment moving.

"Was this good news or bad news, in Mr. Lester's opinion?" questioned Dooley.

"Bad," Scoogs answered almost before the question was finished. "Everett's old man was taboo. Too many scars from the past. Vince didn't want much to do with Everett when he was alive, and Everett definitely didn't want to communicate with Vince from the dead."

"So, what happened?" Dooley strolled toward the jury.

"Endora was very serious about this whole topic, very emotional. She told Everett, 'I tried and tried to block Vince's spirit from coming through, but he persisted.' Everett was mad. He didn't want Endora messing with his past."

"And so, what ensued from there?"

"Finally, she gave in. She said Vince's spirit talked to her and made it completely clear that he was okay on the Other Side, and that he apologized to Everett."

"How did Everett Lester respond to this?"

Scoogs shrugged. "He was ticked."

"How ticked?"

Silence.

"I must remind you, Mr. Scoogs, that you are under oath, and perjury is a felony offense punishable up to—"

"You've got to understand: Endora had problems. She had some totally weird beliefs. I felt like she took advantage of Everett's drug addiction, trying to use him to accomplish her own agenda. She would—"

"Mr. Scoogs." Dooley stood on his toes. "Can you *please* just answer my question? How mad was Everett Lester that December night in Charleston, West Virginia? Did he or did he not threaten Madam Endora Crystal's life?"

"He did, but he was bombed out of his mind at the time."

"What did he say to her? 'I'm going to stab you'? 'I'm going to shoot you'? What exactly was his threat?"

"He said something like, 'Endora, if you ever mention my father again…I'm gonna kill you…'" His voice trailed off with the last words.

Dooley raised both eyebrows and nodded a pompous "I told you so" to the jury. "I have no further questions for this witness."

★ ★ ★

After the fire and stampede in San Antonio came another eventful tour date, the Weekend Music Jam at Arrowhead Stadium in Kansas City. We were the headline group among a bunch of other bands. I had just flown in on my jet and was whisked by limo to the makeshift dressing rooms in the bowels of the stadium.

As usual I was greeted immediately by the short and bouncy Tina Drew, our tour coordinator, who was surrounded by sound people, roadies, promoters, journalists, makeup artists, production managers, and publicists. Tina grabbed my arm and led me past scores of fans who had been herded into special roped-off areas designated especially for those lucky enough to have landed backstage.

As I was ushered past the squealing, reaching fans—a scene I had experienced hundreds of times before—one young lady caught my attention. She stood quietly along the front of the rope, wearing white jeans, sandals, a red short-sleeve knit shirt, and sunglasses that sat atop her shiny blond hair. Her arms rested casually at her sides, where I noticed she held a Bible in one hand and a long-stem yellow rose in the other. I guessed she was twenty-something.

I moved my sunglasses down on my nose to get a better look, but Tina rushed me along toward the dressing room door with a gold star and my name on it. In we went to another small room that looked the same as the last dozen. It featured a small couch, several chairs, a refrigerator stocked with Molsons, several bottles of booze, and a dressing table and large mirror, which was bordered with yellowish lightbulbs. Flowers, presents, cards, and food trays were situated throughout the room.

I grabbed a Molson, lit a Salem, and dropped onto the couch, hoisting my legs up over the side, not bothering to read any of the cards or well wishes from fans stacked in front of me on the coffee table.

By now, fans all looked the same; they were like trees walking. I questioned their motives and feelings. Sometimes I viewed them as wild animals, just wanting a piece of me. At other times, they seemed to care for me genuinely, and I tried to do the same for them. Relationships were a confusing issue for me.

Charlie LaRoche, a friend, employee of the band, and longtime drug supplier, would soon be around to set me up for the weekend. I longed for more of the good hash he'd found recently, and it wouldn't hurt to score some coke while he was here, either.

Who was that babe? I picked at some of the hors d'oeuvres on the coffee table. *And what the heck is she doing toting a Bible in here?*

Within the next hour, Charlie came and left, as did Gray Harris, who had come to check up on his golden boy. Still in my street clothes—which consisted of torn jeans, a white V-necked T-shirt, and black Doc Martens—I was determined to check out the fox with the Bible when I went for the sound check. But when I passed by where she had been standing, hesitantly acknowledging the screaming fans along the way, she was gone.

I would not see Karen Bayliss again for five or six years, but somehow she managed to get this note under my dressing room door that weekend in Kansas City, along with the yellow rose she had brought…

Hi, Mr. Lester!

Do you find it at all intriguing that I, of all people, would be selected by Kansas City's KCFX radio as the winner of two backstage passes to your Weekend Jam concert? I don't even listen to that station, but a friend, who knew I've been praying for you, told me there was a contest—so I entered.

God is behind everything, Mr. Lester. There are no coincidences. The Bible says He has made everything for its own purpose. I am convinced you were made for His purpose. My prayer is that you will surrender your life to Him and allow Him to radically use you for His kingdom, just as He did the apostle Paul (you can read about him in the book of Acts—New Testament).

I did not stay to see the show because I don't care for

your music (no offense!). But I do care about you, your peace
on earth, and where you will spend eternity. Jesus said,
"Come to Me, all who are weary and heavy-laden, and I will
give you rest. Take My yoke upon you and learn from Me, for
I am gentle and humble in heart, and you will find rest for
your souls. For My yoke is easy and My burden is light"
(Matthew 11:28–30).

Are you still hungry for more, Mr. Lester? Jesus can give
you real bread—the bread of life. Do you still thirst for something to quench what's missing in your life? Jesus is waiting
to come and give you Living Water. I know, because I have
drunk of Him and will never thirst again.

I'll write again soon. Until then, may the one almighty
God draw you.

Sincerely,

Karen Bayliss

Of all the…what is this chick's game?
The letter angered me. But it intrigued me at the same time.
How did she get back here?
Unlike all the other hell-raisers who were after me, this Karen had
no interest whatsoever in my music, my money, my body, or my stardom. Why was she pursuing me? *Why bother?* My very existence was
designed to insult people like her—and their so-called God. Yet, she
drove all the way here just to drop off a rose and a note.

It was almost as if it wasn't her at all writing the letters or standing
there along the rope. She was like an angel sending messages from
God. And her words shot a tiny ray of light through the soupy fog that
was my disturbed life.

When I read her letters, I heard Him calling me.

But I ignored the letters and disregarded Him.

I stuffed them all away in the dark attic of my mind, along with all
the other baggage—and then I had another drink.

4

We were in the process of recording our ninth project, this time at The Groove recording studio in Santa Clarita, California, when I got word that Liza Moon was on her deathbed in Dallas. She had been filming her latest movie on location near the Lake Fork Reservoir in Sulphur Springs, Texas, when a crew member found her unconscious in her trailer.

Gray Harris quickly arranged for a limo to take me to the airport and for the DeathStroke jet to get me to Texas. I was determined to see her before she died.

Liza's mother, who was seated outside room 306 at Charlton Methodist Hospital, saw me but made no acknowledgment as I passed her and tapped on the wide wooden door.

After a few moments, Liza's older sister quietly opened the door, gave me a quick half-smile, motioned me into the room with her eyes, then tiptoed back to her sister's bedside.

Liza was a ghost of the woman I had once known.

"She overdosed," said Liza's sister, staring at her sibling's ashen face, closed eyes, and cracked lips.

"What are her chances?" I asked, knowing she couldn't possibly live.

"Not good. I'll leave you alone with her if you want."

"Yes."

When the door to the room clicked shut, I pulled my chair close and touched the fingers of her cold, thin hand. That was the only skin I could find amid all the tubes and tape.

Her appearance upset me. I could see the bones in her face and hands. Her skin was drawn tight against her forehead and cheekbones. The white bedsheet lay smoothly over her, as if there was but a wisp underneath.

Where had Liza gone? This did not look like the same person.

I slipped back in time to the late-night, after-show limo rides and dinners, to the parties and shows, to the long walks and talks. I remembered her at her Hollywood townhouse, wearing faded jeans and oversized sweatshirts with her long brown hair flowing out the back of her Dodgers cap.

"What's happened to us, Liza?" I whispered, surprising myself with the tears that followed, not able to remember the last time I had cried.

We were supposed to be on top of the world, but we had hit the slimy depths. We were supposed to be on easy street, but it was difficult to make it through the day. We were rich, but we didn't have anything of value. We were somebody—and we wished we were nobody.

Liza used to get a kick out of hanging with the band. Everyone liked her. Every guy wished she were his. She was a bright star in an often dark world. And she was the only person I had ever really opened up to about my past and about the failed relationship with my father. He and Mom had met Liza several times. They liked her. To them, she was one of the few things I had ever done right.

Slowly, my sorrow melted cold, like wax drying.

Look at her.

I wanted to smash the equipment that kept her alive.

LOOK AT HER!

I couldn't stay any longer.

Had to run.

"God, why would You do this?" I hissed.

Standing, I took one last look at her and blew out the door, not looking again at the family and friends lined up in the chairs along the hallway.

Gray and the band didn't hear from me for days. The recording session at The Groove stopped in midstream. Liza died two days after I visited her. I did not attend the funeral in California but instead plunged into a weeklong drug binge at my high-rise in Manhattan.

Somewhere near the tail end of the stupor, I flipped through the channels on my TV and saw a thin, elderly preacher addressing a large congregation in Atlanta.

"Listen to me," he insisted. *"Our world is full of sin. That sin nature has been passed down to you and me from Adam and Eve. If you want to know why bad things happen to good people, why tragedy comes unexpectedly, why our world and our country are in such disarray...the answer is sin. It's in you, it's in me, and it's got to be dealt with. Listen, Jesus died to forgive you, right now, wherever you are, whatever you've done. He desires to come into your life and to make His home with you..."*

Those were the last words I remember hearing before pulling the trigger of my 9 mm UltraStar and blowing the picture tube clean out of my 60" Magnavox.

"Yes, he liked guns," our longtime DeathStroke manager, Gray Harris, testified.

Dooley pushed his chair back and stood. "Did he own a lot of guns?"

"Everett was the kind of guy who, once he got interested in something, wanted to be an expert at it, immediately. It was that way with the guns and the knives. Someone turned him on to handguns early in his career, and right away he owned an assortment of them. He took marksmanship lessons and even had a small shooting range built into the basement of one of his homes. But I never saw him misuse guns."

"Mr. Harris." Dooley looked directly from one juror to the next. "In all your years working and traveling with the band, did you ever see Everett Lester threaten anyone?"

Gray had aged incredibly. His hair was white and he was overweight. The bows of his silver glasses bent outward to make it around his wide, red face. Gray had always loved a good steak, and the red meat seemed to be catching up with him. He appeared to be almost out of breath. I didn't know whether that was from his anxiety about the trial, his health, or both.

"Look," he said heavily. "Everett and the other members of DeathStroke were like family. We lived and worked and traveled together, in very close quarters. We were probably closer than many husbands and wives. When you're in these kinds of intimate settings, everyone sees everyone else's weaknesses. And little things take on big proportions."

I was amazed at Dooley's patience. He must have had a good night's sleep, because he remained silent as Gray attempted to soften his answer.

"When Everett was at his worst, drug- and alcohol-wise, he did lose his composure and threaten people. But all in all, I would say he did quite well with his emotions, considering how blitzed he was by the media twenty-four hours a day."

With his arms crossed, strolling about, Dooley asked, "Who did you see Everett Lester threaten, and for what reason?"

"Well, on several occasions he became angered when people approached him in public," Gray answered so quickly that his response seemed rehearsed. "Like when someone would come up to him at a urinal and want to shake hands..."

This brought a relief of laughter from the crowd. I think I even smirked. But Dooley nipped it.

"Did you ever see Mr. Lester threaten the psychic known as Madam Endora Crystal?" Dooley asked, throwing a cloak of silence over courtroom B-3.

"No, I did not."

Dooley approached Gray. "Mr. Harris, what is the most violent act you ever saw Everett commit?"

Boone was on his feet in an instant. "Your Honor, we object on the basis of relevance. What if someone asked that question of your life or mine or of Mr. Dooley himself, for that matter? In each instance, I am certain the answer would certainly be most incriminating."

Boone stared at Judge Sprockett, who debated for several seconds while fiddling with something in front of him. "Objection overruled. I am interested in Mr. Harris's answer."

Gray rubbed his chin with his pudgy right hand, shook his head, and raised his eyebrows. "Geez, I don't know, sir. There was a time once in, I think, Pennsylvania. We were doing a concert with a number of other bands. But it was Thanksgiving Day, and we found ourselves at one of the only hotels in town—a motor lodge of some sort." He breathed deeply. "There were no restaurants open, and we were all kind of ticked off because it was a holiday and we were away from home, apart from our loved ones."

For the life of me, I could not remember what Gray was talking about—or where the story was going.

"Well," he continued, conjuring up the strength in his lungs to continue, "Everett had been deep into drugs to pass the time, and he was totally out of it; I mean, falling-down wasted. We were all in one hotel room. I forget whose room it was. But all of the sudden, one of our roadies burst into the room with a wastebasket.

"He had been collecting all the Gideon Bibles from our rooms, up and down the hallways. And he barged into the room where the band and I were gathered, pulled out the bottom drawer of the nightstand, and yanked out the Gideon Bible. Right then he began ripping out pages and throwing them into the trash can. Next thing we knew, he doused the torn-up Bibles with alcohol and lit the wastebasket on fire."

Groping to remember the incident, I sat dumbfounded, feeling the eyes.

"When Everett kind of came to for a minute and inquired what was going on, what was burning, he went into an outrage. From behind, he grabbed the roadie around the neck, took a knife out of his pocket, flicked it open, and put the knife to this young fellow's throat."

Whispers made their way through the courtroom.

"Please continue," Dooley raised his voice, enjoying the drama yet wanting Gray to finish the gory details.

"The knife slightly punctured the roadie's throat. And Everett ordered him, while still in a headlock, to put the fire out. The young man grabbed an ice bucket, filled it with water, and dumped the ice on the flames. Everett had him in a headlock the whole time."

"End of story?"

"Well…yes," Gray said, almost as if disappointed.

"You hesitate, Mr. Harris. How does the story end? Was the man fired?"

"Not exactly. Everett told him he could keep his job…*if* he fished the legible pages out of the trash can and read every one of them."

Dooley grinned. "Well, you may as well finish." He snickered. "We're all waiting with bated breath. What did the young man do?"

Gray himself laughed now. "Actually, he read every page. The next thing we knew, he joined the Peace Corps."

I guess somewhere in the recesses of my mind I always thought I would marry Liza Moon. Now she was gone. Just another dagger in my heart to prove that life was meaningless, that nothing mattered. You just lived and died and…who cared?

A flood of bitterness and rage filled my soul. I seemed to be walking beneath a dark cloud, unable to break into the sunlight. Sorrow ate away at me. Even though all the world wanted to be close to me, I was so alone. No one really wanted to be a true friend.

I was becoming dangerous.

During a brief break from the DeathStroke Rowdy tour, Endora flew to one of my favorite homes, a waterfront condo in Bal Harbour, Florida, near North Miami, to cheer me up. She promised a full-blown psychic reading, and I was all for it.

After a catered dinner and a few drinks, she shooed me out of the living room while she broke out her bag of tricks. I went to the bathroom, then ducked into the den, clicked on the big-screen tube, and stood channel surfing for a few minutes.

My condo was situated on the top floor, the thirty-second story, of a building complex known as The Towers, whose twin peaks hovered beautifully over ritzy Bal Harbour, providing a breathtaking view of the Atlantic Ocean. One major network news anchorman had a suite in the same building, as did several Hollywood stars.

My unit had three spacious bedrooms, three baths, a kitchen and breakfast area, a large den with a bar, an office, and formal living and dining rooms. Liza had helped me decorate using the finest furnishings money could buy. It was truly elegant and had a style that was all Liza.

By the time I came back, the living room was lit only by dozens of candles, including a large black one that sat just off to Endora's left. Some sort of incense was burning, and Endora beckoned me to sit with her on the floor, insisting I cross my legs Indian-style and remain positive; negative vibes, she assured me, would produce an inaccurate reading.

Next, she opened the lid of a shiny wooden box, which she'd been clutching most of the evening, and removed something that was covered in a square of silk. From beneath the purple cloth she brought out her treasured tarot cards, which she had spoken of often. There were seventy-eight cards in the deck, and I was not allowed to touch one of them. Not yet, anyway.

Looking through the deck, Endora picked out one card—the King of Swords. It was a card that matched my astrological sign, Aquarius, and my skin and hair tones, dark. She placed that card facedown on the table horizontally.

Next, she gave me the privilege of shuffling the deck until the cards felt "warm," which I imagined they did. I cut the deck with my left hand "to invite order from the universe," as she had insisted.

Dealing from the bottom of the deck, Endora carefully set three cards vertically, facedown, above the King of Swords, then one card facedown vertically on top of the King of Swords, then three more cards facedown vertically beneath the King of Swords.

"Okay, let's be quiet," she said, putting on her game face.

Closing her eyes, Endora began to kind of fade away into her own little world. Her posture was straight, but she seemed totally relaxed. Her arms rested on her crossed knees, with her hands open and facing up, as if each hand was about to receive an apple.

The humming began slowly and quietly, immediately making me feel uncomfortable. Then deeper groaning came, mixed with bits and pieces of what sounded like other languages. Slowly, her chanting grew louder.

What the—? Endora had never pulled anything like this before. She revealed remarkable truths to me in the past, but we never "entered in," as seemed to be happening this night, high above the coastline of the Atlantic.

"Say your name," Endora ordered with her eyes still closed.

"Everett Lester."

"Repeat it, *louder.*"

"Everett Lester." I was really concentrating now, really trying to make this work. "Everett Lester…*Everett Lester.*"

Endora reached the far left card in the top line and flipped it over. The words on the card read The Fool. "Adventure…energy…zeal." Endora spoke each word with utter clarity and deep emotion. "You were wild and carefree as a boy. You went in a million different directions. You were gullible. Oh, how you searched for acceptance, taking many risks to find it, not caring about consequences."

A breeze off the ocean swept through the condo, blowing the black curtains at the sliding glass door to the balcony waist-high into the room. The candles flickered. Two went out completely, leaving trails of smoke twisting in the air. Chills ran up my arms.

She turned over the second card in the top row: the Ten of Wands, "Oppression."

A string of unintelligible verbiage poured forth from Endora. Her chanting, the whole setup, gave me the creeps, big-time. It had been a hot day in North Miami, but my apartment was freezing. Endora acted differently than I had ever witnessed, as if she had up and left her body and someone else, a stranger, now occupied it.

"Domination of mind, body, spirit," she groaned, sadly. "You were completely and utterly stifled as a child. Stifled! Your father—insecure, controlling. Although somewhere deep inside he wanted to, he did not know how to love. So he raised you like he was raised. Pure *repression*."

The black candle between us blew out with the wind.

She had my attention.

In fact, I didn't care how all of this looked—she was dead on the mark.

With the flick of two fingers and another string of gibberish, she flashed the Nine of Pentacles, the third and last card in the top row.

In a slow, alluring voice, Endora began almost singing now, her eyes still closed: "You have done it. The higher power within has taken ooooover. Accomplishment, Everett Lester, *accomplishment!* You have overcome your morbid childhood. You have acquired wealth and reached the very pinnacle of success.

"The past has been read," Endora declared with finality, reaching for the card that was facedown in the center of the table, covering the King of Swords, which represented me. "Now, the present."

With a similar flick of the wrist, she flipped over the Ten of Swords, which had one word in bold, black type: "Ruin." I immediately searched her face for a response, but there was none. Nothing seemed to remotely faze her; it was as if she was there with me, but her emotions were not. Eerie doesn't begin to describe it.

Leaning forward with her elbows on her knees, Endora rested her head in her hands, closed her eyes, and exhaled deeply, rocking slightly.

"The moths of cruelty and hatred and loss have eaten away at you. Your life is like a stone wall that's been through wars and turmoil. Some sides of the wall appear strong and unbroken—even glamorous. But much of the wall is crumbling away, decaying…ruined."

Endora's arms slowly lifted upward, and her head rolled from side to side. The chanting came low and deep now. Building faster and faster.

I was startled when she suddenly whipped her arms out to her sides, like an umpire signaling "safe."

"Quiet!" she uttered, eyes closed, head cocked sideways, eyebrows up, as if listening to a voice coming from the other room. "'Move on!' they're telling me. 'Move on!' Let us see what the gods hold in store for your future."

Again, with a flash, she flicked over the first of three cards in the bottom row.

At first, I couldn't read the word at the bottom. My eyes fell instead to its picture: an hourglass.

"Death." With her eyes open now, she looked at the card then at me. "It doesn't mean what you think. Do not worry. It is good. A sign that says, if you do not fear change, if you do not stagnate, if you embrace change, you will be transformed. Death of the old, beginning of the new.

"This is what we've been discussing, Everett. Exactly what we've been talking about! If you are strong and press on and recognize the leader the gods have made you and embrace the afterlife that awaits you on the Other Side, all fear of death will be gone. All of your anxiety will disappear. And you will not only be set free, but so will your massive following."

As she broke into another chant, her head bounced back and forth. "Death to the old, life to the new—let us see what this next card reveals for you."

She reached for the second to last card and flipped it over, slowly this time.

Her eyes grew big.

As quick as a hiccup, rage filled her face as she read the words on the card: "Ace of Cups…the 'Love' card."

Her eyes penetrated mine.

Not a word was spoken for many seconds.

"Well…" She attempted to compose herself. "What do you know about that." She looked almost faint. "Quiet…quiet for a moment, Everett. Give me complete silence."

After placing the card faceup in its rightful position, she held her jeweled hand about an inch above the card. As she did, she shut her eyes and tilted her head back, looking straight up into space.

When Endora's hand started to quiver ever so slightly, I assumed it was just her age. But then the hand that hovered over the Ace of Cups trembled more, and eventually, shook severely.

"What is it?" I asked.

"Silence!"

A fierce wind ripped through the condo. Endora's glass, holding the remains of a bloody Mary, spilled across the glass mantel and down the side of the fireplace. Each candle in the room suddenly blazed one hundred times brighter than normal, brighter than any candle was supposed to burn. The three that had gone out were now torches.

Endora's head was still thrown back; both of her arms and her shoulders were shuddering violently. It looked like she was taking off in the space shuttle.

"No, nnn-no, nooooooo." She shook, yelling, fighting to keep her hand over the Love card.

"Endora, Endora! Stop it! Stop!" I pleaded, my heart hammering. "What should I do?"

Then I saw the smoke. It rolled up in a swirling vapor from underneath her hand.

Instinctively, I lunged for her arm to get her away from the table, and we rolled hard to the ground.

Endora collapsed, her head drenched in sweat, remnants of smoke still trailing from her right hand.

I shot up on my knees to look at the table, to put out the fire.

But there was no fire.

Instead, the Ace of Cups—the Love card—lay there, perfectly in its place, glowing red-hot, like a branding iron. I stared in amazement as its bright orange glow quickly went out in unison with every single candle in my thirty-second-story condominium.

5

Twila Yonder looked just like her name sounded—way-out.

I'd guess she was about thirty-eight. Her face was pale, and her long hair was brown with bleached-blond streaks. She wore stark makeup, including arching black eyebrows that looked as if they were drawn on with a Sharpie. The dark maroon top she wore resembled a cape with webbing under each arm. Her tongue was pierced with a small silver ball. Funny...she looked like a typical DeathStroke fan.

But a fan, it turned out, she definitely was not.

As Miss Yonder clinked to the witness stand with her array of heavy jewelry, I heard the rain begin to come down hard outside. I was tired. It had been a long day.

After all the formalities, Frank Dooley stood beside the witness stand, addressing her as if she were a fragile flower.

"Tell us now, if you will, Miss Yonder, about your relationship to the deceased—Madam Endora Crystal, or, to use her real name, Edith Rosenbaum."

"Endora and I went way back," she said reflectively. "I met her at a mutual friend's house, oh, I'd say fifteen years ago. We became fast friends."

"How often did you see or talk to Endora?"

"During the last few years we spoke at least several times a week," she said, as I wondered how she could chew gum, talk, and avoid having the gum stick to the jewelry on her tongue. "She was like a mother to me and a dear friend at the same time. She taught me a lot about psychics and the profession she was so good at."

"What can you tell us about the relationship between Endora and Everett Lester?" Dooley showed a kindness and patience I didn't know he had.

"Well, Everett had a macho persona, but deep inside, he had problems." She chomped her gum. "Endora became like a mother to him. Without her guidance, who knows what would have become of him long before now? I mean, the man was obviously messed up."

"Explain for the court what you mean by that," Dooley said as he wandered and motioned with his hands for her to tell more.

"Everett Lester was an unstable drug addict. Very insecure. Very unsure of himself, no matter how powerful he came off onstage. The man was a loser. Endora kept his feet on solid ground. He needed her...in more ways than one."

Think of the feeling you get in your stomach when you go over a hill really fast in a car. Do you know that feeling? Or more accurately, when you are suddenly confronted with drastic news—bad news. Your face goes flush. Your body

goes limp. Your lips go dry. Sweat breaks out on your forehead. Do you know that feeling?

That's how I felt, suddenly, in Miami-Dade County courtroom B-3, as I realized something was terribly amiss.

"Wait a minute now." Dooley turned on a dime, facing
the jury. "What did you mean just now, when you said
Everett Lester needed Madam Endora *in more ways than
one?*"

"Simple," said the dragon lady from hell. "Everett was in
love with Endora. She told me herself."

Quiet surprise blazed through the room.

"They were...romantically involved."

Relishing the moment, Dooley paced with his arms
crossed, waiting. I could almost see a smile on his long face.
But no, he was too good to let it shine. He kept his exuberance
at bay.

"Now, Miss Yonder, tell us more of what you know about
the *romance* between Endora Crystal and Everett Lester."

When he emphasized the word *romance* I actually felt
woozy.

"Well, for a long time I didn't know it was going on. It
was only in the last few days of her life that Endora confided
in me that she and Everett had been romantically involved."

My elbow was fixed on the table in front of me, my fore-
head resting in my hand. I shook my head. *Where are You,
God?* Apparently Brian Boone wasn't going to try and stop
Mr. Dooley or Miss Yonder.

"Don't worry," Boone whispered to me while covering
his mouth with a brown leather notebook. "We'll weather
this."

"Endora told me over dinner that Mr. Lester had fallen in
love with her," Twila said, as the bad dream continued. "And

according to Endora, he was very jealous, very domineering."

I closed my eyes in hopes that when I opened them, I would have woken up.

"Did Endora mention whether Everett ever threatened her?"

"She said, just before she died, that if Everett Lester ever caught her with another man, he would kill her."

The courtroom shook momentarily, until Sprockett pounded his gavel.

"How long was the relationship more than friends?" Dooley asked, as I squirmed in my seat.

"Several years, I believe."

"To your knowledge," Dooley asked, ever so strategically, "did anyone else know about this romance between Endora Crystal and Everett Lester?"

"No one but me," she said quickly. "Endora assured me no one else knew."

When I arrived at Endora's private room on the second floor of Baptist Hospital of Miami the day after the incident in my high-rise, she was already sitting up in her bed, surrounded by colorful bouquets from friends and clients. Her makeup was just right, and the room smelled from the new coat of dark brown polish she was applying to her long, fake nails.

"How many times must I tell you," she scolded the thin, shy-looking nurse who was on her way out as I entered, "I want chopped ice and cranberry juice, chopped ice and cranberry juice. A constant flow of it. Is that too much to ask, when it's practically all I'm asking for?"

She turned to see me and feigned innocence, with her head lowered, eyes raised, and lower lip protruding.

"Everett, you've got to persuade the doctors to let me go, darling," she insisted, her usual zeal intact. "I'm fine and I've got business to tend to in southern California. You remember, my niece's wedding is in ten days. I've got to be there to help—"

"You know what the doctor said, lady," I said, revealing a box of chocolate turtles that had been hidden behind my back. "He wants to make good and sure your heart is fine before sending you cross-country on a plane. Just relax. Enjoy the rest."

"Pooh. Easy for you to say." She smiled now at the sight of her favorite candy. "Thank you, sweetheart."

"You're welcome." I removed the cellophane from the box. "Listen, Endora, I need to know what the heck went on at my condo, with the Love card, and your passing out."

I figured enough time had passed. She seemed stable enough.

"To be honest with you, I really don't want to talk about it," she sassed, taking a bite of a turtle.

"I'm still paying your retainer, correct? You need to explain the Ace of Cups to me. What was it telling you?"

She slammed the bottle of polish down amid her other beauty tools on the bed beside her, then looked out the window.

Her wheels were turning.

"It was quite scary, actually," she said, still staring out as if in a trance. "I was shown that *someone* is going to come into your life, posing as a new love—offering new life."

Her head turned toward me, her eyes still in a daze. "But she will betray you. She will lead you down a path you do not want to travel, Everett. Do not follow her."

"Who? Who is this person?"

She looked back down at her hands and newly polished nails, which now rested on her lap. "I'm not sure. I didn't get that yet."

"When will you know?"

"I'll know when I know." She shook her head and looked away again.

"What's wrong, Endora?"

"It's heavy, that's all. Very heavy."

"Why did the card heat up?"

"I told you, it was a warning! Listen to me, Everett. This is nothing to fool around with. *Take heed.*"

"Why? What kind of threat are we talking about?"

She glared out the window. All quiet.

I let her think.

"She will bring an end to your career. Possibly…an end to your life." She finished the sentence in a mean, almost wicked whisper.

I stood and walked to the tinted window. The sun shone brightly on the plush lawn, palm trees, and sidewalks that curved amidst the well-manicured native greenery outside. After watching cars and people come and go for a few quiet moments, I crossed back to Endora, patted her shoulder, kissed the top of her head, and made for the door.

I turned to face her. "I'm glad you're okay."

"Do you believe me, Everett? Do you trust me on this?" She cradled the box of candy against her chest.

"I don't know." I reached for the silver door handle. "I just don't know anymore, Endora. Liza was the only one. And she's gone. I guess I'm still struggling with that."

"Everett," she said, raising her voice as I swung the door open, "I believe you and this individual have already made contact. *Be careful.*"

Confusion clouded the drive back to The Towers, even with the top down and the south Florida sun reflecting off of my slate blue Audi TT Roadster. I waved at the security guard, parked in the cool deck below the complex, and took the elevator up to the thirty-second floor.

The reading with Endora was still bothering me as I picked up a long FedEx package, which was leaning against my door, and keyed my way in. Walking over to the coffee table where we had been the night before, I noticed the tarot cards—exactly where they had been when Endora passed out, as were the candles that dotted the room.

Opening the shiny wooden box in which Endora stored the cards, I removed the purple silk cloth, set it on the table, and began picking up the cards. I shook my head as I recalled the reading and collected the cards in the order in which she had read them to me.

There was one more card still facedown on the table. It was the last in the series describing my future. Endora had never reached this one. Instinctively, I turned it over.

The Moon.

Its wicked-looking artwork resembled that on the other cards, but this one pictured a butter-colored moon shining down on an eerie, snakelike dragon which had wings and a hissing tongue.

My knee-jerk reaction was to call Endora and ask her what it meant, but something stopped me. Instead, I took the card, grabbed a Molson out of the miniature stainless steel fridge, and settled into the red leather chair in front of the computer at my mahogany desk.

Propping the card up next to the computer, I pulled the Internet menu down to Favorites, went to Google, and did a word search on *moon, tarot cards.*

Dozens of websites offered free psychic readings and others sold mystic paraphernalia. Then, *bingo,* I tracked down several sites that, among other things, defined the meaning of tarot cards.

"The moon card leads us into the mysterious realm of darkness…tends to show gloomy foreboding." Another described the Moon card this way: "Another of the cards that is most often viewed negatively, the Moon represents confusion and illusion. Beware!"

The ring of the phone startled me.

"Hello," I answered quickly, not wanting it to ring again.

"Everett, it's Endora. Listen, dearie, I need to make sure you take good care of my cards. Are they still as we left them?"

Odd timing.

"Yeah…they're here." I squinted at the screen.

"Well, do me a favor. Just wrap them as they are in the purple cloth from my box, you know?"

"Uh-huh." I read another description for the Moon card: *"Beware of illusions of the unknown, deception…"*

"And place them inside the box," Endora continued. "Do you understand?"

"Sure. Ah…" I continued reading. *"Lies, trickery."*

"Everett!" she yelled, then began coughing. "Have you heard anything I've said?"

"Yeah. Yeah, sure, I got it. Do you want me to have them sent to you out west?"

"Oh no, dear. Never. I'll send someone by to get them."

Whatever.

I was so tired and confused. I hung up with Endora, shut down the PC, and took the card back out with the others, doing as Endora asked—all inside the purple silk and into the wood box.

Picking up the FedEx package, I wandered into the den. The box's return label was from Jeff Hall, president of the DeathStroke fan club. Setting the package on the bar, I went behind the counter, threw away the empty Molson, and poured myself a tall scotch with ice.

Plopping down on my favorite leather chair, with the kind of worn brown leather you see on a pilot's jacket, I opened the package. Inside was another long, narrow box wrapped in brown paper and labeled with my name and the address of our fan club. The return address simply read: Karen Bayliss—Topeka, Kansas.

The red rose inside was still fresh, thanks to the miniature water tube attached to its thorny stem. The note was written on several small pages of yellow stationery. The paper actually smelled fragrant; whether from the rose or Karen, I wasn't sure. The slanted, bubbly handwriting had become all too familiar…

Dear Mr. Lester,

    In case you didn't know it, the yellow rose I brought you in Kansas City stood for friendship. I hope you will accept my friendship, even though we do not have a lot in common.

The red rose in this box stands for love. I sent it to remind you that while this world and the things in it give us no hope, Jesus gives us hope. Jesus loves you, Mr. Lester.

His blood is red like the rose. His blood ran down His arms and feet for you and me. He doesn't want you to be without Him any longer. He stands at the door and knocks and assures you He will come in and comfort you and live inside you and give you peace if you'll just cry out to Him, confess your sins, and believe in Him.

Today, Jesus is calling out to you. He wants you to understand, clearly, how much He loves you. His love is red like the rose.

My prayers go up to the Father many times each day for you…while I work, while I drive, and while I do chores around the house. It's up to His Spirit to draw you, and I am confident He is doing that as you read this note.

May He bless you and keep you, until next time.

Sincerely,

Karen Bayliss

P.S. The small Bible in this box is for you. Check it out!

I just closed my eyes, shook my head, and smirked.

Unbelievable.

Carelessly, I picked through the tissue in the box till I found the palm-sized brown Bible, examining it for a good long while before opening it to see if she had written a note. Leafing through the first few pages, I found my name written in it, in Karen's handwriting, along with this: John 10:27–28.

After a rather extensive, yet unsuccessful, search through the pages of the small book, I resorted to the table of contents, where I found a list of Old and New Testament books. Finding the page number for the book of John, I thumbed my way to the verses to which Karen had referred me.

"My sheep recognize my voice; I know them, and they follow me. I give them eternal life, and they will never perish. No one will snatch them away from me."

With my finger in the book I slumped into my favorite chair and stared off into nowhere for a long time. Then I read it again.

His sheep follow Him, I thought. *They are well protected. And He gives them eternal life.*

This was not the "Other Side" Endora was selling. I knew it in my bones.

This eternal life was something different. It was forever, with God. And it was for sheep, for those who would quietly follow Him. It was for people like Karen, the polar opposite of the Endoras and Everetts of the world. For Karen, who seemed bright and pure and innocent; who seemed to live so boldly, so cleanly, and with so much refreshing wind in her sails.

Although I wished it could be, this paradise was not for me. No, I would have to put my money on the Other Side. It was for *all* people, including reprobates like me.

The ice in the Scotch had melted. The tall glass was wet. And I sat in my chair until every last drop was gone.

Gray Harris fumed. So did the band. Dozens of business partners and thousands of DeathStroke fans were aggravated as
well. My drug binge after Liza's death had set us way behind
on the recording of our latest album in California. And Endora's unex-
pected collapse had forced me to cancel two shows on the Rowdy tour.

By the time I caught up with the band in Detroit, I was getting the
cold shoulder from everyone. And no wonder. Gray had announced
that on almost every one of the two- and three-day breaks that had
originally been scheduled during the forty-eight-city Rowdy tour, the
band would now be required to fly to the West Coast to wrap up the
recording of our ninth album instead of jetting to our respective homes
for much-needed rest—and time away from each other.

When our normally quiet bassist, Ricky Crazee, approached me
as we convened for a sound check on the black and silver stage at The
Palace in Auburn Hills, Michigan, I knew something was up. He
zeroed in on me like a heat-seeking missile.

"You know what your problem is, Lester?" Ricky jabbed a finger into my chest, his redheaded temper flashing. "The only person you care about is you. It's always been like that. What are you thinkin' of, leavin' us high and dry?"

The sudden loud rip of David Dibbs's drums suggested he concurred with Ricky. And John Scoogs chimed in with an evil guitar riff that spoke louder than words.

Still buzzed from the gin I had consumed on the flight to Detroit and the upper I popped in the limo, I decided not to respond. I had heard it all before and was too high to care. Besides, Ricky could be one crazy cowboy. So, I spun away from him.

"Hellooooooooooo Deeeetrooooit!" I yelled into the mike, nearly causing one of our roadies to fall from a catwalk above.

"You're an idiot, Lester," said Ricky, the strings on his bass reverberating as he stepped toward me again in his pointy gray boots and faded Levi's. "We've all had it. You don't care jack about us or our families, about Gray or Tina."

"*I DON'T CARE too much for money,*" I sang into the mike, "*'cause money can't buy me love. Can't buy me lo–ove—*"

"You don't get it, do you, dude?" Scoogs said, cutting me off. "Everything you do dominoes. You mess up, you don't show up. It affects every one of us, plus staff, crew, fans... We're sick of it!"

"Well, what are ya gonna do, John? Fire me? Huh?" I yelled into the mike. "I *made* you, man. All of you." My words echoed throughout The Palace, as the smattering of vendors and preshow guests froze, their eyes searching each other.

"How would you just like to do it without me, huh, Scoogs? What about you guys? You ready to break this party up once and for all? End the ride?"

"Man, that is *not* what we want." Dibbs stood up from behind his huge drum kit, the large DeathStroke logo blazing bright behind him, generating heat from above.

"I don't know, David." Ricky pushed his suede cowboy hat up high on his red forehead. "Maybe it is time. This thing is wearin' thin."

Tina Drew scrambled off, probably to find Gray.

"You talk about not caring." I slammed the mike stand onto the stage. "How much have you cared? Liza's *gone.* Do any of you care? Have you said a word?" I was yelling.

"Dude, you weren't even at her funeral!" Ricky shot, his small blue eyes locking in on me. "Me and Dibbs were *there.* Gray phoned her parents."

"And I tried to make it, but I couldn't get a flight out on time," Scoogs added.

"Yeah, you know why you went to the funeral?" I laughed. "Publicity. PR. Lights, camera, action!"

"You are so messed up, Lester." Ricky shoved me. "What are you on right now?" Shove. "Heroin?" Shove. "Do you even know what you're saying?" Shove, shove.

Gray practically came flying around the wall of amplifiers with Tina and a small entourage of staff members trailing six feet behind.

"Okay, okay," he huffed, stepping between Ricky and me. "What is going on? Ricky?"

"What's goin' on," I blurted, "is these losers are about to kiss their careers good-bye. They're forgettin' who brought 'em to this dance."

"You are so full of it, Lester," Scoogs yelled. "You're blind. Look at what you're doing to everybody around you. You're *cancer!*"

"Ha. If I'm cancer, then everybody wishes they had it. You guys would be nothin' without me. *Nothin'!*"

"Gray, we've had it." Ricky turned away from me. "This is the crossroad, man."

Gray looked at each band member, getting no argument from the others.

"Okay, look. You guys get the sound check started. Everett, let's take ten." He led the way offstage.

★ ★ ★

After Gray gave me his father-son speech behind several tall stacks of metal trunks backstage, I grabbed a beer from a barrel of iced beverages in the makeshift café and kicked and scuffed my way to the dressing room. I told him I was skipping the sound check. He said he would try to iron things out, as always, with the other band members.

Throwing myself down onto the reddish-brown couch, my head was floating. I was definitely not sober. But I wasn't blitzed enough to pass out, either. I just felt kind of…there. If you've ever drank alcohol or taken drugs, you know what I'm talking about. It was that in-between stage. I either needed to sober up or get some more drugs or alcohol into my system. I chose the latter.

Sitting on the edge of the couch, I examined the room for my black leather shoulder bag, which I carried on trips. It contained my MP3 player, headphones, cigarettes, hairbrush, phone, and an assortment of prescription drugs, which were authorized by my physician and close friend, Dr. Jack Shea.

Finding the plastic orange bottle of Valium, I undid the lid, tapped two into my hand, and threw the bottle back into the black satchel. Then I stopped cold.

What the—?

Bending down, I ripped the bag open a foot wide and stared at the small brown Bible Karen Bayliss had sent.

For the life of me, I couldn't remember packing it. I just wouldn't do it, wouldn't want to be seen with it.

Picking up the black bag, I walked to the bar, set the Valium down amid some booze bottles, and crossed to the large metal dressing room door. After bolt-locking it, I walked over to an empty corner of the small room and eased myself down to the cold floor, with my back against the wall.

From a distance, all around me, I could hear and feel the sounds of the music I had created, the music that had made me filthy rich.

Opening the bag again, I reached in and grabbed the little book. A letter was sticking out. I opened it. The last one from Karen.

Friendship…

His blood…red like the rose…

It's up to His Spirit to draw you…

I opened the Bible somewhere near the middle and began reading.

Oh, what joy for those whose rebellion is forgiven, whose sin is put out of sight!

Yes, what joy for those whose record the LORD has cleared of sin, whose lives are lived in complete honesty!

When I refused to confess my sin, I was weak and miserable, and I groaned all day long.

Day and night your hand of discipline was heavy on me. My strength evaporated like water in the summer heat.

Finally, I confessed all my sins to you and stopped trying to hide them. I said to myself, "I will confess my rebellion to the LORD." And you forgave me! All my guilt is gone.

Therefore, let all the godly confess their rebellion to you while there is time, that they may not drown in the flood-waters of judgment.

For you are my hiding place; you protect me from trouble. You surround me with songs of victory.

I read the words again.

My head dropped to my chest, and I began to sob.

The Bible and letter dropped as my arms went limp at my sides.

Sinner.

I felt the weight.

My life was draining away. I could feel it.

Look at me.

These tattoos.

Filthy.

I could never be good enough.

Wiping my tears and runny nose on the shoulder of my black Knicks T-shirt, I opened the bag again and searched for my phone and a pen. Flipping the phone open, I dialed 411.

"*411 nationwide,*" came the recorded female voice. "*If you need a telephone number, press or say one.*"

"One," I said, clearing my throat.

"*What city?*"

"Topeka, Kansas."

"*What number?*"

"Bayliss. B-A-Y-L-I-S-S. Karen Bayliss."

Waiting.

"*The number is 785-433-8179.*"

After scribbling the number down on the letter from Karen, I flipped the phone shut and sat there.

My heart was drumming.

The crooked wall clock showed 5:45. It would be two or three hours earlier in Kansas. She probably wouldn't be home anyway.

I opened the phone, punched in the numbers, and hit send.

One ring, two rings, three rings.

"Hello," came the lively voice.

My eyes darted about the dressing room.

"Hellooooo."

I clapped the phone shut and threw it in the bag.

Like most days of this trial, when today's session adjourned I was escorted by two sheriff's deputies through double wood doors out of the courtroom and into a stark white holding area. Members of the press strained their rubber necks to find out what goes on back here. But it was plain and simple.

There's a cramped locker room that smells like bleach, where I change from the street clothes I wear at trial into a bright orange prison jumpsuit, which has my prisoner number stenciled in black on the left breast and on the back. It's up to my attorney or family to bring a change of clothes for the next day's trial. One officer is with me at all times when I change.

Once back into the holding area, the deputies, wearing ugly orange-and-brown uniforms, locked leg irons to my ankles. They wrapped a heavy belly chain around my waist and attached its handcuffs to my wrists. Once I was locked down, the two deputies, assigned solely to me, walked me down one flight of stairs in a dark, hollow stairwell lit only by red EXIT signs. Once through a large metal door and down a dingy basement hallway, we entered the eye-watering Miami sun, still burning bright toward evening.

The humidity hit me like a microwave, but I relished it. Who once said that we need at least twenty minutes of fresh air and sunshine every day to keep our spirits up? Liza Moon? I've come to think she was right.

In an effort to cut down on media attention, the Miami-Dade County police department usually set up at least two or three decoy cars around the Justice & Administration Center. However, a number of TV trucks with antennas fifty feet high and good-looking reporters were usually camped all over the cobblestone plaza that we drove past to make our exit for the local detention center.

Some people followed our squad car in their vehicles, just to get a glimpse of the rock star on trial for murder. After we made the five-mile trek to the Miami-Dade detention center, numerous reporters, photographers, and onlookers gathered there as well. They jockeyed for position and yelled for comments, but I only smiled as I was escorted into the building.

The detention center was a sprawling gray concrete structure surrounded by a large parking lot, lawns, and a fifteen-foot-high chain-link fence, which encircled the entire perimeter of the maximum security prison and was topped by rolls of razor sharp concertina wire. The only windows in the complex were narrow, one-yard-wide slits that ran horizontally too few and far between.

After being unlocked and directed through two different metal detectors, I was frisked and taken by a large, heavy-breathing guard to my cell, which is located on the ground floor of the four-story prison.

The cell was designed for one man. It was ten feet wide by ten feet deep with a sink, toilet, and a bed attached to the wall. Nothing else.

I felt lucky I didn't have a cell mate, considering that most of the cells were only slightly bigger than mine, yet housed two bunk beds and two men. Later I was told that the reason they put me alone was because I was such a "high profile" prisoner. Some were even surprised that I hadn't been housed in solitary.

By the time I got back from court, dinner had already been served. Now it's leisure time, which means one hour of gathering around TVs, reading magazines, playing cards, talking on pay phones, and shooting the breeze in each other's cells. All cell doors were open during leisure time.

Donald Chambers, one of the few guards who'd taken a liking to me, brought me dinner on one of the prison's decorative army green cafeteria trays. The meal consisted of one dry hamburger, a handful of soggy salad, mystery bean casserole, and water.

Chambers set a chair outside my cell, turned it backwards, and sat talking to me, his arms resting on the back as I picked at my dinner.

After discussing some of the difficulties from the day's trial, including the false accusations of Twila Yonder, I listened in disbelief as Chambers surprised me with more good news.

"There is a guy in here by the name of Zane Bender." Chambers looked around cautiously. "Nickname is Zaney. You know him?"

"No."

"You need to watch your back. Word is, he thinks this is gonna be another OJ trial—guilty guy walks. Word is, he won't let it come to that."

My stomach was getting used to trouble. I inhaled deeply, blew out long and steady, and reminded myself there was a reason for this.

"Why?" I pushed the tray of food away, feeling flushed. "What's he got against me?"

"Look, Everett, this dude's in for armed robbery and attempted murder. He's doin' a minimum of seventeen years. You think he has to have a reason? It makes him popular, okay? You're a star. He hurts you, it puts the spotlight on him. Guys like this, all they got to live for is having a name in here. Me and the other guards are under special order to watch your back."

"Great..."

"I hear he's into the occult." Donald pushed the green guard hat high on his forehead. "Probably favors people like Endora Crystal. He even does some kind of psychic mumbo jumbo in here—guys pay him for it! Can you believe that? I've heard some pretty weird stuff has gone down."

"Like what?"

"One night during leisure he and about twelve guys met." Chambers inched his chair closer. "He predicted one of the guys in the meeting would be dead within three days. Dude was found hangin' by a bedsheet in his cell."

"Suicide?"

"They're still investigating."

"What kind of guy is this?" I said. "I mean, how big is he?"

"Let's take a walk."

A seductive light sparkled from Endora's eyes as she stood behind the glass partition and watched us lay down a radical new rock number called "Freedom."

She wasn't going to miss this.

We were back at The Groove recording studio in Santa Clarita between stops on the Rowdy tour. Although our frazzled nerves and strained friendships had been pushed to the edge, things seemed to be stabilizing, in great part thanks to the potential we felt in the new *Freedom* album. Although it was by far our most drawn-out recording to date, we also felt it might be our best seller.

Endora made the drive over from her place in Malibu. She was with Gray and three producers in the control room of The Groove, where cigarette smoke swirled beneath track lighting, and dozens of red, green, and yellow lights glowed from a long, sleek soundboard.

The Groove was a great place to record because the equipment and acoustics were top-notch, and it was a comfortable getaway.

Interruptions were kept to a minimum. The facility was small, dark, and well-appointed, with comfortable furniture and a contemporary kitchen that was manned by a full-time chef.

The members of DeathStroke were on the other side of the glass rocking out to "Freedom," a song I had written after spending several days with Endora. It was basically a tune about her spiritual beliefs. I wrote it in fun as kind of a rally-type anthem and really hadn't taken it very seriously—until we started sampling it out on the Rowdy tour. We were taken aback by the response from our fans, who fell into an absolute trance over it, lighting matches and chanting the words in unison.

The song, which I dedicated to Endora, features riveting guitar work by John Scoogs, overpowering bass from Ricky Crazee, slashing drums by David Dibbs, and yours truly screaming louder and meaner than any AC/DC song you ever heard. Here's a taste:

Heeeeeeeeeeeeeeeeeeeeeeeeeeeeeeeeeeeeeeeeeeeeeey!!! (screaming)

Weary traveler
Come into my domaaaaaaaaaain
Hey, weary traveler
I got somethin' to saaaaaaaaaay

FREEDOM, FREEDOM
FREEDOM, FREEDOM
FREEDOM, FREEDOM

Whoooooooooooaaaaaaaaaaaaaaaaa!!! (screaming)

Weary traveler
It doesn't matter where ya beeeeeeeeen
Hey, weary traveler
You are going to live agaaaaaaaaain!

FREEDOM, FREEDOM
FREEDOM, FREEDOM
FREEDOM, FREEDOM

Ahhhhhhhhhhhhhhhhhhhhhhhhhhhhhhhhhhhhhh!!! (screaming)

Weary traveler
The Judgment Day's a liiiiiiiiiiiie
Hey, weary traveler
Every soul will surviiiiiiiiiiiiiiiiiiiiiiiiiive!

FREEDOM, FREEDOM
FREEDOM, FREEDOM
FREEDOM, FREEDOM

"I've got to talk to you." Endora dragged me by the hand out to her white Cadillac during an afternoon break.

"What's up? I didn't expect to see you here. I thought you had the wedding…"

"It's in two days. We're all set," she said, hitting the unlock button. "You know I wanted to see you record this."

"I know. What else is on your mind? Where're we headed?"

"Late lunch, drinks." She buckled up.

I loved Santa Clarita, based on the five or six times I had been there. It was clean, with a small-town feel, a fair amount to do, and close to LA. And it offered a panoramic view of the stark, rocky Placerita Canyon and some of the most breathtaking skies I had ever seen.

"Where's the button to move this seat back?" I asked, as Endora eased the Caddy out of the parking lot. "You see my knees? They're in your glove compartment."

"It's on the right." She puffed on a long menthol as I searched for the lever that moved the seat back.

"Everett," she touched my knee, "I've been getting a woman's initial."

"What?"

"A woman's initial. The spirits are giving me a woman's initial."

"What are you talking about?"

"Remember when I was in the hospital, I told you…"

"Ohhhhhh," I moaned, sarcastically. "This is about the eerie mystery lady. The one who's gonna show up and ruin my already perfect life. Right?"

"It's not funny," she stormed. "I've never been so sure about anything in my life."

"Okay, okay…I'm sorry. Tell me."

"The woman will try to *destroy* you. Her name starts with *K*. Are there any *K*s in your life right now?"

Most of the women I spent any time with probably didn't give me their real names half the time. I had no one serious—not even close.

"No, doesn't mean a thing," I said, enjoying the view.

"She's already in your life, Everett. *I know it.* You need to concentrate on this and figure out who it is. I'm telling you, she's destructive."

"I'm drawing a blank right now."

"This is the supernatural realm we're dealing with. This is about the spirit world. It's real. I can feel it. Someone is encroaching…"

"You give me the creeps when you talk like that," I said.

"The last initial is *D* or *B*." She whirled the Caddy into a parking lot at a restaurant called Diamond Jim's. "I'm not positive about that one. But the *K* is set in stone. You've gotta be watching for this lady."

Endora was out of the Caddy and five steps ahead of me. She threw her cigarette on the ground. "C'mon."

As we walked up the front steps, two attractive women in their thirties recognized me as we passed. I heard the usual giggles and squeals, and then…

"Excuse me." The blonde came up behind me as we entered the vestibule. "You're Everett Lester, aren't you?" She was slightly nervous, yet had one of those playful, "forward" looks about her, which I had come to know well over the years. Her brunette friend was blushing just a few steps below her.

"Yes, I am." I turned and reached to take her outstretched hand. "At your service."

"He's already taken." Endora stepped between us and pushed me inside the door. "Pleasure to meet you ladies. Better luck next time."

She entered the vestibule, pulling the heavy door shut behind us.

Too embarrassed to pursue the lunchtime duet, I turned to Endora. "What do you think you're doing?" I blasted, seeing only darkness as my eyes adjusted to the cavelike vestibule. "That was cold. Don't do that again!"

"Table for two, smoking," Endora barked to the hostess.

"I said, that was cold."

"They'll get over it."

As I left my cell and walked out into the commons area of the detention center with Donald Chambers, I saw dozens of white guys, black guys, Hispanics, and others.

"Yo, Lester!" yelled a stocky white dude, his muscular body stained by more tattoos than mine. "What's up?"

I acknowledged him by raising my chin slightly and then followed Chambers up two flights of stairs. He stopped at the second landing and leaned over the railing. I leaned over, too.

Below, the inmates looked like fire ants, swarming after their hill had been stepped on. Everybody perked up during leisure time.

"I don't see him," Chambers said, both hands on the metal railing, his eyes scanning the busy crowd. "He usually plays poker with that group." He nodded down toward a five-man game.

"Stay here a minute," Chambers said. "I'm gonna walk up to four and go past his cell. Sometimes guys pay him to interpret dreams, read palms, whatever. Hang loose. I'll be right back."

As I perused the orange jumpsuits below, I noticed a few guys pointing up at me. Not sure yet what their consensus was—and I didn't want to know. I just wanted to mind my own business, get the trial behind me, and...

SLAP!

Two hands. Hard. On my shoulders. From behind.

My head turned. My body couldn't.

The viselike fingers tightened into my shoulders.

Then, something drilled into my lower back.

A knee.

My stomach arched forward.

"*Ahhhhhh,*" I yelled awkwardly.

"Are ya singin', Lester?"

The knee ground deeper.

"Stop!"

"I never heard that one," came the raspy voice. "Was that a *Billboard* hit?"

Suddenly, the hands jerked me around quick and hard.

My eyes were shoulder high on this monster, so I only looked down slightly to see the black numbers stenciled on his jumpsuit, 488792.

"What are you lookin' for, rock star?"

My eyes made their way up his sweaty, fat neck and stopped at his blubbery jowls and enormous shaved head.

"You lookin' for me?" He breathed down on me, just four inches from my face.

"Who are you?" I asked, scared, taking in every inch of his red baby face.

"Zaney." His high, cracking voice didn't sync up with the sheer girth of his mammoth physique. "You don't know it yet, Lester, but you and me got a history."

"Hey!" I heard Donald's voice echo from above as he hurried down the hall, pulling out his billy club on his way to the steps.

Zaney stepped back. "I got people inside," he whispered quickly, drilling his thick finger into the middle of my chest. "I got people outside. I *will* finish the job."

The effeminate male waiter brought Endora her second Blue Dolphin. She wasn't eating. The drink came in a glass shaped like a teardrop. It was turquoise blue and contained five different shots of liquor and a pink umbrella.

"Would you mind not smoking while I eat," I said, cutting up the chicken in my salad.

"What do you mean? *You* smoke."

"Not while I'm eating." I focused on the salad.

"Thanks for the raise," she said.

"You're welcome."

"That couple over there recognizes you." She pointed her dripping straw toward a Hispanic couple in the booth to our right.

I didn't look up immediately, but when I did, they quickly looked toward each other shyly and giggled.

"Our waiter was giving you the eye, too." She smirked.

"Did I tell you my mother called?" I asked, ignoring the onlookers.

Endora finally put her cigarette out. "No, what did she have to say?"

"She's worried about Eddie. Thinks he's under too much pressure, depressed… Says he's tryin' to keep up a good front, but she can tell he's miserable. The kids are out of control. The marriage is in trouble, so she says."

"Ewww. I get such darkness from that whole situation," Endora said. "Is he still in the Big Apple?"

"Yeah. And I've got a feeling he's into some stuff he shouldn't be."

"Like what?"

"I don't know, but there's no way they could afford all they have without some kind of extra income. She's a spender," I said. "And he's under the gun to keep up with her pocketbook."

"They've probably got a ton of debt."

"Yeah, and he won't accept anything from me."

"When I think of Eddie, I think anxiety…fear. A tight grip on everything. It's all high-tension."

"He's a wheeler-dealer. Who knows what he's into now. I talked to him a couple weeks ago. He let his guard down a little. He was stressed. In a big hurry, as usual. David, his youngest son, is driving now; he's a wild thing."

"Like you?"

I ignored that.

"What about the older boy?" she asked. "What's his name?"

"Wesley."

"What's he like?"

"A hell-raiser. Eddie says he's probably into drugs. Maybe even selling. I haven't seen them in a long time."

"Weren't you supposed to go skiing with the boys and their dad somewhere?"

"Lake Placid a couple months ago. It never happened. I had to bail."

She shrugged, sipping her drink. "That's life in the fast lane."

"I paid their way," I said, momentarily trying to cover the guilt. "It's not the first time I've let 'em down."

"The boys look up to you, don't they?"

"Yeah, and they shouldn't." I shook my head. "They'll get what I got for lookin' up to my old man. Emptiness…scars."

"You Lester children inherited a lot of your father's baggage, you know?" She stirred the drink with her straw. "He was chronically depressed. He was a womanizer. A drinker. He had a temper—"

"That's enough."

"I'm sorry, honey." She reached toward my hand. "But you're always going to be battling that stuff. You know? It's hereditary."

I nudged her hand away with the back of my fork hand. "Doris doesn't sound good."

Endora didn't inquire further.

"She coughs constantly," I said. "Sounds weak."

"How old is she?"

"Sixty-eight."

"She's young," Endora said.

"Doesn't sound young."

"She misses your old man."

"He was her life."

The Hispanic couple stood. The slightly overweight, dark-complected man clapped the crumbs off of his hands and walked toward us timidly. His wife stood back at the table, watching.

"Hi," he said, smiling and nervous. "I couldn't help but notice you, Mr. Lester. Our son is a huge DeathStroke fan. His name is Hector. I was wondering—"

"I was wondering where you learned your manners," Endora butted in, her head going back and forth with every word. "Can't you see we're in the middle of a meal?"

"Oh, well, I...I'm sorry. I was just wondering if you could sign a napkin for my son, Mr. Lester."

"You're not understanding me, are you, Mister?" Endora said, practically standing up. "Some—other—time. Comprendé?"

I was too ashamed to look up at the man. But as he walked dejectedly back to his wife, I took a snapshot of her face in my mind. It was one of embarrassment and sympathy for her husband.

"Endora," I whispered through clenched teeth, "sometimes you need to *chill*."

"You taught me everything I know."

I kept my head down.

"Oh, come on, Everett. You should be so pumped! This *Freedom* album is going to give DeathStroke a huge second wind. It has the makings of a chart buster."

"That used to motivate me." I wiped my mouth with the thick white cloth napkin.

"You just need some time off, baby," she said in a raspy tone, lighting another cigarette. "Once we get you finished in the studio and wrap this tour up, you can take off a couple months and relax."

That meant nothing to me. "I miss Liza."

"I know."

"Why did I wait till she was gone to realize?"

As she stirred her drink, the long cigarette between her fingers, I could tell she was scheming.

"Liza was the one. I really believe that now. I wish I would have known."

"It's not too late," she said, one eyebrow raised.

I stared at Endora.

"We can communicate with her," she said, moving closer.

Five minutes before leisure time ended at the detention center, a shrill bell chirped off three loud, quick shots. Orange jumpsuits buzzed about like horseflies, as inmates finished up what they were doing and headed for their cells.

After five minutes, the bell sounded one long, stark ring that lasted about ten seconds. One minute later, every cell door in the place automatically lurched forward, clinking, gliding, and banging shut.

Before leisure ended I was in my cell, lying faceup on the cot reading. The meeting with Zaney shook me.

It was 8:40 P.M.

A small black guard named Rockwell ran his billy club along the chipped white bars of my cell. "Evenin' Lester." He stopped at the cell door. "I heard there was a little commotion earlier, and you were at center stage."

"Yeah." I sat on the edge of the cot, my untied generic blue tennis shoes hitting the green linoleum floor. "Some wild man named Zaney introduced himself."

"Zane Bender. Hasn't been in long, but he's making a name for himself."

Rockwell cracked my cell door hard and loud three times with his stick. "Your attorney's here," he said, as the barred door unlocked with a loud echo and jerked open.

Rockwell and I walked side by side up the same steps where Zaney accosted me earlier. At the second story, there was a line of blue metal doors every eight feet or so marked B-1, B-2, B-3, and so on.

Attorneys and clergy were allowed to visit any time, around the clock. Other than that, inmates could have two half-hour visits from civilians during the week and two on weekends. Children were only allowed on Sundays.

We stopped at B-4, and Rockwell opened the door. "Thirty minutes."

I closed the door and turned to face Brian Boone, who was seated and still in the same suit he wore at today's trial. The knot in his tie was completely undone, his tortoiseshell reading glasses rested atop his head, and he looked tired but upbeat.

My side of the visitation room was about four feet by five feet, with a cheap, rust-colored plastic chair and a blue metal desk attached to the thick glass partition that separated us.

The desk looked like my body, much of it scarred with etchings. Only these carvings were from prisoners. There were names, stick drawings, Bible verses, hearts, and profanities. Boone's side of the room was identical to mine.

We smiled at each other beneath the faded yellow light. He leaned into the desk speaker. "How ya holding up?"

"Making it." I nodded.

"I've got questions about Twila Yonder." Brian pulled a

pen from his shirt pocket and turned back five or six pages of
his white legal pad.

"She's a surprise to me."

"And her allegations—?"

"False, of course," I cut in. "I was messed up back then,
but not *that* messed up."

"She's a very good liar."

"Maybe she's not lying," I said, looking into his heavy
eyes. "Maybe Endora really did tell Twila we were having an
affair. Twila is simply repeating what she thinks is true."

"Why?" Boone smacked his pad onto the desk, threw his
hands up in the air, then locked them behind his head. "Why
would she do that?"

"To make me look bad. When Endora changed sides near
the end, it was war. I've told you that. She would have done
anything to trash my name."

"Go on."

"It was like she *knew* something heavy was going to come
down."

"We've talked about this before, but I need you to rack
your brain." He leaned onto the metal table now. "Can you
think of any other land mines we'll run into with upcoming
witnesses? Another Twila Yonder?"

"Brian, it's possible. I've thought and thought. But
again, my memory is fried, dude. A lot of the testimony so far
has shocked me. I guess the drugs have taken their toll."

I thought I heard tapping far away.

But without opening my eyes, I just rolled my pillow into a ball
and plunged my throbbing head back in.

It's hot. I writhed in the unfamiliar bed, sheets strewn everywhere. *What is so…confining?*

Squinting, I looked at the digital clock far across the king-size bed. Ten-forty.

Bright white light sliced through the two-inch opening in the plastic aqua-colored curtains.

Lying there, I noticed the four-inch-wide spiked bracelet still on my left arm. Then I realized my clothes were still on from the concert the night before. Black leather pants and vest. Even my black knee-high boots.

That ticked me off.

Somehow, I swayed myself over to the edge of the bed.

My head reeled.

I rose, took one step, and the legs gave out.

Managing to tear my boots off, I crawled dizzily along the dark green carpet, making it to the bathroom and pulling myself up onto the toilet. My head was drenched in sweat. I was so light-headed it felt as if I had just given ten pints of blood.

It took everything in me just to reach up and rip a large towel from the rack above my head. I wrapped it around my neck and dried my face and forehead. Black makeup smeared everywhere.

I turned to look in the mirror. Ink renderings of spiders and snakes, crosses and daggers, skulls and bones covered my skin.

Wrinkles and creases. Bloodshot eyes surrounded by black.

Long, brown hair, snarled and oily. Earrings and chains.

Waste.

Disgusting waste.

My head dropped into my hands, and black sweat ran to the toilet and floor.

I let my body collapse onto the cold tile, where I curled up and allowed sleep to come again.

It started again. This time, louder.

Tap, tap, tap, tap.

Pause.

Tap, tap, tap, tap.

"Someone's going to die!" I picked myself up from the floor and staggered to the bed, where I flopped down, still fully clothed.

A muffled female voice called my first name from the other side of the door. My people knew better than to allow visitors without my permission, no matter what hotel or city.

"Go away!" I looked for the clock, which read 1:38.

Tap, tap, tap, tap.

"Evie…it's Mary. Open up."

I lay still for a moment, my eyes open wide now.

"It's Mary," said my sister. "Let me in, Everett."

Tap, tap, tap, tap.

"Coming," I groaned, making it to the bathroom, head still pounding. I threw a washcloth in the sink, soaked it, and rubbed the mascara off my face; then I worked a brush through my matted hair. That would have to do.

I took a deep breath, made my way to the door, and pulled it open.

There stood Mary in a full-length denim coat, with a big leather purse over her shoulder and a newspaper under her arm. Her brown hair was as short and sassy as I'd ever seen it, and her crystal clear eyes, white teeth, and glossy smile shone with radiance.

The smile quickly left as I noticed her shiny brown eyes track up and down me. But she walked toward me, and we hugged. She was slender and firm. I opened the door further, and she followed me into the dark room.

"When I heard you were playing Dayton, I made up my mind I was coming to see you. Can I turn a light on?"

"Sure," came my low response.

She turned on a standing lamp, whose faint light revealed empty beer and booze bottles strewn about and cigarette butts on the floor and furniture.

"How'd you get past security?" I asked, coughing.

"Gray let me through." She sat down on the red couch. "I was here at about ten-thirty, but I guess you were still sleeping."

"Hmm." I sat at the other end of the couch. "Sorry I kept you waiting."

"No, that's okay. I was just concerned I would miss you before you went to Cincinnati."

"Are we in Cinci…tonight?"

"Everett, *yes*," she said, impatiently. "What time do you leave?"

"Heck, I don't know, Mary. I'm like an animal in a circus. They'll put me in a limo when it's time. Get the spectacle to the next show."

She gave a half smile, squinted, and shook her head.

"How are you?" I asked.

"Okay. A little lonely, but surviving."

"The divorce behind you?"

"Uh-huh."

"How 'bout the boys?" I asked.

"They're fine. Doing well in school. Jessie's playing football, and Andy is an absolute soccer fiend."

"Ah, I would love to see them play." I looked down, realizing she probably wouldn't want me within a country mile of her boys. "I've neglected your guys, and Eddie's…"

"Oh, they would be thrilled to show off for their uncle Everett. It's been too long. They often ask why we never see each other anymore. Just the other day Jessie said he wished we could have a great big family reunion."

I reached for the pack of Salems on the coffee table, tapped one on the back of my wrist three or four times, lit it, and took a long-overdue drag.

"Would you really want me to come see them play?" I blew the bluish smoke into the room. "I'm not exactly the kind of influence you want for them."

"Of course I would. Everett, I've grown a lot in the past few years."

"How so?" I said, dropping back into the couch.

"I think when I first got saved it was such a black-and-white conversion; I just assumed everyone should choose Christ. Whoever didn't wasn't worth the time of day. That sounds awful, but it's the way I was. Judgmental and legalistic. I judged you."

She was on the verge of tears.

"I'm sorry, Ev. That's what I came to tell you. Will you forgive me?"

I set the cigarette in an ashtray, moved over, and put my arm around her shoulders.

"I forgive you, Mary. It's okay. Don't cry. I love you."

"I love you, too," she squealed. "The boys and I pray for you every night."

"Well, I guess I've changed, too." I wiped the tears from beneath her eyes with my fingers. "A few years ago I would have said I didn't want your prayers."

I felt a kick of emotion. "But now…I know I need them," I managed, a tear slipping out my right eye. "I know I need something."

"Evie." She sat up, sniffing. "Accept Christ now, here, with me today! *He's what you need.* I know, Evie. He's changed my life. Can you see it in me?"

Chills ran up my wrists and the backs of my arms. "I see it."

"You're looking at Jesus, not me!"

I stood, put my hands on my waist, and let out a big sigh. "There are too many obstacles, Mary. Too much to overcome."

"Jesus can wash you clean, Everett. He can forgive every sin, just like He did me, and you can start over!"

"Look at me, Mary!" I faced her, holding my palms out, turning them over. "I'm dirty. Okay? Inside and out. Look at the hole I've dug. All my life, I've dug deeper and deeper. There's no getting out. The mold has been cast! I'm my father's son."

"No, Everett. You're the Father's son. Your life doesn't have to be this way." She stood, holding my hands. "That's why He died. To forgive you. Accept the gift! It's free. Just say yes here with me today."

"You don't know me." I held her tender hands for a moment, then dropped them and turned to the clock. "I'm gonna have to shove off soon."

Mary stood, wiping her nose with a Kleenex. She walked to the windows and pulled the curtains open about three feet. "Ev," she said soberly, turning toward me. "What happened last night?"

"What do you mean?" I started to throw some stuff into my black shoulder bag.

"At the concert." She walked back toward the couch where her purse and newspaper lay.

"We did the gig. Why? You didn't go, did you?"

"No." She picked up the *Dayton Herald*. "No one's told you about this?"

She unfolded the newspaper to reveal the front page and main headline.

DEATHSTROKE SHOW TRIGGERS RIOT
16 Hurt, 1 Critical

Beneath the headline, there was a color photograph of me rocking my whole body forward at the edge of the stage, hair flying, sending a spray of sweat into the crowd.

I took the paper from Mary, dropped down on the edge of the bed, and began to read.

DAYTON—The antics of DeathStroke's lead singer Everett Lester took their toll last night at the Dayton Arena, where 16 of the 17,682 in attendance were hospitalized after a riot broke out when Lester passed out onstage and management stopped the concert.

A 14-year-old Xenia girl is in critical condition at Good Samaritan Hospital. She was struck in the head by a microphone stand, allegedly tossed from the stage by Lester, who witnesses say openly guzzled whiskey from a bottle during the six songs the band performed before the show ended abruptly.

Lester passed out onstage immediately after whirling the heavy black mike stand. The girl, whose name is being withheld, was carried by friends to an outlying concession area where employees phoned 911. Lester was carried from the stage by security personnel, and his whereabouts were unknown at press time.

DeathStroke manager Gray Harris announced that management teams from the band and from Dayton Arena had agreed to cancel the show. Although Harris told patrons they would receive a full refund, fans began yelling obscenities, fighting, and throwing everything they could get their hands on. A race to the exits ensued, trampling dozens of DeathStroke fans in the fray. Of the 16 people taken to the hospital, only the Xenia girl sustained serious injury.

Witnesses say things started getting out of hand when Lester encouraged the frenzied crowd to repeat the lyrics from a new DeathStroke song entitled "Freedom." "Judgment Day is a lie, you know," he reportedly yelled to the audience. "All of us are going to survive. There *is* no hell...only Freedom." Then the band launched into the new song by that name, the last one DeathStroke played before Lester passed out.

Mary was sitting next to me when I dropped the paper and fell back onto the bed, pulling my hair and screaming, "Nooooo!"

9

just saw CNN!" Endora panicked. "What's going on? Are you okay?"

"I'm *not* okay," I said into my phone, sitting slumped in the passenger seat of Mary's Subaru.

"What's the matter? Where *are* you?"

"On the way to the hospital."

"Hospital?" she gasped. "What's wrong? Are you sick from last night?"

"It's not me. Did you hear about the girl?"

"Yes, I told you, I heard about it just now. Are you in Cincinnati?"

"No! I'm still in Dayton."

"Everett, you've got a show in Cincinnati in…four hours."

"Didn't you hear about the girl at the concert last night? That was *my* fault."

"Look, it's just all the pressure you're under. Gray's taking care of this other thing, I'm sure."

"What the heck do you mean . . . that Gray is gonna *pay* this girl's parents so I don't go to jail?! Is he gonna *pay* to make her better? To make her live?"

"Look, Everett, this isn't the first time something like this has happened."

"No, but it's going to be the last!"

"So it is...very good. Good! Calm down. I agree. There's no reason for you to lose control like that. No excuse. But listen, darlin', you've got over twenty-five thousand people counting on you in Cincinnati tonight. Those people love you just the way you are. You don't want to let them down, do you?"

I didn't say a word but instead helped Mary look for a parking place in the visitor's lot.

"Everett, are you going to visit that girl?"

"Yes, we are."

"Who's we?"

"Mary and me." I unfolded myself out of the Subaru. "My sister, Mary. She came to see me today at the hotel."

"Did you tell Gray what you're doing? Because, from a legal standpoint, you need to be very careful about what you do as it relates to that girl."

"Endora, I'm so sick of doing what Gray says, what you say, what the record label says, what the fans say…"

"Listen, honey. I know you're stressed out—"

"Did it ever occur to you that some people don't live with this kind of stress?"

"Everett, your sister's not brainwashing you, is she?"

"Maybe that's what I need, Endora. A good brainwashing."

"Well, she'll be just the one to do it, I'm sure."

"I gotta go. We're walkin' in."

"Everett, you need to make that show tonight. Thousands of people have been waiting for this night for months. They need you. They need the freedom you have to offer."

"I'm not free, Endora." I tried to keep my voice down. "I'm a prisoner!"

Turning around to glance into the audience in Miami-Dade County courtroom B-3, I noticed Donald Chambers, my guard friend from the detention center, seated toward the back of the court in his street clothes. I guessed Donald to be close to fifty years old, about two hundred pounds, with curly grayish black hair and sideburns. He appeared to be alone.

After starting out wearing suits the first few days of the trial, I gradually dressed a bit more casually, today wearing khakis and a navy dress shirt.

Before emerging into the public eye this morning, I checked myself in a mirror in the holding area. My hair was combed neatly. It was cut slightly above my shoulders and was still dark brown, except for a few white hairs at my temples and sideburns, which I usually trimmed when I wasn't in jail.

Brian Boone, wearing navy slacks and a camel-hair blazer, paced in front of the witness stand where Twila underwent her second day of questioning.

"I'm sorry, Miss Yonder." Boone walked away from the witness. "How many years did you say you've known Everett Lester?"

She smirked. "I told you I've never met Mr. Lester."

"Oh, wait a minute. I'm sorry. Forgive me. I just assumed that, since yesterday you said that Mr. Lester was, and I quote, 'unstable, insecure, a loser, and a drug addict,' I assumed that you knew my client."

That made me smile.

"Your Honor." Frank Dooley stood up. "My client told the court yesterday that she never met Mr. Lester. Now...Mr.

Boone is harassing the witness and attempting to discredit her. Let's get on with the cross-examination, shall we?"

"Good idea, Counselor," Judge Sprockett said, looking bored with it all.

"Miss Yonder," said Boone, not fazed by the chastening. "Do you know how much money Endora Crystal was paid by Mr. Lester?"

"I know she was on a monthly retainer. The last time we talked about it, I think she made close to fifty thousand dollars."

"Fifty thousand a year?"

"No, fifty thousand dollars a month," she conceded.

"That would mean that Endora made about six hundred thousand dollars a year from Mr. Lester. Does that sound about right?"

"Your Honor." Dooley stood slowly, calmly. "We object based on a complete lack of relevance. What does Miss Crystal's salary have to do with anything?"

"Where are you going, Mr. Boone?"

"Your Honor, for background and context, I felt it important that the jury realize how much money Endora Crystal was making from my client, not to mention her other clients. It was an exorbitant amount. And I believe it may have played a part in her continued, excessive interest in my client."

"What do you mean, excessive?" Dooley fired at Boone, then swung to Judge Sprockett. "Your Honor, come on."

"All right. Enough already. Endora Crystal's salary from Mr. Lester has been duly noted." Judge Sprockett turned to Brian. "Now, Mr. Boone, let's turn this questioning in a more meaningful direction, shall we?"

Boone wandered back to our table and sat down. Calmly placing his brown reading glasses on his face with one hand, he reviewed his notes, as if he were alone in the courtroom. *This guy is cool, cool, cool.*

"Miss Yonder," he finally said. "You said yesterday you knew Endora Crystal some fifteen years."

"Your memory's improving," she said, blinking, smiling, and searching the room for a reaction, which she got in the form of a smattering of laughter.

"Ah." Boone smiled in response. "Glad to see you are so attentive today, Miss Yonder. You said Endora was so close to you, like a mother, correct?"

"Yes."

"You said you spoke to her several times a week, correct?"

"Yes."

"Well then, my question is—if you knew this woman, this friend, so long and so well, why did you have no clue that she was having this alleged relationship with this world-famous rock star for the past however many years?"

"She obviously wanted to keep it a secret...until the end."

"Ah. Ah. Ah." Boone got the court's attention by spinning around. "'Until the end.' Were those the words you used, 'Until the end'?"

"I guess so."

"Interesting choice of words, 'Until the end.' It makes it sound as if Madam Endora may have known when her end was coming. Did it ever occur to anyone, I wonder, if perhaps she did know? What do you think, Miss Yonder? Is it possible Endora may have committed suicide...?" Boone's words trailed off, as if he knew he was about to be the target of return fire.

Sure enough, Dooley sprang like a jack-in-the-box. "Your Honor, where did that come from? I'm surprised at Mr. Boone. He's grasping at straws. That is pure and undefiled conjecture. It's not a question, and the witness doesn't have to answer!"

"From now on, Mr. Boone, let's keep our hypotheses to ourselves. That is an order, sir."

"Yes, Your Honor."

This was where Boone belonged—moving about a court-room, working a witness, playing a jury. It was like watching a master fisherman as he selected just the right tackle, carefully planned where to troll, patiently deciphered a nibble from a strike, and knew when to set the hook.

"Tell us about your psychic involvement with Endora." Boone casually approached Twila. "Did you work with her?"

I could tell the witness was suspicious of Boone, so she treaded carefully. "When I first met Endora, I came to her for readings. She was obviously good at what she did."

"When you say *readings*, explain to the court what you mean."

"It's when a psychic reads your past, present, or future. She tells you what's happened in your life, what's happening, or what's going to happen. And she gives you advice based on that knowledge."

"So, Endora did that for you?"

"Uh-huh. I had been through some tough times as a youth, and our meetings really helped me."

"Did she do things like palm readings and tarot cards?"

"Yes, and she was amazingly accurate. She had a super-natural gift."

"How was she able to help you personally?" Boone asked.

"When we first met, she immediately realized there was something tragic in my past. She helped me cope."

"Do you mind my asking what that tragedy was?"

"My parents were killed...in an automobile accident," she said coldly, with a sudden glaze over her eyes.

"I am sorry to hear that, Miss Yonder. How old were you

at the time and how, specifically, was Endora able to help you?"

"I was seventeen when they died," she said, snapping out of the daze. "When I met Endora, about five or six years later, she was able to assure me that my parents were okay, that they were…okay, that's all."

"And how did she assure you of that?" He turned to the jury with his arms up in the air.

Frank Dooley rose to his feet, letting out an exhausted sigh. "Your Honor, I am sorry to interrupt, but I just cannot see how this is relevant."

Clearing his throat, the judge spoke to the entire room. "This background may be helpful for all of us. Miss Yonder may answer the question."

"What was the question?" she asked, nervously grasping at her hair.

"How did Endora assure you that your deceased parents were okay?"

"Endora believed in afterlife—for everyone."

"Okay." Boone raised his eyebrows. "So…it's not like she attempted to communicate with your parents after they had died. Because, I know Madam Endora was said to have done that on occasion."

Miss Yonder's head tilted slightly, and her mouth fell open.

"Objection, Your Honor." Dooley stood again. "Leading the witness."

"Sustained," said Sprockett.

Boone focused on Twila like a laser beam. "Did Endora attempt to communicate with your parents after they died?"

"She *did* communicate with my mother. She found out that they are well, that they're in a good place."

"Oh?" Boone hesitated, knowing he was perched atop a

powder keg. "And where is that place? Heaven?"

"No." She set her jaw against the world. "It's known as the Other Side. Endora communicated with many people who had crossed over."

"I see. And did you ever help her communicate with the dead?"

She looked down, fidgeting with her hands. "Actually, I did."

Dooley's head dropped slightly.

"Often?" Boone asked.

"Fairly."

"Did you, by chance, have any part in helping Endora communicate with anyone who may be connected with this case, this trial?"

"Liza Moon."

"I'm sorry, I didn't hear you."

"Liza Moon. Endora asked me to serve as a medium between her and Liza Moon."

"Everett Lester's former girlfriend?"

"Yeah."

"When was that?"

"I don't know, not too long before Endora's death."

"Tell the court what happened in that instance, please." Boone acted as if he already knew.

"For a long time after Liza died, Endora wanted to serve as a medium for Everett, so he could communicate with Liza."

"Why?" Boone asked. "Why would she want to do that?"

"I guess so Everett could have closure after her death." She chomped on her gum. "So he could have some peace, knowing Liza had reached the Other Side."

"And that's the only reason Endora wanted to do this séance?"

"Endora also told me she was getting some bad vibes...about a dark woman coming into Everett's life. She believed doing the séance with Liza might shed more light on that."

The crowd was dead quiet.

"Did Mr. Lester go along with it? Did he take part in this...séance?"

"No," she said. "Everett was changing. He wasn't sure about the power of psychics anymore. He was questioning."

"So, instead of having Mr. Lester in on this séance, Endora asked you to be the medium so she could communicate with Liza Moon? Is that what you're telling the court?"

"Yes."

"Your Honor." Dooley arose, clearing his throat and pulling at his right cuff. "This is getting way out there. Relevance?"

"Yes it is," Judge Sprockett said. "Let's bring this thing back home quickly, Mr. Boone."

"Miss Yonder." Brian looked confident approaching the witness stand. "In a nutshell, I want you to tell the court exactly what happened when you and Endora attempted to communicate with Liza Moon."

"We made contact with Liza," Twila said coldly. "She was sending danger signals to Endora."

"Danger signals about what?"

"Liza was concerned about Everett's future. She warned Endora that an angel of death was coming into Everett's life, a person who would change his life forever. Liza kind of confirmed these bad vibes that Endora had picked up on earlier."

"Anything else about the future, specifically as it related to Everett Lester?"

For a fleeting second Twila's whole body seemed to flinch. Her eyes darted up and down, and she mouthed several words.

I turned to see a slight look of alarm on Dooley's face.

"Are you okay, Miss Yonder?"

She snapped back to reality. "Yes, it is no problem," she said, almost robotically. "Liza said the angel of death was going to lead Everett to a Lamb of some kind and when that happened, everything would change."

"What was Endora's response to that?"

"She became somewhat angry."

"Why?"

"She was concerned Everett would get his mind off his music and his fans and..."

"And what?" coaxed Boone.

"And become some kind of religious zealot, I guess." She threw her hands up. "I don't know. I can't tell you any more than that."

"Okay, Miss Yonder, we're almost done. Let me just go back and ask you one or two final questions about this 'angel of death.'"

Boone stopped just in front of the witness stand, where he placed both hands on the railing in front of her. "In the séance, did Liza Moon indicate who this angel of death was?"

"No," she said, avoiding eye contact with Boone.

"Did Endora indicate to you who *she* thought the angel of death was?"

"Yes, she did."

"Is that person in this courtroom today?"

"Yes, she is...seated directly behind Mr. Lester's defense table."

Mary had waited in my hotel room while I took a steaming hot shower and changed clothes. I didn't tell anyone we were going to visit the girl I had injured. If Gray Harris knew, he would have had heart failure, wanting instead to keep me totally out of the picture.

My sister hadn't asked me to go with her to Good Samaritan Hospital; she simply announced her intentions. I really don't know what made me ask if I could join her. Maybe it was guilt, just knowing that Mary—a total stranger—was going to visit this girl I had hurt. Perhaps there was a faint sense of remorse buried somewhere deep beneath my wicked exterior. Maybe I just wanted to be with Mary longer. Probably, it was all three.

When we left the hotel, Mary ran me by a Wendy's drive-thru, where I picked up a burger and a Frosty. We drove most of the way in silence, with a smattering of small talk about family and old times. Her husband of eighteen years, Rick, had left her for another woman several years ago. The divorce had recently been finalized, with Mary getting custody of the boys. She was relieved that the divorce was behind her.

Heat rushed to my cheeks as Mary and I swung into the visitor's lot and saw a collection of local and national TV trucks. For a moment, I felt that maybe I shouldn't go in. But Mary never flinched. She yanked up the parking brake and was three steps ahead of me as I hung up the phone with Endora.

Warning sirens sounded in my head as we approached the main hospital lobby. Outside, reporters knelt with cigarettes, stood around with Diet Cokes and bottled water, and sat on benches munching snacks. As the large glass doors parted automatically, it was as if we were heading smack into a wasps' nest.

Suddenly, I felt cameras, mikes, notepads, and recorders deflecting off me as I tried to continue along with Mary to the information desk. But I couldn't stay with her. It seemed as if I were snagged in a slow-motion time warp as she paced forward at a normal clip.

When I saw that she made it to the desk some thirty feet past me, I stopped where I was and let the bodies and equipment converge around me. Two, three, four camera lights popped on around the lobby.

"Mr. Lester," one reporter shouted, "are you here to see Olivia Gilbert?"

"How do you feel, Everett?" asked another.

I could feel the sweat spreading on my forehead as I lifted up on my toes to find Mary. She was still at the information counter.

"Have you talked with Olivia's parents?" someone yelled from deep in the room.

The questions scorched me like fire, but I didn't have the answers.

Now on her toes, Mary's arm shot up, a piece of paper in her hand, as if to say, "I got it. Come on!"

"Excuse me," I mumbled, then said it louder, "excuse me!" With both arms bent upward in front of me, I moved ever so slowly through the crowd toward the elevators where Mary waited.

"Have the police contacted you yet, Everett?" asked a short, stocky reporter with a dark beard, moving along next to me. "They tell us she might not make it. Have you heard any more?"

As I broke through to the elevator, Mary hit the third-floor button, the door closed, and I felt sick to my stomach. "Maybe this wasn't a good idea." I turned to my older sister.

Her eyes were closed. "Bring peace, Lord," she breathed, reaching for my hand. "Bring healing."

And there was peace, for a few moments anyway.

"Her name is Olivia Gilbert. She's fourteen." Mary squeezed my hand tightly. "She's in serious condition. Severe trauma to the head."

The nausea began fighting its way back up into my throat as the reporter's words rewound and played again in my head: *They tell us she might not make it…*

10

The third floor appeared relatively quiet as we rounded a corner and headed down a long hallway toward the nurses' station. Next, we took a right down another hall and looked for room 314.

I could tell by the look on their faces that two of the nurses at the central station recognized me. We kept going, making another right and practically stopping in our tracks.

People of all ages lined the hall. Adults stood and talked quietly. Young children ran about while teenagers leaned stoically against the light blue walls. Several elderly people occupied the chairs in the visitors' lounge, which overflowed with guests—most of whom, it appeared, had come to show their love for Olivia Gilbert.

"I'll find out if we can get in." Mary scanned the crowd just outside of room 314.

One by one, I could see the word spreading that Everett Lester was in the house.

"Hurry up," I said, as she approached a handsome, middle-aged man just outside room 314. He wore tan slacks, a black-and-gold golf shirt, and a shiny leather belt.

After whispering back and forth for a moment, Mary pointed at me with a slight turn of her head, and the man's eyes followed, resting on me. She said something else to him, and he touched her shoulder gently, nodded, motioned for her to wait, then slipped into the room.

"Come here," Mary said, as more and more people started to stir because of my presence.

"That's the uncle," she whispered to me. "He's going to ask Olivia's mother if we can go in for a minute."

As we stood there awkwardly, a few people acknowledged me. Some sneered. Others whispered back and forth.

I despised moments like this—under a microscope but not onstage. All eyes on me but no performance; no way to earn their approval. It was stone-cold reality, and it made me overwhelmingly uneasy.

The door to room 314 eased open, and the trim, balding brother peeked out and waved us over with a slight smile.

"Thank you for coming." He shook my hand while gently pulling me into the room. "I'm Jerry Princeton."

With the commotion of the hallway closed off behind us, the room was quiet and smelled like most hospital rooms. The blinds were closed, but the brightness behind them allowed just enough light to silhouette a TV cabinet and a chair in the corner.

As we stepped farther into the room, my eyes slowly adjusting to the light, my gaze fell to a blond woman sitting on the edge of her chair right next to the hospital bed.

"That's my sister, Claudia—Olivia's mother," Jerry said. "Bear with her. She's still a bit overcome."

"Of course," Mary said.

Claudia was about fifty years old, pale, and country-looking. She did not look at us but simply clasped the hand of the girl in the bed and rocked herself back and forth slightly. A dark-haired nurse moved quickly and quietly around the other side of the bed, checking graphs and monitors.

Asleep in the bed, Olivia had a face like an angel, with long, dark eyelashes and a cute ski-slope nose. Her entire head was wrapped in white tape and gauze, with extra bandages bulging on the right side of her head, near the top. Some of those bandages were discolored. Small, clear tubes ran into her nostrils. IVs ran from her wrists to silver stands on each side of the bed, both holding pouches of clear liquid.

This was too much reality.

"Mrs. Gilbert," I said softly. "I'm Everett Lester, and this is my sister, Mary...I can't tell you how sorry I am about this."

Still rocking back and forth on the edge of her seat, the woman didn't acknowledge us. She just stared at her daughter.

"I want you to know...I will pay for everything, *everything* Olivia needs."

Mary patted my shoulder. Had she done so to encourage me to keep my mouth shut? I reflected on my words and determined what an idiot I was to offer money at a time like this, as if it could fix things.

Walking behind his sister, Jerry put his hand on her shoulder. "Thank you. That is comforting to know."

"Is she improving?" Mary asked, staring at Olivia.

"She's stable," Jerry said. "That's what the doctors are telling us. And that's good. They're watching for swelling of the brain, which would not be a good sign. But so far, there's been none. The doctors are keeping a very close eye on her."

"Has she woken up since last night?" Mary asked.

"No. They think she's in...kind of a coma."

Claudia began to weep softly, and Mary and I reached for each other.

"What more do the doctors say?" I asked.

Then several quick knocks sounded at the door, and in came a physician who looked young enough to be in college. He had dark, wavy hair and shiny gold glasses.

Moving quickly into the room he excused himself and grabbed the clipboard at the foot of Olivia's bed. He wore a white lab coat, a dangling stethoscope, Levi's, and white tennis shoes. His name was Dr. Danny Treadwell, according to the green name tag that hung haphazardly on his coat.

"Are these the most recent?" he questioned the nurse.

"Yes, Dr. Treadwell. I'm about to do them again."

Without a response, he unclipped a pen-sized flashlight from his shirt pocket and carefully pulled Olivia's right eyelid up with his thumb, shining the light in and out of her eye. Then he did the other. Next he put the stethoscope in his ears and checked her breathing. "Mrs. Gilbert, will you pull her bedsheets down, please?"

As she did, the doctor gently squeezed Olivia's right arm, bending it back and forth, then the left. He did the same with her legs once they had been tenderly uncovered.

"Nurse, I want the results from the latest Glasgow, ASAP."

"Yes, sir."

"And vitals."

"Yes, Doctor."

He straightened the pages on the clipboard and put it back in its place at the end of the bed. With a quick look and an "excuse me," he headed for the door.

I hurried to catch him just before he left. "Doctor." I tapped his shoulder. "I'm Everett…"

"I know who you are, sir." He turned toward me.

"Can you tell me what's going on…with Olivia?"

Mary joined me from behind, but the doctor hesitated, looking at Jerry, as if to ask permission to tell us more. Jerry nodded.

"Mr. Lester, ma'am," said Dr. Treadwell, barely looking me in the eyes. "Olivia sustained a severe blow to the head last night. She suffered from respiratory irregularity in the ambulance on the way back here, but fortunately we got the airway secured quickly. The wound required a good number of stitches, and we've affixed a drainage tube to the area of impact."

Taking a deep breath and exhaling, he seemed nervous and in a hurry. "There appear to be no skull or depression fractures. That's good. The problem is, she hasn't regained consciousness; that's not good. Her breathing is steady, and her motor activity seems okay. But we're doing tests to reveal any intracranial bleeding or swelling of the brain."

"What would that mean, if those things happened?" Mary whispered.

"It could be devastating," he said quietly. "She could end up in a prolonged coma. Or she could come out of it yet suffer from paralysis, seizures, personality changes, emotional disturbances…"

"So, there could be long-term issues," Mary said.

"Yes, our worst fear is major cognitive deficits."

"What do you mean?" I whispered.

"Loss of ability to think or reason intelligently. This is all speculation."

He turned toward the door. "I'm sorry, I've got to run. Good day, Mr. Lester, ma'am."

The rain came down in pelting waves as the sheriff's deputies bent me into their brown-and-orange squad car and drove toward the Justice and Administration Building.

The spray of water felt refreshing on my face and arms after having been cooped up in my cell all weekend. The dark brown vinyl seat was cold and hard. I felt alive, relishing the short drive and soaking in the glistening scenery.

Even in the downpour, dozens of reporters and camera crews waited outside the courthouse, their equipment covered by heavy plastic, their reporters standing beneath multicolored umbrellas featuring station logos.

I had heard Miami-Dade County prosecutors had subpoenaed former DeathStroke tour coordinator Tina Drew, and
sure enough, she took the stand today wearing tight gray
slacks, clunky black heels, and a lightweight black V-necked
sweater.

Tina was smart and energetic. Gray had originally introduced her to the band back in the late eighties when we were
about to launch *Deceiver*, our third album, and its coinciding
tour. At the time, Tina was single and had an MBA from
Clemson University. Although she didn't consider herself a
DeathStroke fan, the notion of organizing our domestic and
international tours thrilled her.

We instantly fell in love with the petite brunette from
Roanoke, Virginia. Not only was she wholly committed to our
success, she was organized, efficient, and confident, unafraid
of ruffling our feathers. Indeed, that turned out to be the one
thing that really made Tina and DeathStroke gel—the fact
that she was not in awe of us. Her job was to make sure our
tour went like clockwork, and she did whatever was necessary to make that happen, year in and year out.

Tina also saw what went on behind the scenes, which is
precisely why Frank Dooley had her on the stand so long
today. With Tina's reluctant help, Dooley painted the most
sordid portrait to date of Everett Lester—the flamboyant
drug addict who had ladies lined up and waiting for him in
every city.

"Miss Drew," Frank Dooley said, sipping a tall glass of
water and showing five inches of white cuff. "What about
guns or other weapons? Did you ever see Mr. Lester with a
weapon?"

"I did, on occasion."

"What kind of weapon?"

"A gun," Tina said. "A handgun."

"Any others?"

"No."

"Where did you see Mr. Lester with a handgun?"

"At times he would have one in his dressing room at a venue we were playing, or in a shoulder bag as we went back and forth from hotels to concert venues."

"Why did he carry a gun, Miss Drew?"

"I believe, for protection. Mr. Lester's life was threatened on many occasions."

"I see." Dooley looked directly at me. "In all your years working with DeathStroke, did you ever see anyone actually threaten to harm Mr. Lester?"

"Certainly," Tina said. "We often met up with protestors at our hotels, at arenas, at restaurants. Many people hated what DeathStroke stood for and threatened bodily harm to Mr. Lester and the other band members."

"Did the others carry weapons?"

"Not that I know of."

"While he was in your presence, did Mr. Lester ever have his gun available during any of these instances? When he was threatened?"

"Yes."

"Did he use it?"

"He would, ah, usually get it out and show it to people, to scare them off."

"Miss Drew," Dooley said. "Did you ever see Everett Lester fire a gun?"

"One time…we were in Oklahoma City," she said, having obviously expected this. "A group of us had gone out to a section of the city. I think it was called Bricktown. Anyway, it was a pretty night, and we were walking from one club to another when these four guys approached us. It appeared they were intoxicated. They started bad-mouthing the band and harassing me. I do believe they intended to harm us. The next thing I knew, Everett was firing shots into the air. It scared them off."

"Who was there besides you and Mr. Lester?"

"David Dibbs and Endora Crystal."

"Did Mr. Lester ever fire shots at the individuals?"

"No, just into the air."

"I see." Dooley paced the floor, allowing Tina's testimony to soak in. "Did you often socialize with Mr. Lester?"

"On occasion."

"Were you friends with Endora Crystal?"

"Yes. She traveled with us—with DeathStroke—quite a bit. She was just like one of us, part of the family, so to speak."

"So," Dooley said, arms crossed, walking in front of me, "did you often see Mr. Lester together with Endora Crystal?"

"Sure. Like I said, she was around a lot."

"Did you ever see Mr. Lester and Madam Endora argue?"

Tina waited a moment. "Endora and Everett were like a mother and son—they were that close. So in that kind of relationship, yes, naturally I saw them argue from time to time."

"Miss Drew," Dooley said with his back to her. "There is no need to preface the answers you submit. Just answer the questions and let the jury come to their own conclusions. Do you understand?"

"Okay. I just wanted to make sure the jury knew how close they were."

"Oh, we've heard how close they were."

Laughter broke out in spots throughout courtroom B-3. Boone didn't bother to interject. The damage had been done.

"Tell the court, if you will, Miss Drew, can you recall a time when there was ever a weapon present while Endora and Everett were together?"

She let out a slight sigh and swallowed hard. "Yes."

"Tell us about that instance, would you please?"

"We were on tour at a stop in Fort Myers, Florida. We had done an afternoon sound check and were back at the hotel resting before the night's performance," she said methodically. "It was forty-five minutes past the time we should have left for the arena, and no one could find Everett. His limo waited behind while the other band members went on to the venue. I was making phone calls in my room, trying to track him down. That's when I noticed Everett and Endora out on the beach, near the surf. They were arguing. I could tell by their hand and arm motions...he had a gun in his hand."

Dooley approached Tina. Resting both arms on the wooden rail in front of her, he leaned toward her. "What happened then?"

"I knew we had to get to the arena." Tina looked at me. "So I...I grabbed my things and headed down to the beach. I knew they couldn't hear me yelling at them from the balcony, and Everett wasn't answering his phone; neither was Endora."

"Okay. Then what?"

"When I got down to the entrance of the beach, I waved to get their attention. Then..."

"Did you? Get their attention?"

"No."

"So you approached them?"

"No. I just kept waving."

"Why did you stop and wave? Why didn't you simply walk down to them?"

Tina glanced away from me. She bit her lip, looked up for a moment, then back at Dooley. "He had a gun."

"Mr. Lester had a gun. Were you scared of him, Miss Drew?"

Brian Boone stood up fast. "Leading the witness!"

"Overruled," Judge Sprockett said. "Please answer, Miss Drew. Were you frightened of Mr. Lester?"

"I guess so, but I did eventually walk closer."

"And what happened? Was Mr. Lester pointing the gun at Endora?"

"He was waving it," she said, obviously shaken now. "That's the best way I can describe it."

"And did you then approach Mr. Lester?" Dooley asked.

"I got closer, within fifty or sixty feet or so, but they still didn't see me. That's when Endora suddenly stopped arguing and sat down."

"Sat down? In the sand?"

"Yes. She sat Indian-style and put both hands to her temples, like this." Tina bent her head down, closed her eyes, and gently pressed her fingertips to her temples, as if trying to concentrate.

"What did Mr. Lester do?"

"He kept...ranting. Just kind of pacing...yelling."

"Miss Drew, it is every important you tell the court, *did Mr. Lester point the gun at Endora Crystal?*"

She glanced at me, the judge, then Dooley. "He did point it at her several times during all this. But then he dropped the gun. He looked stunned. I...it...it looked as if he had been shocked...by electricity or something."

"Miss Drew, calm down. Tell us, did..."

"She made the gun go into the water," Tina announced in monotone, staring at the rail in front of her. "It lifted up and flew out into the surf, as if someone had thrown it."

A sudden murmur blew through the entire courtroom as I sat staring at the notepad in front of me, remembering distinctly how the gun had scorched my right hand. Remembering how it levitated when I reached for it.

Remembering how it rocketed into the Gulf of Mexico.

"Order," Sprockett commanded. "Be quiet in this courtroom."

"Miss Drew," Dooley took over, "when you were working as the tour coordinator for DeathStroke, did you take social drugs of any kind?"

"Absolutely never!" Tina stated, Kleenex in hand, regaining her composure.

"Because, I don't know what to make of the scenario you just described."

"Endora was a psychic, you know," Tina blurted out.

"In your opinion, was Everett Lester capable of killing Madam Endora Crystal?"

Tina had been looking at me but turned toward Dooley now. "No. Only if he was under the heavy influence of drugs or alcohol, which he wasn't at the time of…"

"Which he *was* most of the time. Thank you, Miss Drew." Dooley headed back to his seat. "No further questions for now."

11

In his own tender way, Jerry Princeton managed to get his sister Claudia to open up to Mary and me during the next several hours that we stayed in Olivia's hospital room.

Formerly a U.S. Marine, Jerry had been married for eighteen years to his high school sweetheart, Susan, until she died from complications caused by breast cancer three years earlier. They had no children, and Jerry lived by himself in nearby Grayson, Ohio, where he was the director of admissions at a small, private liberal arts college.

"Do you remember, Jerry, how Olivia used to love to swing with you when you came over to our place, like on holidays?" Claudia's eyes twinkled up at her brother.

"Ohhh," Jerry moaned, pretending to faint from exhaustion. "She would wear me out on that thing. 'Uncle Jerrrry, Uncle Jerrrrrry, give me another mile-high drop, pleeeeease,'" he imitated Olivia.

Claudia slowly opened up and told us all about Olivia's life. She was a solid B student in the ninth grade who loved cheerleading, swimming, music, movies, and friends. She was the light of everyone's life, a young lady who took an interest in others, even adults.

Olivia was the life of the party, and very loyal to her family. Claudia made it clear, too, that Olivia's father, Raymond, wasn't coping well with his daughter's injuries. He and Olivia were very close, and he was "out of sorts."

That made me feel squeamish.

The DeathStroke show in Dayton was the first big concert Olivia had ever attended. She did so with her older sister, Veronica, and a group of their friends.

Jerry took an interest in us, especially in Mary, probably because it would have been awkward for him to ask much about me. What could he have said? "So, are you still struggling with drug addiction? How long has it been since you injured someone as badly as you have my niece?"

Mary and Jerry, it turned out, had a great deal in common. They were both avid readers, loved to play racquetball, and were very involved with their churches. After Jerry lost his wife, he told us he had almost taken his own life. Instead, he turned to a friend from work at Gladstone College who cried and laughed with him—and helped him make it through the grieving process.

Ah, what it would be like to have such a friend.

The letters from Karen Bayliss shuffled through my mind. *I will call her. I will.*

Meanwhile, Mary had given Jerry her phone number and asked that he keep her informed about Olivia's condition. Jerry assured her he would and even suggested perhaps they meet for dinner sometime in the near future, since they lived only about an hour apart.

"Claudia," Mary said quietly as we were about to leave, "would it be okay if we pray for Olivia quickly before we leave?"

"Of course," she said, with a dazed look on her face. "That would be fine."

Before the uneasiness had time to engulf me, Mary had taken my hand and led me toward Olivia's bed. Jerry extended his left hand toward me, and I took it. Claudia reached up and grasped her brother's free hand.

Mary bowed her head, closed her eyes, and rested a hand on Olivia's shoulder. I shut my eyes as well.

"Father in heaven…this is a precious life, here in this bed. A dear lamb of Yours." I could hear Claudia fighting back the emotion. "Please, Lord, *please*…will You come and restore her? Please, heal this wound, we pray. Let there be no internal complications. Move in power to wake her from this sleep and let there be no lasting problems from this injury."

A moment of silence passed.

"Father," Jerry added, "You have Your reasons for everything. I know that." He paused, composing himself. "Thank You for bringing Everett and Mary here today. We see You at work here, God, in some mighty way that we don't understand. But Your Word tells us to trust in You and lean not on our own understanding. So, instead of worrying about what we see, we trust in You for her healing and for everything else You're going to do as a result of this accident. May Your Spirit heal Olivia and richly bless Mary and Everett. Strengthen Claudia, give her faith in You… God, bless Raymond. Calm him. Help him find Your peace in this storm."

"Oh, dear God!" Claudia burst in. "Please heal my baby."

She cried, and Mary's hand squeezed mine tightly as the tear that escaped my right eye caught me off guard.

"Please, God, heal my little angel. I'll do anything…"

The door to room 314 swung open, and just as I turned toward it, my nose and upper lip were smashed by the swooping, iron fist of Raymond Gilbert.

The floodgates in my nose burst open. Blood let loose everywhere as I saw neon stars whirl by, and then I collapsed to the floor.

Raymond Gilbert was all over me.

"How dare you come here!" He pummeled me with his boots.

"Stop, Raymond!" Jerry staggered to get between me and his brother-in-law.

"Get him ouuuuut!" Raymond shoved Jerry out of the way then jacked me in the face with another right.

The room spun.

"Stop it!" Mary screamed. "Stop!"

Still down on the floor, I felt Raymond kick me again, then grab me underneath my armpits and drag me to the door.

"You dirty…filthy…" he inhaled deeply after every word, "piece of garbage. I knew I never should have let her go!"

With what had to be all of his might, he slammed me against the inside of the large wood door. My head and the top of my neck cracked hard, and I dropped to the floor, blood all over the front of me.

Mary squealed and dashed to my side. Jerry locked Raymond in a bear hug from behind, but he didn't fight.

"Don't ever come near us again," he gasped, spitting every word, his sand-colored hair sticking to the sweat on his forehead.

"Sorry," I managed, out of breath, my whole body aching. "So sorry…"

"You're gonna pay." He pointed a long, crooked finger at me as Jerry continued to harness him from behind.

"No…Raymond, *please!*" Claudia cried. "Stop. This is *too much*…"

"I'm gonna ruin you." He ignored the pleas of his wife. "I'm gonna sue you for everything you got. Now, git outta here, before I—" another flying boot came toward me but missed—"put you in intensive care."

"Isn't it true that you carried a 3.95 grade point average in high school?" Brian Boone cross-examined Tina Drew, who was still licking her wounds from Dooley's attack.

"Yes."

"And is it true that in just three and a half years, you earned a bachelor's degree in business from Columbia University?"

"That's right," Tina said.

"And what did you do next?"

"I held a job with a Fortune 500 company while working my way through graduate school at Clemson. There, I earned an MBA in international business."

"Have you ever seen a psychiatrist, an analyst, or a hypnotist?" asked Boone.

"No, sir."

"Have you ever been arrested, accused of a crime, or even been pulled over for an auto violation?"

"No. None of those."

"And tell the court, if you will, the condition of your eyesight."

"I see twenty-twenty."

"And Miss Drew—" Boone spun around to face me—"did you ever, in all your days with DeathStroke, or at any time, see Everett Lester kissing or hugging or showing any kind of romantic affection whatsoever for Madam Endora Crystal?"

"Never even close," Tina said, getting the wind back in her sails.

Boone smiled at Judge Sprockett. "Your Honor, I need it to go on record that Tina Drew is an exemplary witness. This is a smart, honest, upright citizen. She has no reason to make up a story about a gun flying into the ocean. No, she is telling us the truth about what she saw on that beach in Fort Myers. And that is why I need to impress it upon your heart that there are some very...very strange circumstances shrouding the life and death of Edith Rosenbaum—Madam Endora Crystal.

"Miss Drew," he turned to Tina, "have you ever heard of telekinesis?"

"Yes I have," Tina said, bending her shoulders back. "After the episode I described in Fort Myers between Everett and Endora, I researched telekinesis."

"And what did your research reveal?"

Frank Dooley tossed his pen onto the table in front of him but remained seated. "Your Honor, I object. Madam Endora Crystal is dead. She is not on trial. But the man seated at the table next to me, the man with the gun, Everett Lester, is on trial here—for murder in the first degree. May we try his case? What's the relevance of Mr. Boone's line of questioning?"

"Point well taken." Judge Sprockett removed his glasses from the end of his long nose and leaned forward in his tall, black chair. "However, I think you would agree, this is a most unusual case. We are dealing with a victim who dealt heavily in mysticism, the psychic realm, and the occult. Therefore, as Mr. Boone has said, this case is likely going to take us some places we don't normally go...some places we may not feel comfortable going. I believe it will have to be that way. Objection overruled."

I exhaled deeply and relaxed slightly as Boone stood up from the edge of the table in front of me where he had been seated for a moment. He strode to the witness box. This was clearly his most poignant defense to date. He delivered each question to Tina like a mouthwatering home run ball, which she hit over the fence. And as she did, Boone looked directly into the eyes of juror after juror, one by one, right down the line.

"Miss Drew, you were about to tell us what your research revealed about telekinesis."

"Yes, sir. Telekinesis is the ability to move an object with the power of the mind only, with no physical touch."

"Are you suggesting that's what happened in the incident on the beach between Everett Lester and Endora Crystal? That Endora moved the gun by using telekinetic powers?"

"That's the only explanation I can come up with. I've read that people who have this ability—telekinesis—can learn to control it and even *use* it, especially in emotional situations where there is substantial fear or anger."

"I cannot believe what is happening here." Dooley groaned, crossing his arms in disgust.

"That's enough, Mr. Dooley," Judge Sprockett said.

"And that's all I have for now." Boone headed back to the table with a slight grin on his boyish face.

I didn't know where I was, and I didn't care. It was nothing new for me to wake up feeling drugged or to be in a strange place. What was new and what I did care about, however, was the sheer pain that pulsated from my face and body.

As I cracked open my eyes and lifted my head from the big pillow to look around the dark, unfamiliar room, pain scorched my neck. Then I noticed a bulk of white bandages on my nose. It had to be broken, the soreness told me. I reached up to feel a boxy splint on my nose and gauze and tape on my jaw.

Dropping my head back onto the pillow, I stared up at the white ceiling and recalled seeing Olivia Gilbert asleep, covered in tubes and tape and bandages. Fourteen years old…swimming…cheerleading…*coma*.

I remembered praying over her bed with Mary, Jerry, and Claudia.

I remembered the boy doctor, Danny Treadwell.

Cincinnati! *I'm supposed to be in Cincinnati.*

What time was it?

Wincing, I propped myself up on the edge of the bed.

Two thirty-five and light outside.

People and companies and cash registers…*counting on me.*

Dibbs and Scoogs and Crazee…Gray Harris.

I've got to go! *But there's no way.*

My father's displeasure.

Liza…gone.

Endora.

My head reeled from it all.

Death would be better than this.

A sick feeling rolled through my stomach and up to my throat as I remembered the enraged face of Raymond Gilbert.

A father's passionate love…

Disregarding the pain that coursed through me, I dashed into the small bathroom where I fell to my knees, vomiting violently into the toilet.

Unrolling a wad of toilet paper from the holder next to me, I swiped my mouth and dropped back against the wall of the cramped bathroom. I was burning up. The pain in my neck and face was almost unbearable. Feeling the sickness coming again, I hoisted myself up and vomited.

Grasping the front edge of the sink with trembling hands, I looked into the mirror. This was not my shirt. Someone had changed me. The splint appeared huge over my swollen cheeks. Even worse were the dark purple half circles that had settled beneath my eyes.

A pit deep in my stomach screamed out. My head pulsed.

Drugs.

I crawled to my black shoulder bag, which sat on a chair in the corner. My hands shook almost violently as I rummaged through.

Nothing.

I groaned and felt the weight of the world.

So alone.

Sleep…just let me sleep.

I started to fade out but then remembered the promise I had made to myself. "I will call Karen Bayliss. I *will.*"

My phone was off. Holding down the red button with one hand to power it back up, with the other I found the letter on which I had scribbled Karen's number; it stuck out of the small brown Bible in my bag.

I didn't hesitate to dial the number this time but punched it in quickly, as if Karen was the drug I had been longing for a moment ago.

Two rings…

"Hi, this is Karen. I can't make it to the phone right now, but leave a message if you like. Hope to talk to you soon… Bye!"

Beeeeeep.

"Hi…" I sniffed. "This is Everett…Everett Lester. I…I get your letters. They mean something to me. Uh, I don't know… I've been meaning to contact you. I need help, I really do. I'm just messed up. Um…uh…thank you…for caring. Good-bye."

I turned the phone off and slept.

12

When I woke up again, my face and sides were sore to the touch, and my neck felt as if I had been in a car wreck.

After lying in bed for a few minutes thinking about Olivia, our packed concert schedule, the recording project in California, and all my other commitments, my heart raced. Sheer anxiety forced me up.

I walked gingerly to the window, moved the curtains open about six inches with the back of my hand, and peered out. My room overlooked a picturesque backyard, nicely mowed and filled with trees and greenery. The long shadows told me it was late afternoon.

My black bag was still in the chair in the corner.

In the bathroom, I patted my mangled face with a wet washcloth, rinsed my hands, and brushed my hair. Then I eased open the door to my room, which led out to a cozy family room lit by skylights and a tin lamp. It featured wood floors, a dark brown couch, fireplace, built-in bookcases, and rustic exposed beams overhead.

"Hello," I called out, walking into the room.

The largest of the framed pictures sitting upright on the built-in desk showed a young Jerry Princeton with his arm around a beautiful blond woman, probably the wife who died. Their hair was blowing in the wind. They were both tan, wore sunglasses, and held drinks. It looked as if they were on a boat.

"Hello," I said louder.

Another photograph, a black and white, showed Jerry and four other uniformed Marines, smoking cigarettes and showing off their tattoos and rifles. There was also what appeared to be a family portrait with Jerry and Claudia, their parents, and two other men who I guessed were brothers. Then I picked up a small framed photograph of Claudia and Raymond Gilbert with their smiling daughters, Olivia and Veronica.

Memories of the dysfunctional Lester family began to emerge, but I quickly suppressed them. Olivia glowed in the photograph. She was so completely different than she looked lying in the hospital bed.

"Anybody home?" I yelled, walking into the kitchen.

The island in the middle of the room was clean, except for an orange bottle of pills, which sat on a sheet of white paper. I picked the note up and read:

Everett –

After you were treated at the hospital in Dayton yesterday, Mary didn't think you should travel far and agreed to bring you here to my home in Grayson, Ohio. It is just east of Dayton and should give you adequate privacy during the media coverage.

In case you didn't figure it out yet, you have a broken nose! You've been quite heavily sedated, and more pain medication is here, should you need it. Don't worry about upcoming concerts. Mary is handling everything with Gray

Harris. I am at work, will be home around five-thirty. Help yourself to food in fridge and pantry.

For now, rest.

Fondly,

Jerry Princeton

I picked up the bottle of pills prescribed in my name. One every four to six hours. I tapped two into my hand, found a glass, and swallowed them with tap water. Then I put the orange bottle in my pocket and casually opened a cabinet here and there, hoping to find a bottle of wine or something to wet my whistle.

On top of the white refrigerator, I noticed a maroon Bible and a small, black hardbound notebook. I got the books down. Leafing through the worn Bible, I noticed that many of its words and verses had been highlighted with yellow and orange markers; others were underlined and circled in ink. Words were written up and down the margins. The black notebook appeared to be Jerry's personal journal. I put both books back as they were atop the fridge.

Opening a door in the kitchen, I looked down several steps into a clean two-car garage. Jerry had a nice workbench, with lamps, cabinets, and shelves full of tools. Next, I opened the door to the pantry, found a box of Ritz crackers, and helped myself, taking the box with me.

I peered into the small dining room, then walked into a nicely decorated study, with a maple desk, a comfortable reading chair and ottoman, and a wall full of books—complete with a rolling library ladder. One wall was filled with unique paintings, watercolors and oils.

There was a painting of an orange sunset, a fisherman repairing a buoy, sea oats at the beach, and one of a lighthouse at night. Another showed Jesus and his disciples in a boat, surrounded by a raging storm. Christ stood with his arms stretched skyward, and the sun began to shine in the background. Words were written in calligraphy below: *"He got up, rebuked the wind and said to the waves, 'Quiet! Be still!' Then the wind died down and it was completely calm."*—Mark 4:39.

So this is where Jerry gets his peace… Even the tough Marine is a sheep.

Heading back to the family room, I found the remote control on the arm of the couch and turned on the TV. Flipping through the channels, I stopped at CNN *Headline News*, thinking I might see something about the events of the past two days.

During a commercial break, I pulled up the white T-shirt Jerry must have loaned me and examined several spots that were particularly painful. Slowly lifting the tape that covered a large bandage on my left side, I saw a red welt about the circumference of a softball. It was hot to the touch. Several ample purple and yellow bruises decorated the middle of my chest. Reaching behind me, I felt another warm lump on my lower back.

"Real news. Real fast. This is CNN Headline News *with Linda Stockton and Chuck Richards…*

"Management for the heavy metal band DeathStroke announced today that it will cancel at least the next ten shows of its forty-eight-city Rowdy tour. This news comes one day after fourteen-year-old ninth grader Olivia Gilbert of Xenia, Ohio, was struck in the head by a microphone stand thrown into the audience by DeathStroke lead singer Everett Lester at a concert before thousands of people at Dayton Arena.

"The young girl remains in a coma, in guarded condition at Good Samaritan Hospital.

"Fifteen other people were treated and released from local hospitals after suffering from breathing difficulties, cuts, and bruises sustained in a riot and stampede that ensued when Lester passed out onstage, and the concert was abruptly cancelled.

"Further developments have revealed that Lester was badly beaten by the Xenia girl's father when attempting to visit her at the hospital. Unconfirmed sources say Lester sustained a broken nose, cuts, and abrasions in the tussle.

"Numerous reports indicate that Lester was intoxicated before the concert began and continued to imbibe openly during the show. Dayton

police have questioned numerous people in the case and have said they are looking for Lester in order to question him. However, his whereabouts at this time are unknown.

"Insiders say the parents of Olivia Gilbert are considering filing charges against the bad boy rocker. For more, here's CNN's Byron Pinter…"

"Good evening, Linda and Chuck," said the handsome black reporter, standing outside Good Samaritan Hospital. *"Dayton police are investigating this case, which could lead to aggravated assault and other charges against Lester—even manslaughter, should the young girl die.*

"Meanwhile, her father has made it clear he wants Lester punished for his actions. Gilbert could file suit against Lester right now for battery, compensatory damages for the wrong done to his daughter, and hefty punitive damages—designed to dissuade the guilty party from repeating his actions.

"Although Gilbert is anxious to file suit, his attorneys may advise him to wait until Lester is brought to trial by the Dayton district attorney, if indeed he is. This way, Gilbert's attorneys could use to their advantage all of the pertinent material gathered in the case by the district attorney's office—including evidence, witness transcripts, and factual data.

"We'll keep a close eye on this one, Linda and Chuck. For now, this is Byron Pinter reporting live from Good Samaritan Hospital in Dayton, Ohio."

Setting the black bag on the floor in my room, I lowered myself onto the chair, found my phone, turned it on, and held down the button programmed with Endora's cell phone number.

"Endora Crystal," she picked up, sounding as if she was on speakerphone.

"It's me."

"Where *are* you?" she hissed.

"Sounds like the cops are looking for me."

"Them and everybody else. Are you okay?"

"Pretty banged up."

"You poor thing. Where on earth are you? I know you're not at your sister's."

"What am I gonna do? This girl's in a coma."

"Everett, you need to listen to me very carefully," she said, pronouncing every word slowly, systematically. "This may be the most important conversation we ever have. Do you understand?"

"I'm here."

"You need to get yourself to the Dayton police and cooperate with them—however they want."

"But…"

"I'm not finished," she yelled over the sounds of traffic. "Then…we're going to get you back in the studio to finish *Freedom*. We've cancelled ten concerts so we can get that monkey off our backs. You can sing, can't you?"

I didn't say anything.

"Are you there?"

"Yeah."

"Once we're done with *Freedom*, hopefully you'll be well enough to finish the Rowdy tour."

"There's a girl in a coma, Endora! Do you live in the real world? My nose is broken!"

"Gray and the attorneys are handling all the legal stuff. All of it. Okay? To you, it doesn't exist."

"That girl exists! I saw her… She may never be the same."

"She'll make it," Endora said coldly. "I really feel she's going to make it."

"We're talkin' aggravated assault, battery…"

"Everett, I just hung up with Gray."

"Manslaughter!"

"No suit has been filed," she shot back. "The district attorney hasn't charged you. And if any charges are filed, our attorneys will get you off. The worst you'll have to do is pay damages."

"How do you know I'm not at Mary's place?"

"I called her," she said, followed by a deep drag on a cigarette.

"When?"

"She knows where you are, doesn't she? Why are you keeping it such a big secret?"

"I need to figure out what to do…"

"I just told you what to do! Don't be freaked out and don't go on some heavy guilt trip about this thing. Remember…judgment, condemnation—they're lies from hell, Everett. Don't be hard on yourself. Move on. Rest in the security of knowing that your friends are going to get you out of this mess. Soon it will all be just a blip on the screen."

"What else did Mary say?"

"That the two of you went to visit the girl at the hospital, and that's the last she saw you. Listen, I don't care where you are, as long as you do what I tell you! Number one: Go to the Dayton police. Number two: Call Gray and tell him how soon you can be back out to The Groove. Is two more days enough?"

I stared blankly out the window at the falling darkness. It reminded me of the shade of my soul.

"Well…you decide," she snapped. "But make it quick. We need to finish this record. Tina says sponsors are chomping at the bit to bid on the Freedom tour. That thing could launch as early as a month after the Rowdy tour ends. Listen, get some rest. You'll feel much better in the morning. And leave your phone on! I want access to you."

"Are the guys ticked?"

"They'll get over it. They're probably glad to have another few days off. None of us could believe you went to visit that girl. Great PR move."

"*It wasn't PR!*"

"I'm just teasing," she said. "Do you need me to come to you?"

"No…where are you?"

"I'm in a cab on my way to a reading. A high-ranking official with the New York Stock Exchange in Manhattan… Hey, by the way, if I decide to stay over, can I crash at your place?"

"Help yourself."

"You're a doll. Be happy now, pumpkin! Everything's going to be fine."

She hung up, and I held the phone in my lap and stared outside.

It was the kind of yard where children would love to run and play hide-and-go-seek. Had Olivia ever romped in this backyard?

The clock by the bed showed 5:25. Jerry was due home. I couldn't decide whether to ask him to drive me to the Dayton police, to leave the house on foot and run from all this, or to take every pill in my pocket.

The stench in my cell was overwhelming tonight. What I wouldn't give for some fresh air. Ever since I was incarcerated on murder charges, and throughout the trial, my life had become abysmally sedentary. I couldn't stand it. I was used to moving, going, doing. But now, I was either sitting in an uncomfortable, straight-backed wooden chair in courtroom B-3 or lying on this soft, lumpy mattress behind these chipped white bars.

But I would say this—I'd grown in the past few weeks. I was forced to learn about trust and hope, about patience, about being content in the here and now. There was plenty of time to read, which is what I did most of the time when I wasn't writing these memoirs. I also did several sets of sit-ups and push-ups when I got up in the mornings—just to keep the blood flowing.

Although they wouldn't let me have my guitar in here (Brian was working on that), I still managed to scribble down quite a few new tunes and lyrics. Perhaps I'll share those with you later.

The lights were dim in here. It was depressing. Like I said, the smell was always bad. At night, when the lights

flickered off at 10 P.M., I could hear men crying, screaming…laughing wickedly. The sounds echoed off these
concrete walls like bad dreams.

I had a friend in here named Scotty; didn't know his last
name. He'd served four years of a twelve-year sentence for
armed robbery. He had a wife and two young children at
home and struggled with depression. Scotty was strung out
on drugs when he did the crime and needed the money to pay
for his fix.

I understood. And I hoped I could encourage him.

A large shadow crept up my legs and darkened my chest
and the pages of these memoirs.

I looked up to see the outline of Zaney's massive body
covering what little overhead light came in from outside my
cell. He held a mop in one fist and a bucket in the other.
Looking both ways, he set them down and pressed his pudgy
nose between the bars.

He stared in at me for what seemed like a minute.

"I am anti-Christ," he finally whispered. "So was
Endora… You know that, don't you?"

My stomach tanked and I froze to the bunk.

"You were doin' so well, Lester." He leaned his head back
a few inches. "We were settin' people free…legions of people!
Through the wide gate, down the broad road—"

"To destruction," I said, surprised by my own words.

He squeezed the bars next to each side of his head with
both mitts and sneered at me. "That's right…*to destruction*.
And when you found that out, we started losing you, didn't
we?"

He backed up, looked all around, then smashed his fat
face between the bars.

"We couldn't let that happen, Lester. We couldn't *lose*
you. We had to do something."

"What are you talking about…Endora Crystal's death?"

"The ultimate sacrifice."

"I don't know what you had to do with Endora, but whatever it was, it's backfiring."

"We're not done yet," he spewed. "I told you, we *will* finish what we started. Sleep with your eyes open, Lester, and tell your lovely to do the same."

He picked up the bucket, grabbed the mop, and took several steps. "And don't bother havin' Boone call me to the witness stand." He smirked. "After all, I'm the father of lies."

He managed a sick laugh and lumbered away, repeating the words, "That's just my nature… That's just my nature…"

13

Mary took the day off from her many real estate calls to pick up my attorney at the Dayton International Airport. Brian had flown in from New York to be with me as I turned myself in to the Dayton police department for questioning in the Olivia Gilbert incident.

Jerry Princeton couldn't have been more kind. He saw to it that I was well fed and rested at his comfortable home. We talked at length during meals and while watching ball games. It turned out that during his days in the service, he was a rock 'n' roll junkie and even had a bent for DeathStroke music, in his rowdier moments.

That first night, when Jerry returned home from work, he found me sitting in my room, staring out the window with the bottle of pain pills in my hand. He sat on the edge of my messed-up bed, and we talked about life, about family, about growing up, about love—and about his beautiful wife, Susan, who was snatched from him by cancer when she was just thirty-seven.

That's when Jerry had considered suicide…with his service revolver…right here in the same room, staring out the same window, wondering the same things: Why was life so cruel, so lonely? What was the meaning of life? Why was I here?

I had known Jerry less than a month, and I considered him a warm and honest man. In fact, I had never been exposed to such love and interest from another human being; therefore, I wasn't certain I could trust it. But Jerry had been on the front lines of war, he'd done drugs, he'd lost a young wife, he'd contemplated suicide. And yet…he was sane. He was standing. His life even seemed to flourish.

Just by being there and being transparent, Jerry enticed me to open up and share things I hadn't shared with anyone.

"My old man and I argued all the time," I confessed. "He beat me often."

"How did those skirmishes make you feel?"

"Terrified…of the next time."

I cried, flooding his waiting heart with my deep-rooted feelings of inadequacy, hatred, incompetence, bitterness, and fear of man.

Jerry listened. He related. We became friends.

"I have so much rebellion inside. Even though I'm famous, I'm so lonely. There's no contentment. I feel depressed and guilty all the time. It ticks me off."

"And you've become determined never to be hurt again, haven't you?"

"In a way, yeah. I live a defensive life, that's for sure."

"Maybe that's why you developed a love for guns."

During one of our chats, Jerry explained in a casual, heart-to-heart way that God had come into his life when Susan died. He said that Christ could be my lifeline, too. Although I listened intently out of courtesy, I just could not get my head around what he was telling me; I couldn't bring it into focus. It seemed far off, untouchable—something for other people. However, Jerry's countenance and compassion toward me didn't change as a result of my lack of response—and that intrigued me.

He took the morning off from his job at Gladstone College to drive me to meet Mary and Boone at the Dayton police department. On the way, he told me he had seen Mary the night before at Good Samaritan Hospital and that his niece remained in serious condition. There had been no change.

Mary and Jerry had seen each other almost every day at the hospital and had shared dinner and walks several times since the incident with Olivia. Claudia and Raymond Gilbert hadn't filed charges yet and, to my knowledge, had no idea I was staying at the home of Claudia's brother.

Unbeknownst to me, Gray Harris flew in, rented a car, and met us at the police department. While Brian, Gray, and I met with a jazzed-up, four-person team of Dayton investigators, Mary and Jerry took off to find a good cup of coffee and enjoy a morning out together.

I won't bore you with all the details of the interrogation with the police. My initial impression was that they were four rednecks on a witch hunt. Then again, a fourteen-year-old girl lying in a coma had been injured on their watch—and they wanted answers.

The three men and one woman plainclothes team of investigators escorted us into a dark, windowless, smoke-filled room where, just like in the movies, a lone overhead light dangled low over the table between us.

With tape recorders rolling, I told the investigators how I had slept in late the day of the concert at Dayton Arena, my normal routine while on tour. "I was especially tired that day, because we had been recording in California, had flown in for a show in Toledo, then jetted down to Dayton in the wee hours of the morning.

"When I woke up in my hotel room, it was about 2:15 or 2:30 P.M. I ordered room service, watched TV, and ate alone. Then Gray Harris, David Dibbs, several staffers, and I played cards down the hall.

"Limos took us to the arena for a sound check at 4:30. After ninety minutes at the venue, I met up with Charlie LaRoche, a friend and DeathStroke staff member, and we had a driver take us to some clubs in downtown Dayton, the names of which I can't remember. From there, it was back to Dayton Arena for the concert."

Naturally, the investigators grilled me about my drug and alcohol consumption that day. Knowing every eye was on me in public, I told them the truth about drinking several beers and mixed drinks that afternoon and evening at the clubs. I did not mention, however, the excessive amounts of cocaine and marijuana Charlie and I had consumed during the hours before the show.

Was I swigging from a bottle of Jack Daniels onstage during the concert that night in Dayton? I knew I couldn't deny it, so I said yes. When the investigators—especially the strong, young black woman named Tammy—pressed me for details about the concert, I told them I only remembered bits and pieces. That was the truth.

"What is the last song you remember performing the night of the concert?" she asked.

"I just can't remember," I said, trying to comply. "It may have been 'Souls on Fire,' I'm just not sure."

"You did do that song, fourth in the set," she confirmed. "Do you remember doing the new song, 'Freedom'?"

"No…I don't."

"No recollection about your interaction with the crowd during that song…your making statements about your beliefs and the crowd chanting back?"

"No."

"No recollection of talking about breaking free from bondage to God?" Her temperature seemed to rise with each word. "No recollection of having the audience repeat after you, something about a vow to lash out against Christians who forced their religion on you?"

"No." I laughed innocently. "I mean, I don't remember that. You've got to understand how absolutely fatigued I was from all the travel and pressure—"

"What we understand, Mr. Lester," lead investigator Bernie Novak raised his voice, "is that you came into our city out of your mind on drugs, spewing your anti-religious mumbo jumbo. The next thing we know, a young girl is in critical condition from a blow to the head, fifteen others are transported to the hospital after almost suffocating to death, and dozens more go home with a newfound fear of crowds. Do you remember slinging the microphone stand into the audience?"

"No." I looked at Gray, then Boone.

Novak eyed his colleagues and paused. "That's all the questions we have for now, Mr. Lester."

The investigators remained seated as we stood and began shuffling out of the dark room, hoping no more would be said.

"Mr. Lester," came Novak's deep voice.

The three of us turned around.

"We are going to do all in our power to put you behind bars for this heartless crime."

Gray put his arms around my waist and Boone's and continued prodding us out the door.

"Pray Olivia Gilbert doesn't pass away, Mr. Lester." Novak's voice boomed as we rounded the corner. "Pray that little girl doesn't die!"

During an urgent late-night phone call to my attorney's rental home in North Miami, I filled Brian in on my close encounter with one Zane Bender, aka Zaney. In the hundreds of hours of research Boone had done in the case thus far, Zaney's name had not surfaced—until now.

Boone said he would look into it.

For a few minutes, I felt exceptionally good in courtroom B-3 this morning. Boone had brought me a large cup of Starbuck's breakfast blend with just the right amount of cream and sugar—still hot. I could have kissed him.

Unfortunately, the coffee buzz lasted only so long.

My old pal Charlie LaRoche—with his patented five o'clock shadow and greasy jet-black hair—leaned coolly to one side of the witness stand, the same way he leaned while steering his old, rust-colored Impala.

I used to call Charlie "Jewelry Man." Straight from Queens, this guy was your stereotypical, tough-as-nails New Yorker. Thick gold and silver chains. Big, heavy rings. Shirt unbuttoned halfway to his belt. Lavender tinted glasses. Black leather jacket and shiny black shoes. He reminded me of one of John Travolta's cronies in *Saturday Night Fever.*

I warned Boone early on that Charlie's testimony could be damaging, and Frank Dooley did his best to make sure of that.

As it turned out, Dooley forced Charlie to reveal to the jury—and the world (the media hype surrounding the case was mounting daily)—that he was a paid employee of DeathStroke. Once Dooley stripped away the facade that Charlie was some kind of pyrotechnics consultant or special tour assistant, all that was left was the glaring truth.

"And so, Mr. LaRoche," Dooley said with his arms crossed, pacing in front of the jury in his shiny gray suit, "it was your job to score drugs for Everett Lester, mainly while DeathStroke was traveling—correct?"

"Yeah," Charlie said nonchalantly, in his low New York accent. "And the other guys in the band who wanted 'em. Ricky didn't do drugs; the others did."

"Why was this? Why couldn't Mr. Lester and the other band members score their own drugs?"

"One…they didn't have time to be messin' with that. Two…they couldn't transport their own drugs from city to city while traveling by plane—airport security."

"And that's where you came in." Dooley made sure his silver cuff links were on snug and showing.

"That's right." Charlie slid the palm of his hand through his shiny hair and exhaled loudly. "I was a step ahead of the band, scoring drugs in upcoming tour cities, providing whatever they wanted, and moving on to the next city to do it all over again. Whatever drugs they didn't use in a given city, they were supposed to trash, so we wouldn't leave a trail."

Charlie had barely made eye contact with me today, and the few times he had, it seemed to be with disgust.

"What drugs did you supply to Everett Lester?"

"Most of those mentioned already in this trial."

"Tell the court again, please, Mr. LaRoche," Dooley said, tightening and straightening the small knot in his maroon tie.

"Marijuana. Cocaine. Hash."

"Heroin?" Dooley asked.

"Sometimes…when he was really depressed."

"Mr. LaRoche." Dooley walked toward him. "Did you ever supply Mr. Lester with weapons?"

Charlie paused from picking at his cuticles, raised his dark eyebrows, and searched the room with his eyes. "Weapons weren't my specialty. But on occasion I would find him a gun if he felt he needed one or didn't have access to one."

"You say, 'If he felt he needed one.' Would you describe Everett Lester as paranoid, Mr. LaRoche?"

"He could get a little wigged out at times, kind of lookin' over his shoulder a lot, but it never struck me as excessive."

"Did you know Madam Endora Crystal?"

"Yeah."

"Would you say you knew her well?"

Charlie frowned. "Not really."

"Were you ever together with Madam Endora and Mr. Lester?"

"Sure," he said, suppressing a burp. "'Scuse me."

Dooley flashed him a look of distaste. "Did Endora use drugs?"

"Sometimes. Not much."

"Of the times you were together with Endora and Everett, did the two ever argue?"

"Frequently," he said.

"Did you ever see Everett threaten Endora in any way?"

"Sort of. They were so close; it was like they had these little family squabbles. He would tell her to knock it off or shut up, you know, things of that nature. And she wouldn't back down to him at all. She was a tough old gal."

"Did you see them hit each other?"

"There were little flare-ups," Charlie said, bored. "He would push her arm away, she would slap him on the back of the head. Things like that."

"Mr. LaRoche," Dooley said, turning to look directly at me, "do you believe Mr. Lester and Madam Endora were romantically involved?"

Charlie froze sarcastically, staring straight ahead. "I don't think so." He laughed. "Then again, I guess that question did cross my mind over the years. It just seemed odd, with the age difference and all—and all the other women Everett had access to…"

Charlie knew very well Endora and I weren't involved romantically. He was trying to get back at me. But for what? We had been friends, or so I thought. Perhaps he just didn't like the Everett Lester he was looking at across the courtroom today.

"Mr. LaRoche," Dooley said, sipping his water. "Can you tell the court, are there any other times when you saw or heard Everett Lester threaten the life of Endora Crystal?"

He hesitated ever so slightly. "One time…Everett and I and the band were on a private jet headed from New York to

Nashville for some TV interview. This was fairly close to the time of Endora's death. Everett told me Endora was messing with his head. He said he was going to get rid of her, but he was afraid she wouldn't leave him alone, wouldn't go quietly."

I moved uncomfortably in my seat as the crowd whispered.

"Okay, why did he want to 'get rid of her'?"

"I guess she had been trying to communicate, or whatever you call it, with people from his life who had died...like his old man and Liza Moon. He was sick of it. He felt she had just come way too far into his personal life. He didn't say these words, but he implied he was being manipulated by her."

"So, Mr. Lester said he was going to 'get rid of her,'" Dooley repeated. "'But he was afraid she wouldn't leave him alone, wouldn't go quietly.' What else did he say to that end?"

One glance at me and Charlie looked down and spoke. "He said the relationship with Endora was going to end and that, lately, it had been like a bad dream. In fact, during that trip to Nashville, he told me they were on the outs. She had disappeared for a few days. He was scared, I think—"

"Scared of what?" Dooley pressed.

"I think he was apprehensive because he felt she had some kind of evil power that she might use against him. That's just my opinion."

Dooley stood in silence, waiting, knowing a good witness for the prosecution when he had one in his clean, well-manicured hands.

"On that flight I told you about, he told me he would do anything to end the relationship with Endora." Charlie raised his head toward Dooley.

"To the best of your recollection, what did Mr. Lester say about that, exactly?"

"He said something like, 'I've got to get rid of her. No matter what it takes…she's gone.'"

Clenching my teeth and closing my eyes, I lowered my head dejectedly—and prayed.

14

By the time everyone met back at The Groove in Santa Clarita, several days after I was questioned by the Dayton police, almost every single person was high on something.

The recording had dragged on for months, and the tension was as thick as the smoke floating in the studio.

A few forged attempts at sympathy were made toward me, with the splint on my nose and the dark bruises beneath my bloodshot eyes, but mainly I felt resentment zeroing in on me from every direction—the band, Gray Harris, Tina Drew, Pamela McCracken, even the production staff.

Maybe I was just paranoid, but it seemed like my performance in Dayton and the injuries that ensued, along with the concert cancellations, were just the latest cause for embitterment.

Everyone sought their own way of escape. Even Gray Harris, our dependable leader, had begun to use cocaine to whiteout the dark and frantic strain of recent weeks.

One of the few people not high was bassist Ricky Crazee, who had amazingly kicked his past addictions to drugs and alcohol several years earlier. He had done it cold turkey and was still clean.

Ironically, Ricky was perhaps more miserable than any of us, as he attempted to lend soberness and leadership to the chaotic task of wrapping up the recording of *Freedom*. In his attempt to organize the final leg of the project, he was met by pride, stubbornness, and apathy from a bunch of people who were half stoned out of our minds.

Me…I had decided to imbibe a slow, steady flow of Scotch and painkillers to extinguish the fiery darts of those around me. Alone in the dark, denlike studio lounge, which was lit by several mod lamps and decorated with a floor-to-ceiling rock waterfall, I poured myself a Dewar's, settled into a comfortable recliner, and lit a Salem.

Although the splint on my nose was a nuisance, the whiskey numbed the pain in my face and neck. Resting my head back and blowing smoke, my eyes fell to a black electric guitar that hung on the wall, a gift the band and I had signed and given to the owners of The Groove. It was one of many instruments, plaques, and framed records that hung neatly on the walls and glowed impressively beneath the low-lit track lighting.

Then I thought about Olivia Gilbert in room 314. My mind kept returning to her—the tubes and tape and bandages and drainage device—and her mother Claudia rocking bemused by her bedside. Nor could I erase the memory of the days spent with Jerry Princeton and Mary—a time that had made me feel accepted, hopeful…refreshed.

With the Scotch and cigarette in one hand, I casually fingered my way through a basket of mail that sat on a small table next to my chair. When I realized it was DeathStroke fan mail that had been forwarded from fan club manager Jeff Hall, I rocked the leg rest up on the recliner and sat forward in one motion.

Setting my drink on the table and putting the basket in my lap, I picked through the stack letter by letter, searching for the familiar envelope, handwriting, and postmark from Topeka.

There it is.

Finding one envelope from Karen, I searched the remainder of the stack for others. There was only one.

Rubbing the Salem out in the ashtray next to my chair, I set the basket of mail on the floor and gave the letter from Karen my full attention.

Greetings Mr. Lester,

Sorry it's been a while since I've written. I've been extremely busy with my job and helping out with the youth group at my church. But I haven't stopped thinking of you.

What a surprise it was to hear your voice on my answering machine! I only wish I could have been there to speak with you. When you called, you sounded discouraged and confused. I am sorry.

I read about Olivia Gilbert. The teens at our church are praying for her to pull through. It was kind of you to visit her at the hospital. I'm sorry about what happened to you there and hope you are healing quickly.

Mr. Lester, I feel in my heart that there is a spiritual battle being waged over you right now—even as I write this letter. Each time I pray for you, tears come to my eyes because of the emotion bucking up inside me.

Do you feel the battle going on in your life?

I know the word *Satan* probably sounds ridiculous to you, but the Bible tells us he is real, and it warns that he is out to "kill, steal, and destroy" each of us. Satan will fight powerfully to stop you from believing in Jesus Christ. He will manifest himself to you in the allure of drugs, women, money, and power; he will make you feel like you're not good enough to be God's child; and he will use devastating circumstances and evil people to thwart you.

But I sense God is calling you, Mr. Lester. Do you hear Him?

He's using me to call out to you, and probably others.

Don't ignore Him. Please! Call out to Him. Are you tired of your life? Fall into His arms of love. Open up to Him like a friend. He is waiting.

When I first believed, I said a prayer, something like this: "Lord, I'm a sinner. I've done so much wrong. But I know the Bible says You died to forgive my sins. I repent of them. I turn away from them. And with Your strength—with the power that raised Jesus from the tomb—I vow to follow You, and to give the rest of my life to You. Amen."

I'll be in touch again soon. Until then, warmest regards from Topeka!

Karen

Dropping back into the chair, I considered reading the prayer in Karen's letter, saying it to God, just for the heck of it. What could it hurt?

In fact, I did.

Leaning forward, with my elbows resting on my knees and the letter there in my hands, I read the words to the prayer quietly, thoughtfully, sending them up…into the sky. "Amen."

Had I prayed?

But I'm drunk. He won't accept it.

You didn't just pray, something told me.

Besides, you need to count the cost. What's it going to cost you, Lester, to become a Christian? The music would have to go, the women, the drugs, and booze, the adoration, the money—anything I wanted, anytime.

Forget it! Those things are my life. They are who I am.

But…have they made you happy? Have they satisfied?

They're supposed to! Everyone who didn't have those things thought they satisfied.

But what about in your case, Lester?

I looked down at the letter again, then closed my eyes.

"I am a sinner, God. A messed-up sinner," I whispered. "Karen says You'll cleanse me. Is it true? Will You?"

The familiar voice from behind scorched me like a flamethrower. "I suppose *that's* from Karen Bayliss."

I turned my head to see the rage in Endora's small black eyes…her silk jacket still on…keys in hand…out of breath.

For a flash, I saw that she was taken aback by my damaged face. But she ignored the impulse to sympathize. She had come too far… *"You lied to me!"* She strutted toward me, ripping the letter out of my hands.

Reading the words on the page, she sassed: *"'I'll be in touch again soon…Karen.'* Why didn't you tell me about Karen Bayliss? KB. Huh? This is the K that I warned you about!" She crumpled the letter.

As I rose from the chair she shoved me as hard as she could back into it.

"Take it easy," I warned in my nastiest voice, standing again. "I'm covered with bruises!"

"I found letters at your place in New York! A bunch of them. Why didn't you tell me?"

"I didn't even think about Karen being the K person," I said in a nasally, innocent voice. "It's just fan mail."

"Yeah, fan mail that comes with pretty roses, fan mail you keep in its own separate compartment in your desk…with no other fan mail?" she barked out. "What is going on, Everett? Is this woman getting to you? Have you talked to her?"

"Calm down," I said, annoyed. "I've been getting letters from this chick for ten years."

"This chick, this person, *this thing,* is out to destroy you. Do you understand what I'm saying to you? Don't you know by now that you can trust me on things like this?"

I laughed. "You're crazy. She wants me to be a Christian. That's all. She's not interested in me…as a man."

"She is what the Love card was all about." Endora opened up the crumpled letter. "I swear to you on my mother's grave, Everett, this woman is out to ruin your life and career. She's out to stop everything we've fought for!"

"What are you talking about?" I yelled. "What do you mean…'Everything we've fought for'?"

"Leading people to the truth about freedom on earth, about life on the Other Side."

"That's *your* truth. Those are your beliefs." I snatched the letter from her. "Stop pushing your agenda on me."

At the same time, we both looked at DeathStroke publicist Pamela McCracken, who ducked her head into the lounge for a moment but quickly realized she was in a war zone and disappeared.

"Liza Moon can tell us more about this, Everett; I just know it. I've been getting these incredible feelings. They wake me up at night."

"You're nuts! Liza's dead. Karen Bayliss was writing me letters long before Liza died."

"Something's going on!" she whispered in a rage. "Liza can tell us more. I know she can! We need to contact her. I want you to do a séance with me. We can reach her."

"No! I have no interest in talking to the dead. And I'm getting sick of your psychobabble."

"Don't do that, Everett. Don't turn on me. You *do not* want me against you."

"What is that? Some sort of threat?"

She set her purse in the chair and began taking her coat off. "I'm warning you about this girl. If you pursue her, I will *not* be by your side. You'll be on your own. And she'll bring death to your door. You've been warned."

"I've never talked to her," I said innocently.

"Have you tried?"

"I called, but she wasn't there." I took a swig of my drink. "Let's change the subject."

Endora sat down, found a compact in her purse, and checked her mascara. Then she snatched a cigarette and lit it.

"You have everything you need!" She turned and stared at me, smoke jetting out her nostrils. "Do you understand that? So many people would *die* to be in your shoes. People worship you—just the way you are. You don't *have* to change."

"Does it matter to you that I'm not happy?"

"Stop questioning so much. *That's* your problem. Can't you just enjoy yourself, enjoy your music and all that you have, like you used to?"

I felt the warm, crumpled letter in my hand. "Things aren't like they used to be." I stared at the rock waterfall. "Something's wrong. I'm…changing."

"But it *can* be like old times, Everett." She scooted closer to me. "Where is that rock 'n' roll god I first met in LA? You were so bold and confident back then, knew exactly what you wanted and where you were going—straight to the top."

"And now…rock bottom," I said blankly. "I need help."

I watched the clear water shimmering over the different levels of multicolored rocks.

Yes, I need help.

"You're getting tired, aren't you, Everett?" Her voice cut to monotone. "Getting sleepy. So tired from all the hard work and travel, the worries and pressure. Drowsy, Everett. Close your eyes and rest. I'll wake you in good time."

I could hear the water, trickling and gurgling over the rocks, but I was fading.

"You're drowsy." She sounded like a mother speaking to a three-year-old. "You're so tired that you're giving yourself up to me… Sleep now, child… Simply allow me to impose my will over you."

It was as if I were draining away, into the water.

"We're doing a little test," came the distant voice, zoning in and out. "Gain dominion over your mind…take the guitar…smash…black out…will not remember…"

I was out of breath and flat on my back when I came to, with red-faced Ricky and Gray frantically pinning me down.

A small crowd had gathered at the doorway to the dark lounge, each person staring in bewilderment.

Pain in the knuckles of my hands.

"What's happening?" I said to the faces glaring down at me.

"You tell us." Gray breathed hard, raising his sweaty head toward what used to be the rock waterfall.

Now it was a pile of broken slate mixed with stones and pieces of the black Les Paul that used to hang on the wall. The hoses that formerly powered the waterfall were mangled, one shooting straight up into the air like a drinking fountain.

Looking to my right and left, I saw blood trickling from my knuckles, the neck of the guitar still in my clenched right hand. I, too, was out of breath.

"Did…I do that?"

Ricky shook his head in disgust and collapsed to the floor next to me.

I stared up at the familiar faces, some wearing looks of shock, some of sympathy, and others of repulsion.

"It's a wrap," Gray announced, still panting. "Make sure everyone knows we're through. We'll start tomorrow at nine."

"What happened…Gray?" I asked, my heart pounding.

They let me sit up on the floor.

"Are you trying to tell me you don't remember what you just did?" he said, ticked.

"I don't. Honestly. What happened?"

"What do you think?" Ricky said. "You demolished that waterfall."

"Cursing God the whole time you did it," Gray added.

"Was I alone?" I said, almost scared to ask.

Gray handed me his handkerchief. "Just you and your demons, Everett." He got to his knees, then his feet, and walked out of the room. "Just you and your demons."

15

Your Honor, I'd just like to make it perfectly clear that my client, Everett Lester, in no way denies his former drug use or dealings with weapons," Brian announced just before beginning his cross-examination of the Jewelry Man, Charlie LaRoche.

"These details—about Mr. Lester's drugs and weapons, brought about by Mr. LaRoche and others—should no longer shock any of us. They are a factual part of his past." Boone walked in front of me as I sat as innocently as possible with my hands clasped and resting on the large wooden table in front of me.

"However, as we continue questioning witnesses, there are several vital facts none can overlook. First, the fact that Everett is not on trial for drug usage. Second, the undeniable changes in his life slightly before, during, and after the death of Madam Endora Crystal. And third, the extraordinary occult powers this woman possessed and unleashed against Mr. Lester during their acquaintance."

Boone's stealthy and opinionated introduction ticked off Frank Dooley, who arose quickly to appeal to Judge Sprockett.

"Mr. Boone," Judge Sprockett said, "please get on with your questions and save your summations for closing arguments."

"Yes, Your Honor." Boone turned from the judge to the witness stand, not missing a beat. "Allow me to ask you, Mr. LaRoche, if you ever witnessed any strange or mystic-type behavior—any abnormal displays of psychic power—by Madam Endora Crystal?"

Charlie demonstrated the kind of boredom you might see on the face of a high school kid in a physics lecture. "Endora was definitely a Gothic-type individual." He shifted in his seat to perk himself up. "The average person may not know it just by looking at her, but she had a dark side. And yes, she obviously knew magic…or something."

"What about specifics? Can you tell us some of this magic you saw?"

"One time she broke a glass that was about five feet away from her, without touching it," Charlie explained. "She could make the hands on a clock move from across the room."

The crowd began to stir.

"She would tell us the phone was about to ring and even knew who would be on the other end when it did…"

"Did these things surprise you?" Boone asked, flowing with the tide of emotion swelling up in the room. "I mean, *I've* never seen anyone do such things and, probably, neither have most of the people in this courtroom."

"Sure it freaked me out. She did most of that stuff when we were stoned. I guess I really never thought that much about it afterward…until now, until I knew I'd be testifying at this trial."

"How did Everett Lester react to Endora's magic or telekinetic powers?"

"Oh, he was blown away by it, too. Like I said before, I
think that's one of the reasons he kept her on retainer so long.
He knew she had these freaky...powers. I think he was
scared. He didn't want her to turn against him."

"Now, you told Mr. Dooley that Everett mentioned 'getting rid' of Endora Crystal. Isn't it true that he was talking
about firing Endora and not killing her?"

Charlie shook his greasy head. "I honestly don't know."

"Oh, come now, Mr. LaRoche. You know darn well he
wasn't talking about hurting Endora. Tell the court, what
have you got against Everett Lester?"

"Nothing! I've told you what he said. I don't read minds
like Endora, so I'm not positive what he meant when he said
he wanted to get rid of her! All I know is, Everett didn't like
the way Endora was messing with his head."

"When you say 'messing with his head,' what do you
mean by that?"

"On more than one occasion, he told me he'd done things
that he had no recollection of doing."

Slight laughter rolled through the room.

"No," Charlie said defensively, in response to the crowd.
"I mean, things he wouldn't normally do, even if he was
high...weird things."

"Like what?"

"Oh, geez. One night they found him sitting on the end of
a diving board, staring into the water. This was at a pool on
top of a building in downtown Chicago where the band was
staying. He was muttering something about being able to
walk on water... I don't know."

"And wasn't there a time during a recording session?"

Charlie nodded. "He demolished some kind of waterfall

display at a studio where the band was recording, near LA. He told me he wasn't even that stoned. Just did it. No reason. When he came to, he told me it wasn't like coming to after being stoned. It was totally different—really scared him."

"To what did Mr. Lester attribute his behavior in that instance?"

"He said it wasn't him doin' those stunts. He thought he either got some bad drugs or was hallucinating, you know, having flashbacks. He said it felt like he wasn't in control of himself. Heck, I didn't know what to believe. Still don't."

"Wasn't it shortly after this that Everett Lester drew back from you?"

"He began calling on me less and less," Charlie said.

"For drugs, you mean?"

"For drugs, for friendship." He shrugged. "Everett blew me off, big-time."

"Why do you think he did that?"

"He became too good for me. I don't know, ask him. He's sitting right there. Put him on the stand. Maybe he'll do a little preaching for you."

After I destroyed the rock waterfall at The Groove, Tina Drew gently washed my bleeding knuckles in warm, soapy water, and Gray arranged for a driver to pick me up.

As I rode alone in the black limo that glided toward our hotel in Santa Clarita, I stared out the dark window at the bright blue sky and rocky canyons.

People driving cars alongside the limo peered in, as usual, to see if they could catch a glimpse of whatever "star" might be sipping champagne and basking in glory behind the black glass.

Little did they know how lonely such a life could be.

I brought the cigarette in my fist to my mouth, took a long drag, and knocked the ashes to the floor.

This is no good.

I remember feeling confused. Frustrated. Alone.

No good.

My phone rang and I let it.

The driver, a fidgety young man with big brown eyes and high, bushy eyebrows, kept peering into the rearview mirror.

I dug in my bag and snatched the phone. "Yeah."

"Everett? It's Mary," my sister said in a jovial tone.

"Hey."

"Can you hear me?"

"Yeah," I said, sounding like a zombie.

"Are you okay?"

"It's always about me, isn't it?"

"Where are you? What's the matter, Everett?"

"How's Olivia?"

"No change. Dr. Treadwell says it's very good that there's still no swelling."

"Have you seen Jerry?"

"Oh, Ev...yes! I've seen him every day."

That got a shot of laughter out of me. "He's a good guy," I managed.

"He's fabulous! I can't believe what's happening. We just want to be together all the time. We have so much in common."

"Sounds like a winner."

"What about you?" she said.

Dead silence filled the air.

"I've been getting letters from a girl in Kansas."

"Yeah..."

"She's a Christian. She's not a fan. Hates our music. But she's been writing to me for years. She sends roses...sent me a Bible."

Mary tried to say something but gasped.

"I don't have anything left, Mary. I'm empty."

"What's her name? The girl in Kansas?"

"Karen…Karen Bayliss. She's from Topeka. Works with her youth group."

Mary fought to compose herself. "Have you met her?"

"I've tried to call a couple times, but…no."

"You've got to talk to her, Everett! That's so neat. What does she say in her letters?"

I could tell she was crying, as if she already knew what was in the letters.

"She's been praying for me. Shoot. It's been ten years."

Silence on Mary's end.

"She says there's some religious battle goin' on over me. Satan versus God. Do you believe that?"

I could hear Mary covering her phone and weeping at the same time.

"I said a prayer today, kind of. It was something Karen prayed once. Didn't feel like God heard it, though."

"He heard," she blurted. "I promise. He heard."

"But nothing's changed." I raised my voice. "I want to get wasted right now. I made a fool of myself today. I'm an idiot. I hate myself."

"Ev," she said, calming herself. "Is Endora still with you? Still on retainer?"

"Yeah."

"Listen to me. You've got to get rid of her. She's evil. I could hear it in her voice when she called looking for you. Did she tell you she called me?"

"Yeah."

"I don't know what's going on, Ev, but she wants to *own* you and *suppress* you. I've prayed about this. She's bad news. It's time to cut the cord."

"Karen says there will be people like that."

"Would you consider coming back here? You can stay with me and the boys, or Jerry says you can stay with him to dry out and get your feet on the ground. Oh, Ev, please!"

"I've got obligations…on this record. Then the tour…"

"Ev, you can't go on like you are. You could die. Please. Come be with us. We'll take care of you. Jerry has offered his house—"

"I can't answer. I don't know!"

"Please."

"It's like a scary ride at a fair. It's going fast and furious. I can't get off."

"You *can* get off! Just do it, Everett. It's your life. Jump off the ride. You can do whatever you want. Call the shots! Tell the jet to meet you at the airport and fly to Dayton. Jerry and I will meet you."

The sleek ride eased to a stop in the circle drive outside my lavish hotel, and a cluster of fans descended on the limo like ants on a puddle of Popsicle juice.

"There's a rehab clinic in Columbus," she said. "We could take you there."

The crazy-eyed driver opened his door, then turned around to see if I was ready to be escorted inside. I nodded that I was.

"Mary, listen. I've got to go. Let me get back to you."

"Ev, call Karen Bayliss. Get to know her…"

"I will."

"Are you still there?"

"Yeah, but I gotta run."

"Get rid of Endora Crystal! Do you hear me?"

"I hear." I ducked out of the limo and into the arms of the adoring fans.

"I love you," I heard Mary say, as I clapped the phone shut and put on my best smile.

Not much is clear after that.

I got high. There were dark nightclubs, floating limos, spinning purple lights, smoky rooms, spilled drinks, crowded dance floors, and women…

Then there was Endora. Dragging me off when I could barely walk. The sleep-filled ride in her white Cadillac, the dreamlike walk up the sidewalk to her small beachfront home in Malibu.

It must have been the middle of the night. I took the pills she gave me, then slept in a large, soft bed with cool silk sheets and a heavy down comforter.

But I was not allowed to sleep long.

It was still dark when she woke me and led me to a sleek recliner in a small room lit only by candles, dozens of them at all levels. She served wine and the strange, low sounds of what reminded me of funeral music filled the glowing room. The chair felt like it was filled with water. I floated. Smoke arose from four or five stands of incense around me…cinnamon, spice.

I was on something, but this was not a normal buzz.

In and out.

Endora was wide awake, holding my left hand, talking to me very intensely.

Double vision.

She and a friend had contacted Liza Moon.

I fought to stay awake, to keep my eyes fixed on Endora. To keep my head from nodding to the sides and backward.

Liza had spoken of an angel of death in my life…it was Karen Bayliss.

Endora was my only true friend. She was here to help me with this spell.

Karen wanted me to become a slave of the Messiah, and to lead people to Him through my testimony.

Endora would not allow it. She would preserve my life and lead me to the contentment for which I longed.

Karen desired to bring an end to me.

Endora whirled her hands in the air and summoned her spirits to fill me and use me for Satan's purposes—and his alone.

16

The initial jolt of the hotel phone rocked me. I smacked the pillow over my head to get back to sleep. But after eight or ten rings, I flung the pillow and fumbled for the receiver.

It was Gray Harris. I was more than an hour late for the recording session at The Groove.

What else was new?

I called room service for coffee, good coffee. Then I meandered into the living room of my penthouse suite and over to a large picture window.

Easing onto the couch on my knees, I leaned over the back, squinting out over the city of Santa Clarita and the surrounding canyons. The sun was bright, and the colorful flags surrounding the shining blue fountain below showed a steady breeze. Just another normal day in southern California.

After going to the bathroom and taking a Valium, I began brushing my teeth when there was a knock at the door.

It was the coffee.

The graying, middle-aged gentleman came into the dining room and set me up with a hot carafe of freshly brewed Columbian, cream, and Splenda. I told him to put fifty dollars on the room for himself. Made his day.

The limo would be here in another thirty minutes, he assured me.

I sat at the large dining room table, poured a cup of coffee, doctored it up, and looked around at the plush accommodations. This was supposed to be "the life."

I remembered having drinks with several women the night before, and dancing, and cocaine. Endora came to mind, but only the ride in her car. I guessed she must have met up with me and brought me back here.

The conversation with Mary came back to me. The report on Olivia Gilbert. And Mary's invitation to go to Ohio to be with her and Jerry.

I took the coffee with me when I heard the muffled ring of my personal phone. After finding it buried in my black bag, I snapped it open.

"I'm coming, I'm coming!" I said, peeved, knowing it was someone calling again from the studio.

"Hi…is this Mr. Lester?"

"Who's this?"

"Um. Mr. Lester, this is Karen Bayliss calling, from Topeka, Kansas. Do you remember my name?"

I stopped what I was doing and walked away from my coffee, back to the window.

"How did you get my number?"

"Mary," she said hurriedly. "Your sister called me yesterday. She gave me your number. If this is a bad time, I can…"

"Mary," I said.

"Yes, she was…she wanted me to have your number. She said you had mentioned me, and that…well…she figured you would be too busy to contact me. She's very sweet."

"Yeah," I said with a slight laugh. "You two would get along."

"She told me you're in California."

"Yeah. Doing some recording. I'm late right now…"

"I can let you go."

"No. It's okay."

"It's good to hear your voice, in person," she said.

"Thank you for the letters…and gifts."

"You're welcome."

"Why'd you choose me?"

She was quiet. "What do you mean?"

"Why did you start writing to me in the first place?"

"The kids at my school, a lot of them idolized you and DeathStroke. I guess I felt sorry for you," she said quietly. "I saw in you someone who was…desperate, someone who needed to be loved and prayed for."

It turned out, Karen would never fail to mention me during prayer meetings among friends. She later confessed that some of her peers grew uncomfortable continuing to lift up one of the most sinister bad boys of rock 'n' roll.

"So, it was kind of a quest to save the carnival freak, huh?"

"No! I saw you as someone crying out for God's affection. Just like me."

"That was ten years ago."

"Something like that."

"Good people like you are supposed to *detest* people like me."

"I'm not good," she said. "I'm a sinner, just like everybody else."

"But you're a Christian."

"Yes, I'm a Christian. That's why I can relate to you. Because Christ reached down to me when I was in a dark pit and plucked me out. He gave me new life."

"I find it hard to believe you've ever been in a dark pit."

"Well, I have."

"When?"

"I grew up in a Christian home. My father used to be a pastor. I got pregnant when I was fifteen. *That's* a dark pit."

"Yes…it is." I shook my head in embarrassment. "I'm sorry. You'll notice I tend to think only of myself."

"Tell me about Endora."

"What do you know about Endora?"

"Magazines," she said. "I've followed your career like a diehard DeathStroke fan. Plus, your sister mentioned her."

"Thank you, Mary. Endora's my psychic. She's also a friend."

"She sounds dangerous."

"That seems to be the consensus," I said, a little ticked. "What would you know about it?"

"Isn't she behind a lot of the things you claim to believe—about no God, no judgment, no heaven or hell?"

"Look…"

"Just live for the moment. Live free. Do whatever you want. We're all going to have an afterlife. Isn't that what you preach to your fans?"

"To me, that's all there is. Okay?"

"I know you don't believe that," she shot. "And I know it's not up to me to force Jesus Christ down your throat. God's calling you, Mr. Lester—in His way, in His time."

"Call me Everett. How old are you, anyway?"

"Twenty-seven."

"So, you started writing me when you were, what? Seventeen?"

"Around there. How old are *you?*"

I laughed. "You're not shy, are you?"

"Not usually."

"I'm thirty-four, as far as I can remember. Do you know what people would think if they knew I was having this kind of discussion? About religion?"

"What people think has never seemed to stop you before."

"Ha." I laughed aloud again, noticing how good it felt.

"I really should get going," she said. "But listen, something happened I wanted to let you know about."

"What's that?"

"I got a call a couple days ago. I said hello several times, but all I heard was breathing…and some sort of evil laugh."

"It wasn't me."

"I know it wasn't you," she insisted, laughing. "Let me finish. This guy told me to stop meddling in your life."

"What?" I froze. "What did he say, exactly?"

"It was kind of creepy. Something like, 'Karen Bayliss, *you will* leave Everett Lester alone. No more letters. No more contact.'"

A chill went through me, and suddenly I longed to hold and protect this young lady I'd never seen.

"What else?" I asked anxiously.

"He said if I disobeyed, I would suffer. I think those were his words. But listen, don't worry about it. This is just—"

"See what happens when you get near me?"

"Everett, don't worry," she said, almost jokingly. "This guy sounded harmless. You know who he reminded me of? Do you ever watch the reruns of *Green Acres?* This guy was Mr. Haney, the traveling salesman! High, squeaky voice…"

"I can't believe you."

"Why?"

"That call was supposed to scare you. It's a threat! Maybe you didn't get that."

"Mr. Lester," she said in a most charming voice. "Greater is He who is in me than he who is in this world."

"What's that?" I said, really trying to understand her words.

"Greater is He who is in me than he who is in the world," she said slowly, with what sounded like a substantial grin on her face.

"You're one very different young lady."

"I've got to go," she said.

"You better stop writing, for now."

"We'll see about that," she said casually. "You better get going, too."

"No, seriously. Don't contact me anymore until I find out who was behind that call. I think I know."

"There's one more reason I called."

"What's that?"

"This morning, I felt God asking me to share a Scripture with you. May I read it to you?" she asked, a bit nervously.

"If it will make you feel better," I teased.

"It's from the book of Romans." She paused a moment. "It says, 'If you confess with your mouth Jesus as Lord, and believe in your heart that God raised Him from the dead, you will be saved.'"

I rubbed my forehead. "Saved, huh?"

"Yes, saved…forever. And protected, and loved, and forgiven."

"I would like that," I said, more seriously.

"Then, believe in Him!"

"That sounds like the easy part."

"That's the *only* part."

"You're crazy! Look at my life. It's chaos. You know that. You've seen the stuff I've been through."

"So, what do you want to do, try and become perfect in your own strength and then go to God and say, 'I'm ready to become a Christian now'? It doesn't work that way! You're not strong enough, and God won't accept that anyway."

"Why not?"

"Because we're not saved by our own works or cleanness. We're saved only by believing in Him. That's it. End of story."

I stared out into nowhere. "That's too easy."

"That's what's so amazing about God! He gave up His only child, *His boy*, to die on a cross. That was done to forgive our sinfulness. Your sins. My sins. All sins. But listen…it was a *gift*. And God's terms are that we simply accept the gift. Just believe. That's what makes us right with God. If we try to earn His favor any other way, it's no good in His eyes."

I had never heard anything like this before and began to wonder if

Karen knew her religion as well as I had perceived.

"In the Old Testament," she said, "the Jewish people tried to get right with God by doing things—following rules—instead of depending on faith. They didn't understand God's way of making people right with Him."

"Hmm," I managed, half bored and half trying to process it all.

"When someone offers you a gift, what do you do? Do you tell them to hold on to it until you've had a chance to earn it? No! You just say, 'Wow! What an awesome gift. Thank you!'"

"You don't know me, Karen," I said, succumbing to the heaviness of my heart. "My life is trash. To the core. Do you understand? You think you know me, but you don't."

"The Bible says *all* who believe in Him are made right with God. That includes you!"

"You don't understand. *I'm* the exception. Okay? *I'm* the black sheep. God will not accept me. I prayed that prayer, the one in your letter—and nothing changed. In fact, I got so high that very night that I don't even know where I was or who I was with."

"What do you think, that God's looking at you going, 'Oh my! This Lester is a bad one… I better stay away from him, or he'll rub off on Me'? You think you scare Him? You think He doesn't know your problems or can't overcome your sin? He's God, for heaven's sake."

I dropped onto the couch and said nothing.

"Everett, you can't worry about all the details of getting off drugs and cleaning up your act, or whatever you're worried about," she pleaded. "Christ stands at the door and knocks. Just let Him in! You probably already have, by praying that prayer. He'll do the rest. The Bible says, 'To the one who does not work, but *believes* in Him who justifies the ungodly, his faith is credited as righteousness.'"

"That's all! No more for now."

"I'm sorry," she shot back. "I'm sorry. Darn it! I promised myself I wouldn't do that. My fault. Please…will you forgive me?"

"You're okay. It's me. It's not you. I enjoy listening to you."

"Let's say good-bye, for now," she said.

"Yes, good-bye…for now."

With each day, the hype surrounding my murder trial grew to epic proportions, and county prosecutor Frank Dooley relished every moment. TV coverage for the case had grown from a few minutes per day to full-time, blow-by-blow coverage. I was sure Dooley must be thinking this was his "breakout" case—the one that would launch him to worldwide stardom; it probably already had.

Apparently enjoying the balmy south Florida evening, the mob scene of camera crews, and the scores of microphones jammed in his face outside the Miami-Dade Justice and Administration Center, Dooley closed the day by virtually assuring victory for the district attorney's office as the prosecution rested its first-degree murder case against me. I watched it all on TV from the detention center rec area.

Dooley's confidence was not unfounded. For the past three days, he had questioned the lead investigator in the case, Harry Coogle, the forensic technician, and other Miami-Dade crime scene investigators, all of whom had been at the crime scene in my North Miami high-rise that fateful day last November.

During that three-day marathon, the testimonies of these experts had proven extremely incriminating, especially when the forensic technician testified that slight traces of gunpowder residue had been found on my right hand and sleeve after swipes were taken several hours after Endora's death.

However, I had seen nothing yet. A mild-mannered medical examiner by the name of Leonard Morris took the stand—and proceeded to tear me to shreds.

Wearing a light brown suit that matched the color of his

skin, Morris appeared a bit antsy on the witness stand, always perched right out on the edge of his chair. He had a light smattering of freckles beneath his round, smudged, gold-rimmed glasses, and one of those sparse mustaches that sat right along the top of his thin upper lip.

Although Morris appeared anxious, constantly shifting and leaning awkwardly over the edge of the rail in front of him, his testimony was quiet, concise, and damaging.

"We've heard already today that the murder weapon used to gun down Endora Crystal was a .45 caliber semiautomatic," Dooley said, standing, hands on his lean hips. "A gun owned and registered to the defendant, Everett Timothy Lester. A gun with only his fingerprints on it, and fresh ones at that.

"Now we're going to hear more vital details from Dr. Morris, who is a…" Dooley swiveled on a dime to face the attentive witness. "How long have you been medical examiner in Miami-Dade county, sir?"

"Twenty-two years."

"That's a long time and a lot of experience. Dr. Morris, please begin by explaining where the bullet from Everett Lester's gun entered Endora's body and the distance of the murder weapon from the victim's body at the time of the shooting."

"The, ah, single .45 caliber bullet that killed Ms. Crystal entered through her abdomen, ah, just to the left of her naval," he said. "By the looks of all of our reports, photographs, and research, I estimate that at the time the gun was fired it was approximately, ah, three to five feet away from the victim."

"In your estimation, what does this confirm to us about Madam Endora's death? Was this a suicide?"

The doctor smirked and wiggled on the edge of his seat.

"Most definitely not. In most suicides committed with handguns, the weapon is fired well within twelve inches of the body, which was clearly not the case here. In addition, in most suicide attempts committed with handguns, the bullet is fired into the mouth or into one side of the head."

"Interesting. And tell the court if you will, Dr. Morris, if the bullet that entered Endora Crystal tore through her clothes or not—and what that means in your assessment of the case."

The doctor pushed his glasses up onto his nose with the pads of his fingers, directly on the lenses, smudging them even more. "The bullet that killed Ms. Crystal, ah, did indeed travel through her clothing before it entered her abdomen. Rarely ever do we see a suicide bullet that enters through clothing. In the rare instance that a suicide shot does enter into the lower body, the shooter virtually always, ah, unbuttons his clothing first."

"And Endora's clothes were not unbuttoned."

"Correct."

"And in most suicides by gunshot, Dr. Morris, where is the gun almost always found?"

"The gun is found in hand, ah, or very close to the body."

"And Mr. Lester's .45 caliber Glock—the one used to kill Endora Crystal—was found where?" Dooley turned to peer into the sole TV camera that fed all the major networks.

"In a chest of drawers in Mr. Lester's bedroom, ah, apparently where he always stored it."

17

Endora was oddly missing from the remainder of the recording sessions at The Groove. I repeatedly attempted to reach her by phone to confront her about the telephone threat to Karen Bayliss, but to no avail. Instead, I was forced to leave messages on her voice mail, and she didn't return my calls. I even had a limo take me down to her place in Malibu where I sat for several hours, but no sign of her.

Well, at least the *Freedom* sound track was finally finished.

I flew back to New York where my friend and physician, Dr. Jack Shea, gave me a full checkup and rebandaged my nose, but with no splint this time. The bruises were healing nicely, and the blood that had settled beneath my eyes was clearing.

Although we were due back on the Rowdy tour in Indianapolis the following night, Dr. Shea recommended that my nose needed at least two more weeks to heal properly, possibly more. He didn't believe my head was ready for the noise or acrobatics of a night onstage with DeathStroke.

When Gray and Tina received the report from Dr. Shea, the remaining twelve shows of the Rowdy tour were cancelled. Our management, promoters, and fans were furious, and the boys in the band went ballistic, accusing me of jeopardizing their future success. Although I was sorry about the strain between us, I was not disappointed that the tour was cancelled.

After a quick, tension-filled flight to Nashville with the DeathStroke entourage for a TV interview, I crashed after returning to my Manhattan high-rise. Waking several hours later, I sat in the corner of the living room, where two enormous picture windows converged to overlook Central Park and the city skyline. Night was falling.

Before I had time to instinctively pour myself a gin and tonic, I threw on a Yankees cap and a dark wool coat, grabbed my black shoulder bag, and headed out the door. I didn't know where I was going exactly but knew I didn't want to be left to my own devices. It had been several days since I had taken a drink, and I was curious to see if I could keep the streak going.

It was a Thursday night, and the city was alive in anticipation of the weekend.

I walked for a long time without being recognized, because it was dark and I had flipped my coat collar high around my neck and face. The chilly air made steam rise from the manhole covers along the city sidewalks. Later, the homeless would lay on those sewer covers in hopes that the steam would warm them through the night.

Deciding a cup of hot coffee would taste good, I headed for an old favorite, Bean's coffee shop. As I hustled down the sidewalk toward Bean's, I approached a black man in a wheelchair. He wore several layers of tattered sweatshirts and gloves with no fingers. His black ski cap, turned upside down next to him in the wheelchair, held an assortment of bills and change. He had a mangy beard, a graying afro, and no legs.

As I approached him, I pulled out my wallet, found a hundred-dollar bill, folded it several times, and dropped it in his hat. Without looking at my gift, he grabbed my hand in both of his. The gloves felt threadbare, almost damp; his fingers, like sandpaper.

"Whatever you do for the least of these," he looked up at me with the whitest eyes I had ever seen, "you do for Me… Thank you, brother. God be with you this night."

As I began to back up, his hands gripped mine tightly, blatantly, and his shining brown eyes locked in on me. "In this world, you *will* have trouble—perhaps even tonight. But take courage; I have overcome the world."

Instead of looking around to see who might be watching, and making a concerted effort not to be embarrassed by the man, I let go of his hand and stared.

He had no legs.

Do you understand what I'm saying?

NO LEGS.

Only dirty, frayed, brown corduroys—cut off like shorts and flapping in the mean New York wind.

He was thin, practically toothless, and probably slept in a box.

Yet…he was happier than I, more content than a millionaire.

I turned, thrust my hands into my pockets, and continued down the sidewalk. There was a card in my hand, the size of a business card. He must have handed it to me.

Ducking into Bean's, I shook off the cold and put a finger to my lips so Mrs. Fagan would keep my presence a secret.

"Long time no see, stranger," she said quietly, with a sparkle in her gray eyes.

"Too long." I approached the counter. "It's good to be back."

"What on earth happened?" She pointed to her nose with a pained expression.

"You didn't hear?"

"No."

"Good," I said, "maybe the whole world doesn't know after all."

"The usual?"

"Sounds good." I took off my coat and walked toward an empty table and two chairs by the window.

Placing the coat on the back of the chair, I reached into its pocket and pulled out the card the legless man had slipped me. It was white with black type and looked like a Bible passage. I put it back and went to the counter for my coffee.

"This one's on the house." Mrs. Fagan handed me a white mug, steam swirling.

"Get out of here," I said, opening my wallet. "I know I still owe you."

She mouthed a *thank you* as I handed her a large bill and headed back to my table.

Then I saw her.

In the backseat of a yellow cab that crept past the storefront. She stared in at me with those black marble eyes.

Instinctively, my free arm shot up.

"Endora..." I started to yell.

The cab kept going as I clacked my coffee cup down on the nearest empty table, dodged several clusters of people, and ran to the door and out into the night. By then, the rear of the cab was getting smaller in the distance, steam churning from its dangling muffler.

The sidewalk and streets were wet. It had begun to drizzle.

Opening the heavy glass door to Bean's, I noticed several patrons staring at me now, talking among themselves.

Mrs. Fagan called me over with the tilt of her head as she was drying some mugs. "That's a good way to blow your cover," she said softly. "What's up?"

"Nothing." I looked back out at the street. "I thought I saw someone I knew, someone from out of town."

With a gray towel in her hand, Mrs. Fagan propped herself up on her tiptoes for a moment and looked out over the counter toward the half-full café.

"That's not your phone ringing by any chance, is it?"

"Probably." I ignored my coffee mug and zigzagged back to the table with my head lowered.

Retrieving the phone from my satchel, I sat down and gave an out-of-breath, "Hello?"

"Hello, Everett? It's Karen..."

I looked out the window, turning my back to the café in hopes that the people inside would stop gawking.

"You're not supposed to call me," I said, glad to hear from her.

"Gee, I didn't figure anyone would be tapping my phone."

"Have you gotten any more calls?" I peered out the window, thinking I must have been mistaken about seeing Endora.

"No, but I did get a package today. That's why I called. It's a little on the weird side."

Mrs. Fagan appeared with a fresh cup of the house blend. I nodded thanks. "Why? What is it?"

"Are you ready for this?" she said. *"Black roses."*

"What?"

"On the doorstep when I got home from work. A dozen *black* roses."

"What the heck?"

"You know what the black rose means, Everett?" There she was—*again!* This time, across the street in the third-story window of an office tower. Wearing the same black overcoat she had on in the cab. Arms crossed, looking right at me.

"Everett? Are you there?"

I turned back into the room, rubbed my eyes and stared at an empty table, then a chair, then at Mrs. Fagan grinding espresso beans. *Okay, everything is okay. I'm hallucinating or something. She is not in New York. Your mind is playing tricks.*

I turned back to the window and Endora was gone.

Just like I thought.

"Everett?"

"I'm here," I said, thinking that if this was what it was like to be off drugs, I didn't want any part of it. "I'm sorry. Um, I haven't had a drink in a few days, and I'm dealing with some…some stuff. Never mind that. What's this about black roses?"

"They mean *death*."

"What?"

"*Death*."

"And someone delivered you a dozen of them?"

"Yep."

"Endora knows about the roses," I mumbled. "She's got to be behind this. I can't get in touch with her. I've been trying ever since you told me about the phone call. And now I'm sitting here thinking I see her outside where I am."

"Where are you?"

"New York. A coffee joint."

"She wouldn't be there, would she?"

"No. She wouldn't. She hates the cold. She's just been on my mind a lot since you got that call. It's weird she hasn't been around. That's just not like her."

"That's good," Karen said.

"Yeah, probably. I've just depended on her for so long… She found some of your letters. She was furious."

"The letters I wrote you?"

"Uh-huh."

"*See*, that's what I mean about being dangerous," Karen said. "Why would she be mad about my letters? They're good!"

"She thinks you're going to ruin me," I said with a laugh, still searching the city outside the window.

"She's afraid you're going to become a Christian. That's what she's afraid of."

I finally sipped my coffee.

"You've got to be careful, Everett. This is a dangerous thing for you. I really believe with your popularity there's a war going on.

Endora may have Satanic powers. That stuff is real…"

There!

In the breezeway, half a block away, above the street, gazing down at me with her arms crossed, like some kind of wizard.

"There she is! I gotta go!" I shot to my feet. "Don't write or call. I'll be in touch. *I see Endora!*"

"I'll pray!" I heard her say as I snapped the phone shut, threw my coat on, grabbed my bag, and took off.

Endora calmly watched me from above as I dodged pedestrians, splashed through puddles, and ran toward the breezeway. She was expressionless.

Looking up at her one last time, I gauged which building to enter and plunged through a set of heavy revolving doors. In the center of the giant silver and glass atrium filled with plants and trees, I saw an escalator that I was certain would take me up to the breezeway where she stood.

Dashing up the moving stairs two and three at a time, I arrived at the top, turned back toward the breezeway, and stood frozen, staring down the long, empty corridor.

Looking in all directions and not spotting her, I sprinted across the breezeway and searched the area on the other side.

Not a trace.

Dejectedly, I walked back out onto the crosswalk and stood where I was sure I had seen Endora standing only seconds ago. I looked down on the sidewalk toward Bean's coffee shop. Was I losing my mind?

Leave me alone.

Then as I stood there on that empty breezeway, spotlights shining down, night engulfing me, I was directed to go to the rooftop. She was telling me she was up there.

I had to confront her, had to protect the only pure and innocent thing in my life: Karen Bayliss.

Damp and chilled from the rain, I went back the way I had come and found the elevators near the top of the escalator. A heavy, blond female security guard eating a Baby Ruth looked at me from behind her desk.

"Everett Lester?" she inquired wide-eyed, with her mouth full.

"Yes, ma'am," I said, doing my best to hide the confusion and rage.

"I can't believe it! I'm a *huge* fan of yours."

"You're kidding," I managed. "Wow. Small world. Listen, I'm just heading upstairs for an appointment, is that okay?"

"Hmm." She rolled her eyes and talked way too slowly. "I'm not supposed to let anyone up who hasn't been called in by someone upstairs. Who are you here to see? I'll call up…"

"Oh. This is kind of a secret business meeting, if you know what I mean." I tried to manage a laugh. "Listen, will you let me up if I set you up with an autograph and some CDs?"

She looked both ways and smiled shyly. "I think we can arrange that."

I left the girl an autograph and Jeff Hall's phone number and assured her he would send her a nice package of goodies. Then I headed for the elevator and pushed the biggest number I could find: fifty-seven.

After wandering the quiet halls on the top floor, I went through a white door and entered what looked like a boiler room. Then I found some concrete steps that had once been blocked off by chains, which now dangled at each side of the steps. Making my way to the top, there was only one way to go—through a big rust-colored metal door. I had to bang hard against it with my hip, and it flew open into the howling wind.

Heading out onto the dark, wet rooftop, lit only by the surrounding city lights, I yelled into the wind, "Where are you?"

Turning all around, I finally saw her some fifty feet from me, seated atop a large silver box, and looking the other way—out over the city.

"What's your game, Endora?" I yelled loudly through the rain.

She acted as if she didn't hear me, so I walked toward her, running a hand along the wet concrete ledge, trying to get used to the height. The sky spun slightly, and I felt light-headed. Never did like heights.

Coming up behind her, I was still a good four feet beneath Endora, because she was perched on top of this shiny piece of exhaust equipment, steam billowing into the sky beside her.

"What's going on, Endora?" I yelled with no patience left, the rain coming steady now, wind gusting. "Who's *messing* with Karen Bayliss?"

Without turning around, she yelled, "You'll have to come closer, near the edge, Everett. I can't hear you."

When I got closer to the very corner of the building and turned to look up into her face, I noticed the fingers of her left hand were pressed hard into her forehead. Her eyes were closed.

"Who called Karen Bayliss and threatened her to leave me alone?"

Ignoring me, she raised her other hand to her temple and lowered her head in meditation.

Then it struck me.

She was dry as a bone.

"Who sent the black roses?" I shouted.

No response.

Infuriated, I reached up to grab her arm, but my hand swept through air. Nothing was there!

I let out a gasp.

But…she *was* there.

"If you hurt Karen…I'll *destroy* you!"

The rain came harder.

Ever so slightly, with her fingers still pressed into her forehead, her hands and arms began to shake. "You've had enough of this world, haven't you, Everett?"

Slowly, I reached up to touch her again.

Nothing.

"You're all alone, Everett," she moaned. "I'm not even here. You've lost touch with reality. It's time to call it quits."

My hands dropped to the ledge at my waist, and I looked out over the massive buildings and thousands upon thousands of sparkling lights all around me.

"Sit on the ledge," she said. "Look below."

The cold rain soaked the seat of my pants as I did what she instructed.

"Now…if you are a Christian, throw yourself over the edge, because the Bible says, 'He shall give His angels charge over you.'"

A shiver ran through me from head to toe, and my hands found the pockets of my drenched wool coat.

"If, on the other hand, you are *not* a Christian, throw yourself down, for you will find the contentment you've been seeking…on the Other Side!"

I leaned the upper half of my body out over the ledge, looking straight down at the slivers of street below.

Maybe there will *be contentment in the fall. Maybe this is where I will find my peace.*

"Either way," she sneered, "you are not meant for this world, Everett. You're no good to Satan anymore. And you'll never be any good to God. You know that…"

I felt the card in my pocket.

"Go ahead!" She nodded, glaring at me now with the outstretched arm of someone presenting a performer. "Do something right for a change. Push off. Make your father proud, for once…"

When I pulled the card out of my pocket, a thousand screams pierced my ears, the likes of which I had never heard before.

I dropped my head to read, silently:

When tempted by Satan, repeat the words of your Savior, Jesus Christ.

Then I began to read aloud the words the legless angel had given me, getting louder with each word, for all the demons to hear:

> "Go, Satan! For it is written, 'You shall worship the LORD your God, and serve Him only.' Then the devil left Him; and behold, angels came and began to minister to Him."

Slowly turning back over the ledge, I let my body drop onto the rooftop.

Lying motionless for a moment on the cold, wet concrete, I lifted my head.

She was gone.

And I felt the presence of God's angels all around me.

18

It was past lights-out and I had a difficult time sleeping. My friend the guard, Donald Chambers, walked past my locked cell and whispered, "I thought you'd be asleep by now. Pretty tough day." He referred to the damaging testimony of the medical examiner, Dr. Leonard Morris.

"Were you there?"

"Yeah, near the back. Standing room only."

"I suppose it couldn't have been much worse," I said.

"It will be better tomorrow."

After taking several steps, he stopped again. "Remember that inmate I told you about a couple weeks ago? The one who died after Zaney predicted he would?"

"Yeah."

"It *wasn't* suicide," he whispered. "They found a bruise at the base of his neck, definitely caused by pressure from the killer's hand."

"Zaney."

"Had to be."

"Boone is trying to have him subpoenaed as a witness at my trial, since he knew Endora," I said. "We've got to get the judge's approval first."

"I'm afraid he'll flat-out lie, even if you do get him to the stand."

"I know."

"The word is, he's out for you—big-time."

I remained still and silent on my bunk.

"You just gotta watch your back," he added, perhaps realizing he may have burdened me with fear.

I exhaled deeply, closed my eyes, and pictured Zaney coming for me in my cell. Then I thought of Karen, all alone.

It was too much to shoulder. "Thanks for the heads-up, Donald." I rolled onto my stomach. "I think I just need to let everything go—and get some rest."

The usual sense of guilt and remorse engulfed me when I woke up the morning after chasing Endora's ghost around Manhattan. But what wasn't normal was the sweat-covered pillow beneath my head. Even after coffee, I was shaking on and off—at times, uncontrollably. My head was filled with the most excruciating pain. It had been three days since I had taken a drink or used any drugs.

I called Gray Harris to let him know I was taking off for a few days; then I chartered one of the DeathStroke jets for Dayton, Ohio.

Jerry and Mary did a good job of hiding their alarm over my appearance when they picked me up at the airport. I was shivering and sweating profusely when they greeted me hand in hand near baggage claim.

As we drove to Jerry's place in Grayson, they treated me with kid gloves. I fell asleep during the ride. Just before I did, however, I noticed how their conversation and body language shouted that they were madly in love—and probably would be for a long time.

The weeks that followed were remarkable.

Jerry took time off from work, then Mary; then they each did it again. As I battled my addictions, they saw me through fits of rage and times when I literally wanted to die. There were tears and hallucinations, sickness and endless sleep, threats and loving talks. And a whole lot of prayers going up from two of the most unselfish people I had ever met.

During that very foggy, nightmarish season, thoughts of Karen, Endora, Olivia, and rock 'n' roll were left far behind. I was just trying to stay alive, fighting to take another breath, attempting to stir up the desire to live another minute and keep my body free of the substances that had poisoned it for more than two decades.

I guess it must have been into the fourth week of my "homemade" rehab program when Mary and Jerry felt I was mentally stable enough to have a serious talk about some things that had transpired while I was out of commission.

First Mary said, with a beautiful smile, that Karen Bayliss had called almost every day to follow the progress of my recovery. Mary said the two ladies had become fast friends, and she advised me not to get too big a head about Karen's interest, because they had talked about much more than just me. Mary also assured me that Karen had been praying steadfastly, which I had already taken comfort in assuming.

Although still extremely weak, I wondered rather anxiously whether Karen had received any more threats, or if Mary even knew about that, but decided to let it ride for the moment.

Next came a double dose of bad news. The Dayton police department had formally filed aggravated assault charges against me, and further charges were pending. They would bring manslaughter charges should Olivia Gilbert die. Meanwhile, Olivia's father had made a formal statement that he would file suit against me for battery, compensatory damages, and punitive damages as soon as the case by the police department was completed.

Even darker, Olivia's condition had gotten worse. Signs of brain edema had developed, meaning there was an abnormal buildup of serous fluid between the tissue cells in her head. This could be bad, Mary warned, and doctors were watching for symptoms of rigidity to form in her limbs, trunk, jaw, and neck. These would serve as signs of a potential long-term coma and, possibly, death.

My heart plunged.

There in Jerry's family room, we prayed—the three of us. We prayed for Olivia to recover, for her mother and father's well-being, and for the charges against me to fall by the wayside. We prayed for blessings toward Karen Bayliss. And Mary and Jerry prayed for me to have the power to stay off drugs and to find life in Christ.

I didn't know exactly what they meant by "life in Christ," but I knew that if it meant becoming more like them—I wanted it.

After chatting with Donald Chambers tonight, I tossed restlessly in my lumpy prison bunk for hours. The mustiness of the cell, the screams in the night, and thoughts of Zane Bender and a potential guilty verdict pummeled me.

Keep in mind, I was not up on second- or third-degree murder charges. This was murder one, which would result in one of two outcomes if I was found guilty: life in prison or death. Anyone who's never been smacked square in the face with the bitter reality of those two scenarios probably wouldn't understand the heaviness and utter despair I felt in my soul.

When I finally did doze off after reading by flashlight, I dreamt I was out of prison and living in a house in the coun-

try. Children were there with me. Everything was right with
the world.

And then Endora began stalking us.

I heard noises in the barn one night, went out, and found
Endora in the loft. She was evil to the core; I can't begin to
explain how wicked. I shot her with a rifle, but the bullets
went right through her body, which was arched grotesquely
backward as she moaned with laughter.

Then I woke up.

The morning brought refreshment. And believe it or not,
I was somewhat excited about the day's trial, as Brian Boone
continued the battle to prove my innocence in the death of
Madam Endora Crystal.

Twila Yonder looked like a ghost in noisy courtroom B-3
this morning, as Boone called her back to the stand as a rebut-
tal witness, with Judge Sprockett's prior approval. Her skin
was powder white, with black and silver eye makeup and two
silver balls pierced through her right eyebrow. A slight tint of
pink streaked her brown hair, and remnants of dark lipstick
smudged one of her front teeth.

Boone started by refreshing the jury's memory about
Twila's friendship with Endora, but he wasted no time pursuing what he'd brought her here for.

"Miss Yonder," he said, with a bounce in his step, "does
the name Zane Bender ring a bell?"

She cleared her throat. "Yeah...he was a friend of
Endora's."

"Do you know where Zane Bender lived?"

"Oakland, I think."

"And what was the relationship between Zane Bender
and Endora Crystal?"

"What do you mean, 'What was the relationship?'" she
wisecracked.

"Were they friends, lovers, business partners?"

"Zane was into psychics, but he was kind of a wannabe." She looked down, fidgeting. "He heard of Endora and came to meet her one time. I guess you could call him a fan of hers, more than anything."

"I see. And did Endora teach Zane Bender about psychics?"

She delayed. "Yes...he wasn't really cut out for it, but she did the best she could with him."

"What do you mean?"

"Some people are gifted in the psychic realm and others aren't. Zaney wasn't very gifted, but Endora was able to help him along."

"Where are we going, Your Honor?" blurted a frustrated Frank Dooley from his seat at the table next to mine. "Relevance, relevance, relevance."

"Mr. Boone," Judge Sprockett said, "Mr. Dooley raises a reasonable question. We have a long day ahead of us. Let's cut to the chase."

"Your Honor, this friend of Endora's, who I'm questioning Miss Yonder about, is currently incarcerated in the very same prison where my client is imprisoned for the duration of this trial."

Dooley and his cronies were sent shuffling back through their many ledgers. Twila, however, chomped her gum, examined her nails, and looked unfazed by Boone's words.

"His name is Zane Bender, better known as Zaney," Boone announced. "He is serving seventeen years in the Miami-Dade detention center for felony charges of armed robbery and attempted murder. And it is our belief that Zane Bender may play a key role in proving the innocence of Everett Lester."

Brian glanced at his notes on the table and cruised off

toward the witness stand. "Miss Yonder, you say Zane Bender wasn't 'gifted' in the psychic realm. What exactly was it that he tried to learn from Endora?"

Ever so slightly, a blush tried to make its way to the surface of Twila's chalky face. Her eyes shot to Dooley, to Judge Sprockett, then back down to her lap.

"I just want to remind you, Miss Yonder, that you're under oath here today."

"He wanted to learn about hypnotism," she said quickly and quietly, not looking up, as if her comment might just scoot right past us.

But Boone's body jolted slightly as a result of her response. Neither of us was expecting it. We didn't know what we were fishing for. But suddenly, things started clicking.

"You're saying, Miss Yonder, that Zane Bender sought out Endora Crystal to learn how to perform hypnotism?"

"I guess that was his main reason for initially contacting her." Her tone turned bitter. "But they became friends after that. They were just friends, okay? There's nothing to hide."

Boone walked confidently beside the jury box, shook his head, and smiled. "I've got to ask. I mean, the whole court, the whole world, wants to know...did Endora Crystal perform hypnotism? And, if so, for whom?"

Twila moved uneasily on the hard wooden seat. The gum-chomping slowed to a soft chew. Frank Dooley, who had been buried in notebooks, suddenly became all ears. His sidekicks, who had been buzzing around him like moths on a floodlight, grew still.

"I don't think it's any real secret Endora worked with a lot of wealthy people, a lot of stars," Twila confessed. "But one thing people didn't realize is that hypnotism was kind of her forte. With it, she helped people overcome weight control problems, drug addiction, insomnia, phobias...all kinds of serious stuff. She was a humanitarian, for goodness' sake! That's what's such a bum wrap about this whole trial. You're painting her to be some kind of...witch."

"Whoa, whoa, whoa, wait a minute." Boone put up a hand like a stop sign. "You're telling us what? That she would hypnotize these people, and they would go away with their problems solved?"

Twila shifted uneasily. "If you don't believe me, ask some of the Fortune 500 companies that called on her. Go ahead, ask them. They used her to hypnotize entire employee groups to reduce fear and anxiety, increase productivity. She's hypnotized pro athletes, CEOs, movie stars—even the disobedient children of rich parents."

Spots of murmuring rose up behind me.

"Did she hypnotize Everett Lester?"

Stone-cold silence.

"I don't know the answer to that."

"You are under oath."

"Yeah, and I still don't know the answer!"

"Were you ever present when she hypnotized anyone?"

Her eyes darted toward the jury and back to Boone.

"Do I need to repeat the question?" Boone asked.

"She hypnotized me once. When she was trying to teach Zaney." Twila twirled her hair around her index finger. "I was still having nightmares about my parents' car wreck. Endora hypnotized me and put me in a state of...oh, what did she call it? Selective amnesia. So I could forget about the accident, or at least not dwell on it so much."

"And did you forget?"

"Yes, I did." She dropped her head. "The nightmares have never returned."

"So Endora's hypnotism worked. You are proof of that?"

"Yes…Endora was good at what she did."

"Indeed," Boone said, patting me on the shoulder as he came to take his seat.

It actually felt good to turn myself over to the authorities in Dayton, Ohio, on the aggravated-assault charge for Olivia Gilbert's injury. I was quickly booked and released on four hundred thousand dollars bond.

From there, I took a limo to nearby Grayson to see Jerry Princeton and my sister, Mary. It was then that I realized why Jerry loved his town, as he and I strolled down Grayson's clean, wide sidewalks, past the bakery and the bookshop, the post office, and the corner café. Attractive awnings covered most of the storefronts. There were American flags flying, parents pushing baby strollers, and elderly folks relaxing on park benches. A nice, slow pace.

Jerry told me he had thought about leaving after Susan passed away because of all the memories they shared here, but he treasured the college where he worked, which was right in town. Plus, he had made many new friends at his church—a beautiful rustic brownstone building he pointed to with pride across the street.

Earlier, Jerry had turned me on to one of his favorite neighborhood delis, where at his suggestion we enjoyed pita sandwiches stuffed with chicken, onions, feta, and Greek dressing. Delicious. I also found myself relishing the simplicity of browsing several art galleries, one owned by a friend of Jerry's and the source of several of the paintings that hung in his den.

My phone rang in the back left pocket of my Levi's as we walked past the town park toward Jerry's Mercury Sable, parked along Wooster Avenue. When I heard it was Gray, I excused myself, went up the steps to the park, and sat on a long bench near a swing set. Jerry waved and ducked inside a clothes shop, probably to talk to the owner. He seemed to know everyone in town.

Gray was polite, asking where I had been and how I was doing. I didn't tell him about my newfound sobriety because, frankly, I wasn't sure it would last. But I did offer that I was visiting my sister's place in Ohio.

"Listen," he said, "I hate to rush you back, but Tina's been working night and day lining up promoters and venues for the Freedom tour. It's gonna be incredible. She's got us booked for at least forty cities, probably more like sixty, including a swing through Europe."

My stomach turned.

"Fairly soon, I've got to get you guys back to the bubble to practice the new set."

The "bubble" was an enormous jet hangar at JFK International Airport in New York that Gray rented for us when it was time to practice for upcoming tours.

"Hmm." News that once would have made me pump my fist in exultation, now made me literally sick to my stomach.

He staggered through the silence. "So…how is everything? How's Endora?"

"Haven't seen her," I said, my mind rocketing back to the rooftop mirage in Manhattan.

"Oh, really? That's unusual. What's the deal? You two haven't gone your separate ways, have you?"

Suddenly, I felt anxious, almost light-headed. My heart raced, much like it had atop the fifty-seven-story skyscraper the other night. But this time, my feet were firm on Ohio soil, which scared me even more.

"We may be." I focused on the thick gray trunk of a nearby tree to stabilize myself.

"Listen, I'm glad you turned yourself in to the Dayton PD," he said, waiting for a response but getting none. "Eventually, you're gonna have to head back for a hearing on that thing…unless the attorneys can pull a rabbit out of the hat. But don't worry, it's gonna be fine. We'll take care of it."

"Okay," I said, pacing amid the playground wood chips, my heart drumrolling. "Is that all?"

"Yes, I guess that's it." Gray sounded confused by my abruptness. I shut the phone.

Look at you, Everett Lester, came the voice. *You're never going to change. Your sobriety is temporary. You see? Now, it's back to the tour and records, back to the pot and booze and pills, back to the strange women, and yes, back to Endora—the only one you will ever be able to trust...*

The tires that squealed around the corner two blocks away snapped me out of the funk. Then an engine opened up about five times as loud as it should on such a quiet street. I looked up to see Mary's Subaru swerve sharply before it veered toward me and lurched to a halt in a parking space twenty feet away, her driver's door bouncing open almost before the vehicle stopped.

"There's been an accident! There's been an accident!" She ran toward me. "Oh, Everett...we've got to get to New York!"

The bells on the shop door rang, and Jerry raced over from across the street. I ran down the small hill from the park, and we both met Mary at the sidewalk.

"It's David!" she said, out of breath, turning toward Jerry. "Eddie's youngest boy!"

"Calm down, Mary, calm down!" Jerry grabbed her at the elbows. "Slow down, sweetheart. It's okay. It's okay. Tell us what's happened." He was out of breath, too. So was I.

"Jerry!" She clamped onto his face. "It's my nephew, David. Oh, dear...he may not make it!"

"Ev." She turned to me. "He's been in a terrible accident. We've got to get up there...for Eddie."

"Okay, okay," I said, getting my bearings. "We'll go to him. Let's get your car back to Jerry's. Then...Jerry, can you drive us to the airport?"

He was already in motion.

19

A limo whisked Mary and me from the cold runway where we landed at LaGuardia through the Bronx and Yonkers and up to White Plains Hospital Center in White Plains, New York.

What we found there was not good. Not good at all.

Our brother Eddie was nowhere to be found when we arrived at the hospital. However, his red-eyed wife, Sheila; silent nineteen-year-old son, Wesley; and stunned sixteen-year-old daughter, Madison, were camped outside the intensive care unit, along with about a dozen family members and friends.

The torn body of seventeen-year-old David lay in an adjacent room, where he was monitored constantly by a staff of all-business nurses and physicians.

One of Sheila's brothers, Bill, explained to Mary and me that David had been in a horrific car wreck following school that afternoon. He was driving his black Camaro with three passengers in the suburbs of White Plains, when he lost control of the car and hit an oncoming vehicle head-on.

David's mangled body was found twenty feet from the scene, actually *behind* the car he had hit. Nearly every bone in his body was broken, a foot had been severed, and he had lost a dangerous amount of blood. Two of David's passengers, a seventeen-year-old boy and a sixteen-year old girl, were pronounced dead at the scene. The other passenger, a nineteen-year-old male, was in good condition two floors up.

An elderly couple from Scarsdale, New York, married forty-seven years, probably didn't know what hit them when they were killed instantly by David's roaring Camaro. Worst of all, an excessive amount of alcohol and drugs—including methamphetamines—were found in or around what was left of David's car. This just served as more proof that the drugs I had once craved as a vice were poison.

The hospital's intensive care unit was a nerve center of activity. Strategically situated in the middle of the third floor, it was encircled by a carpeted hallway and decorated with low-lit lamps, oversized couches, coffee tables, telephones, and magazines. No TVs.

A quiet setting—for those who grieved.

Approaching 10 P.M., Mary was curled up beneath a blanket with Eddie's daughter, Madison, on a large red couch in the hallway outside the ICU. Madison, who had turned into a beautiful young woman since I had last seen her, was dozing off as Mary softly stroked her frizzy brown hair.

When I first saw Eddie's oldest son, Wesley, I literally didn't recognize him. His once full and toned body was rail thin. His face was ashen, with pink rings beneath his bloodshot blue eyes. His baggy, beltless cargo pants rode well beneath his waist, and his nylon Nike jacket appeared two sizes too big.

Wesley seemed paranoid and angry. I felt his fury directed at me and immediately the guilt rose in my soul over the repeated times I had stood up him and David. After refusing to say hello to me, he gave me the evil eye for a long time before dropping to the floor in the dark at the end of the couch, putting his headphones on, and burying his shaved head between his knees. The fuzzy tone of acid rock pulsated from his direction.

I rested in a chair next to Eddie's wife, who sat with her legs folded up beneath her slender body. Sheila held a cup of hot tea someone had brought her but she hadn't tasted. Her shoes were off; her face was pink from rubbing away tears from the past six hours. She wore a soft white V-necked sweater and Calvin Kleins. Though I couldn't tell for sure, I thought she had undergone quite a bit of plastic surgery since I had last seen her, at least on the lips and nose—and probably more.

"This is going to be *it* for Eddie, you know," she said, not quite making eye contact with me. "He was already a mess…before this."

"What's been going on before this?" I asked quietly.

"What hasn't? He's lost tons of clients in the past year, because of the economy. No fault of his own. But he beats himself up for it. He works too long to overcompensate. The kids barely see him…"

"What about you?"

She shook her head, and her pretty face grimaced. "He used to be such a good husband…father. Our marriage is dead," she moaned. "We're barely making ends meet. The kids have been *bad*. Wesley's into who knows what. Just one thing after another. Now this."

As she lost control once again, I bent down to one knee and put my right arm around her in silence.

"I don't want to lose my baby boy, Everett," she cried. "My baby is dying in there."

No words. I had no words, only my presence to offer.

The remainder of the day's events in courtroom B-3 paled in comparison to the stunning testimony of Twila Yonder— which centered around Zane Bender and Endora Crystal's apparent proficiency at hypnosis.

As promised, Brian was here tonight at the detention center to quiz me about Endora and hypnotism. Did I ever see
her hypnotize anyone? Had she ever hypnotized me? Was
there ever talk of hypnotism? And the eight zillion dollar
question: Could I have been under some sort of induced
trance at the time of Endora's death?

Naturally, I cooperated wholeheartedly. But Boone
seemed frustrated by my inability to come up with a dramatic
confession, perhaps that Endora had sat me down in some
dark room and swung a crystal before my eyes until I fell into
a deep trance. I just didn't remember any such thing. And
time was running out.

It seemed to me that the majority of our current defense
had dwindled to a smoke screen. We were trying to buy more
time to either produce evidence that would clear my name, or
to somehow show that the prosecution had failed to meet its
burden to prove me guilty beyond a reasonable doubt.

Unfortunately, neither scenario seemed likely.

I was getting negative, even beginning to doubt my choice
of Brian Boone as lead counsel, doubt his legal team—and
even doubt myself and my actions November 11, the day
Endora was killed in my condo.

I was sorry about the negative trip.

Brian hadn't given up hope, and he did have a plan. I just
didn't know what it was because we hadn't had time to talk it
through. He'd spent sleepless hours researching telekinesis,
and I knew he still had witnesses he wanted to recall, and
several new ones Dooley hadn't questioned. Zane Bender was
at the top of the list, and we were awaiting a response from
Judge Sprockett right now to see if he would approve a subpoena to bring Zaney from prison to the witness stand.

With an armful of tattered paperwork, weathered
notepads, and two carrying cases, Boone just raced out of the

tin can visiting booth across from me, down the polished white hallways, by the guards and metal detectors, and back into the real world.

He would be up most of the night, researching the topic that appeared to be one of our last hopes in the first-degree murder trial of *The State of Florida v. Everett Timothy Lester*: hypnotism.

It appeared that my nephew, David Lester, wasn't going to make it.

As news of the accident spread through his world, the crowd at the hospital grew, the phone calls increased, and the disbelief that this young man soon might be just a memory slowly became stark reality.

It reminded me all too much of the terribly uncomfortable scene outside Olivia Gilbert's hospital room in Dayton, Ohio.

How is she tonight?

Oh, please...heal her.

After many unanswered phone calls and too much speculative chatter, I finally tracked down my older brother right under my nose. Eddie was upstairs from ICU, checking on the condition of the only other survivor in his son's crash—Tom Schlater.

Eddie and I hugged, and he insisted that I duck into Tom's room for a moment, because the young man claimed to be a DeathStroke fanatic. He looked the part, too. Long, stringy brown hair with a black stocking cap (yes, even in his hospital bed). Beard stubble. Tattoos up and down his arms. One, a skull and crossbones that read, *"Sworn to fun, loyal to none."*

A battered-looking Eddie waited outside Tom's hospital room for a few minutes, speaking in hushed tones with the young man's lethargic parents, while I spent a few minutes with the boy who reminded me very much of a young Everett Lester.

Tom Schlater looked in good condition, great condition, considering what had happened to the other three people in the vehicle with him. My guess was that he was admitted simply so they could make sure he didn't go into shock after the accident. But the only shock he experienced was seeing me at his bedside.

"This rocks, man! No one is even gonna *believe* I met Everett Lester. I've been a fan of yours since I was ten."

He spoke of the upcoming *Freedom* album and tour. As he did, I recalled being somewhat disturbed by how quickly he seemed to have forgotten the events of the day.

I smiled hesitantly. "How well do you know David?"

His bottom lip went out and he shook his head. "Not very well. I'm older than him. He's...he's still in high school, ya know. I'm nineteen. I know his brother Wesley better than I know David."

"Oh? You run with Wesley?"

"Not really. I see him now and then."

"Were you friends with the other kids in the car?"

"Nah," he said. "I barely knew them. Why all the questions?"

"Just wondered."

"You look like you're almost better." He pointed to my healing face. "I swear, if I ever met the guy who did that to you, I'd kill the sucker."

I stared at him.

"So, do you live around here?" he asked. "I mean, nobody really knows. I've read you've got a place in Manhattan, but heck—"

"Tom," I interrupted. "You know...you're lucky to be alive."

"Oh, heck yes I am! It's just like your song, dude. *'I got ten lives, ten lives. Just watch me fly. Ain't never gonna die, never gonna die...cause I got ten lives...'*"

As he mimicked the hit song, I grew impatient. "If you didn't know David or the other kids that well, what were you doing in the car with them?"

"We were hangin', man. They were giving me a ride."

"Well, which is it? Were you hanging out, or were they giving you a ride?"

"Ha." He smirked and looked away. "What difference does it make?"

"None really, I guess. Not now. The police said drugs and alcohol were in the car…and meth."

"Got me, man. Like I said, I was just along for a ride."

"Were there drugs in the car, alcohol?"

"Let's put it this way," he said, casually. "We weren't doin' anything *you* wouldn't do."

"Was David high when he wrecked the car?" I asked point-blank.

"He was up there, laughin' all the way 'til we hit."

"What do you mean?"

"Other than the fact that he had 'Ten Lives' cranked and was singin' it at the top of his lungs when we crashed—nothin'."

My song. He was singing my song when it happened.

"He'd been blabbin' to his buds about the Other Side. He was a big fan of yours, man. Knew everything about you, Endora… I mean, at the end, it was almost like he knew he was about to go."

"What did he say about the Other Side?"

"It's where everyone goes when their number's up."

My heart broke, and there was a long, quiet silence.

"What was he on?" I finally asked.

"Ice." Schlater shrugged. "What else? His brother's rollin' in the stuff."

"Meth? He got meth from Wesley?"

"Bro, I can't say any more. And I'll deny what I have said."

I stood to go.

"Listen, can I get your autograph or something?" he said with seemingly no remorse about the things we had just discussed.

I stared at him for a moment, forced myself to remember that I had traveled a similar road, and looked around to find a pen at the end of his bed. Then I found paper, signed, and handed it to him.

"Thanks, man. You're awesome for coming." He looked down at the autograph. "I'll be watchin' for you on the Freedom tour."

I opened the door to leave.

"Hey, what's this below your name?"

"A Bible verse." I looked back in at him. "A friend sent it to me…a long time ago."

I had memorized one of the first scriptures Karen sent me: Matthew 11:28–30.

"Cool. What is it, about Jesus or something?"

"Yeah, it is," I said, wanting to remember Tom Schlater—his face, his tattoos, his words…his heart. "I think it's starting to mean something to me. Maybe it'll mean something to you, someday."

Prison guard Donald Chambers was excited tonight. He was at the trial again today and thought Brian was really on to something—pursuing Twila Yonder, Zane Bender, and the whole hypnotism lead.

I wish I could tell you I was equally enthused.

Chambers said his wife of thirty-one years, Della, was about to have a coronary because he'd been away from home so much. Lately, he was working the night shift here at the detention center, sleeping a few hours at home in the morning, then coming to my trial for a good portion of the day, before going back to work at the prison. Chambers was so enthralled by the trial that he said Della was beginning to watch it on TV and might even join him in the courtroom one of these days.

Brian left the prison about an hour ago to do his homework, and we were in the last free time of the day before lights out. I was in my friend Scotty's cell upstairs from mine, playing a game of poker with him and three other inmates. It was boring, but it beat TV.

They played for cigarettes in here. So although I didn't smoke anymore, I still tried to win as many smokes as I could. You never knew when you might need a favor or two.

Most of the inmates had been keeping up with the trial, especially because it's here in Miami-Dade County and one of their very own "homeboys"—yours truly—was at center stage.

My two aces just got beat by three jacks that were proudly presented by a guy named Radar (I guess because he strongly resembled the little guy from *M*A*S*H*). There went seven more Marlboros…

"Looooo-ser! Oh, Looooo-ser!"

The sound of Zaney's high, cracking voice came somewhere from behind and instantly produced a vacant feeling in the pit of my stomach.

"You'll never be anything but a loser, Lester," he said, as I turned to watch him duck into the cell.

I kept my cool, brought my leaning chair to the ground, and didn't say a word.

"I told you not to call me to the stand." He moved in to hover behind me.

The card game stopped, but I continued looking straight ahead. "Deal," I said to Scotty.

"What does a courtroom 'oath' mean to me, Lester?" He tugged the hair on the back of my head. "Huh? An oath to who?" He pulled again. "To God?"

I flashed back to my father taunting me in similar fashion, in front of my friends.

"Don't pull my hair again," I said through clenched teeth, still looking at the card players frozen around me.

"Ooooh, the rock star defends himself."

"Deal the cards," I said again.

"Remember the guy who hung himself a couple weeks ago?" He came around to cast a shadow over me. "That's gonna be you, Lester."

My eyes went up his orange jumpsuit and settled on his

fat face. "You can't kill me, Zaney. I've got too much to live for, too much preachin' to do. I told you once, whatever your involvement was with Endora, it's backfiring. What she planned for evil, Somebody is using for good."

Instantly, he was on top of me...my chair, over backward. A viselike fist ripped my hair toward the ceiling, then smashed my head against the floor. Then he did it again, as my upper and lower teeth cracked together. I felt like a mannequin. This could be it, right here. Today...to paradise.

But Radar and the *M*A*S*H* unit were tougher than I thought.

At once, they crashed into Zaney, rolling him off me and smothering him to the ground. It took all four of them to keep him down.

I scrambled to my feet, tasting blood in my mouth, feeling it wet my chin.

No guards in sight.

They had Zaney pinned down. He screamed like a maniac, the words unrecognizable.

"I don't know why you got it in so bad for me," I said, bending over, my hands to my knees, catching my breath, "but it needs to stop."

"You are so *dense!*" he screamed from beneath the pile of orange-clad inmates. "You are an *idiot*, Lester. Your brain must really be fried." His squeaky words and sick, strained laughter taunted me. "I only wish I could spill my guts, but it's too soon. The time will come, though. You'll see..."

I had never seen my brother, Eddie, quite like this before. As we walked the sterile halls of the fifth floor, two up from where his son lay fading in and out of existence, I realized how incredibly vulnerable Eddie was...I was...life was.

David's accident—his fateful condition—wasn't real yet to Eddie. I don't think he had cried in all the hours that followed the accident. He just looked empty, dying, as if nothing mattered anymore.

The noticeable bags beneath his sad brown eyes said volumes. His once curly brown hair was straighter, shorter, and mostly gray now, but he still used some kind of gel to make it look wet and hip. As usual, he was dressed in fine clothes—an expensive blue silk shirt, black slacks, and a shiny black leather belt. Walking beside me, he seemed to have gotten smaller in stature since we'd last met.

"Sheila says things have been rough," I said, feeling weird to be the counselor instead of the counselee.

He looked over into my face. "We're about to divorce."

"Is it that bad?"

"Worse."

"Why? What's the problem? If it's debt, I can—"

"Sheila would say it's me; I'd say it's her," he said, hands in pockets. "My job stinks. I'm a crummy father. Now I think I may know how Dad felt."

"You're not like Dad."

"Have you seen Wesley?" he shot.

"Briefly."

"He's one messed-up young man—and where did that come from?"

"When I saw him downstairs he seemed mad at me, maybe for blowing him off one too many times…"

"He's mad at the world, Ev. Sheila and I feel like we've completely failed as parents. And that's put an end to our marriage."

"I'm sure being a parent isn't easy."

"Being a parent," he spit, "is too big for any man—or woman." His voice began to quiver now. "David's been an accident waiting to happen for years."

"Eddie, do you realize how badly Dad *abused us*—physically and mentally? It wasn't right! You had no example to go by. Zilch. It's not your fault!"

We walked slowly in silence. Eddie sniffed back the emotion.

"This life, Ev," he whispered. "It's a bear."

"We've been underdogs since we came into this world. The odds have been stacked against us since day one. I know how you feel. It's tough to get your head on straight when you don't know what straight is."

"Ev," he said, not looking at me. "I may have a gambling problem."

Obviously, the days when Eddie masked himself with a joyous facade were gone. Maybe that was a good thing.

"What? Gambling? Like…on what?"

He kept walking, looking down at the floor. "Mostly Atlantic City. You know, cards, craps, the machines. And when I travel…Harrah's, the casino boats."

"You need to get help, Eddie, that's all. I'll pay your debts. I'll pay for the treatment to get you cleaned up. You can kick it."

He stopped walking. So did I. He turned to look at me and did so deeply. "You've changed."

I didn't say anything.

"When have we ever had a conversation like this?"

"I love you, dude."

That's when he broke down. There on the fifth floor of White Plains Hospital Center. To his knees. Hand on my shoulder. Brothers.

"I just want one more chance," he sobbed. "With David…one more chance."

Boy, did Eddie and I get some looks when we reappeared down at David's ICU station. Everyone knew Eddie was at the end of his rope, even before his son's catastrophe, so all eyes naturally searched him to see how he was coping. Then there was me, the long-lost black sheep who had somehow hit the big-time. Quite a spectacle, the two of us.

Eddie went over and hugged Mary and caressed his sleeping daughter's soft, pretty cheek. He and Sheila glanced at each other but didn't speak. Wesley remained where he was, head down in the darkness.

I checked with Sheila's brother, Bill, for the latest report on David. The prognosis was not favorable. In fact, the doctors said he might not have long. If he died, would he go to Endora's Other Side or Karen's heaven?

Before I hunkered down with Eddie and Sheila for what appeared to be a long night ahead, I grabbed my shoulder bag and took a walk.

Finding a quiet, dimly lit area in another portion of the ICU corridor, I sat down and found my phone. It was approaching midnight, so that made it just before 11 P.M. in Topeka.

I had been longing to call Karen. So much had happened since the night we last spoke, when I dashed out of Bean's coffee shop to pursue Endora's ghost. I was anxious to tell Karen, firsthand, about my stay at Jerry's and all he and Mary had done for me. She needed to know about David, too—so she could pray.

I dialed the number, hoping she was still awake. Her phone rang three times, four, five… I thought about hanging up.

"Hello," she said in a soft, groggy tone.

"I am so sorry to wake you," I whispered. "It's Everett."

"Oh, hi," she said, perking up slightly. "It's good to hear your voice. Where are you?"

"I'm back in New York."

"I was so glad you went to be with Mary and Jerry. Are you doing okay?"

"They were incredible," I said. "And I'm doing good, better than I've been in a long time. Listen, though, I'll tell you more about that in a minute. There's been a bad accident in my family."

"Oh, no…"

"It's my brother's son David. He's seventeen. He was in a really bad wreck today."

"Wait a minute…oh my gosh. Everett, *I smell smoke!*"

"What?"

Her phone dropped. "Oh my gosh!" came her shout from a distance. *"Oh my gosh! FIRE!"*

Her scream terrified me.

My mouth dropped open, my eyes darted. "Karen!" I yelled into the phone. *"Karen!"*

I stood up, but…what could I *do?* My mind went in a thousand directions.

I listened hard. Several more slight screams. Then footsteps.

"Gotta call 911!" she gasped. "Place is burning!"

The line went dead.

Just then, Sheila's brother came dashing around the curve in the quiet corridor.

"Everett, come quick," Bill said, his face cloaked in panic. "David's not good. This may be the end."

20

The moments that followed were surreal, like I was outside my own body, watching from someone else's point of view.

My oldest brother, Howard, had arrived from Ohio with our ailing mother, Doris. They were locked arm in arm with Mary a few feet from David's bed. I fell into their arms when I entered the white, antiseptic-smelling room.

Eddie and Sheila were bawling, smothering their boy, one on each side of the bed, clutching his hands, stroking his thick hair. Wesley stood alone behind them, his arms crossed, jaw locked shut, staring wide-eyed at what was left of his brother. My mother could barely look at her grandson; she was coughing, mumbling, and beginning to say things that made no sense. Madison was too young to be in the room.

The severe trauma David had suffered and the vast amount of blood he lost proved to be too much for his frail body to bear. His life was indeed but a vapor that appeared for a little while—and vanished.

The steady beep we had grown accustomed to that day, the beep that subconsciously gave us hope, became a steady, cold, fatal buzz.

More commotion. Nurses and doctors zipping about. And the official pronouncement: David Anthony Lester was dead.

When he realized his brother was gone, Wesley burst out of the death chamber.

Then came the weeping, the cursing, the grief.

I had never been so close to death, and never wanted to be again.

The Lester family embraced as we never had before. Surrounding David's bed, we cried, we swayed, we squeezed one another tightly. And Mary prayed. The bond of family, the ties that bind.

I felt guilty that my thoughts were divided.

There lay my brother's dead son. And yet, at that very moment, a fire burned in Topeka.

She's okay. She's awake. She's called 911. She will get out of there.

I couldn't leave my family.

Oh, please, God…take care of Karen. Please.

Sure enough, Donald Chambers and his wife, Della, were seated in the fourth row of courtroom B-3 as Brian continued to present his case for my defense. I was able to smile and acknowledge Della before today's proceedings, and Donald told me later that that one brief gesture won her heart; she would be praying against the odds for an innocent verdict the rest of the way.

Boone's work today was nothing earth-shattering, but he wasn't at fault. After all, we were facing a substantial amount of extremely incriminating evidence. Namely, a .45 caliber Glock, registered in my name, with my fingerprints— the very gun used to kill LA psychic Madam Endora Crystal. And to make matters worse, I argued with the victim and even threatened her life in front of other people—many others, many times.

Boone presented a fairly nice dog and pony show, calling several solid character witnesses to the stand. However, it didn't escape anyone's notice that he had no follow-up questions for the Miami-Dade police, crime scene investigators, or the medical examiner, Leonard Morris.

We were, in fact, still buying time to scrape together more detailed research about hypnotism, telekinesis, and the possible part they may have played in Endora's murder. We were also waiting on the edges of our seats for Judge Sprockett to decide whether or not he would subpoena Zane Bender as a witness for the defense.

When I returned to the detention center a few minutes ago, I was pleasantly surprised to find one of my favorite acoustic guitars leaning up in the far corner of my cell, with a note slipped beneath the strings at the neck.

> Everett,
>
> I know this has been a long time coming. Sorry it took so long. Now you can make the new music you've been telling me about. I look forward to hearing it. Enjoy!
>
> Your friend,
>
> Brian Boone
>
> P.S. Excellent news! Judge Sprockett has approved the subpoena for Zane Bender! We will have him on the witness stand tomorrow. Everett, I am convinced his appearance before the court will be most damaging to the prosecution and beneficial to your defense. Possibly, the one key witness we've been waiting for.
>
> Rest well and keep the faith.

Slowly, I picked up the guitar, almost as if I'd never held one before, examining every inch of this tool that made me famous, rich…miserable.

Setting the instrument on my bunk, I slid to my knees, sifting through a stack of paperwork below. Finding a group of folded song sheets, I sat back on the bunk and searched for the tune I scribbled just a few days ago. My fingers played the notes softly, as I tried out the words.

I led you down a dead-end street,
I didn't care if you would die,
I took your money and I stole your heart,
I pushed you out when you—

A tiny flash of light caught my eye, over at the front edge of my cell, but I looked and it was gone.

I picked up the song where I left off.

The light flickered once more.

Quickly, I looked again.

It was a match. Held by a mallet fist. The fist shook out the flame.

"Smell smoke, Lester?" came Zaney's high, breaking voice from around the corner. "That smoke you smell, *boy?*"

I stood, set the Gibson down gently, and crept toward the voice.

"*Boo!*" Zaney jumped out from around the corner.

I staggered back, and he roared with laughter, then turned suddenly somber.

"I smelled smoke," he whispered, grabbing the bars between us. "That night…in Kansas. When your pretty was all alone…I watched her."

I lunged through the bars, getting hold of a piece of his

orange jumpsuit. Jerking with all my might, I slammed him against the cold bars between us.

I had his jumpsuit inside my cell, pinching, pulling, with both hands, smashing his chest and face against steel.

"Remember, Lester?" he squirmed with a sweaty, pained smirk. "When pretty Karen's house went up in flames? I was there!"

I cringed as I tried to improve my grip, but his hands slithered in like tentacles, one clawing my face, another gouging the back of my neck.

I moved quickly to dodge his paws, then one of his hands squeezed my neck and tried to slam my head against the bars, but he didn't have the leverage. His arms were too fat; they could only make it through up to his elbows.

I thought about yelling for guards. Chambers must be near. But I resisted, realizing I had to hold out to hear more of his confession.

"I used gas, you know," he cackled uncomfortably. "I watched her squirm in that inferno, watched her from my truck as long as I could."

Taking his jumpsuit with my right hand now, I reached through the bars with my left to grab whatever I could. Wrapping my forearm around his wet neck, I muscled his big head toward me, up against the bars.

"Did Endora hire you?" I gasped, tightening my grip in short jerks.

Suddenly, he shifted all of his weight against my arm, the one sticking through the bars. It bent backward, and I screamed, losing my grip on his jumpsuit.

Realizing he'd snap my arm, I socked through the bars again with my free hand, trying to force him off me. But his heavy frame wouldn't budge. Instead, he grabbed my free arm as well.

"Whoops." He ripped both my arms toward him as hard as he could.

I turned my head away, but my shoulders and sternum crashed into the bars. The impact dropped me to my knees, but he still clenched my wrists with his powerful fists.

"Karen Bayliss is the one," he growled, yanking me up against the bars. "She's the wench who caused all this...*all of it!*"

Get through this...he'll be in court tomorrow.

"You're gonna die, Lester," he whispered. "Whether it's in here or outside, you *will* die." He jerked me against the bars again. "And your—"

Crack!

Donald thumped Zaney from behind with his billy club, square in the middle of the back. My body dropped limply to the floor of my cell.

"You won't learn, will you, Zaney?" Chambers shoved him with his boot. "Not to mess around on my watch? And playing with matches..." He shook his head and clicked his tongue three times. "This is going to get you a nice little vacation in solitary. That is, as soon as you get back from testifying at your buddy's trial tomorrow."

"What's he doing out?" I managed.

"He had mop-up," Chambers said. "Somebody took his eyes off him."

"You can't do that," Zaney breathed. "The minute you take your eyes off me...you're dead."

All of us left David's hospital room, except his mother and father.

Quite a few visitors still remained in the lamp-lit waiting area, and I knew they would be seeking an update on David. As Mary spoke quietly with Mom and Howard, and they prepared to share the distressing news with the others, I ducked into the men's restroom.

With my face in the far corner, my heart rate increasing, I dialed Karen's home phone number.

Staring at the black and green designs on the walls, I waited anxiously. One, two rings. *"The number you have dialed is not a working number,"* came the recording. *"Please check the number and dial again."*

My insides ached. I was far away and helpless. I didn't know Karen's cell phone number. So I called information for the Topeka police department and waited to be connected.

Rubbing my sore eyes, I asked if they had any information about a fire within the last hour. Had any police, fire, or rescue squads been sent to a Bayliss residence, Karen Bayliss…?

I got zero answers from an uppity young officer. A brick wall.

"Listen," I said, frustrated, "there's a fire burning, probably right this minute, at the home of a Topeka resident. Her name is Karen Bayliss. B-A-Y-L-I-S-S. I do not have her address, and I'm calling from out of town. But I just spoke with her, and her home is *on fire.*"

"You told me that already," said the officer. "And I told you that I would check into it."

"May I wait…to see what you find?"

"No, you may not," he shot back. "First of all, it's going to take me a while to get to it. Second, I am not at liberty to give out that kind of information over the phone. You'll have to call back in a half-hour or so."

"Can you give me the number of the Topeka fire department?"

"Just dial 911."

"I am not in Kansas! I'm in New York! Look, someone's life is at stake here. Now I need you to get me a local number for the Topeka fire department, or—"

He interrupted, reading the number.

I dialed and, yes, stations 10, 15, and 21 had dispatched units to a house fire in suburban Topeka about an hour ago. The Bayliss residence. At last report, four tanker trucks were at the scene, and the house was fully engulfed.

I bolted out of the restroom and went to Mary like a paper clip to a magnet.

With tissues waded in her soft hand and red patches beneath her eyes, she sat quietly, visiting with Sheila's brother, Bill, and four or five other people I did not know, several of whom were in tears as well. Teenager Madison was there, looking fatigued and confused, her dark mascara smudged at both eyes.

They politely understood when I excused myself and called Mary away, probably thinking I needed to consult her about family matters or funeral arrangements.

That's when I spilled my guts about Karen and the fire.

"I don't know what else to do," I said anxiously. "Maybe I should fly out there, but I can't leave Eddie…"

"My gosh, Everett, what is going on? Is Endora Crystal behind this?"

"I think so. She's disappeared. I haven't heard from her in weeks."

"You need to keep checking back with the fire department for details and keep trying Karen's number. I would tell you to fly out there, but…people are going to need you here."

"I know." I searched her eyes for more answers.

Then she hugged me, and I squeezed her like a boy does his mother.

"She's going to be okay," Mary said, holding me. "Father in heaven, we pray for Karen right now, that You will protect her from danger. Get her out of that house safely, we ask. Let her be safe, Lord… And take special care of our family right now, as we grieve."

My phone rang.

"That's me." I left Mary's grasp and headed around the corner to a vacant waiting area pulling out my phone at the same time.

"Hello!" I shouted.

"Well, hello, stranger," came the jovial voice. "You sound in good spirits."

Mary had come around the corner to see if it was Karen, but she caught my glare instead. I mouthed to her: *Endora.*

"Everett…can you hear me?"

"I hear you," I said coldly.

Mary was at my side now. She covered up the phone and whispered, "Be *nice*. You need to play her game, so you can find out what's going on."

"What's happening with you?" Endora said. "I'm sorry I've been out of touch. I was visiting my sister's place in Sedona, taking kind of a sabbatical. You know what I mean?"

Hearing her voice made me sick.

"I've been taking some time off, too," I said, afraid she would pick up on the suspicion, the hatred in my voice. "Listen, Endora, there's been a bad accident. It's my brother Eddie's son, David. He just passed away a few minutes ago from a car wreck he was in earlier today."

"Oh, no," she whined. "I'm so sorry."

"I just need to be with Eddie and the family right now. Maybe we can get together in a few days. Would that be okay?"

"That's just what I was thinking, hon. You be with your family now. When we meet, we can catch up. Hey, maybe we can go to your place in Miami. I'd love to get down there where it's nice and warm."

"That's possible. I'll call you."

"Everett," she said, catching me just before I hung up. "David is all right, you know… He's on the Other Side now."

21

I hoped my physical presence was good enough to comfort Eddie, his family, and my mother, Doris, because my mind was far from the third floor of White Plains Hospital Center.

That sounded cold, but Karen had grown to mean a great deal to me. She probably didn't know that, but it was true. I wasn't at all myself not knowing where she was, if she was okay, and whether she was still smiling.

Don't get me wrong, my heart broke for our whole family. Losing David would be the hardest thing most of us would ever have to deal with. For Mom, of course, that was when my father died. But this, this was bad. A parent never thinks he'll outlive his children. Eddie existed in another world.

The call from Karen came at 2:20 A.M., and when it did, my lips quivered as I held back the strains of joy. After saving all she could from her burning home, she was taken by paramedics to a local hospital in Topeka, treated for smoke inhalation, then released shortly thereafter. She was calling from the Residence Inn just outside Topeka, near her home, which was now smoldering ashes and wet, black soot.

"I've had my eye on this cute little white house in Vinings, anyway," came the voice I had come to adore. "It's got a big front porch with a swing and a separate garage out back."

"Karen, you've lost everything. And it's my fault," I whispered, from around the corner of where Eddie's family gathered. "Endora's behind this. I've brought this trouble to you."

"I got the important things. My photo albums and Bibles, and the keepsakes from the kids at church."

"Karen," I said, exasperated. "Endora—whoever did this—he or she is not messing around."

"I know, I know. This is a war…"

For the first time, I heard her break down.

"I'm sorry," I pleaded into the phone. "So sorry I can't be there."

Her breathing turned to short, choppy gasps.

"There's a reason God put you on my heart so long ago," she cried. "I'm not afraid. I just don't want anything to happen to you before…"

I shook my head. "I'm going to find out what's going on. I'll take care of it, I promise you."

"Everett." She inhaled deeply. "There *is* a heaven and there *is* a hell. There is no Other Side! Do you understand me?"

She *knew* this was true. It was no theory to her. And she cared enough about me to share, to warn…

"I'm the messenger," she managed, "your messenger. And before another minute goes by, I want to be clear to you that there is only *one way* to the Father—to God—and that's through Jesus Christ, believing in Him. The Bible says that, Everett."

"Karen, we can talk…"

"He's gone to prepare a place for us. In heaven, forever." She was regaining her wind. "If you reject Him, there is a hell. It's darkness and fire—and it's forever, too."

"Karen, I'm not used to this. Someone caring. I'm thinking about what you're telling me…"

"You need to do more than think about it! You may not have much time. Who knows what Endora has planned."

"I'm not going to do it halfway, Karen! Okay? If and when it happens, I want it to be real."

Quiet descended, and then she blew her nose.

"Okay, fine," she bounced back. "Just don't wait too long. There *is* an urgency. That 'Other Side' stuff is complete mysticism, and you need to be radical enough to follow Christ. That's it. That's all I'm going to say."

"Phew." I laughed. "You've got some fire little lady."

She laughed, too, and finished crying at the same time.

"I'm setting up a meeting with Endora."

"Have you talked to her?" Karen asked.

"She called tonight. I was ready to ream her out, but Mary said I need to get close to her again, so I can find out what's going on, who's after you…"

"Everett, you've got to be so careful. This is Satan himself you're dealing with. Do you hear me? Endora *is* Satan."

"I hear what you're saying, Karen, but I've got to get into her mind."

"No! It's not worth it. Don't give her an inch. I'm telling you, don't put yourself in a position to be under her evil authority. She'll suck you in!"

"I'll be careful," I promised. "Look, I want to come to you, to help you."

"That's not necessary. I got a lot of my clothes out. My folks have helped set me up in this nice hotel. I'm going to take a week off to square the insurance away and find a new house. It's gonna be okay, really."

"It's your safety I'm concerned about."

"I know," she said. "Believe me, I'm keeping my eyes open. I know this is real. Don't worry. I'm being careful."

"Maybe I should hire you a bodyguard."

"Oh, right!" she moaned. "You've been in showbiz too long."

"I'm serious. Or maybe I should come out there in a day or two to help you."

"That's kind of you, Everett, but my folks are here. They'll help me find the right place and get some new furniture and stuff."

"Can I send you some money?"

"No!"

"If anything out of the ordinary happens—phone calls, black roses—you call me. Anytime, day or night."

"Okay," she agreed.

"One of these days I'm going to show up there, you know."

"Is that right?"

"That's right."

I wondered if she felt the same way I did precisely at that moment.

Cloud nine.

"There's a reason I'm not there right now, Karen. It's one of my brother's boys, David…"

"Oh, my gosh. That's right! You were just starting to tell me about it."

"Yeah," I said, slumping back to reality. "He died tonight."

"Oh, Everett, no!" She sighed. "Tell me what happened."

The days that followed were long and difficult.

Although Eddie and Sheila invited Mary, Howard, my mother, and me to stay with them at their large home in White Plains, we all felt a bit awkward and exposed. Mary was the exception, of course. She seemed happy in the moment, content wherever, whatever the circumstance. I admired her immensely.

During our stay, Madison remained in her room upstairs most of the time, only joining us for meals once in a while. When she did come around, she was shy and reserved, usually only giving one- or two-word answers when spoken to.

Wesley was seldom home. Every now and then, a loud car would pull up in front of the house, especially in the early-morning hours, and he would run out or run in through the side garage door, often with a backpack on his shoulder. He was nineteen, didn't have a steady job, and had no interest in college. Eddie still gave him a weekly allowance. I wondered what was in the backpack.

David's funeral was terribly sad. It took place on a dark, cold, drizzly fall afternoon. There seemed to be virtually no color in the universe that day, only gray and black, silhouettes and shadows.

I was surprised by the weight of the casket, as I helped hoist if off the rollers from the back of the shiny black hearse and carried it through the wet grass, up to the knoll that Eddie and Sheila had decided would be David's resting place.

The dirt taken from the eight-foot rectangle in the ground sat in a low pile nearby, with a green blanket over it that read "Relova's Funeral Home" in embroidered white letters.

Awkwardly, we eased the casket onto a stretcher that rested directly above the crevice in the ground. Most of the crowd gathered beneath a large green open-air tent, which also featured the name of the funeral home. Some of the mourners, however, spilled out beyond the tent, their umbrellas adding splashes of color to the gray hilltop graveyard.

The tall, thin priest who delivered the eulogy stood stoically, his thinning brown hair wet from the drizzle, his glasses dotted with raindrops. You could see wisps of his breath in the frigid air, and his hands shook while holding the Bible from which he read, "The Lord is my shepherd; I shall not want. He makes me to lie down in green pastures; He leads me beside the still waters. He restores my soul…"

The words are so peaceful. Like an oasis. But what about David? Where is his soul right now? Is he resting in peace? Could he be where Karen warned me about?

Many of David's friends were here. And although I spotted some paparazzi with two-foot lenses, shooting photos from behind distant tombstones, most of the kids seemed more concerned about bringing their condolences than seeing a rock star. I scanned the crowd but did not see Tom Schlater, the nineteen-year-old crash survivor I had met at the hospital.

Eddie, Sheila, Wesley, and Madison sat solemnly in the front row next to the casket, draped with beautiful purple, white, pink, and yellow flowers. A recent eight-by-ten of David in a wood frame sat on a small table next to the family. In the photo, he wore a Rangers hockey jersey and cutoffs as he washed his Camaro barefooted in the driveway.

When it was all said and done, the cars lined their way down the hill and around the curves with headlights on and windshield wipers whirring. Those of us left here included only the immediate family, the priest, a few funeral officials, and David. The priest gave a final prayer, and the suited men from the funeral home—who resembled Secret Service agents—lowered David's casket into the ground.

Before walking to our cars, we each approached the opening in the earth, paid our last respects, and gently tossed a light pink rose onto the casket.

Light pink, for sympathy.

Eddie and Sheila wept while Madison sat frozen with a glossy stare, looking out over the rain-soaked hillside, probably asking the same question we all do at times: *Why?*

A sad day, indeed.

As I stood alone with my thoughts and questions beneath one corner of the funeral tent, chilled from the rain, a low voice spoke fast from behind.

"I hate you. You know that, don't you."

I turned to find Wesley standing there, legs locked shoulder-width apart, arms at his sides, forearms braced in front of him with fists clenched.

"You did this to him," he seethed.

He was about four inches shorter than me, wearing a new, dark blue blazer with a crooked tie and gray corduroys. One of his black rubber shoes was untied. All I could do initially was stare.

"David *worshiped* you," he growled. "He bought into you, big-time. The whole scam. So did I, for a while."

I shook my head in sorrow. "Wesley, I—"

"He was a miserable person, you know that? He *wanted* to die—because of you! He wanted your afterlife. Your…your…your stupid life on the Other Side!"

Some of the family beneath the tent glanced our way, but no one approached.

"I'm sorry, Wesley. I've made some bad decisions, and I've surrounded myself with some bad people—"

"You and your 'Ten Lives' and your 'Own Religion' and your so-called 'Freedom,'" he hissed. "Look where it got your biggest fan. He's gone! Dead. Cold and lyin' in a box. And that's as far as he's goin'."

He looked at his watch and scanned the hillside. One lone car was heading up the winding driveway: a purple SUV with black windows and two tiny yellow lights at the bottom of the windshield. As it got closer, Wesley turned to me one last time.

"You let him down, 'Uncle Everett,'" he whispered. "All those times you said you'd be there for us. You and your afterlife…"

"Wesley, please try to under—"

"I hope you sleep well tonight, *Uncle Everett*—" he pointed his finger two inches from my chin—"knowing David drove to his death counting on you and your fictional tomorrows."

Then he whirled around, took one last look down into his brother's grave, and marched into the downpour toward the SUV that had come for him.

★ ★ ★

The little white house Karen had her eye on was now hers, front porch and all. She signed a contract the day of David's funeral and would be closing on it and moving in within a few weeks. This girl wasted no time.

Whenever I phoned her, Karen was like a kid in a candy store, running about town, choosing new furniture and enjoying time off from work in preparation for her move. Although I wanted desperately to fly to Kansas to meet her in person and help her after the fire, it did not feel like the right time.

Perhaps she needed to be alone after such a devastating experience. Maybe beneath the cool exterior, she was scared and vulnerable and felt she needed to keep her distance from me. I hoped that wasn't the case.

Investigators soon determined that the fire had been set deliberately, starting with gasoline in the carport and spreading fast to the kitchen and remainder of the two-story home.

My anger toward Endora was palpable. Yet, I knew Mary was right; somehow I needed to keep my cool and draw close to Endora again so I could find out what was really going on behind the scenes, especially as it related to Karen.

Throughout the days surrounding the funeral, I thought long and hard before contacting Endora, racking my brain to figure out how I could get her to tell me all she knew about Karen and the dangerous events that had plagued her.

That's when I remembered the séance.

After my one-time fiancée, Liza Moon, passed away, Endora had pestered me repeatedly about joining her for a séance to try to communicate with Liza. But each time I refused.

Suddenly, I knew what to do.

Reaching Endora by cell phone, I asked if we could meet at my condo in North Miami in two days. "Yes," she said. Then I told her why: "I'm ready to contact Liza Moon."

Endora was delighted.

★ ★ ★

10:30 P.M.

With Zane Bender taking the witness stand tomorrow, Donald allowed me to phone Brian and fill him in on the incident that occurred earlier tonight with Zaney. I told Boone how Zaney claimed to have set Karen's house on fire. He assured me he would pursue it in court.

In the meantime, Chambers offered to take me to the infirmary to have my cuts cleaned and bandaged. Normally, I wouldn't go for such minor injuries, but the deep scratch where Zaney got me on the back of the neck stung like crazy.

Not only that, but I felt like getting out of my cell.

I guess I was on edge. So much was riding on Zaney's testimony.

Chambers told Rockwell where we were going, and we headed out. Through two large metal detectors, about fifteen feet apart, and down a short hallway to some steps. We went up, made a left, and went down a long hallway of mostly darkened offices.

Stopping at the door of the infirmary, Chambers and I looked in on a short guy in green scrubs seated at a desk. His knees bounced up and down as he ate Cheetos and played solitaire on the computer in front of him. Aerosmith blared from the boom box on the credenza next to him.

His small eyes finally sensed us standing at the door. "Oh, my goodness," he said loudly, turning down the music and wiping his orange fingers under his armpits. "My goodness, my goodness, Everett Lester."

He approached us nervously with an extended orange hand. "My name is Jimmy...Jimmy Pierce, physician's assistant. At your service. Hello, Donald."

Chambers and I smiled, said hello, and explained the incident with Zaney.

"My, my, my...I'm sorry to hear about that, Mr. Lester. Why don't you just hop up here on the examining table and let me have a look-see." Pierce patted the table, shaking noticeably as he snapped on some rubber gloves. "You know this Zane Bender fella, he...he's been in a number of scrapes."

"Believe me, we know," said Chambers.

"Boy, he-he got ya g-good on the neck, Mr. Lester." Pierce fidgeted with a bag of cotton balls. Pierce had a large forehead with a few strands of dark hair plastered across the top of his shiny dome and wore round glasses with no rims.

"So, you've heard about Zane Bender?" I winced a bit as he dabbed the big cut with hydrogen peroxide.

"Oh...oh, my, yes. People are saying he's some kind of...of wizard or something." He scanned the empty room and whispered, "I heard he made one inmate levitate. Do you hear what I'm saying...*levitate!* We're talking, the guy is seated in a chair, and both he and the chair rise four feet off the ground."

I looked at Chambers. "What more have you heard?" he asked.

Pierce glanced around the room and out the door. "You didn't hear it here." He smudged the cut on my neck with Neosporin. "I've heard wind that something big is going to come down...within the next few days."

"Like what?" Chambers whispered now too.

"An attack." Pierce cleaned up after himself while repeatedly peering at the door. "Maybe a riot. Something involving Zaney. That's all I know."

We stood to leave.

"Do me a favor, Pierce," said Chambers. "Keep your ears open. Let me know the second you hear any more about it."

"Will do...will do." Pierce walked us to the door. "Pleasure to meet you Mr. Lester...a real pleasure."

11:50 P.M.

In my bunk, I just finished some new lyrics that I began jotting down during today's trial. I guess I'll continue writing the memoirs for a few minutes until I get tired. (Between the lumpy bunk and the noise in the night, you had to be *really* tired to sleep in here.)

I received a special letter today. Let me share it with you...

> Dear Mr. Lester,
>
> When is the last time you remember receiving a letter from me? It's been quite a while, I know.
>
> I wanted to write to you for old time's sake, simply to remind you how much your loving Savior cares about you. You have withstood a great deal during this trial and in the months leading up to it, and I am very proud of you.
>
> As I was looking at some old notes of mine while watching your trial today, I came across the following Scripture. I know you're familiar with it. But I just wanted to share it with you again in hopes that it will uplift you and give you hope:
>
>> "Then I heard a loud voice in heaven, saying,
>> 'Now the salvation, and the power, and the

kingdom of our God and the authority of His
Christ have come, for the accuser of our
brethren has been thrown down, he who
accuses them before our God day and night.

'And they overcame him because of the
blood of the Lamb and because of the word
of their testimony, and they did not love
their life even when faced with death.'"
—Revelation 12:10–11

The evil one has been overcome by the blood of
the Lamb! And the evil one is being overcome because
of the word of your testimony. I know God has big
plans for you, and your testimony.

I am excited about the future!

Yours truly,

Karen

She had always brought me a smile, like the one I wore
now.

She had been so faithful…to her God…to me.

I was falling asleep now.

More tomorrow.

CLANG…CLANG…CLANG…CLANG…

RRRRRrrrrrrrrrrrRRRRRRRRRRrrrrrrrrrrrrrRRRRRRRR…

Floodlights and sirens.

Footsteps…running…one guard after another. Rifles
engaged.

CLANG…CLANG…CLANG…CLANG…

RRRRRrrrrrrrrrrrRRRRRRRRRRrrrrrrrrrrrrrRRRRRRRR…

Dogs…panting, wagging, running.

"Fourth floor, fourth floor!" came the guards' screams.

I staggered out of my bunk, squinting beneath what appeared to be stadium lights. Standing dazed, looking out my cell…searching for Donald Chambers.

Inmates began banging and clanging in their cells, cheering…screaming.

Someone is out!

Now I saw Chambers running toward the main guard station; he slid to a halt, just down the corridor from me. He wore a green helmet and was armed with a black rifle. The radio clipped to his shoulder emitted static, then voices…loud.

"One inmate…we have one inmate *down*."

Static…

"He's in custody."

Static…

Volume and alarm of the voice increased… "We got bedsheets!"

Static…

Chambers's eyes locked in on mine. It was a grave, fleeting look.

Static…

Another voice on another radio. "We're outside at the perimeter."

Static… "We got a…mattress. I repeat, a mattress at the top of the fence."

The place went bonkers. I'd never heard it so maddeningly loud.

I turned to throw on another shirt, and something on the floor caught my eye. A yellow piece of paper, folded down to wallet size.

I picked it up and unfolded it. Dark red liquid ran off the edge of the paper onto my left hand. Revolted, I shook it off. Then I read the childlike handwriting:

Watch out, Lester.
Me and my demons are loose.
I've made a blood oath to get you.
Tell my pretty Karen I'll see her soon.
Z

22

Mary's phone call came as I was preparing for Endora's arrival at my condo in North Miami. When she told me young Olivia Gilbert was moving back to Xenia, Ohio, to be with her parents, I was ecstatic.

But Mary hadn't finished yet.

Olivia was still in a coma, a state in which her doctors feared she would remain—indefinitely.

I imagined the rage and anguish of Claudia and Raymond Gilbert as the hospital bed was delivered to their meager home and set up in the family room. A nurse would be on duty twelve hours a day, Mary said, to bathe Olivia, brush her teeth and hair, to reposition her stiffening body in order to prevent bedsores, feed her by tube, administer physical therapy, and…change her diaper.

"Stop, Mary! Stop. Don't tell me any more…I can't take it. My gosh…*what have I done?*"

She was crying, too. Loudly. Both of us were.

I hung up and fell to my knees between the living room and the balcony.

The floodgates opened.

I remembered the picture at Jerry Princeton's house—the one of Olivia and her older sister, Veronica, cutting up in the summer sun, along with their mother and father. I examined it often the weeks I was there.

Yes, I remembered the picture. Raymond was admiring Olivia. The father. Gazing at his little girl with a light in his eyes. A look of thankfulness. A reason for being.

Wake up from this nightmare that is your life, man!

YOU did this!

And David…he believed in you. And now his blood was on your hands.

This is REALITY.

A girl lies in a bed, almost a vegetable, probably for life!

What kind of person are you? ANIMAL!

As I crawled out to the edge of the balcony, the sun that engulfed me did not warm the chill in my soul. It was the coldness of evil. Of death. Of everything that was wrong in the world. This was me.

The thirty-second floor seemed dizzyingly high.

"My God. My God. What have I done to this girl's life? Oh, Lord, *please*…You can still save her. I'll give my life for hers, Lord. Will You accept that? Will You make a deal with me? One time? One…time."

I had never cried like that before. Out of control.

"Please, Father. Please…I'll give You my life, if You'll heal Olivia. I want You, Lord. *I need You!* I'm so full of sin. Please…come in. Come into my life. Right now! I give it up to You. Please…forgive me. Make me Yours. Oh, please, make that little girl well again…"

I did not want to commit suicide that day, but I did want to die.

I did not want to leap from the balcony of The Towers complex, but I was finally ready to lay my life down.

"You're going to need to help me, God," I cried, still lying on the floor near the balcony. "I don't know anything about being a Christian, but I'm ready…I'm ready to try."

With my nose running and tears all over my shirtsleeves, I began to laugh and weep at the same time.

This is so radical.

Karen will be beside herself. And Mary, and Jerry…

I smiled, then laughed again and dried my eyes and nose with the front of my untucked shirt.

The fans, the band, Gray—no one will believe it.

I couldn't ever recall feeling as I did at that moment: completely drained but thoroughly refreshed. Alert. Clean. *Resurrected.*

Then the doorbell rang, three quick shots.

Before I could even react, footsteps rushed about the condo.

"Everett?" came Endora's panicked voice. "Everett…what's going on?" Her feet paced to and fro as I remained silent on the floor. "Oh, dear, Everett! Oh, dear Satan, tell me I'm not too late. Can't be too late…"

A local AM radio station was the first to have the story, which I picked up on my small black and silver transistor radio as I lay on my bunk before breakfast.

"Authorities launched a massive manhunt in the predawn hours today for a dangerous felon who escaped from the Miami-Dade detention center by shimmying down a thirty-foot rope made out of bedsheets.

"At least seventy-five officers using dogs and boats pursued the thirty-eight-year-old escapee, Zane Bender, who had recently begun serving a seventeen-year sentence at the facility for armed robbery and attempted murder. Bender was set to serve as a key witness for the defense in the highly publicized Everett Lester murder trial in Miami today.

"According to authorities, Bender and another inmate

broke a thirty-six-by-twenty-four-inch window on the fourth floor and stuffed a mattress out the opening. The other inmate was critically injured, apprehended, and hospitalized, but Bender squeezed through the window, slid down the home-made rope, dropped some fifteen feet to the ground, and used the mattress to scale a tall, razor-wire fence.

"Authorities were concentrating their search in the Kendall area, but a state trooper and spokesman in the case says Bender may be farther than that by now. 'Who knows? This guy may be headed for the Everglades, which is really one of his only choices. We've got dogs on airboats right now, combing the Glades. But if he went that route, he may have a difficult time with the gators and all.'"

"I guess you don't believe in letting someone answer the door," I said, my voice startling Endora from the floor of the balcony that over-looked Bal Harbour.

"Oh, my gosh," she said, out of breath. "What are you doing down there?" Then she blinked in surprise, probably noticing my puffy eyes and runny nose.

Setting her purse on the table, she knelt. "Hey, what's the matter with you? Are you okay?"

But they were just words, empty words. I knew that now.

She could no longer disguise the revulsion she felt toward me; it was all over her face. And likewise, my hostility toward her had to be a dead giveaway.

"What did you mean just now when you said you hoped you weren't too late?" I surprised her by taking the offensive. "Too late for what?"

She stood and put her hands on the railing, looking out at the Atlantic, shimmering white from the high south Florida sun. "Oh…nothing. I've just been in such a hurry, juggling a zillion clients, talking to Gray about the new tour. I wanted to make sure I didn't miss you."

"Seemed pretty urgent, the way you barged in here." I knew clearly that she was against me now, that she was indeed my enemy, that somehow she knew what had just transpired in that room, and that she had intended to stop it.

"I just care about you," she said, without turning around. "Is that such a crime?"

She made me want to gag. I could only think of Karen, the black roses…the fire. "Let's get on with this thing."

"Fine." She spun around, throwing her shoulders back and heading into the condo with her lips pursed. "Let's darken this place up and talk to the dead."

Everyone on our defense team was on edge this morning. Earlier, Judge Sprockett had instructed his bailiff to dismiss the jury temporarily. We didn't know why but assumed it had to do with Zane Bender's escape from the detention center the previous night.

Even the usually calm Brian Boone was antsy and pacing, as we waited for Judge Sprockett to enter the courtroom from the judge's chambers. Meanwhile, Frank Dooley, standing with his arms folded and wearing an overconfident grin, scanned the crowd for fans and admirers.

The media crew was literally overflowing from its designated area, and there was a distinct frenzy among today's crowd. Dooley tugged at his starched white cuffs and smiled enormously as Judge Sprockett strode into the courtroom.

After breezing through some formalities, Sprockett motioned to Brian to determine how the defense wished to proceed, following the eventful night at the detention center.

"Your Honor," Boone said, looking a bit pale. "Everyone

is well aware that one of the key witnesses in our defense, possibly *the* key witness, Mr. Zane Bender, will not appear before us today. Although we are confident and hopeful Mr. Bender will be apprehended quickly so he can testify before this court, we must regrettably request that the court recess for a day or two so we may redirect our research efforts and line up several more witnesses."

Boone, wearing a khaki blazer and dark blue slacks, sat down hard beside me and waited for the repercussions.

"Your Honor, if I may." Dooley stood and approached the bench. "We, the prosecution, believe we have been extremely patient, if not long-suffering, as we have painstakingly waded through Mr. Boone's uninspiring defense proceedings. I can see clearly," he smiled into the TV camera, "that Mr. Boone and Mr. Lester are in a bit of a pickle today, seeing that their big star witness decided to choose today of all days to escape from a maximum security prison..."

Dooley was right in thinking the line would bring a laugh, as courtroom B-3 erupted like a Letterman audience.

Even Judge Sprockett gave in to a half smile. "Okay, Mr. Dooley, enough bantering. What's your point?"

"My point is, Your Honor," Dooley turned to look directly at Boone and me, "let's not drag this thing out. The facts have painted a blatantly clear picture. We're asking that you not allow this case to be watered down by sheer...aimlessness."

Glancing toward the media pit, he pulled his chair out and sat, careful not to crease the expensive duds.

"Your point is well taken," Sprockett said. "I'm going to grant a one-day recess, Mr. Boone. We will meet back here precisely at 9 A.M. tomorrow. Everyone, please be on time. And please, Mr. Boone, let's get things rolling at a good clip tomorrow. Bailiff, tell the jury they have the day off."

The crowd came to its feet, and the reporters blew past their boundaries within three feet of Boone and me, as we huddled close to talk before I was escorted away.

"Let's not worry too much about this yet, Everett." He raised his voice. "They'll catch him. In the meantime, I've been doing some research. Found a good witness—an expert hypnotist. He may be able to help."

I looked into Brian's eyes and nodded but detected an uncertainty I hadn't seen in Boone before. "Pray we can get this guy to the stand by tomorrow," he said. "We're running out of time—and leads."

Things began as I had planned. Endora pulled the black curtains closed and lit more than a dozen candles. She positioned herself on the floor, with me opposite her.

"Here, drink this." She handed me a glass of dark red wine and sipped one herself. "It will help you relax."

Karen's words came zinging back to me: *"Don't give her an inch… Don't put yourself…under her evil authority. She'll suck you in!"*

At the same time, I believed Karen's life was on the line. I had to dupe Endora.

"Cheers." I hoisted the glass to my lips to pacify her and pretended to take a big swig.

"More," she bossed, drinking herself.

Again, I lifted the glass, yet drank as little as possible.

Silence fell over the room as we closed our eyes and waited.

After a few minutes had passed, Endora slowly broke into a low, evil chant. It became louder. Soon she began to break into deep moans paired with sudden, stuttered shrieks. *"Liza Moon…Liza Mooooooooon. Come and meet us."*

As I cheated, peeking through squinting eyes, the floor spun slightly, and I noticed Endora had begun to tremble. Her face was milky white, in stark contrast to her dark purple lipstick and the brown mole painted on her right cheek.

"*What?*" Endora shouted, as if she had seen a ghost. "*Yes. YES…I hear you, Liza!*"

"What did she say?" I asked anxiously.

"*Silence!*"

I quickly shut my eyes and pretended to listen harder.

Then Endora began laughing wickedly, practically shrieking. I couldn't help but glimpse at her again. I had never seen anything like it. It was as if her body had been taken over by someone else. Every inch of her was shaking. I didn't know what had hold of her, but whatever was rocking her body seemed real.

"'The…angel…'" Endora nodded toward the sky, as if holding a conversation with someone above her. "'The…angel of death, she must…'"

I had heard this term, "angel of death," before. I didn't know where, but I knew Endora was talking about Karen.

Alarm set in. My head swayed.

Get hold of yourself.

Endora's face was wrinkled in contortion, her head tipped sideways, as if listening to someone floating above her. "'She—must—die. The angel of death must die!'"

"Why?" I barked, fighting off dizziness. "Why must she die?"

Endora paused, as if staggered by an unwanted intruder. "Why must the angel die, Miss Liza?" she finally asked, throwing her arms up in the air, demanding quiet as she waited for Liza's response.

Speaking in another voice, almost as deep as a man's, Endora said, "She will lead Everett to the Lamb. Then, everything will…change."

It was now or never.

I hoped Endora was fully caught up in the spirit realm.

"How…will…the…angel…of…death…be…slain? By whom?" I asked, as if mouthing the words to a deaf person.

That's when it happened.

Like a huge switch shutting off its power, Endora went silent. I peeked and saw the color returning to her face. Her eyes were still shut, but her body stopped trembling.

"Liza knows you've been through a great deal, Everett," came Endora's evil monotone. "She knows you're tired…you need rest. Therefore, you must sleep now, as we've practiced in the past. You must rest…"

Tranquilizers.

That's all I could think of.

It feels like tranquilizers…

"I knew it would come to this, sweet Everett." The voice grew distant now. "When my friend Twila and I first contacted Liza, we knew it was bad, that you were going to become a Christian. Now it's happened, hasn't it? Just before I arrived. I can see something different in you."

I struggled to fight the sleep, but my body was heavy, going limp. I was paralyzed, and I thought of Olivia Gilbert, wanting to speak, to shout, but unable to function.

Trapped.

"Maybe it wouldn't have mattered so much if you were the only one," came Endora's robotic voice. "But Liza informed us you would lead others to the Lamb. Thousands of others. No, no, no, Everett." She laughed. "We mustn't have that. You see, I am loyal to my god, as well," she droned, as if in a trance. "And I am prepared to die—for him."

The rest was bits and pieces, as I became utterly powerless.

"You will…dresser…loaded…shoot me…return…telephone Gray…no recollection…"

23

When I awoke on the floor of my Miami high-rise, the first fumbled, frantic call I made was to Gray Harris in New York. It took me what seemed like forever to find a phone number and drum up enough composure to push the right buttons. I couldn't control my hands from shaking.

Gray forced me to slow down and explain everything. After listening to him for five minutes while staring at Endora's lifeless body, I hung up the phone, followed his instructions, and dialed 911. The truth would be the best way, he had insisted.

Miami-Dade County police converged on the condo like a pack of wolves as I sat dazed and silent on the balcony overlooking the bluish-green Atlantic. Soon, crime scene investigators followed.

Lead detective Harry Coogle was surprisingly kind and patient. He sat with me on the balcony, prying mostly one- and two-word answers from me about what exactly happened surrounding the death of

Endora Crystal. Then he transported me in his unmarked car to the police department for further questioning.

Hours later, the interrogation continued in a small, stuffy room with fluorescent lights, a Formica desk, and dirty plastic chairs. One of the DeathStroke attorneys, Brian Boone, had flown in from New York and was by my side. But I still sat in a state of shock.

Three hard-nosed investigators grilled me for information, obviously assuming that, because I was the infamous Everett Lester, I was high on drugs, filled with rage, and guilty of Endora's murder. Coogle, a handsome, dark-haired man of about fifty, came back into the tiny room with a fresh cup of coffee and cooled off his colleagues.

"The bottom line, the thing these men want to hear from you, Mr. Lester, is—did you kill Edith Rosenbaum?" Coogle asked. "You've told me, but I would like you to tell them—in your words."

Looking at the floor, I shook my head. "No, I did not." Brian patted me and told me it was okay to go on. "The last thing I remember was that we sat down to do a séance, to try and communicate with my old girlfriend, Liza Moon, the actress. The next thing I knew, I was calling my manager to tell him about the…Endora."

I also explained my motives for pretending to participate in the séance, to find out who was trying to hurt Karen Bayliss. But they weren't interested in Karen or the fire at her home halfway across the country.

When it came time for urine and blood samples to be taken, I told the investigators that Endora had obviously put something in my drink before the séance, because I was dizzy and eventually must have passed out.

When the results from the tests came back, they confirmed the presence of a foreign substance, which chemists couldn't specifically identify. They could, however, conclude that properties from the substance were consistent with those found in certain psychotropic drugs, which are often used to aid hypnosis.

Soon after Brian refused to allow me to submit to a polygraph test, my phone began ringing with calls from loved ones who had started to hear or see the news. Mary called from her car, Jerry Princeton from his office, and Karen phoned in tears from her new home.

"I can't talk now," I said, as investigators signaled for me to end the call and get back to business. "I'm sorry. I did not do this, Karen."

"I know…I know. I was afraid of this, so afraid. But it's going to be okay, Everett. Do you hear me? Don't give up on me, and don't give up on God. He's with you. I promise He is. I'll be watching—and praying."

"I know He's with me…I've got more to tell you, good news. But I've got to go now."

My trial had recessed for the day. About thirty minutes ago, I decided to play a few of my new songs during leisure time. So I took my acoustic guitar to a corner of the main recreation area and quietly began strumming and singing.

To my amazement, more than three hundred inmates gathered on the floor in front of me, on chairs and couches, and standing along the perimeter and upstairs hallways of this packed atrium. Most of the guards were looking on as well.

"I met a nineteen-year-old kid in a hospital in New York a while back," I found myself sharing with the crowd. "He had tattoos, drug problems, a bad attitude, no conscience—a lot like me." I smiled. "And maybe a lot like you…"

The place was silent, except for my voice echoing across the atrium.

"When I left him, I signed my autograph with a Scripture from the Bible. And do you know, that kid—with all his anger and vileness—said to me, 'Hey, cool. What is this,

about Jesus?' And I said, 'Yes, it is.' And it struck me since that night that my goal in this life should be to share what Jesus Christ has done for me—and what He can do for you.

"By the way—" I began to strum softly—"that Scripture is from the book of Matthew, chapter 11, verses 28 to 30. It goes like this:

> 'Come to Me, all who are weary and heavy-laden, and I will give you rest. Take My yoke upon you and learn from Me, for I am gentle and humble in heart, and you will find rest for your souls. For My yoke is easy and My burden is light.'"

Several screams and catcalls echoed about the atrium, as I launched hard into the new song I'd been working on, called "Blind/Faith."

> I led you down a dead-end street,
> I didn't care if you would die,
> I took your money and I stole your heart,
> I pushed you out when you didn't know how to fly.
>
> It was the blind leading the blind, my friend,
> Will you let Jesus in?
> It was the blind leading the blind, my friend,
> Will you forgive me for my sin?
> It was the blind leading the blind, my friend,
> This is your chance to be born again.
>
> Don't say you don't believe in Him,
> Don't say He's just a lie,
> Listen to His voice it's callin' you,
> "I am the Way, the Truth, and the Life."

It was the blind leading the blind, my friend,
Will you let Jesus in?
It was the blind leading the blind, my friend,
Will you forgive me for my sin?
It was the blind leading the blind, my friend,
This is your chance to be born again.

A warm, breezy night had fallen by the time Miami-Dade police agreed to release me. Gray Harris had flown in from New York, rented a car, and driven to the police department. Although Mary and Jerry wanted to come down from Ohio to be with me, I urged them not to. I was ready to be alone.

Together, Gray, Boone, and I dodged the plethora of reporters and photographers that had camped out in front of the precinct. Staying close to each other, pressing through the crowd, we wormed our way into Gray's rental and took off into the night.

I sat in the backseat, staring at the passing lights, as Boone filled Gray in on the details of the case. Although physically and mentally spent, I felt different than usual. The facts swirling around Endora's death were incriminating, yet I felt an unexplainable peace.

"What'll happen next?" I asked from the dark.

"You'll be brought in for further questioning." Boone hesitated. "There may be an arrest."

"You mean Everett?" Gray asked.

"Yes. The police are likely to come after him with everything they've got. Between his persona and the evidence at the crime scene, things aren't in our favor at this point."

"What then?" I asked.

"Hopefully, the judge appointed to the case sets bail so you can be out until the trial. But that's not definite."

The sound of the Lincoln's tires against the clean streets filled the car.

"Your condo is off-limits, Ev," Gray said, looking for me in the rearview mirror. "I've rented a house in Bal Harbour Village. It's plenty big. Bigger than you need, but it's all I could get. We have it indefinitely. I figured the three of us could stay there tonight until we see how this thing plays out."

"I need to go somewhere tomorrow," I said. "Is that okay, Brian?"

"Ah, Miami-Dade didn't place specific restrictions on you yet, but they—"

"Good," I said.

"They *did* say you should be readily available, in case they want to bring you in for more questioning, which I'm certain they're going to do."

"I need to make a one-day trip, that's all. Then I'll be here for the duration."

"Where are you going?" Gray asked.

"Kansas." I turned to look into the night. "Topeka, Kansas."

Brian walked quickly from the jury box to the witness stand and back to our table, as if he had just consumed a large portion of superhuman protein breakfast food. Spinach, perhaps.

Boone was on a roll. Earlier today, he brought Jerry Princeton to the stand as a character witness and, as expected, Jerry's testimony couldn't have been more glowing. Boone compared my old, selfish, destructive lifestyle to the man Jerry had come to know. Jerry explained how I had reached out to Olivia Gilbert's family and shown remorse for my action toward the young girl. He also spoke at length about how I had kicked my drug habit and become a Christian.

Most recently, Boone finished questioning the chemist who found traces of psychotropic drugs in my bloodstream following Endora's murder. The young man confirmed that

the chemicals could indeed have had an altering effect on my "mood, perception, mind, and/or behavior."

That was a good thing. And now Boone was out to further prove Endora's desire to control me.

"I would like to take us back to the testimony of Charlie LaRoche, Everett Lester's friend and the former drug dealer for DeathStroke," Boone announced. "You may recall, Mr. LaRoche told this court that Everett confided in him that he felt like his mind was being manipulated in some way by Madam Endora Crystal."

Frank Dooley rolled his eyes and began conferring with the attorneys to his right and left.

"It just so happens that we have with us today a gentleman who can further enlighten us about things such as mind manipulation. He is known the world over as a master hypnotist. His name is Dr. Cary Golde."

After outlining Dr. Golde's long list of academic credentials—including degrees from Stanford and UC Berkeley—Boone read various testimonies from clients who had previously called on the good doctor for experiments with hypnotherapy, astral voyages, dream therapy, and self-hypnosis.

Boone clasped his hands together. "Like it or not, there is a whole spectrum of New Age metaphysical activity going on all around us. After you hear the testimony of Dr. Cary Golde, I want you to ask yourself—is it possible that Everett Lester is an innocent man who was unknowingly caught up in this…bewitching spirit realm."

Dooley was on his feet before Boone finished the sentence. "Your Honor," Dooley practically yelled, raking his hair with his hand. "Is this Mr. Boone's closing argument? Because if I'm not mistaken, there's a witness on the stand, waiting to be questioned."

"Enough interjection, Mr. Boone. Let's go ahead and proceed with your witness."

"Fine, Your Honor," Boone said, easily shaking off the interruption. "Dr. Golde, let's get down to it."

Dr. Golde sat relaxed and smiling at the stand, probably thrilled to be the recipient of so much free PR. He was about fifty-five years old, with curly black hair, bleached white teeth, and an expensive olive-colored suit.

"Let's keep this as simple as possible, shall we?" said Boone. "Give us a brief background, if you will, on hypnosis and its popularity today."

"Hypnosis has been used for centuries to treat pain and illness and to control bad habits, enhance performance, and combat phobias." Golde rubbed the tip of his long nose with a bright white handkerchief. "It's far more popular today than most people realize."

"Briefly, what is hypnosis?" asked Boone.

"The mind works at two levels—conscious and subconscious." Golde used his large hands to help explain, the hankie still in one of them. "At the conscious level, the mind causes the body to perform daily activities, such as washing the car, going to work, or cooking dinner. Meanwhile, the subconscious mind causes the body to perform daily functions that we don't even think about, like breathing, swallowing, heart beating, and such.

"During hypnotism," Golde continued, "the conscious mind is subdued, making the subconscious mind more readily open to instruction, or manipulation. In essence, the subconscious mind can be instructed what to do and, in turn, can preside over the body accordingly."

"You used the word *manipulation*." Boone took his jacket off and laid it across the back of the chair. "Can a mind be manipulated while under hypnosis?"

"I don't mean to make your question sound...repetitive or trite, but that is basically what hypnosis is: manipulation of the mind."

Dooley squirmed ever so slightly in his chair.

"Dr. Golde, most hypnotherapists would say that hypnosis is all good, that it is a science that has helped thousands of people overcome their problems," Boone said. "One of our previous witnesses, Twila Yonder, even testified under oath that Madam Endora hypnotized individuals to help them conquer problems such as weight control, drug addiction, insomnia, and other phobias. So while some believe no harm can come from hypnotherapy, you disagree. Is this correct?"

"Strongly." Golde nodded. "Hypnotherapy can be a marvelous tool, when used appropriately. That's one of the ways I make a very good living." He grinned, getting a few smiles from the crowd. "However, I have personally been made aware of a number of cases in which hypnotism has been terribly abused."

"How has it been abused?"

"Under hypnosis, the minds of innocent people have been programmed, if you will, to commit robberies, to purposefully forget things, to become sick, to slander, to lie, and to assume other people's identities. I've even heard of several cases in which people have been hypnotized and convinced to take their own lives. All of these things fall under the umbrella of what we in the profession call criminal hypnotherapy."

Boone clasped his hands, took a few steps, and glanced around the room, giving the jury plenty of time to digest Dr. Golde's testimony.

"Is there more?"

"Unfortunately, yes," Golde said, sniffling and dabbing his nose again with the hankie. "We've heard of cases in which people's minds have been manipulated to make them hallucinate, to make them feel unbearable pain, and to perform all kinds of inexplicable behavior."

"Including...murder?"

"Yes, including murder."

Finally, a score for our side, as the courtroom lit up with surprise.

"Dr. Golde, why would a person allow himself or herself to be hypnotized in such a way?" Boone walked away from the doctor.

"Therein lies the enormity of the problem with criminal hypnotherapy. Through what we call disguised induction, a person can be hypnotized without even knowing it. It can happen fast, and it can happen in any number of ways."

"What ways?" Boone asked, eyeing the jurors. "Tell us more about this *disguised induction*."

"A good hypnotist can induce someone—and I mean gain *complete* control of him in a deep trance state—while that person sleeps, while he shares a conversation, even while he talks over the phone."

The people in courtroom B-3 seemed stunned and excited by Golde's testimony.

"And the subject of such hypnosis would never know he or she had been hypnotized, is that what you're saying?" asked Boone, on the tips of his toes.

"Objection!" yelled Dooley from his seat. "Leading the witness."

"Overruled." Sprockett looked at Golde for an answer.

"Yes, that's what I'm saying. It's on the rare side, but it is reality."

Boone walked toward me. "Dr. Golde." He turned to face the jury and positioned himself right next to the chair in which I sat. "Please answer a very important question for the court today. Would it be possible for a good hypnotist—a professional—to hypnotize a man, have that man commit a murder with a gun, and have that man not remember one iota of that heinous crime?"

Dooley scrambled past his table to get to the bench.

Boone raced toward Judge Sprockett right alongside Dooley.

"Your Honor, what is going on here?" Dooley tried to whisper but failed. "Are you going to allow this, this…freak show? I object! Hearsay. Leading the witness. *Conjecture!*"

I felt chaos, relief, and tension all mixed together.

"Mr. Dooley, be seated." Sprockett looked directly at the doctor over the top of his thin glasses. "Dr. Golde, answer the question."

His face was slightly red as he concentrated on giving the answer he'd been trying to hold for the past minute. He cleared his throat. "Yes." Golde leaned toward the mike. "Yes, I consider that murder scenario feasible indeed."

With this, several reporters actually broke out their cell phones and began making calls.

"Let me say," Golde raised his voice above the frenzy, "I've seen enough criminal hypnosis to sympathize with Mr. Lester's case—"

"You were not asked your opinion, Doctor." Dooley stood up with his arms outstretched. "Can we have some order, Your Honor?"

Sprockett cracked his gavel repeatedly as Boone and I grabbed each other's shoulders and laughed.

24

Neither Gray nor Brian thought I should go to Topeka. Boone was vehemently opposed. In fact, we ended up arguing about it into the night, when the three of us were way too tired to speak seriously—about anything.

In my heart, however, I had a hunch this would be my last opportunity to meet Karen in person for quite some time. I was already in hot water. And if this trip would turn up the heat more, then so be it.

The next morning in the back of a white limo on the way to Miami International, I phoned Mary to give her an update on the police interrogation and to tell her of my plans to visit Karen. I also asked about Olivia, whose condition remained the same.

I could tell Mary was surprised by my attitude that morning. She probably expected me to be in a deep state of depression over the circumstances in which I now found myself. However, there had been an evil about Endora so subtle, yet so eerily real and powerful…I must confess, I was relieved she was gone.

I felt as if my life was beginning all over again.

Certainly, I was concerned about the future, about the very real possibility of going to prison. Boone had made it sound as if he was surprised I wasn't locked up already. But something was different that day. A peace had settled over me. It penetrated my soul and surpassed understanding.

When I told Mary I had finally surrendered my life to God, I thought she had literally passed out. The phone went silent for a long time. Then I heard her sobbing. She said she would call me later, when she could talk.

Meanwhile, I had a mission to accomplish—in about the next twelve hours.

The DeathStroke jet provided a beautiful view of the shiny lakes and flat farmlands of Kansas before it touched down at Forbes Field mid-day. I decided to rent a car, grab a bite, and run an errand before trying to locate Karen's new residence at 1585 Primrose Lane.

Amid brochures for the "World-Famous" Topeka Zoo, the Kansas Museum of History, Gage Park, and other local attractions, I found a Topeka street map in the lobby of the rental car company. Soon, I pulled away from Forbes Field in a dark green Chevy Lumina and headed straight into town on Topeka Boulevard.

For a state capital, Topeka seemed fairly small, probably around 150,000 people. It had that familiar Midwestern feel, with many traditional, low-rise government-style buildings and slightly dated architecture.

I stopped at a cozy local café to study my map over a cup of soup and a sandwich, then I ducked into a shop next door to pick up a surprise for Karen.

Back in the Lumina, I cracked the windows, because the skies were sunny and the fall air was crisp and refreshing. After driving across the peaceful Kansas River, it was another twenty minutes or so before I spotted Karen's street and found my heart beating a mile a minute. I checked myself in the rearview mirror and made the left-hand turn on Primrose Lane.

The houses along the wide, tree-lined street were mostly older, two-story traditionals with rocking-chair front porches. They were midsized homes and quite close together. The huge trees and small, well-manicured front lawns made it look like a wonderful, peaceful place to live. Uneven, cracking sidewalks ran down both sides of the leaf-filled street.

Karen's house appeared freshly painted in white, with glossy black shutters. Some kind of pretty white, yellow, and orange flowers filled the area in front of the house along the sidewalk that led to the front porch; I thought they were chrysanthemums. The door to the separate, single-car garage out back was down, and my heart sank when I realized she might be at work or church or wherever she went during the day.

I held her gift delicately behind my back and rang the doorbell anyway, nervously looking around at the porch swing, rocking chairs, and wicker furniture. After several more rings, I walked around back to peer in the garage. It was indeed empty.

Bummer.

Backing the Lumina out of the double concrete driveway, I eased it along the opposite side of the street and stopped to glance back at Karen's house. Sitting there for a few moments, a brilliant idea came to me.

I jotted down a note to Karen and ran it to her mailbox, placing it with the rest of her mail. Then I resumed my position in the car and, with the windows down and the seat tilted back, closed my eyes and waited.

The sound of the street getting busier as the workday ended roused me a bit, but I was still snoozing when I heard a car pull up. Raising my seat but staying low, I watched the white Honda Accord come to a stop in Karen's driveway. As the driver side door slowly opened, I found myself completely mesmerized to finally see Karen and have the chance to meet her in person.

I must have gulped aloud when I saw the lady who now unfolded out of the little white car. She was about five foot seven, with long, shiny blond hair, wearing a dark blue skirt, matching jacket, white blouse, and dark high heels. The spring in her step and the cheerful way she carried herself confirmed this was the Karen I had come to see.

News flash from Topeka: Karen Bayliss is gorgeous!

Why had I envisioned her so much younger? All this time I pictured myself coming to meet a college-age student. But why? She had told me not long ago she was twenty-seven. It had just never registered until that moment, in front of her home.

Okay, Lester, keep your mind on the business at hand…

Juggling a stack of folders, a briefcase, and a coffee mug, she made her way to the side of the house where she keyed her way in. Although tempted to run up to the front door and ring the bell again, I stuck to my plan and remained slouched in the rental car, waiting for her to get the mail.

The next half hour felt more like three hours. But finally I saw movement in the front room downstairs, and then the heavy front porch door unstuck and opened wide. Karen wore blue jean overalls, a red sweatshirt, moccasins, and a wide, white hair band that pulled the bulk of her light hair back so you could see her bright face.

She bounced down the front steps, waved to two boys riding past on their bikes, then—of all things—she stopped to talk with an elderly lady watering her flowers in the lawn next door.

The suspense was too much.

After another grueling ten minutes, she said good-bye and finally made her way across the street to the black mailbox. I was several houses down and tilted way back in my seat so she wouldn't see me. She gathered the thick stack of mail, looked both ways, and crossed back over the street toward her house, sorting through the mail on her way.

That was my cue to move out.

Quickly, I eased out of the car and nudged the door shut. Next, I quietly assumed my position, leaning casually with my behind against the hood of the car, cradling the gift gently in front of me.

Holding several pieces of mail in her teeth and flipping through the remaining stack in her hand, Karen made her way up the steps to the porch, opened the screen door, and went back inside, closing the big wooden door slightly with her foot.

I waited, my heart thumping.

About three minutes later, I saw a reflection in the front window. She was looking out, I thought, directly at me. Slowly, the silhouette disappeared. It was another minute or so before the curtain in the other front room moved slightly. She must have read the note I left:

> Dear Miss Bayliss:
>
> I was here with a special delivery for you today, but you were not home. If you will kindly look across the street, however, you will notice that I was able to leave the delivery with that kind man you see leaning against the green car.
>
> Along with the dozen white roses he is holding, he sends special thanks to you for your many years of prayer and devotion. By the way, Miss Bayliss, since you seem to know so much about roses and their colors—do you know what the white rose means?
>
> Sincerely,
> The Delivery Man

Ever so slowly, the heavy front door opened. She must have been in shock or scared or something, because Karen didn't come out right away. Instead, she just stood there, still well inside the house, peering out at me. I could only smile and nod my head as if to say, "It's true…yes…somehow it's true!"

Finally, she eased the screen door open and crept out onto the front porch, never taking her eyes off me. She still held the note in her right hand as she walked to the top of the steps.

"The white rose means purity," she yelled across the street.

"That's right," I yelled back, enjoying this immensely.

After a pause, she walked down two steps and stopped. "What does the yellow rose mean?"

"I know that one from Kansas City—it's friendship!"

By now the elderly lady next door was standing in two inches of water, paying no attention whatsoever to her garden.

Karen reached the bottom of the steps and stopped again.

"What does the red rose mean?" she asked quieter now, somewhat hesitant.

"To you and me, it will always mean…the love of Jesus."

After the words sank in, Karen fell to her knees, buried her head in her arms on the sidewalk, and started to sob. Her heart went out to the Lord in thanks and amazement and praise.

I hurried across the street, up the short drive, and knelt beside her. She started to stand and I helped her.

"Thank you, Karen Bayliss." I held her at the elbows, tears streaming down my face.

She looked up into my eyes, as if to confirm it was me. We nodded yes to each other amid the blurry tears, then we hugged and wept aloud, rejoicing.

Although he was vain and obnoxious, Frank Dooley was good at what he did. And that was bad for me.

Very bad.

In his cross-examination of Dr. Cary Golde, Dooley for the most part dismantled the excellent case Brian had built in my favor, which implied that I could well have been hypnotized when Endora Crystal's murder took place.

Dooley's destruction centered on the fact that Golde could produce no hard evidence—no formal case history—in which someone had been cleared of murder charges based on the fact that they were hypnotized when the crime was committed.

In other words, we would be setting a precedent if we won our case based on that theory.

Looking as sharp toward the end of the day as he had at the beginning, Dooley paced back and forth directly in front of Golde, who had lost his smile and his enthusiasm.

"We have exactly zero factual cases to substantiate your theories about minds being 'hypnotized' and 'manipulated' to murder," Dooley said sarcastically. "We have exactly zero proof that Endora Crystal's murder was the result of some 'New Age metaphysical' scam. This is a smoke screen, plain and simple. Why are we getting a smoke screen from Brian Boone? Because he and his client, Everett Lester, haven't a leg on which to stand."

Boone stood. "Your Honor, may I ask, is *this* Mr. Dooley's closing argument? Because, if it is, he's begun too early."

"Quit pontificating, Mr. Dooley."

"All right, all right; we'll get back to Dr. Golde." He approached the fatigued doctor. "What percentage of reputable hypnotherapists believe the way you do in things like criminal hypnotherapy? In other words, hypnotism that leads to criminal activity?"

"A small percentage."

"How small?"

"Quite small."

"*How* small, Dr. Golde? Be specific."

"Maybe 5 percent."

I tried to hide my feelings of defeat.

"Isn't it true, Dr. Golde, that a majority of reputable hypnotherapists—virtually *all* of them—would say that what you have presented to this court is outright fallacy?"

Boone stood up. "Leading the witness."

Sprockett overruled.

"They haven't seen what I've seen," said the frustrated doctor.

"Let me put this in the form of a question to appease Mr. Boone." Dooley tucked in his shirt beneath his jacket and glanced at our table. "How would most every single professional hypnotherapist—besides you—react if he or she were told that a person under hypnosis is a slave who will automatically do whatever he or she is instructed to do by the hypnotist?"

"It's not that simple," said Golde.

"Answer the question, Doctor," said the pit bull.

"Most would not agree."

"Isn't it true they would passionately *disagree*?"

"Yes, but…"

"This witness—his character and premise—tells us a little bit about Mr. Boone and Mr. Lester and how very desperate they've become. Where did they find Dr. Golde, underneath some—"

"That's enough!" Boone stood and slammed his pen down on the table. "He's harassing and argumentative."

"That *is* enough, Mr. Dooley," Sprockett said.

"That *is* enough," Dooley mumbled as he walked toward his seat. "I can't believe we've even had to broach this."

As Dooley looked at Boone and me as he sat, I realized how much he hated me. It was in his eyes. Just like Endora. Just like Zaney. He wanted me out of commission.

25

Karen Ruth Bayliss grew up an only child in Topeka with her Christian parents, Jacob and Sarah Bayliss, with whom she was still very close. She later attended Sterling College, a Christian university about two hundred miles from home in the heartland of central Kansas, where she graduated with a degree in business management.

When I met her that first time, Karen had recently switched jobs and was one of the top business managers for a promising start-up software firm in downtown Topeka. She lived and breathed the Christian faith, helping with the teens at her church as well as with several exciting mission trips that had taken her to various parts of the world.

Karen got us two Popsicles, and we continued rocking the afternoon away. I mean, what adult still buys Popsicles? But that was Karen, just bright and innocent, charming, actually. I was refreshed and invigorated just by being around her. Every now and then being with her would remind me of my days with Liza Moon. Yet, this was so much different, because Liza and I had been prisoners, but Karen and I were free.

There was a nice, long comfortable pause as we rocked. The elderly neighbor lady, Mrs. Krance, was watering her plants again, quite close to where we were sitting. The fall breeze was cool but pleasant. I liked it here.

We discussed Endora's death, and I told her my side of the story. Karen allowed me to share my feelings of grief and guilt over my nephew David's death, as well as the self-reproach I harbored following the Olivia Gilbert incident. We talked about the fire at her old house, how scary it had been. And she assured me there had been no more threats.

"So, what will you do now?" she asked.

"My attorney didn't even want me to make this trip, so I need to get back…tonight." I hoped that was a touch of disappointment I detected in her eyes. "He's sure they'll want to bring me in for more questioning."

She looked into my eyes but said nothing.

"I may be charged with Endora's murder," I said, as if expecting her to have some magical insight or answer.

"So…what do you like to eat for dinner?" she said, cheerfully changing the subject. "You can stay for dinner, can't you?"

I chuckled. "I'd like that."

"You're in steak country now, you know. Do you like a good steak, or are you a vegetarian, like everyone else in show business?"

"I love steak, if it's cooked right."

"Do you cook it right?"

"Yes, ma'am. Got my own special marinade."

"Well, let's go grocery shopping." She stood and shuffled into the house in her moccasins.

★ ★ ★

On the way to the store, I insisted we drive by Karen's old house to see what remained after the fire. She didn't want to, and when we got there, I realized why. The charred property literally took my breath away. The only portion of the structure that still stood was an inside corner where the garage met the house, and it was only five feet tall. The rest looked like black toast, and the smell of smoke was still overwhelming.

We couldn't even walk the property, because it was so thick with soot and ash. But as we strolled along the street in front of the burnt remains, Karen pointed to where different rooms used to be. Then I noticed her eyes puddle up.

"This is the first time I've cried about it." She lowered her head and accepted the arm I put around her shoulder.

"It must have been so hard for you," I whispered, squeezing her tighter. "I'm so sorry."

My insides burned with anger toward Endora and whoever she coaxed to strike the match.

"Let's go," Karen said.

She drove us in her car to Lance's Market, where I bought steaks, baking potatoes, and a bag of salad. Although it was cold outside, I grilled the steaks on her little hibachi out on the patio, which overlooked her private backyard, complete with a variety of bird feeders.

Karen dazzled me over a wonderful dinner, which we ate by candlelight in her kitchen. She struck me as carefree, yet pure; completely independent, yet undeniably obedient to God.

"So, what does your future hold?" I pried, looking for some small sign that she wanted to see me again. "Do you want to go on more mission trips? Settle down and have a family? What are your desires?"

"Oh, I love kids," she said. "My real passion is working with teens, getting to know them, and helping them through the tough years. It's hard to be a kid these days, harder than when I grew up."

"Why haven't you married?" I finally managed.

Her head turned sideways ever so slightly, and she smiled a beautiful, curious smile.

"It's never been right." She closed her eyes shyly.

"Not even close?"

"I've had a few relationships that got kind of serious over the years, but nothing ever panned out."

"I suppose you want to have children of your own someday."

"Absolutely!" She smiled. "I'd love to have four or five. Being an only child was good but lonely. I want my kids to have each other, you know, to love each other and take care of each other when they get older."

"And take care of *you* when they get older." I smiled.

"That's right!" She laughed.

It was quiet for a moment. My mind faded back to the memories of my troubled upbringing. *Could I ever be a good parent?* Doubt flooded in. I even thought of my dad, in that fleeting moment, how he would have thought Karen was way too special for a tarnished loser like me.

"I really feel like God has given me a gift to relate to kids, to teens," she said, snapping me back to the present. "I told you a little about when I was fifteen, the abortion. It was a nightmare. There were weeks and months when I felt hopeless—like dying. I just didn't want to go on.

"But when God brought me out, He set me on a rock. If I hadn't gone through what I did, I never would have known Him like I do. Hopefully, now I can draw others closer to Him. At least, that's where He's shown me I can be pretty effective."

"I know you can." I looked deeply at her. "You sure helped this kid."

She stared back into my eyes, and I can't describe how I felt at that moment. It was like a whole new world to me, so clean and pure and exciting—and right!

"What about you? Ever think you'll marry? Settle down?"

"Ha! You know my story. Every relationship I've ever had was when I was on drugs. None of them ever meant anything, except Liza. She was the closest thing I ever had to a wife…but I'm thankful we never got married; it wouldn't have been good."

I paused thoughtfully and wiped my mouth with my napkin. "To be honest with you," I said hesitantly, "I've never known what it was like to truly love someone, you know, purely, in the right way."

"Well, I'm sure that will happen for you, Everett Lester." Her eyes twinkled. "Because now you're a new creature in Christ, and God has made all things new."

The day had gone like the snap of my fingers, and I stayed longer than planned. It was dark and getting Kansas cold outside.

As we walked to my car, still parked on the street in front of Karen's house, I felt like an old friend of hers. We had bonded quickly, maybe because I had been hearing her voice for so long through her letters.

"Well, this is it." I looked down at Karen as we stood at my rental car beneath a yellowish streetlight.

"Yep. It's been a great day!" She peered up at me. "I'm glad you came. Really glad."

"Let's talk again soon." I didn't want this to end.

"Sounds great. You've got my number." She laughed.

"Listen." I looked deeply into her eyes. "I can't thank you enough. For your prayers. I'm so grateful."

"It was all Him, Everett. It's always all Him."

"I think I'm going to miss you," I said, hoping it didn't sound too romantic, not wanting to rush the one good and innocent thing in my life.

"I may miss you a little bit, too."

We stared into each other's eyes for a long time.

"I'm going to be praying that everything works out fine," she whispered.

"Please do. I need your prayers… They work!"

We laughed together.

"When will I see you again?"

Maybe never, I thought that instant as my eyes locked in on a large, black pickup truck barreling straight for us.

"Run!" I barely had time to yell, jerking Karen by the wrist.

CRUUUUUNCH.

Metal to metal. An explosion of plastic and glass. Smoke, hissing, and the smell of antifreeze…

We had just made it around the front of the Lumina, a split second onto the sidewalk, when the pickup plowed into my rental car.

Running Karen up several concrete steps and down a long sidewalk that led to a neighbor's house, I quickly rang the doorbell four or five times.

"Stay here!" I commanded, not wanting to but letting go of her wrist. "Call the police!"

"Don't go!" she yelled as I ran back down the sidewalk toward the street.

The truck was roaring and rocking, back and forth, trying to jerk its way loose from being embedded in the side of the Lumina.

This has to stop.

With fear and anger heaving up to the base of my throat, I made it to the driver's door of the wicked-looking truck and yanked on the door handle, but it was locked.

I pounded on the jet-black driver's window as the giant pickup revved and lurched, loud as thunder.

"Open up!" I pounded with the bottom of both fists.

When the door suddenly blasted toward me, I had no time to react. It slammed me backward, off my feet, and skidding into the street. Then a torturously loud metal to metal peeling sound, getting more deafening and, *RRRRIIIIIIIIIPPPP,* the black truck jolted backward.

I just made it to my feet again in the middle of the street when I heard Karen's piercing scream. *"Look out!"*

The front of the dented pickup truck rocketed toward me, its hot engine within four feet of me when I dove atop the Lumina, rolling off the other side.

This time, the truck bashed the rental car sideways, bouncing off and coming to a chilling halt. Then it shot backward and screeched to a stop. Its engine revved and roared. I heard sirens, and the driver must have too, for the truck squealed away, no license plates to be seen.

The Topeka police officers who stood with us in Karen's yellow and blue kitchen were typical-looking cops. One was a male, the other female. They were both tough looking, with broad shoulders and superhuman posture, hands on their thick black leather belts.

No license plates, no names...not much they could do, they told us, besides promise to cruise the area more frequently. A real comfort.

"You can't stay here," I stated, after the police cleared out. "You're not safe."

"I thought this would end, with Endora...dead."

"I did, too."

She sat in a chair at the kitchen table, appearing tired and dazed. "I'll go to my parents'."

"I don't feel good about this," I said, pacing. "Come back with me to Miami."

She said nothing.

When I asked her again, she got upset.

"I can't go to Miami! I've got a job and...commitments. It's not realistic."

"I've hurt too many people, Karen. I won't let anything happen to you. Come with me. I've got a big house with lots of rooms. Or I can rent you a place in the Village...please."

"Everett," she said painfully. "This is my home. I've got to get through this."

"Yeah, this is your home. Do you want to die here? Something's come up, okay? You've got to be flexible. You can't stay here. Come with me…"

9:20 P.M.

I looked at Brian through the thick glass partition; he was pale and unanimated. "We took a beating today."

"Still no Zaney?" I asked.

"Nada. The guy's disappeared…thin air."

"Great."

"We *need* him."

"What if they don't find him?"

"That's bad," said Boone. "We can ask Sprockett for a mistrial because of Zaney's escape, but I know he won't buy into that. I've been thinking of other options."

"Like what?"

He paused for a long time. "I'm thinking maybe we should change our plea, Everett."

"What? Since when? You've never mentioned anything like that."

"Since this deck is so heavily stacked against us."

I looked down at the carvings on the blue metal desk in front of me. "It's that bad?"

"It's serious. Look, Everett, I've pursued every lead. Yes, we've had some success. Raised some good questions. Got some doubt going in the jury's mind. But we're stretching everything, trying to… Our case just isn't as solid as I'd hoped it would be at this point. I'm afraid where this thing may be going. I'm not giving up hope, but…"

"What would we plead?"

"Guilty."

"By reason of insanity?"

"No," he said softly. "It's too late for that. Just guilty to reduce your sentence."

"What, so I would get seventy-five years instead of a hundred? What difference will it make?"

"Capital punishment is alive and well in the state of Florida. If we change our plea to guilty, we may be keeping you out of the electric chair."

Why was it that before now—before this precise instant—I had never actually entertained the thought of dying for Endora's murder?

I sat, stunned.

"Dooley's out for blood. If he doesn't put you in the chair in Starke, Florida, he'll try the next best thing, which is life without parole. They believe in that down here. A guilty plea will give you some hope for the future."

That didn't deserve a comment.

"We've got to examine this thing realistically," Boone said. "My job is to look out for your best interest. We're quickly approaching a time when a guilty plea may be better for your future."

"I see compassion in the jury, Brian. I saw it today."

He didn't say anything.

"I want to take the stand."

"No."

"Brian, why not? What can it hurt us?"

"If you *did* actually see compassion in the jury, your testimony would erase every bit of it!"

"How?"

"Everett, I know you're a born-again Christian. I know

you are a godly man, and I've come to admire you for that. But most of your life has been the opposite. Dooley will nail your coffin shut if you testify."

"I know you're the lawyer. And I trust you...very much. But I've been praying about this. I think I may be supposed to take the stand."

He shook his head and exhaled loudly. "I want you to *keep* praying about it, because only an act of God is going to change my mind about allowing you to testify."

26

It had been an emotional day—flying into Topeka to meet Karen for the first time, seeing the home where she almost perished, and running from a maniacal death machine. A lot had happened in the past fourteen hours, but perhaps none of it compared with sitting across the room from Jacob and Sarah Bayliss.

After the police left Karen's home on Primrose Lane and a tow truck hauled my rental car away, she insisted we go to her parents' house in suburban Topeka, about a fifteen minute drive from her place.

I did not want to go. After all, I was the sinister rock star for whom Karen had chosen to pray all those years when she was a teenager. I was supposed to be a larger-than-life character from another world, someone none of them would ever actually meet. Instead, I had traipsed into their daughter's world, bringing with me fallout from the remnants of my past—including things like phone threats, black roses, fires, and now…blatant attempted murder.

Needless to say, I expected a chilly reception from Karen's parents. But what I received instead was something I did not deserve. Love. Rejoicing over my newfound salvation.

Now I was beginning to see what made Karen so special.

Her father, Jacob, was about six foot four, rugged and handsome, with a thick brown mustache. Karen had mentioned that he was once a pastor, but wearing faded Levi's and an untucked blue-and-white-checked flannel shirt, he looked anything but. Karen's mother, Sarah, a foot shorter than Jacob, was blond, fit, and radiant.

As we sat by a crackling fire in their warm den, I guessed Karen's parents were in their mid-fifties. I also presumed they were extremely close to their daughter, since they knew everything about the events leading up to that night.

Karen and I sat next to each other on the toasty brick hearth, while Jacob sat nearby on a loveseat, waiting for Sarah to join him after she finished passing out warm white mugs full of steaming hot chocolate.

"You've been a big part of our family for a long, long time now." Sarah smiled at me from the kitchen. "I feel like we've known you for years."

"I'm grateful. I just can't tell you how sorry I am about what's happened…with Karen. It's my fault, all of it. I mean, I'm responsible. I know you're ready for things to get back to normal."

There was an awkward silence.

"Everett, to see you come to Christ… It's obvious God has been at work," Jacob said. "It's amazing to me how Karen heard from the Lord all those years ago. The thing we need to do now is just trust Him the rest of the way, with whatever's going on."

"I admire your faith."

"Don't think of us as super spiritual." Sarah sat close to Jacob, putting her hand on his knee. "We've struggled. The fire was…bad." The memories of the blaze rose in her eyes.

"We're human, Everett." Jacob clasped Sarah's hand. "We've had to battle questions and doubts in all this…bitterness …and fear."

"I understand. Again, I can't tell you how sorry I am. If Karen were my daughter, I don't think I'd allow her to have any part of the person who brought all this on."

Jacob closed his eyes and smiled. "Believe me, it's been a trying time for us." He looked at Sarah and squeezed her hand. "But who are we to question God? We've made up our minds. We're just going to trust Him. That's all we can do."

At that moment, I felt embarrassed and ashamed about what I had done to this family. Again, I had been thinking only of myself, wanting to get closer to Karen. The thought crossed my mind that if I really cared, I would get out of their lives.

"So, what happens from here?" Jacob asked.

"Everett's attorney thinks he's going to be called back for more questioning in Endora's death," Karen said. "They didn't even think he should leave Miami."

"I had to come." I felt a jolt of emotion. "I had to say thank you."

Karen slipped her arm around my shoulder. Her mother sniffed back the emotion and ran an index finger under her tearing eyes.

"We've still got a problem, don't we?" Jacob looked at me, man to man.

"We do," I said, facing the music.

"Who is it?" Sarah asked. "Why are they after Karen?"

"It's all connected to Endora," Karen said. "When she lived, her whole purpose was to stop Everett from becoming a Christian. Whoever was helping her is after me now, probably because they think I helped lead him to Christ."

"But that's not all," Jacob insisted. "The deed is done. Everett *is* a Christian. These people are still after you, honey, because they think you'll continue to play a part in his life. Maybe they think if they can hurt you, Everett will fall away from the faith."

The emotion in the room was powerful, and the clarity of the moment struck me. It was like an appointed moment, a moment of revelation when it dawned on the four of us that Karen and I had been brought together for a greater purpose than my salvation, or even our relationship.

"Satan hates what's happening to you, Everett," Jacob said. "He hates Karen for being part of it. And he hates the prospect of what you're going to do with your faith in the days ahead. You're a very influential man."

"I can't stand what's happening," Sarah cried. "But it's exciting." Her sobs turned to laughter.

Looking intently at Karen's parents, I said, "I can't believe you people." I paused to keep my composure. "You love God...so much." I was stopped short by the sentiment.

Karen's arm drew tighter around my back.

"I'll be right back." Jacob squeezed his wife's hand, stood, and walked into the living room.

"Everything is going to work out," Sarah said, assuring herself, Karen, and me.

When Jacob returned to the warm den, the blue, digest-sized Bible he held seemed small in his large hand. He sat next to Sarah and flipped to the back of the worn book.

"A few months ago, my pastor gave a message to our men's group about how important our testimony is. Before then, I never thought much about my testimony: how I came to the Lord or what I was like *before.* But I learned something powerful that night. It may be good for you, Everett."

Karen found my hand, and the warmth that coursed through my body at that moment was indescribable.

"In Revelation 12 it says that you overcome the accuser—Satan—because of the blood of the Lamb and the word of your testimony," Jacob said. "My pastor felt so strongly about that text, that he made us write down our testimony on one page and turn it in to him the following week. And when he had us read those aloud... I mean, tears flowed, the truth came out, and men accepted Christ—many men."

"I never heard that story," Karen said.

"Before, I would just kind of ramble when I tried to tell people what God had done in my life, but this forced me to nail down my testimony, to know it, and to be ready to share."

"That's hip," I said enthusiastically. "What is your testimony anyway, Jacob? Karen had told me you were a pastor at one time."

It was past lights-out, but the sobering conversation with Brian several hours ago kept me awake. Lying in my bunk with pad, pen, and flashlight, I racked my brain to recall the people who had and had not been called as witnesses thus far in my trial.

I still couldn't fathom that Boone might want us to cop a guilty plea. That was a real blow, mainly because I trusted him so much. It scared me to think that an attorney of his caliber was considering such a drastic measure. What Boone said to me through that recommendation was, "Everett, in all likelihood, we're going to *lose this case*. I don't want you to die for this crime. I want you to be able to get out…someday."

Maybe I'd just been naive, thinking all along that the jury would believe my story and side with me. After all, I was used to getting my way.

When I began to think about spending the rest of my life in prison, I got a terribly sick feeling of helplessness and claustrophobia. There was just no way. I couldn't even continue that train of thought. Then again, could it be that God had chosen *this* as my destiny? They say He had a sense of humor, but frankly, I didn't know if I was mature enough to handle that.

By 12:22 A.M., I'd listed every single person I could think of who might or might not have a positive influence as a witness in my case. A few minutes later, I'd scratched off the name of every person who had already testified, as well as each of those who I didn't believe would have any relevance at this stage of the trial.

I was left with a sheet of paper filled with chicken scratch and five surviving names, each circled in blue ink, in different places and angles on the page. They were: Ricky Crazee (DeathStroke bassist), Dr. Jack Shea (my personal physician), Jeff Hall (DeathStroke fan club president), Pamela McCracken (DeathStroke publicist), and...Everett Lester (yours truly).

"When Karen was young, she grew up in a very legalistic, very *religious* home," Jacob explained to me as Sarah and Karen cleaned up the kitchen. "It was our home—mine and Sarah's—but we were different people back then. I was the proud pastor of a church of seven hundred members here in Topeka."

Karen smiled beautifully at me as she entered the room to pour her dad and me more cocoa. She patted me on the shoulder before leaving.

"Basically, I was one of the Pharisees you read about in the New Testament," Jacob told me. "I had all the college degrees, I had a deep knowledge of the Scriptures, I had a flourishing church with all the popular programs—but I had no love, absolutely none. And no real relationship with God."

I shook my head in amazement.

"I could point a ridiculing finger at people and tell them to read their Bibles more, to serve more, and to work harder in the church," he said. "I could lay down the law to troubled couples about why their marriages were failing, from a Biblical perspective... You see, Everett, in my sick eyes I was above everyone spiritually. I was at a higher level." He raised a hand above his head, then lowered it as he said, "Then came the elders, the deacons, and the rest of the sheep—who hadn't *arrived* yet spiritually."

"Whoa."

"Without realizing it, I pictured myself as spiritually elite," he explained. "Even when it came to the elders and deacons, I always had the last word. I couldn't receive anything from them. Why? Because I was deceived into thinking I was better, more spiritual, closer to God."

I had never heard anything like this and was thoroughly immersed in Jacob's story.

"Then, one day, it happened." He stared off. "Karen was fifteen. She and her mother came into my study at our old house after dinner. In utter fear, they explained to me that Karen was pregnant. It shattered my world. *My world*, you see! It was all about *me*, and what people thought of *me*."

"I can't believe that," I murmured, thinking of my own self-centeredness. "What happened?"

Jacob sat on the very edge of the loveseat now with his elbows on his knees and his hands clasped together. Karen and Sarah were out of sight.

"I drove Karen to get an abortion."

Chills engulfed my whole body.

Tears came to Jacob's eyes.

"The night after the…operation, in my study, I had an encounter with God. It was the first time. I had never actually known God before that moment. But that night, He met me. For hours I cried, there on the floor, my door locked. And Christ came and showed me, through that awful experience, what kind of person I was."

My poor Karen.

"But by His mercy, that's when everything began to change," he said quietly. "I asked Karen's forgiveness, and Sarah's, and God's. They were each merciful. I repented and prayed for God to change me, and He began to, that very night. And when I changed, there was a glorious change in Karen and in Sarah. I stepped down from the pastorate. In fact, we gradually left the church and found another one, where we worship today."

"Have you ever gotten back into leadership…in the church?"

"No," he said, smiling. "I never will, either. I have no titles, and I don't want any. I simply serve my Savior, quietly. I just try to love, like He did. Thank God it turned out the way it did, for Karen's sake, and Sarah's."

"And mine."

It was well after midnight by the time the flames went out in Jacob and Sarah's fireplace. As the embers glowed orange and the remnants of a few charred logs flamed out, Karen's parents insisted we stay as their guests for the night. I figured I could fly out first thing in the morning.

Karen, of course, slept in her old bedroom, which she showed me after we crept up the hardwood stairs, leaving her mom and dad to their quarters below. Karen's room was soft pink, with frilly white curtains, pillows, and a twin bed. There was a pretty, white corner cabinet filled with her favorite childhood books, some old framed photographs of Karen and her parents and relatives, and several shelves filled with memorabilia and knickknacks.

Sitting on her bed together by the soft, golden glow of a bedside lamp, we went through page after page of her childhood scrapbooks, photo albums, and yearbooks. They made us both want to howl, but we tried our best to suppress the laughter so Jacob and Sarah could sleep.

Karen had been voted "Most Friendly" in her high school graduating class. As I reviewed the yearbook and all of the faces and signatures, I wondered which boy she had been with…and what the circumstances had been.

When she was about ready to show me to the guest room, she whispered, "Oh, wait a minute! Wait a minute. You've *got* to see this!" She opened the cabinets in the bottom half of the bookcase and pulled out a large brown book; it was three inches thick with papers and pictures overflowing from its yellowed pages.

"This is the scrapbook," she said as she smiled and plopped down next to me, "where I kept all of my DeathStroke stuff."

"You've got to be kidding me," I said, anxious to see inside.

She opened the cover to reveal a large, color magazine photograph of me flying through the air onstage; the caption said it was taken in Chicago. I did not remember that moment, nor most of the others Karen had captured in her heavy memory book.

"It all seems like a lifetime ago." I turned from one page to the next, reading bits and pieces of the stories, feeling dirty about some of the antics highlighted in the clippings.

"Why did you do this?" I asked, still not grasping the freedom of her unconditional love.

She smiled shyly. "I don't know. I guess I knew, someday, you would be different; I knew. And I kept this so I could remember what God did in your life."

"Thank you." I stroked her cheek and rounded her silky hair behind her ear. "*Thank you.*"

I gathered her head against my chest. "You are the most precious person I have ever met, Karen Bayliss," I whispered, with tears just behind my eyes. "Your God put an evil, renegade rock star in your heart…and you believed in Him enough to dream a very big dream. And now it's come true. How do you like that?"

She reached up and fiddled with a button on my shirt. "I like it very much," she said quietly. "And I'm going to keep dreaming big dreams for you, Everett Lester. Big dreams in which God's the star…"

27

Never before had I felt like I did that brisk November morning in Topeka, Kansas. The smell of pancakes and sausage filled Jacob and Sarah's warm home. Karen and I met outside her room and sauntered downstairs together, joining her mom and dad at the candlelit kitchen table for coffee.

We were like a family that morning—eating, talking, laughing, and sharing more stories. Being among those three people, I felt clean and new. No hangover, no need for drugs or booze. I had truly begun anew.

Amid the joy and camaraderie, however, two problems still loomed: Endora's murder investigation and the people still stalking Karen.

I broke away to call Brian Boone in the living room after breakfast and told him I wasn't back in Miami.

"Everett, you said one day! These investigators think you're in town," he hissed. "They're going to want you down at the precinct at the drop of a hat, probably today. Are you on your way?"

"Believe it or not, what I'm doing here is important," I said, trying to calm him. "I can be back there in two or three hours, whenever you say."

He said nothing.

"Besides, the way you make it sound, they may make me stay in Miami, because of all the questioning and stuff. Is that right?"

"They may, yes!" he stammered. "And it's not going to look good if they find out you've skipped town."

"This is something I have to do," I said. "I'm staying today. If they want me for questioning, call my cell phone. I'll be on a jet in no time."

"I wish you wouldn't do this."

"I have to, Brian. This is probably the most important thing I've ever done. Trust me. I'll come back pronto the second you need me."

"You keep that phone with you and turned on at all times!"

"Yes, sir!"

After Karen called her boss and got permission to take the day off, she and her folks and I went for a long walk in their neighborhood. The air was cold, but the sun warmed my face and hands.

Around a sharp curve on Jacob and Sarah's peaceful street, there was a community park with a shimmering, dark blue lake. A flock of geese had gathered along its grassy edge. As we strolled on a black cinder path around the lake, Karen's hand slipped around my arm and rested at the crease of my elbow.

Is this really happening?

That morning nothing more was said among us about the truck that had catapulted out of the dark toward Karen and me the previous night. But I was remembering and even found myself turning around several times to look behind us. Was Karen worried? She seemed a bit tentative.

Soon, Jacob announced that he had to get back to make some

business calls. He ran a small insurance agency from his home office. Karen told me he was a well-respected community leader. Her mother didn't work outside the home but enjoyed gardening, housekeeping, reading, and various women's ministries at their church.

Once we drove Jacob and Sarah back to their house in Karen's Honda, we swung by her new place, just to make sure everything was okay after the previous night's activities. As we went inside we found things were fine, and I tried to convince myself that Karen was safe now, that we had seen the last of fires and menacing black pickup trucks.

Karen tossed together some delicious chicken salad sandwiches with chips and carrots, which she served on wooden plates. We sat at her small kitchen table, overlooking the backyard, and watched the many different birds feast at her feeders. The house was so quiet. I wasn't used to such tranquility.

"You make a mean sandwich."

"When will you go back?" she asked, seeming preoccupied.

"Tonight, or I may take your folks up on their offer to stay one more night and leave early tomorrow."

"Why don't you stay? It'll be fun. I'll be there with you."

I peered into her gray-green eyes, thinking how gorgeous she was.

"Well, that sounds like a pretty good invitation. We'll see."

Karen insisted we buzz downtown next, so she could show me the city she had grown to love so much. She parked the white Honda near some kind of government building where we threw pennies in the Fountain of Justice. I didn't know what Karen wished when she splashed hers in, but my wish was that we could be together like this the rest of our lives.

Topeka was a small but busy city, with a surprising amount of traffic buzzing by as we stopped to admire the state capitol, a marvelous white stone structure with mighty columns, a wide expanse of steps, and a slightly tarnished light green dome.

I was enjoying immensely the fact that hardly anyone recognized me. And those who did weren't quite sure where they had seen me before. Very nice.

It proved to be a fantastic afternoon, as we wandered by the local Performing Arts Center, the Kansas Museum of History, and on down the boulevard to one of Karen's favorite spots—the First Presbyterian Church.

"This is special." She tugged my hand. "C'mon."

We entered the large stone structure through an arched doorway at the bottom of a huge bell tower. The vestibule was dark, dry, creaky, and smelled like mothballs.

"My dad and I used to walk through here all the time when I was a girl. And after…when he stepped down as pastor, he came here a lot to think and pray."

We walked through another set of heavy wooden doors, and as my eyes adjusted to the darkness, I began to see the old, cushioned pews.

"Look up, silly." She laughed, pulling me along. "The windows. Look at the windows! They're all stained glass. One of the only sanctuaries in the country with all its windows done in Tiffany."

Many shades of light and brilliant colors poured through the intricately fashioned glass, and my heart soared with joy and wonder. Those feelings came not only from viewing the stained glass, but from the sheer honor of knowing this special young lady before me.

"Each window is a sermon, and a prayer, and a treasured work of art." She looked at them again herself. "Isn't it cool?" Her love for God—for everything that had to do with God—was contagious.

"Yes…it is." I enjoyed watching her as she admired the handcrafted Favrile glass, just like she used to do as a girl.

When we crossed the street to head back to Karen's car, we strolled past Topeka High School, where she graduated more than a decade ago. She shared a few memories and pointed out several familiar spots on campus. Then she got quiet.

"Where to next?"

"I thought I was in love." She turned her back to me and stopped. "I just want you to know…I thought I loved him—the boy who…"

"Shh, shhhh," I said with a finger to my lips. "I understand, Karen. You don't have to explain."

"I want to!" she said, suppressing tears. "I was hurting. Confused. Dad was double-minded—a hypocrite. You wouldn't have recognized him. He would quote Scripture in every other sentence, but there was no…gentleness. He didn't forgive. There was no real love."

She was staring at her old school now. I thought it best to let her share.

"I don't know why I let it happen. He wasn't a Christian, but he was gentle and kind. We met up at the football game that night and left in his car." Tears raced down her white cheeks. "It was my fault…"

"Karen…Karen," I whispered, coming close and wiping the tears away with my thumbs.

"Let me finish, please. In hindsight, I realize I was rebelling—against Dad, against his religion, I guess even against his God."

She looked away and cried hard now.

"I want you to know," she moaned, "there's never been anyone, after that."

I shook my head and gazed at Topeka High School as the cold wind whipped through the Kansas plains. "Karen," I whispered, cupping the back of her slender neck in my hand. "Do you realize where I've been? What I've done?"

She looked up into my eyes. "I just wanted you to know."

"If anyone has any explaining to do here, it's me." I smiled. "And I have no excuses. All I can tell you is I'm different now."

"God restored my purity, Everett. He's already done the same for you."

At the same time, we came toward each other, hugging tightly. I turned my head sideways, resting it atop her soft blond hair, as she gently laid her head against my chest.

"What's going to happen?" she said as we stayed like that, swaying slightly in the wind.

"I don't know, but whatever happens…I want it to be with you."

Saturday afternoon I sat at one of a dozen pay phones that lined a white concrete wall on the first floor of the detention center. Beneath each phone was a marred wooden desktop attached to the wall, along with a dark green plastic chair.

For the past twenty minutes, Boone and I had been discussing the comprehensive witness list I created late last night in my cell. He agreed to take an in-depth look over the weekend at four of the five people remaining on the list who might be helpful witnesses in our defense. However, Boone continued to refuse to allow me to testify in my own defense.

As I hung up the phone and headed back toward my cell, I felt dejected. Boone sounded tentative. He made me agree that if he investigated the remaining names on my potential witness list, that I would consider pleading guilty to Endora's murder. That would assure me a spot in this can for a long, long time.

As I walked through the open atrium, past dozens of inmates in orange jumpsuits, I felt a bit uncomfortable. Looking around, I noticed inmates…watching me. Some were smiling as they whispered back and forth. Others, it seemed, hesitantly inched toward me. There were sporadic claps and calls of "Owwwww!"

As I passed two guards standing erect at their central station, I ducked into my cell and noticed two pieces of mail awaiting me on the floor. There's nothing like getting mail when you're incarcerated.

The first one was from my sister, Mary.

Dear Ev,

Just wanted to drop a quick note and let you know Jerry and I arrived back home safely. We're both going to work a couple of days, make sure things are under control with our jobs, and see if we can't get back down to Miami for more of the trial ASAP!

I still can't believe how God has brought Jerry into my life. It's a match made in heaven. He brings me so much joy and laughter.

Jerry and I drove over to see Olivia yesterday, and her condition is the same. Unless God intervenes, it looks as if she will remain in this semi-comatose condition, which is extremely difficult. But I believe in miracles.

Olivia's mother, Claudia, is not doing well under the stress of it all. Jerry spends a lot of time visiting with her in person and on the phone. After Claudia's husband got over the shock that Jerry had befriended you and fallen in love with me—Raymond has grown, how do I put it…silent.

If you will, please pray for that family. They need God so much right now. Pray for Olivia. I know you are.

Keep your chin up and fight the good fight. We hope to be back down there with you in a few days. See you in court.

Love,

Mary

Before I left my cell to see what the growing commotion was about (much clapping and yelling), there was another letter to check out first, in a white business envelope with a Miami postmark and no return address.

Lester,

Terribly sorry I couldn't testify at your trial.
It appears your following has begun.
That is why you must die. Karen too.
Only then will I rest.
Z

The chanting became almost thunderous.
"*Les-ter…Les-ter…Les-ter…Les-ter…*"
I stood, dropped Zaney's letter on the bunk, and walked slowly to the entrance of my cell. The place exploded in one enormous ovation. I looked out to see the hallway and atrium beyond filled with orange jumpsuits, hundreds of them. Then the chanting began again, everyone in unison: "*Les-ter…Les-ter…Les-ter…*"
A smile broke out, and my head moved side to side in disbelief.
As I turned and disappeared into the cell to retrieve my guitar, the chanting was replaced by a deafening roar. And now I would play for them…*and for Him.*

After Karen finished her famous tour of downtown Topeka, we drove back to her parents' house and both decided to take naps. By the time I woke up in the guest room, it was getting dark, and I had to check my bearings to remember where I was. The clock read 5:35 P.M.

Karen was already awake and downstairs, assisting Sarah and Jacob in the kitchen. I joined them and helped set the table.

We had an informal dinner. The homemade lasagna and garlic bread Sarah prepared from scratch were mouthwatering, as was the tossed salad that Karen sliced and diced. We told her folks what we had done the rest of the afternoon, and then we talked about Karen's work,

Topeka, their church, and Jacob's business. I felt like the boyfriend who had come to call.

"Will you be able to stay longer, Everett?" asked Sarah. "We'd love to have you, at least one more night."

When I glanced over at Karen, she wore a huge smile, and her eyebrows were arched high. Her expression made me break out laughing, and then she began laughing too.

"That is so nice of you, Mrs. Bayliss. Yes, I would love to stay tonight. I'll be heading back early tomorrow morning."

"Please, call me Sarah."

"And Jacob," said Karen's father.

"Thank you," I said. "You've made me feel like part of the family, a special family. It feels good."

The coffee we enjoyed was strong and hot, and the apple pie was warmed and served with a wedge of cheddar cheese and vanilla ice cream. Over dessert I learned that Jacob was originally from Guelph, Ontario, and was a hockey fanatic. The next thing I knew, the four of us made the trek back downtown to Landon Arena for a minor league hockey game between Jacob's hometown Topeka Tarantulas and the visiting New Mexico Scorpions.

The past two days I had spent with Karen and her parents were, hands down, the best days of my life. This was family; this was home—warm and safe. Something I had never known before. The thought of going back to Miami made my stomach ache. It was another world back there, another life. But if I stayed with Jacob and Sarah, I felt nothing could go wrong. My father must have gone to his grave having never experienced that feeling. What a shame.

We were on our feet, screaming like crazy as the Tarantulas came from behind to beat the Scorpions 3–2 in a game that went down to the wire. When we filed out of the arena with the other fans and made our way to Jacob's dark brown SUV, Sarah suggested we drive through something called the Winter Wonderland Celebration of Lights, which had just opened for the holiday season.

Jacob kind of frowned on the idea, and I was neutral, but the girls were giddy with excitement. So we decided we'd better take them. Sarah liked to support the holiday light display, because the money raised went to help local mentally handicapped children.

When we approached the guardhouse at Lake Shawnee, I offered to pay for our car to enter and did so through the passenger window directly behind Jacob.

"I love coming here," Sarah said from the front seat, as she scooted closer to Jacob. "This is a fabulous lake. You can't see it well at night, but it's like seven and a half miles around. There's a campground. It's beautiful."

"Daddy, turn your lights off." Karen handed Sarah a blanket from the back and got us one as well. She tossed the wool throw over me, then got beneath it herself and snuggled close.

Jacob squinted into his rearview mirror. "The guy behind me doesn't have his off."

"He didn't read the sign 'All Headlights Off,'" Karen said. "Everyone in front of you has them off."

Jacob switched his lights off as we drove slowly behind a line of other cars.

The light display was magnificent. Dozens of large and small Christmas trees were decorated to the hilt. We passed myriad lights created in the shapes of large animals, stars, planets, trains, and a beautiful nativity scene.

"Check that out," I said. "The nativity scene. It has a whole new meaning this year."

Without a word, Karen clung tightly to my arm and rested her head against my shoulder.

"This guy behind me has his lights on again, his brights." Jacob sighed. "Get with the program, mister."

When I turned around to look, headlights from the high-riding vehicle blinded me. "I can't see a thing," Jacob said, as the girls squirmed slightly in their seats.

"Pull over, Dad. Let him go by."

That's when the car's bright headlights started blinking.

"What the—he's flashing his lights at me now."

"Honey, pull over," Sarah urged him. "Just let him go past."

Without saying anything, Jacob eased the SUV off the right shoulder of the long, curvy road into the grass. We were right next to Shawnee Lake, which had a huge, lighted dinosaur protruding from its dark waters.

"He's following," Jacob said cautiously. "Right behind me."

As we came to a stop at the side of the road, I looked back to see the bright headlights—four feet from our rear bumper.

"Uh-oh," I said. "That may be the truck from last night."

"A black pickup?" Jacob barked out, adjusting his rearview mirror.

"I can't tell, but it's big, whatever it is." My heart banged inside my coat.

"I'm going back there."

"You are doing no such thing, Jacob," Sarah insisted.

"I'll go with you." I opened my door and jumped out. "That's him, Jacob!"

Karen screamed as Jacob shot out of the SUV.

The engine from the black pickup revved.

With anger and precaution boiling together, I approached the driver's-side door of the high black truck. Tall Jacob was at my side.

"Are you sure it's him?" Jacob yelled over the revving engine.

I nodded. "It's him."

Jacob pounded hard, right in the center of the driver's window.

The hot engine howled even louder.

I ran behind to double-check—no plates.

Suddenly, gears cranked, white reverse lights flashed, and mud spit as the giant truck heaved toward me.

"*Look out!*" Jacob yelled as I dove into a patch of tall, wet grass.

I heard the girls' muffled screams.

Jacob saw that I was okay, ran to his SUV, and jerked the door open.

"Call 911 and lock the doors!" he yelled, slamming the door shut.

I was back on my feet at the passenger side of the truck, pulling at the locked door handle and pounding on the black glass as hard as I could with my fists and elbows, trying to break it. Jacob kicked at the driver's door with his strong legs.

The truck roared, vibrating loudly, shaking and buckling.

"What do we do?" I screamed across the cab.

"Stall till the cops get here!" Jacob bashed the driver's door with a powerful kick.

Gears shifted and the truck jolted forward.

"Stop!" Jacob yelled. *"Stoooooop!"*

BASH.

The ugly black tank crunched the SUV from behind as the girls' piercing screams rang out from inside.

Jacob raced to the driver's door, and one of the girls hit the unlock button. He ripped the door open and jumped in as the SUV was bull-dozed forward by the menacing truck.

Meanwhile, I jumped up onto the side of the lurching monster and rolled myself over onto the truck bed. The back windows were black too, but I didn't think they would be as thick. I started kicking with my booted feet, still hearing the girls' frightened screams over the bellowing truck engine.

Determining I couldn't break the glass, I shot to my knees to look forward. Jacob must have had the emergency brake on, but the SUV was slowly being steamrolled toward the lake.

Where are the cops?

Then I saw the wheel. A big, fat, silver car wheel, vibrating on the floor at the rear of the truck bed. I crawled back to it as the truck screamed and rocked. It was heavy, but my adrenaline was pumping.

Balance would be the key.

Please God…DO THIS!

Jacob's SUV was almost to the water.

Working on my knees, I dragged the wheel to the middle of the bed. Then I locked one hand on each side of that thing, took a couple of deep breaths, and hoisted that sucker as hard as I could, like a cannonball, right through the back window of the cab.

Even with the mighty explosion of glass, the heavy masked man inside didn't seem to flinch. Feeling the crunch of glass against my clothes, I stuffed my upper body through the window, got my hand on the gearshift, and ripped it upward with all my might into Park.

My body jolted forward, then back, as the truck locked up.

Blow by blow by blow, the huge driver smashed and thumped my body with elbows and fists.

I had to get out.

Pushing backward through the glass shrapnel, I fell to the back of the bed, and the truck roared to life again.

Forcing myself to ignore the searing pain from the broken glass, I made it to my knees briefly, long enough to see that Jacob's SUV was gone.

They made it!

Then the pickup suddenly bolted forward and careened left, throwing me against its tailgate. He knew he had me.

I grappled my way to my knees, froze for a second, and rocked off balance. I had to get out.

Now or never!

Throwing myself over the edge of the truck, I hit the ground hard and rolled a good fifteen feet, through the cold grass and right down to the shore of Lake Shawnee.

The black pickup accelerated fast, fishtailing up the embankment and rocketing past the line of cars that sat at a standstill.

He was gone.

28

You've got to do something," Jacob told the short Topeka police officer, one of six now gathered at the dark shore of Lake Shawnee. "This same guy tried to run over my daughter and her friend last night in Vinings, right in front of her home on Primrose Lane. They filed a report with *your* department."

"Mr. Bayliss, I can assure you," the acne-faced officer said with clipboard, pen, and flashlight in hand, "we will do all we can to find the individual responsible for this. However, without a license plate or name, it's going to be difficult. Topeka's a fairly good-sized city. But we do have an APB out right now for a black Chevy pickup truck, badly dented, with dark windows."

Static and monotone voices blared from the four black-and-white Topeka police cars parked at various angles along the lake's soggy shoreline, some with their doors open, all with their blue lights still whirling. One officer with a bright orange glow-in-the-dark vest and flashlight kept traffic moving through the Winter Wonderland Celebration of Lights.

I was seated on the back end of an ambulance with Karen bundled up by my side while two young paramedics cleaned and bandaged the cuts on my arms, hands, and stomach. Initially, they insisted I accompany them to the hospital, but I had no intention of leaving. After thanking the paramedics, Karen and I said good-bye and strode over to Jacob, Sarah, and the police.

"I want you to understand, this person is *tormenting* my daughter," Jacob blared. "Her house in Prospect Commons burned to the ground just a few weeks ago. The fire department ruled it as arson. The same person is responsible. What do I need to do to help nail this guy?"

"Sir, you've done just about all you can do. You've filed a report for each incident; you've given the best description possible of the perpetrator—large, white male; you've—"

"You need an investigator on this."

"Mr. Bayliss, investigators are usually called in on murder cases and drug trafficking. Believe me, you've done the right thing. We've got your reports, and we'll be watching for the truck."

"If something happens to my daughter…" Jacob stopped himself from saying more.

The officer turned his back to confer with his colleagues, whose flashlights were scanning the muddy skid marks at the shore of Lake Shawnee as well as the dents and black paint remnants on the back of Jacob's SUV.

"I want to *find* this guy," Jacob hissed, as Sarah, Karen, and I drew close to him.

"Let's go home, honey," Sarah said. "I just want to go home."

I paced in Jacob and Sarah's quiet kitchen as they sat at the picnic-bench-style table with Karen. Sarah had just closed the blinds in the bay window. The fluorescent light above the island was the only one on in the dark house. Somehow, the room didn't look or feel as cozy as it had the previous night.

Jacob rose and walked to the coffeemaker. "Anybody want decaf?"

"I can't let you guys stay here like this." I turned my back to the kitchen cupboards and rested my palms on the beige counter. *"I'm responsible!* I got you into this. I need to get you out."

"We've been over this, Everett," Jacob said, removing a white paper filter from the cupboard. "We are where we are, okay? It's where God has us. We're not going to dissect the past."

I walked to the table and pulled out a chair. "I want the three of you to consider coming with me to Miami."

"Ha!" Jacob laughed as he dipped the small blue scoop into the green coffee bag. "Where did *that* come from?"

"I've got a huge house in Bal Harbour Village." I rested my elbows on the table and animated the sales pitch with my hands. "You guys can take a vacation. Lose this wing nut for a while. Give the police a chance to track him down. C'mon. It's on me, all expenses paid."

"Fine with me," Sarah said surprisingly, in a high-pitched tone.

"What are you saying?" Jacob set down the coffee supplies and faced us. "We can't just…leave."

"Why not?" Karen said. "I've got vacation time coming. And you can do your job from anywhere."

"You guys are dreaming," Jacob's voice rose. "We'd come back and find *both* houses burned down."

He realized too late how much that hurt.

I stood up and went to get a glass, filled it with tap water, and got some ice.

"Honey," Sarah said softly. "Let's leave for a little while. The house will be okay. We leave it to God."

"I'm ready." Karen perked up in her chair. "I'll call my boss bright and early. We're not that busy anyway." She shook her shoulders and giggled.

"Jacob?" I said. "How 'bout it?"

"Okay, okay, let's just pray about it. Can we do that?"

"Absolutely," Karen said. "I'll start."

After leaving Brian with my sparse list of potential witnesses and the letter I received from Zane Bender two days ago, I had no idea what to expect when I showed up in courtroom B-3 on Monday morning. Wearing a light green suit and a yellow dress shirt, Boone looked fairly well rested and quite a bit more confident than the last time I saw him.

"Good morning, Everett," he whispered, shaking my hand as I approached our table. "We've got a friend of yours on the stand today. I think it'll be interesting. Thanks for the leads."

"What about the note from Zaney? Can we admit it?"

"Problem is, anyone could have written it." He shrugged. "Hang in there. We're gonna have a good day."

After a weekend breather, the courtroom was alive with chatter and movement as the media began to mega-hype the fact that the sensational case of *The State of Florida v. Everett Timothy Lester* was winding down.

I didn't arrive a second too soon. We remained standing as Judge Henry Sprockett strode into the courtroom with his black gown flowing behind him. He immediately told the press corps to back up within its allotted boundaries.

As I sat in my all-too-familiar wood chair, I noticed two things that came as pleasant surprises. One: the cup of Starbucks positioned on the table directly in front of me. Two: the glimpse I got of Donald Chambers and his wife seated about ten rows back.

I mouthed a *thank you* to Boone for the coffee, and he stood to proceed with our defense.

As former DeathStroke bassist Ricky Crazee walked

toward the witness stand, I offered a humble smile, but he glanced at me and looked away quickly. When Ricky first stood up to come forward, I recognized his wife, Alesia, seated next to him. She wore dark glasses and was dressed in brown leather from head to toe.

Ricky seemed the same. He wore jeans and a white T-shirt with pointed cowboy boots, a thick black belt, a fist-sized Harley-Davidson belt buckle, and a black leather sport jacket. His reddish-blond, shoulder-length hair resembled a bird's nest, which is what we always used to tell him, but he still never brushed it.

Boone reviewed the history of our relationship and asked Ricky questions about our friendship in order to set the stage for his next line of questioning.

"How well did you get to know Madam Endora Crystal, during your years with DeathStroke?"

Ricky sat erect, with his hands clasped tightly against his stomach, as if bracing for a storm. I had seen him sit like that a million times at press conferences.

"Fairly well, I guess."

"Would you say you were friends with Endora?"

"Yeah, I guess."

"Did Endora ever give you a psychic reading, predict your future, delve into your past—anything like that?"

Frozen in the same position, Ricky said, "Once or twice, for the heck of it, she gave me readings. But it was just for fun."

"What did the readings tell you?"

He laughed, pulling his clenched hands tighter toward his belt buckle. Then he pursed his lips, and his shoulders jumped up. "I don't really remember, actually."

Boone walked quietly along the railing in front of the jury. "So…you don't remember what the readings were about? I mean, you weren't on drugs like everybody else in the band, right? You were known as the sober one. Tell the court, please, what Endora's readings revealed to you. I'm really expecting you to remember."

Frank Dooley popped up. "Your Honor, is this relevant to the murder of Endora Crystal?"

"It may be," said Sprockett. "Answer, please, if you can."

Ricky looked at me momentarily. "Back when I was still on drugs—a long time ago—Endora talked me into letting her give me a reading. It was all casual, you know, I did it for fun. But in the middle of the thing, she got serious on me. Way serious. Told me there was...some sort of dragon in my life that needed to be slain. 'Slay it,' she said, or it would slay me."

"And who or what was that dragon? Did she say?"

"No. She said I had to figure it out myself."

"Did you figure it out?"

"Yeah, eventually."

"And who or what was that dragon, Mr. Crazee?"

Ricky's nostrils flared as he inhaled deeply, his chest out, his shoulders pointing backward oddly. "Drugs and alcohol. I'm not ashamed to say it. The so-called dragon in my life was drugs and alcohol. I was addicted. It's no secret."

"And so," Boone strolled in front of our table, jacket off, "what kind of drugs did you do and how bad was your addiction?"

"From the minute I got up till I crashed, I was on something," Ricky said, perturbed. "Heroine, coke, uppers, downers—you name it."

"Tell the court today, Mr. Crazee, how you ever came clean from such addiction. Did you check yourself into a rehab center? Some sort of clinic?"

Ricky shot Boone a look of disgust.

I glanced over and noticed his wife on her way out of the courtroom.

Something was definitely cooking.

"I think you know the answer," Ricky said to Boone.

"That's not the point, Mr. Crazee. The point is, I need you to tell the jury how you came clean from your debilitating drug addiction."

"Okay! Endora hypnotized me. That's what you wanted to hear, isn't it?"

"Yes, in fact, that is what I wanted to hear," Boone said, with his arms crossed, standing right in front of Ricky. "Why don't you tell us more about your healing."

"This is a farce, man…"

"Mr. Crazee," Sprockett said. "I'll remind you that a man's future is at stake here. I'll also remind you that you are in a court of law and may be held in contempt if you're not fully compliant here today."

"Just explain, Mr. Crazee." Boone walked toward a bewildered Frank Dooley.

"She knew what the dragon was," Ricky gave in. "Once I figured it out, I went to her. She told me she could help…by hypnotizing me."

Ricky tried to continue, but the turbulence in the courtroom was too much.

Crack!

"People…" Sprockett yelled.

Crack!

There was a pause as the crowd quieted. The noise was reduced to the sound of an audience before a play—quiet chitter-chatter everywhere.

Boone didn't want to lose his momentum. "Keep going, please, Mr. Crazee."

Ricky seemed to relax with the bedlam. "We were in LA. Endora invited me to her place in Malibu."

"For the specific purpose of hypnotizing you?"

"That's right."

"And how did that unfold? What happened? How did it work?"

"She gave me a couple of pills; I don't know what they were. Then I just laid on a couch, and she told me I would be getting tired," Ricky said. "Basically, that's it. I woke up about an hour later and really didn't feel any different. Really didn't think it had worked."

"But, had it…worked?"

"I haven't had any illegal drugs since." Ricky leaned toward the microphone. "I'm not ashamed of what I did. I'm clean and sober today because of it."

"I'm glad for you, Mr. Crazee." Boone walked away from red-faced Ricky, making sure it was good and quiet before he spoke again. "Tell the court, if you will, exactly what you remember about the time you spent under hypnosis with Madam Endora."

"I told you, nothing." Ricky shrugged. "I didn't think anything had happened. It felt like I had taken a short nap, got up, and went on my way. Later I realized my drug cravings were gone."

"But to clarify, you cannot tell the court one thing about what happened while you were under the power of Endora's hypnosis?"

"No."

"So you wouldn't have known if she asked you to walk somewhere?"

He hesitated. "No."

"You wouldn't have known if she instructed you to call someone on the phone or go someplace in your car?"

Looking around uncomfortably, he said, "No."

"And you wouldn't have known if she told you to smash a rock waterfall or…shoot someone in the stomach?"

Dooley's table actually moved slightly when he barged into it, shooting around the corner, objecting all the way to Judge Sprockett's bench.

But it was too late. Boone had already opened the can of worms, sat down, and braced himself for Judge Sprockett's scolding, which came in the form of a verbal lashing and a strict warning about being in contempt of court.

As far as I could tell, Boone's strategy scored points for our side.

Karen usually got what she prayed for. That explains why, the morning after the incident at Lake Shawnee, she and her mom and dad found themselves lounging with me in the back of a gleaming white DeathStroke jet, sitting on the runway at Forbes Field ready to take off for Miami.

"I can't believe we're doing this," Jacob said, staring out one of the small, round, tinted windows while seated on a beige leather couch.

"I can't believe it's going to be warm enough to swim!" Karen said, as she examined the contents of a nearby refrigerator.

"I've never been to Miami," Sarah said. "How did you end up with a place down there, Everett?"

"It started out as just another investment." I accepted a cup of coffee from the brunette hostess. "My financial advisors told me I needed to buy more real estate. So, we did. Finally, I got down there one time on a video shoot and loved it. Then I started going there regularly."

When the hostess had served each of us, we sat in silence for a few minutes as the three-person crew prepared for takeoff.

"I wonder if there are any good churches in Miami," I said, looking at Jacob.

"Sure there are. You just need to start visiting some and see what fits you best. Maybe we can do that while we're there."

"That would be fun," Karen said.

"I've been thinking about the story you told, Jacob, about knowing your testimony," I said. "I want to write mine down."

"Yours is going to be a doozy," he said, smiling.

Karen reached out for my free hand. As she did, Sarah smiled ever so slightly from her seat in one of the soft captain's chairs. Then she swiveled and took Jacob's big hand in hers.

My phone rang, and I grabbed it quick, almost as if I had been expecting it.

"Where are you?" asked a rigid Brian Boone.

"On the tarmac at Forbes Field in Topeka, preparing for takeoff, you'll be glad to know. We should be back to you in two, three hours. What's up?"

"Who's we?"

"Oh, did I say *we?*" I said jokingly to Karen and her folks, who looked embarrassed. "No, really. My friend Karen is coming back with me, and her mom and dad."

"Hmm."

"What's wrong, Boone?" My stomach rose and fell. I realized in that moment I had been denying might have arrived. "Do they want me in for questioning?"

Nothing.

"Boone? Are you there?"

"You haven't had the news on this morning, have you?"

"No." I motioned for Karen to turn the TV on.

"It's not good, Everett."

"Tell me...what?"

At that moment, CNN lit up on the small screen. My picture was frozen in the upper left corner while a live feed showed a reporter outside Miami-Dade police headquarters.

"A warrant has been issued for your arrest, for Endora's murder," Boone said. "The whole world is watching. Are there camera crews on the ground at Forbes Field?"

I looked out my window and saw a lone white, blue, and yellow satellite truck racing down an access road. Then another one, farther back.

"They're on their way."

"Miami-Dade police want you to turn yourself in and surrender your passport," Boone explained.

"Fine, what do I need to do?"

"Just come back to Miami International as planned. It's going to be a zoo. They'll take you in and book you. I'll be there. We're already trying to arrange bail. Not sure what's going to happen with that."

"What do you mean? Could I go to jail?"

"The county prosecutor, a guy named Frank Dooley, says they may be seeking murder one charges… Yes, you could go to jail."

"Murder one?" I repeated, feeling faint.

Jacob had his arm around Sarah, who was in tears in front of the TV. Karen had come to my side and put an arm around my shoulder.

"Do you want me to make a statement for you to the press?" Boone asked.

"Just tell them…" I stopped. "For now, tell them I heard about the warrant and am coming back right away to comply in any way I can. I'll write up a statement on the flight and have it ready by the time we get there."

"Everett, are your friends prepared for this kind of media coverage? It could change their lives. It's not too late for them to turn around."

"We'll talk it over," I said, feeling a touch of sweat on my forehead.

"Sorry about this."

"Me too, Brian."

"I'll see you when you get here."

"Hey, Boone, while I got you…is there any more word on Olivia Gilbert?"

He was quiet for a moment. "She's the same. It's good of you to ask, though."

29

I t was somewhat embarrassing to say, but I believed Jacob, Sarah, and Karen felt it was their responsibility to look after me. After all, I was a new Christian. This was what they had spent the last ten or fifteen years praying for. Perhaps they wanted to make sure I would be okay in the tumultuous days ahead.

In any case, they expressed no hesitation when I asked if they were certain they wanted to continue on the journey to Miami with me. I wouldn't have blamed them if they had accepted my offer to be driven back to Jacob and Sarah's house.

Anyway, when the wheels of the Gulfstream G450 touched down on the warm Miami runway, we were all together. I was glad to have them along for the ride and away from whoever had been chasing us. As we bounced toward the jet's private hangar, we could see what looked like a massive sculpture of media clutter awaiting us.

Speaking with airport officials via radio en route to Miami, our pilots had already planned to pull the nose of the Gulfstream into the hangar, so we could exit the plane in private. Reporters and camera crews did not have access to the inside of the hangar.

When the steps to the jet lowered, Gray Harris and Brian Boone were there to greet us, as well as a handful of other DeathStroke staff and personnel. I introduced the Bayliss family to Gray and Boone.

"Is it going to be any problem getting my friends someplace where they're comfortable?" I patted Gray on the back.

"I've got it all arranged." He smiled at the Baylisses. "We'll have you to the house in Bal Harbour Village in no time."

A weight had been lifted.

As I watched two of our suited security people lead Jacob, Sarah, and Karen across the sprawling floor of the large hangar, I smiled, waved, and blew a kiss to Karen when she looked back at me for the last time.

"Are you ready to do this?" Gray asked.

I turned back around to see Gray, Brian, and the others peering out through the opening in the large hangar doors at the mob scene of reporters, microphones, camera crews, and satellite trucks.

"Let's rock 'n' roll." I walked toward the bright white light.

The lead investigator in Endora's murder, Harry Coogle, reintroduced himself to me with a polite nod and handshake as I came into the sunlight and in view of dozens of cameras and hundreds of people—including law enforcement officials, fans, and onlookers.

As people converged around me, I heard various screams ring out. "We love you, Everett!" A small group of people were chanting, "Killer, Kil-ler, Kil-ler!" Reporters shouted, "Did you murder your psychic? Did you shoot Endora Crystal?"

Coogle leaned close and spoke loudly so I could hear. "Thank you for coming. We'll need to search you and use the handcuffs, then drive to Miami-Dade police headquarters for booking." With my hands clasped behind my head, one officer patted me down from head to toe in search of weapons or drugs, I supposed. The cameras went wild.

Then, with my hands behind my back, a tall black officer handcuffed me and escorted me to a waiting squad car, then helped me duck inside. Boone and Gray followed directly behind in a chauffeured black Lincoln.

As we pulled away, a handmade sign stood out in the sea of people and equipment. It was way in back, on a big white placard, written in large black and red letters: *"DIE SATAN!"* Behind the sign, I noticed some ominous clouds looming high on the horizon, rolling our way.

All eyes were on me inside the police precinct, where my pockets were emptied, my passport was taken, and I was quickly fingerprinted and photographed.

"Everett," Boone whispered, as a short uniformed woman wiped the black ink from my fingers, "the judge has set bail at five million dollars. Gray had a check drawn for five hundred thousand, which is what we need to provide today to get you out."

"Okay." I nodded.

Gray leaned in. "We'll be out of here soon, Everett. Are you going to want to say anything outside?"

"Yeah, I've got something to read, but you need to get it for me. It's with the stuff from my pockets. White sheet of paper, folded up."

Outside, the skies had grown mean and dark, and a strong wind was kicking up. I could hear outcries about my fast release among the throngs of people covering the steps of the police headquarters. Even more media crews and people had gathered here than at the airport. Questions were being fired from all directions about "special treatment," "another O. J.," and "letting the rock-star killer go free."

"Ladies and gentlemen," Gray said, his white hair whipping in the wind, and his voice echoing as he stood behind a makeshift podium where there must have been fifty microphones hooked, taped, and hanging overhead. "Everett has a few words he would like to share today."

The crowd went nuts.

"Before he speaks, I just want to say that we are confident he will be cleared in a court of law of all charges filed against him." Gray's voice seemed to bounce off the stormy sky.

A mixture of cheers and boos arose from the crowd.

Gray gestured for me to step forward.

I hesitated just a moment, forcing my shoulders back and taking in a deep breath. Slowly I walked to the podium, adjusted the microphone, and unfolded the piece of paper that had grown warm in my hands. I was nervous, not used to being in front of people without the influence of drugs and alcohol.

"Good day, ladies and gentlemen. What I want to say today does not have to do with the death of Endora Crystal."

I paused, chilled by the resonance of my own voice. "As my friend, Gray Harris, stated—we are confident the truth surrounding the details of her unfortunate death will come out in the days ahead, and our condolences go out to her family.

"What I would like to talk to you about for a moment has to do with a young lady named Olivia Gilbert, who lies in a hospital bed in her home in Xenia, Ohio. She is a young lady I hurt very badly… What I'd like to talk to you about has to do with my nephew, David Lester, who was killed suddenly along with two other young people and an elderly couple in a tragic car accident in New York recently… What I want to say has to do with the overwhelming amount of fame and fortune I have amassed due to the success of a rock group known as DeathStroke."

I paused again as the wind whipped across the microphone. "What I want to say is, it has all been too much for me. Too much selfishness. Too many drugs. Too much sinfulness. Too much hurt. Too much guilt. Too much…bad influence."

Just then a huge gust of wind ripped across the landscape. I stepped back and squinted as papers flew, baseball caps danced across the crowd, and three or four mike stands crashed to the ground. I had to hold the sheet of paper I was reading from in both hands.

I found myself almost yelling to be heard over the wind. "Not long ago, I made a decision to surrender my life to Jesus Christ."

A flash of white-hot lighting cracked across the Florida sky. For a split second, I thought I could taste aluminum foil in my mouth, the lightning seemed to have hit so close. No rain yet, but the tall antennas atop the TV trucks rocked and bent due to the enormous wind. I couldn't hear anything, except the roar of the air current hitting the mike.

"I want you to know, I have found peace, joy, and the promise of eternal life in Jesus Christ. To you, the public, and to the many DeathStroke fans who will hear this message, I apologize to you from the bottom of my heart for misleading you with evil intent during my DeathStroke days. Although my sins have been forgiven by Christ, I also want to ask for your forgiveness as well."

Suddenly, we were engulfed by the menacing clouds I had noticed back at the airport; it was black as night. Cold drizzle began to pelt my face and arms as I saw a beautiful, thin white horizon all around me.

"The new life I have in Christ is a living, breathing miracle. Only God can change a man so that he is literally born again as a new creation, as I have been. Today, I urge you to see what Christ has done in my life and to seek Him with all of your heart so He can have His way in your life as well."

As I paused one last time, gazing out over the crowd and the umbrellas, I noticed the cheering and bedlam had ceased. They were replaced by expressions of fear, perhaps about the brewing storm, and looks of confusion, probably about my statement. Turning around momentarily, I noticed Gray and Boone were wearing similar expressions.

"Again…please accept my apologies for the poor example I have set for you. I hope with all my heart that God will allow me to make up for all of the destructive years—in the days to come. Thank you for being here with me today."

I'd never forget the shock on Gray's face when I turned to be escorted off the podium to the black Lincoln. He kept staring at me but said nothing. Brian made eye contact and shot me a quick smile, then went on, business as usual, as police motorcycles revved their engines in preparation to escort the Lincoln toward Bal Harbour Village.

"Mr. Crazee." Prosecutor Frank Dooley slowly approached former DeathStroke bassist for cross-examination. "Before this trial began, were you aware of anything known as 'criminal hypnotherapy'?"

"No sir," Ricky said, still rigid.

Dooley held no legal pad or notes. When he spoke to Ricky, he stood directly in front of him, reaching one hand out to rest on the wooden rail that separated the two men.

"Look," Dooley said. "I'm going to make this brief. Did Endora Crystal help you?"

"She changed my life."

"And she did that by…?"

"I guess you could say she helped my mind overcome my body's need for drugs and alcohol."

"And in the years you knew Endora, did you ever know of an instance in which she hypnotized anyone for negative purposes—to hurt people or commit crimes?"

Ricky looked straight at Dooley. "No."

"No," Dooley confirmed. "In fact, other than the desperate allegations made by Brian Boone, we have neither heard nor been presented with one shred of evidence suggesting that Endora ever—in any way—hypnotized anyone with criminal intent."

Boone stood and started to speak but was cut off by Dooley.

"In fact, Madam Crystal only *helped* people." Dooley squeezed in the last line before Boone objected.

"Your Honor, it seems that Mr. Dooley is drawing conclusions and lecturing the jury instead of questioning the witness. Has he concluded his cross-examination?"

"As a matter of fact, I have not." Dooley turned from Boone back to Ricky. "Mr. Crazee, what was your take on the relationship between Everett Lester and Endora Crystal?"

"She hung out with Everett and the band for a long time—years. They were very close."

"Were they…romantically involved, in your opinion?"

Ricky took in another enormous breath, letting it out audibly. "I don't think so." He shook his head.

"You don't think so," Dooley repeated. "But the fact is, you're not absolutely positive they were *not* involved romantically, is that correct?"

"Well, I guess that's true."

"Did you see them argue?"

"Once in a while."

"Did Everett raise his voice to Endora?"

"Yeah, I mean, they—"

"Is that a yes?"

Ricky hesitated. "Yeah."

"Did Everett Lester ever strike Endora?"

"Well, they would kind of slap each other around, but it was pretty much in fun, most of the time."

"Most of the time," Dooley said. "But what about the other times? Did you see him hit her?"

Ricky shot a glance at me, then looked back at Dooley. "Once in a while I saw him shove her or push her down onto a couch…something like that, when he was really high."

"Uh-huh," Dooley said, back at his table, leafing through a notepad with one hand. "And what about guns? Did you ever see Everett carrying a gun?"

Ricky put his head down. "We used to do some target practice at a shooting range he built in one of his houses."

"Any other instances when you saw Mr. Lester with a gun?"

"He sometimes carried one with him between hotels and concert sites…for protection."

"So, we have arguments with Endora, we have drugs, we have guns." Dooley stood. "Is there any doubt in your mind, Mr. Crazee, that Everett Lester pulled the trigger that day last November?"

Boone stormed to his feet. "Objection, Your Honor! Speculation. Mr. Dooley is…"

"I know exactly what he's doing." Judge Sprockett glared at Dooley. "Objection sustained. Mr. Dooley, no more of that."

When I walked through the door to the sprawling rental home at Bal Harbour Village, Karen ran to greet me and was quickly followed by her parents and, to my surprise, my sister, Mary, and Jerry Princeton, who had flown in from Ohio earlier in the day.

We hugged and laughed. They couldn't say enough about my "speech" on CNN, which had become the talk of the networks. Then quiet reigned, as we each settled in, embracing the seriousness of the moment and our thankfulness for my current freedom.

While I was gone, Karen and her folks had become well acquainted with Mary and Jerry. At Mary's insistence, they all found rooms and put their luggage away. Jerry had a bedroom of his own, while Karen and Mary shared a large bedroom, as did Jacob and Sarah. They saved another single bedroom for me.

I sat in wonder as Jerry and Jacob carried on a deep conversation, something about the media coverage surrounding my arrest. Karen and Mary felt like old friends after having spoken on the phone so regularly during my drug rehabilitation. They sat on a couch drinking Diet Cokes and gabbing with Sarah.

For a moment or two, I stood at the kitchen sink, staring out at the rain as it watered the tropical foliage and sprayed the Atlantic surf in the distance. I had searched all my life for happiness and content-ment—and now, finally, I was surrounded by it.

But I also faced murder one charges.

A desperate feeling took hold.

Then, a soft hand on my shoulder. "Penny for your thoughts," Karen whispered.

I turned and put my arms around her waist, but did not speak.

"Dollar for your thoughts?" She smiled, tilting her head to the side.

"Just can't believe what's happened to me."

"Bittersweet, isn't it?"

"Yes…bittersweet." I kissed her softly.

We looked at each other for a long moment.

"What if I go to jail?"

"Then God goes with you…and so do I, in spirit."

"I don't want that to be the plan."

"I don't either," she said, her hands squeezing the backs of my arms. "But we're gonna make it, no matter what happens."

"I want you by my side, Karen Bayliss. I need you."

Our eyes searched each other.

"I'll be there, Everett Lester."

I held her close. "After the trial, if I get out…I'm going to ask you to marry me." I set her away from me to look at her. Tears fell with her smile.

"Why wait?" she managed.

My heart leaped as I pushed her back a few more inches, and gazed into her eyes. "What are you saying?"

"I'm saying, I want to be your wife."

Then we embraced and my tears came.

"I can't marry you if I'm going to spend the rest of my life in prison. It wouldn't be fair…"

For the longest time, we just held each other.

"Oh, Everett," she said finally, hugging me tight, her head buried in my chest. "We've got to pray."

I closed my eyes. "I know…I know…."

"God, please, give us victory," Karen whispered, "We pray you'll set Everett free. Oh Lord, we long to share a life together. Please, have mercy. Find favor, dear Jesus…find favor. And let Everett use his testimony to win many others to You."

30

woke up early the next morning at the house in Bal Harbour. Quietly, I made my way downstairs to the foyer. Peeking out the slats in the plantation shutters at the front door, I saw dozens of cars and TV trucks lining the parklike street. Several dozen press people mulled about, smoking, eating doughnuts, and sipping coffee.

"May I help you, Mr. Lester?" came a whisper from around the corner.

The voice of the little woman startled me.

"Hello!" I said. "What's your name?"

"I'm Sonja," she said through bright red lipstick and a beaming smile. "Mr. Harris asked that I be here to serve you and your company today."

"Well, wasn't that nice of him. I bet you make a good cup of coffee."

"Yes, sir. Coming up." She hustled off to kitchen in her white apron.

"A tiny bit of cream and sugar," I whispered, as her round little frame bounced out of sight.

The day's newspaper lay in the foyer on a table beneath a stained-glass lamp. I picked it up and began perusing section A when Sonja came back with my coffee.

"I'm going to go to my room for a bit, but I'll be back for more of this, I'm sure."

"That will be fine, sir. I'll be making a breakfast buffet today. Is there anything in particular you would like?"

"Let's see…I know some of the guests like pancakes and sausage. Plenty of coffee, and you'll be all set."

After closing the door to my room and propping my pillow against the headboard of the bed, I crawled in, pulled the covers up to my waist, and read the top story of the day in the *Miami Herald*. It featured a small, full-color mug shot of me, the one taken the day before at police headquarters.

LESTER SURRENDERS ON MURDER WARRANT
ROCKER IS BOOKED, POSTS BAIL, SPEAKS

MIAMI—Shock rock legend Everett Lester flew from Kansas to Miami yesterday on a private jet to turn himself in to authorities who had issued a warrant for his arrest on murder charges a day earlier.

Lester is being accused of murdering LA psychic Madam Endora Crystal, who was found dead from a single gunshot wound in the singer's North Miami high-rise last November 11. Miami-Dade Prosecutor Frank Dooley said the county will likely seek a murder one conviction, a felony punishable by the death penalty or life in prison without parole.

Once Lester's jet pulled halfway into a hangar at Miami International Airport yesterday, he and friends deplaned in privacy; then he surrendered to authorities, was handcuffed with his hands behind his back and was escorted by squad car to police headquarters.

As reporters and fans swarmed the police station, Lester's attorneys immediately posted his five-million-dollar bail. The rocker was in and out of the precinct in less than one hour amid complaints of "special treatment" from onlookers.

Before leaving in a black Lincoln Continental, which was escorted by a police motorcade, Lester spoke beneath lightning-filled skies of his recent conversion to Christianity, an event that has rocked the world.

"I have found peace, joy, and the promise of eternal life in Jesus Christ," Lester told the rambunctious crowd. "To you, the public, and to the many DeathStroke fans who will hear this message, I apologize to you from the bottom of my heart for misleading you with evil intent during my DeathStroke days."

Prosecutor Dooley said a grand jury is currently reviewing evidence in the case, and that he expects a formal indictment within days. At the indictment, Lester will have the opportunity to plead guilty or not guilty to the murder charges.

"Everett Lester has been in and out of trouble ever since he was a youth," Dooley told reporters outside police headquarters yesterday. "The drugs, the violence…they've caught up with him. The evidence in this case is extremely damaging. Our goal is to get this man off the streets, out of the public eye, before he hurts others."

Of Lester's claim that he has become a born-again Christian, Dooley said, "That's what they all say, once they get caught. It's typical foxhole religion."

Lester will likely be free on bail until his trial begins but unable to leave the Miami-Dade jurisdiction. Once the trial starts, Lester will be incarcerated at the Miami-Dade detention center until he is either found guilty or exonerated.

Due to Lester's monetary holdings and worldwide fame, his trial promises to be one of the most sensational in history, with cameras in the courtroom and twenty-four-hour cable news channels making a blitz to show all.

I folded the paper, rested it on my lap, and sipped my coffee—reading but not really thinking about the story in the small box on the lower left-hand portion of the front page. It was about a six-foot, eleven-inch white male who robbed a firearms store near Miami International Airport the day before.

The man overpowered one employee, got two guns from behind a glass counter, loaded them, and attempted to flee. When another employee reached for the security alarm, the perpetrator fired shots, seriously wounding both employees, a father and son. The gunman was captured three blocks away, hiding in an abandoned office above a bakery. He was arrested and charged with armed robbery and two counts of attempted murder. His name: Zane Bender.

Discarding the *Miami Herald*, I picked up my brown Bible from the nightstand and read in silence for fifteen or twenty minutes, then slipped out of the bed and onto my knees.

Dear God, thank You for this day. Thank You for who You are and what You've done. You are mighty. You are alive. I feel You here with me.

Lord…I need Your help. Please, Jesus, clear my name. Give me a good name. Set me free of these charges. I pray for Karen and her parents, for safety. Please give Karen and me life together here on earth. I know it's selfish, but that's what I long for. And give me a mighty testimony, so I can help many people find You.

I'm thinking of Olivia this morning, God… My heart aches for her, for her mom and dad. God, please, would you heal that girl? Let her arise out of the condition she's in—just like You helped so many people do in the Bible. Let her parents feel Your love and comfort. Help them to forgive me.

Bless Mary and Jerry. May they find happiness together, with You as the center of their relationship.

Help me be like You today. Amen.

I had never seen Brian Boone as desperate as he appeared after Dooley had finished cross-examining Ricky. Following the day's trial, Boone and I were given thirty minutes to meet in a stark white holding area, just off of courtroom B-3. We sat in two plastic chairs with a small, dingy yellow table between us, and a Miami-Dade police deputy standing at attention near the door.

"I'll be straight with you, Everett. I'm worried. We've played all of our cards."

"No, we haven't. I haven't testified. You need to put me on the stand tomorrow, Boone. That's what I want!"

"I think we need to change your plea to guilty," he said, staring hard at me. "It's not too late."

"Why? So I can get out when I'm ninety? Come on. I want to take this chance."

He dropped his head.

The red-cheeked, baby-faced deputy looked straight ahead the whole time, as if he weren't listening.

"I just want a chance to tell my side of the story. All they know of me is the past. They need to see who I am today."

"Dooley will eat you alive."

"I'll take my chances."

"I need to think about it some more," Boone murmured, his head still down.

"Will you be at the prison tonight? Will we talk again before tomorrow, or what?"

"I'll get in touch with you, one way or another." He

stood, looking at the guard. "Let me know if you have any more big ideas."

I found some cream-colored stationery and a black pen in the drawer of the desk in my bedroom at the house in Bal Harbour. I pulled out the desk chair, sat down, and began to write.

> Dear Olivia, Claudia, and Raymond,
>
> As you probably know by now, I am in serious trouble with the law here in Miami. I'm sure these latest charges have confirmed your worst thoughts about me. I'm sorry you feel the way you do and must admit, I cannot blame you.
>
> I did want to let you know, however, that I have changed. My love and concern for Olivia grow each day, and I can't express the sorrow I feel about her condition and the fact that I am responsible. With Jesus Christ now living in my heart, I pray that our mighty God will heal your lovely girl—that He will raise her up to walk and talk and swim and cheerlead again.
>
> Please also know that it is my desire to pay for all of your hospital expenses and medical costs. If you continue your plan to file suit against me, I will gladly pay the amount determined by the courts.
>
> Claudia, my prayers are with you for strength and peace. Raymond, I pray that someday God will allow us to be friends. Olivia, I pray God will restore you.
>
> Again, please forgive me for the heartache I have brought to your world. I think about your family often and will never give up hope for healing.
>
> Warm regards,
> Everett Lester
> Matthew 11:28–30

★ ★ ★

The breakfast Sonja drummed up was scrumptious. Not only did she come through with thin, golden pancakes and sausage in maple syrup, but she created a fresh fruit bowl, egg casserole, and biscuits with white sawmill gravy. (She's from the South.)

The mood was upbeat and festive as we gathered around the huge dining room table, which was garnished with two crystal vases full of fresh flowers. Jacob and Sarah were still in their pajamas, but Karen and I were showered and dressed. Mary and Jerry were in their sweats, having just returned from a morning walk.

"We sneaked out the back door and went down to the beach," Mary said. "It was *wonderful*. I love this setting."

"Did the photographers follow you?" I asked.

"For a little while," Jerry said, "but we kept going and lost them. I think we did about four miles."

"I hope you guys can sneak out and visit the shops in the Village today," I said to everyone.

"Oh, I'm up for that!" Karen said. "How 'bout it, Mom? Are you with me?"

"Absolutely."

"What about you, Mary?"

"Well, I don't know…" Mary hesitated with mock sadness. "I'm not sure I can be away from my fiancé for too long."

With those words, Mary lifted her left wrist up to her forehead, pretending to be distraught and at the same time revealing a sparkling solitaire diamond ring.

"*Yes!*" I jumped up to hug my sister. "Congratulations! When did it happen?"

Karen was up hugging Jerry in an instant, while Jacob and Sarah beamed and clapped from across the table.

"This morning, of all times!" Mary blurted out, looking at the ring again. "Can you believe it?"

"When will the wedding be?" Jacob asked.

"We don't know," Jerry said. "We're open to anything. Who knows, we may get hitched while we're down here."

"Well…we can't do that," Mary said, acting like a wife already. "We'll want to have the boys there. But other than that, it's pretty wide open. Sometime within the next year, I hope."

I caught Karen's glance from two seats over. She looked right into me. The grin on her face was warm and loving, a forever smile. I knew what she was thinking—about us and when our day would come, if ever.

As I left the Justice and Administration Center under heavy guard after speaking with Boone, the press coverage was insane. Miami-Dade deputies began escorting me to their car, but as they did, we were overcome by reporters to the extent that my feet actually left the ground in the crowd's sway. Panic sparked in the eyes of one of the deputies in front of me, who pushed with all his might to forge a path to the waiting car.

On the ride back to the prison, I relished the sight and smell of temporary freedom. I made a point of remembering the passing palm trees, bright sidewalks, and polished buildings. I thought of Karen and Olivia, Mary and Jerry. I wanted to do so much for them. How I longed to be free. How different things would be if I could live on the outside again, but now as a Christian.

Dinner in the big house was pink-looking meatloaf, mashed potatoes the consistency of applesauce, wet spinach, cheap white bread, and good old H_2O—all served on the finest of the detention center's army-green meal trays. I ate with Donald Chambers, Rockwell, Scotty, and a couple of other friends.

Once back in my cell, I began having a difficult time taking a deep breath. I plopped down on my bunk, concentrating hard just to breathe and swallow normally. I couldn't fathom life in this concrete confine. I began rocking, rubbing the top of my thighs. My face felt flushed. I was weak and sweating, a cold sweat.

Forcing myself up, I paced the perimeter of my cell, fighting to wake up from the nightmare of having my freedom stripped away. My knees were about to give out. I fell back on the bunk, pummeled by thoughts of lethal injection and the smell of my burning flesh in an electric chair.

What is happening to me?

It used to be that I didn't care if I lived or died. But now I knew about hell—and heaven. And even though I had the promise of eternal life because of Christ, I did not want to die. I wanted Karen…a full life with her.

I wiped the sweat from my forehead with the blanket on my bunk.

Breathe deep.

"*The Lord is my Shepherd… I shall not want.*"

"Hey, man," said Donald from outside my cell. "What goes on?"

"Nothing." I avoided eye contact.

"Are you okay?"

I finally turned to face him and watched his eyes grow bigger. "You don't look good. Want to go to the infirmary?"

"No," I blurted, turning to face the concrete block wall. "I'm just dwelling too much about how this trial is going to play out."

Donald moved as close as he could outside my cell. "I understand. If I were you, I wouldn't torture myself thinking about worst-case scenarios."

"It's hard not to. This is one of the first times I've really started worrying about what might be, what really could happen."

Chambers held the cord to his billy club and twirled it as he spoke. "King David said, 'I would have despaired unless I had believed I would see the goodness of the LORD.' He was under a lot of pressure, too. So much that he was about to faint from despair, maybe like you feel. But one way or another, you are going to see the goodness of the Lord, Everett. Take rest in that."

I faced him once more. "Hmm..." I nodded, clinging to the words, wanting the peace I drew from them to last.

"You dudes think you spend enough time together?" Rockwell sauntered down the large hallway outside my cell.

"We brothers gotta stick together," Chambers jested.

Rockwell and I laughed.

"Lester, man, your attorney's here again," said Rockwell. "Dude has got ants in his pants tonight."

"Oh, yeah?" I sat up on the edge of my bunk. The fear had fled. I was myself again.

Rockwell clacked the crossbars of my cell three times. The locks inside the steel door clanged, the door bumped and slid open to the sound of clinking chains.

"Maybe Boone got lucky," Rockwell joked. "I'll tell you, he needs to make somethin' happen. Odds in here are running against you, big-time. There's a lot of guys bettin' a lot of dough on Frank Dooley and the state of Florida."

I peered through the small, square window in the blue metal door.

Boone was standing. He smiled and waved me in.

I pulled the heavy door open, and Rockwell left me. "Thirty minutes, rock star."

"We may have something!" Boone held up a small piece of yellow paper between his index and middle finger.

"What?" I didn't bother to sit.

"This showed up addressed to me in an unmarked envelope a couple of hours ago."

He carefully unfolded the paper and pressed it against the glass for me to read. It was small, about five by seven inches. And the writing looked like a female's, in blue ink.

Dear Mr. Boone,

I saw something several months ago...and may be able to help Everett's case. Contact me.

Sincerely,

Pamela McCracken

Former publicist, DeathStroke

31

The days and weeks ahead at the house in Bal Harbour were bittersweet, indeed.

Karen, her folks, Mary, Jerry, and I prepared meals together (including a huge Thanksgiving feast), sat around and read, sneaked away for day trips (including the dog races and an airboat ride through the Everglades), and talked extensively, sometimes well into the night. We also prayed together as I had never prayed before—for Mary and Jerry's future, Olivia Gilbert's healing, recovery and restoration for my brother Eddie and his family, and for success in the upcoming trial.

After about ten days, Jerry and Mary flew back to Ohio so they could return to work and get back to her boys, who were staying with close friends. They promised to hand deliver a unique seashell mobile to Olivia Gilbert, which I had found at a sidewalk shop at Hallandale Beach.

Within a day or two of their departure, the hammer dropped. The grand jury announced that it had compiled sufficient evidence for the state of Florida to prosecute me, and I was formally indicted on charges of first-degree murder in the death of Madam Endora Crystal.

Accompanied by Jacob, Sarah, and Karen at the arraignment, I pleaded innocent before presiding Judge Henry Sprockett.

Miami-Dade Prosecutor Frank Dooley made it clear that day that his intent was to remove me from society for life, whether it be via the death penalty or life in prison without parole.

"We will prove without a doubt that the defendant, Everett Timothy Lester, had every intention of killing Madam Endora Crystal," Dooley told the judge in his syrupy Southern twang. "This was cold-blooded, premeditated murder if ever there was such a thing. Celebrity or no celebrity, Everett Lester deserves to be punished severely for his crime."

In private, my attorney voiced his shock at the murder one charges. "I'm surprised Dooley didn't go for second-degree murder or even manslaughter," Boone explained to Gray Harris, the Baylisses, and me, shortly after the arraignment. "He must have some rock solid evidence. And he must have witnesses lined up who he believes are going to show that Everett had requisite intent to kill Endora."

"What's requisite intent?" I asked.

"Indispensable intent. In other words, Dooley thinks he can prove without a doubt that you had the reason, the motive, and the necessary intent to kill Endora."

"But I didn't."

"Tell Frank Dooley that. He's out to hang you. And he wants to do it fast. He's gonna ramrod this thing to trial."

Not long after my arraignment, the Baylisses packed their bags and headed back to Topeka on the Gulfstream. Karen and I had talked about the possibility of getting her a condo near my house in Bal Harbour, but she needed to get back to work for as long as possible if she hoped to return for the trial—and the media circus of the century.

All I can tell you about what happened next is that I became silent.

The press coverage was so smothering, I didn't feel like leaving the house. For days I stayed alone, quiet, thinking. Brewing a fresh pot of coffee every now and then, I read the Bible. When a verse stood out to me, I read it again, sometimes praying. I read night and day, sleeping whenever sleep came.

I found great hope in those days of solitude.

One day, a box was delivered to the front door. It was from Jeff Hall, president of the DeathStroke fan club. *"Everett,"* his note read. *"Among the tons of stuff pouring in, this came for you today. Thought you would want me to forward it along—just like the old days. Best regards, Jeff Hall."*

Ripping the brown paper from the long box, I flipped off the lid and stared at a large, pink rose, the stem of which was carefully attached to a miniature water bottle. It was wrapped in green tissue and surrounded by baby's breath. A loose note on a small white card was lying in the tissue.

> Dear Mr. Lester,
> Do you know what the pink rose means?
> Sweetheart. It means sweetheart!
> Missing you, sweetheart. Looking forward to a bright future.
> Love from Topeka,
> Karen

The newspapers those days told me that thousands upon thousands of people within Christian circles had embraced the discovery about my new identity in Christ. According to an in-depth report on *20/20*, however, many in the church still condemned me for the man I used to be. That was between them and God, I decided.

As for the secular world, those who had not yet believed in Christ, there was a diverse and widespread response. Some found joy and curiosity in my newfound faith, while others expressed utter animosity and resentment. Hate mail and love mail came in by what seemed like the truckload, according to Gray. Even a few death threats trickled in via snail mail.

It was then that Gray told me about a prominent New York publishing house that had expressed an interest in publishing my memoirs. Years ago I wouldn't have been interested in such a project. But now that I had something—Someone—important to share with the world, I agreed to speak with the vice president of the company by phone. In doing so, we came to terms on the new book, which would tentatively be entitled *Dark Star: Confessions of a Rock Idol.*

During those very quiet days in Bal Harbour, I began compiling the memories of my life that you read here. It was also then that I began jotting down the new lyrics and melodies that overflowed from my soul.

Pamela McCracken wore dark green slacks and matching jacket over a white blouse. Her long, sandy blond hair was soft and full. Her thin, tan face looked calm. When she crossed her legs, revealing ankle-high zippered boots, she exuded confidence as she awaited her call to the stand.

When the call came, Brian began by questioning her about her job as the former publicist for DeathStroke. She shared openly about her eight years with the band: the friendships, joy, hard work, and sometimes displeasure.

"There were a lot of drugs," she told Boone. "That made it difficult, at times, to get information from the band, to provide on-time interviews to the press, etcetera. But overall, it was a great experience for me and I hope for them."

"Miss McCracken, how familiar were you with Endora Crystal?"

"I knew Endora quite well, simply because she was around so much."

"Would you say she was a friend of yours?"

"Sure, I would call her a friend."

"And what would you call the relationship between Madam Endora and Everett Lester?"

"They were friends," she said flatly. "Everett was not romantically involved with Endora."

"Did you ever do a 'reading' with Endora? Ever have any involvement with her from a...shall we say, *psychic* perspective?"

"No, never." She shook her thick hair.

"Were you ever present when Endora performed readings for other people?" Boone still stood beside our table.

"I was always kind of floating in and out. I would see things, perhaps what you described, but was never really invited to participate, nor had any desire to do so. My role with DeathStroke was always kept at quite a professional level."

At that point—I remembered it as if it were yesterday—I noticed one member of the jury, a black man with extremely dark, shiny skin, looking at me very intently. I had noticed him before, but not like I did that day. He was tight-lipped, had a very erect posture, and wore a simple dark blue work jacket zipped up halfway. All of the other jurors seemed to be watching Boone or Miss McCracken, but this juror, in the first row to the far right, zeroed in on me.

"Tell the court, if you will, Miss McCracken, about the encounter you witnessed several months ago between my client and Madam Endora Crystal at The Groove recording studio in Santa Clarita, California."

With that, Boone swung around and walked directly toward Frank Dooley, who was seated with a sick smirk on his face, flicking the dust off the shoulders of his gray jacket.

"I ducked my head into the lounge portion of the studio and saw Endora and Everett. It appeared as though they were arguing."

"What were they arguing about, could you hear?"

"Endora was saying how Everett needed to keep emphasizing to his fans that there was life for all people...after death. She called it life on the Other Side. It was weird, but you know, that's what she was all about. That's what she spent her time talking about, arguing about, living for."

"What was Mr. Lester's response?"

"He told her those were *her* beliefs, not his," Pamela said. "He insisted she stop pushing her agenda on him."

"And what happened next?" Boone crossed his arms.

"I left the room at that time. I had just ducked in for a second and saw that they were arguing."

"And?"

"Well, after I left the room, I walked down the hall, but..." She looked down. "My curiosity got the best of me. I walked back to the door to listen."

Dooley squirmed noticeably, practically standing up as he shifted uncomfortably. The juror I mentioned earlier continued to pierce me with his brown eyes.

Pamela put her head up and forged ahead. "Endora was trying to convince Everett to take part in a séance in order to communicate with his old girlfriend, Liza Moon."

"What was Everett's response?"

"He said no, he wasn't interested," Pamela testified. "And when he did, Endora became very angry. She warned him not to turn against her."

"Really?"

"Yes, I believe she said, 'You do not want me against you.' I keep playing those words over in my head."

Chills ran up my spine with her words, which ignited the crowd in courtroom B-3.

"Keep it down!" Judge Sprockett ordered.

"What then, Miss McCracken?" Boone prompted, with a distinct tone of drama.

"Endora began to warn Everett about a lady who she predicted would come into his life and destroy it. I think she used the words that this lady would 'bring death' to 'his house.' I did not hear Endora mention a specific woman's name, but I assume it was—"

"Objection!" Dooley ripped to his feet. "Conjecture, Your Honor!"

"Sustained," said Sprockett.

Pamela looked at Boone.

"It's okay, Miss McCracken, you're doing fine. Tell us, what did Everett and Endora talk about next?"

"Endora was trying to convince Everett that he had all he needed, you know—in money and popularity. But he told her he needed help, that he had hit rock bottom. I remember feeling good that he was admitting to someone that he needed help."

Pamela's testimony sparked my memory. Suddenly, that day came back to me as I returned the glance of the dark juror on the far right. I remembered confiding in Endora. In my own way, I had been crying out for help.

"And what was Endora's response to Mr. Lester saying he needed help, telling her he had hit rock bottom?"

Pamela took a deep breath and faced me. "She began to...to tell him he was getting tired."

It was church quiet, so Boone just let her roll.

"She kept repeating that he needed rest and that he was getting drowsy…"

Her words just hung out there, dangling above the

silence. Then somehow, I sensed what was coming and so did the crowd.

"I remember, she said something like, 'Sleep little child…and let me impose my will over you.'"

Roar!

On their feet, every person in the courtroom.

Pamela sat frozen on the witness stand, perhaps suddenly realizing the crucial part she had stepped forward to play in my future.

Amid the bedlam, the black juror was still staring at me when my head dropped, my shoulders sagged, and a backlog of emotions rushed to my eyes.

The noise around me had become so loud that the sound of Judge Sprockett's banging gavel sounded like he was only clicking his fingers.

"We will have silence in this courtroom, or I will close this case to the press and public!" stormed Judge Sprockett, now standing and leaning forward over the courtroom like a hood ornament, with both hands clutching the desk in front of him.

Boone paced the main floor. "Miss McCracken," he yelled in an attempt to silence the storm. "Miss McCracken!"

The place was a nuthouse.

I had just finished wishing Jacob and Sarah a Merry Christmas and hanging up the phone with Karen when the doorbell rang. From the cherry-colored wood floors in the living room of my house in Bal Harbour, I heard a commotion outside the front door.

The doorbell rang again twice, then loud pounding.

I hurried to the foyer and peered through the shutter slats.

It was my brother Eddie, with his face practically pressed against the front door. Reporters and camera people were packed around him. This was the first time they had ventured down the front sidewalk or anywhere near the front porch. Didn't these people have anything better to do on Christmas?

When I pulled the door open for him, shutters raced and strobes flashed. Some photographers even stuck their arms into the house, holding down their motor drive buttons as they did.

Eddie and I managed to get the front door shut, took a few deep breaths, and laughed. Then we hugged, clutching each other for some time and exchanging Christmas greetings.

"I can't believe you." He pulled back to examine me. "You always find a way to keep the heat turned up, don't you?"

I smiled and shook my head.

"What are you doing here?"

"I just needed to see you, man." Eddie turned away, taking his jacket off.

We made our way into the living room and sat on a couch by the empty fireplace.

"Well...how *are* you?" I asked, sensing a fragileness about him.

"Hey, this isn't about me." He feigned a smile. "You're the one in the spotlight. How are you holding up?"

"I'm good, man." I nodded, assuring him. "I'm hanging in there. But I can tell you're not. What's up?"

He fumbled for words, not making eye contact. "I guess you'd say I'm in kind of a tailspin," he mumbled, his handsome exterior still intact. "Ever since David died...a light's just gone out."

"I can't imagine, bro."

"I mean, even before that, things were bad. But now. This. It's... Life is just...it's just rotten."

"Are you still gambling?"

"Yeah."

"How much, Eddie?"

"'Bout the same." He searched my eyes. "Wesley's gone off the deep end. Running with a wild crowd. We have no control over him anymore. He's an adult, of course..."

"He's mad at me, isn't he?"

"He thinks you let David down. But I don't put any blame on you…"

"I let them *both* down," I said, shifting uncomfortably. "That's something I've got to try and make right."

"Good luck." Eddie shrugged. "He actually wants you to be convicted."

I felt myself go flush.

"He's a very dark young man." Eddie dropped his head. "There's no getting through to him."

We sat without words for a moment.

"What about Sheila and Madison?"

That made him turn and look out the window. "Healthwise, they're fine, but we're still not doing good. Sheila's depressed, wants out of the marriage. Madison's bitter and just stays completely to herself. We're totally dysfunctional. Remind you of anything?"

"Yeah, it does." I nodded, as several snapshots of our childhood appeared and vanished in my mind. "You need to give it time, Eddie."

"It's not getting better with time, though," he snapped, laughing sarcastically. "It's getting worse."

"Is there other stuff you're not telling me?"

He brushed the dust off the top of his shoe, and twisted the lace.

"I'm just feeling the pressure from all sides, man. That's all. I've just made a mess of things."

"As much of a mess as I've made?" I asked, slowly breaking into a smile.

He looked at me. "I told you I saw something different about you…at the hospital."

I smiled. "You were lookin' at a new man."

"I know. Then when I saw your statement outside the police station, everything clicked. I knew what had happened to you."

"It's real Eddie. *He's* real."

He closed his eyes, frowned, and let his head drop back on the couch.

I remembered that same frown, that same defeated spirit from the face of my father.

Putting his palms to his temples, Eddie opened his eyes slowly. "I'm just tired, Ev. Just plain tired. I know you've been there."

"Don't feel like goin' on, do you?"

"No. I don't."

I patted his knee. "It's good you came. Let's just hang out. You can rest here."

With the help of the Yellow Pages, we found a Chinese restaurant that was open and placed an order that would be delivered within the hour. When Eddie called Mom at my brother Howard's house in northeast Ohio, we were surprised to hear that Mary and Jerry had joined them by making the short trek from Dayton.

They were all elated to hear that Eddie had made the flight to Miami, and that the two youngest Lester boys would be together on Christmas.

When we were all on the line and the conversation wound down, I figured there would be no better time to tell the family my news.

"Hey…you probably haven't heard this yet, guys, but my trial is set to start January fifth."

All the voices on the various phones in Ohio and Miami fell silent.

"They're keeping me in custody for the duration of the trial. I check into the jail January second or third," I said, trying to keep it light. "So get your TVs warmed up for the news event of the year."

Quiet cloaked the phone lines, until Mary broke the silence.

"Everett, Jerry and I will try to make it down, at least for some of it. Can we stay at the house?"

"I have your rooms reserved," I said. "Karen and her folks will be here, too, for as much of it as possible."

When Mom got off the phone, Howard explained that her health was deteriorating steadily. They wouldn't be able to make the trial, and I didn't expect them to.

"Mary, did you tell Everett about the mobile…and his letter?" Jerry asked on one of the many phones they had going at Howard's house.

"No, you tell him."

"Claudia was so grateful to get your letter and the mobile for Olivia.. When she gave Olivia the mobile, she actually smiled; she stares at it all the time. It's hanging from the ceiling, right by her bed. Claudia also said she read your letter to Olivia, and that when she did, Olivia began to moan. Claudia thinks she was actually crying, which is the first time that's happened since the accident."

I fought off the vision of that scene. "What about Raymond?"

Jerry paused a moment. "He doesn't like the contact from you. But Claudia insisted on reading the letter to Olivia and keeping the mobile. So you've won a fan in my sister, anyway. And that's the first avenue to Raymond's heart."

I ushered in the new year alone, eating microwave popcorn, sipping Diet Coke, and watching *New Year's Rockin' Eve* with Dick Clark and special guest, my old pals, the Rolling Stones—live from frigid Times Square in New York City.

When New Year's Day came, I spoke with my whole family again and, of course, with Karen and her folks. Things had completely cooled down since the scare the night we were all together at Lake Shawnee. In fact, Karen had moved back into her house, with no further disturbances. We were beginning to rest a little easier, but none of us had our guard down.

As the plans stood that day, Karen and her parents, and Mary and Jerry, would all fly into Miami the night before my trial began. Gray and Brian were taking care of their transportation and security needs, as well as special credentials for the trial.

"I'm actually excited to finally get this show on the road," I told

Karen on New Year's Day. "I can't take it cooped up in this house much longer."

"Yeah, well, that house is probably going to look pretty good after about five hours in the Miami-Dade detention center," Karen snickered.

"I can't wait to see you."

"Me too," she said. "Hopefully, this will be the beginning of the end of the Madam Endora saga."

"Hey listen, I'll need a change of clothes each day for the trial. I had all my stuff moved over here to the house from the high-rise. Do you think you and Mary could pick something out each day and bring it to the courthouse?"

"You mean I'm going to have something to say about what the world-famous Everett Lester wears to his world-famous trial?"

"Just make sure it matches, okay? Brian wants me looking like a gentleman, if that's possible."

The next afternoon, more reporters and news crews had converged on the house at Bal Harbour than I had ever seen in one place before. They canvassed the sandy ground beneath the palm trees in back of the house, trampled every inch of the centipede front lawn, spilled over into the neighbors' yards, and rolled right up to the front door.

This was the big day.

Brian and Gray arrived together in another chauffeured black Lincoln similar to the one that had transported me to and from the Miami-Dade police precinct weeks ago. With the help of police, they prodded their way through the grid of bodies to the front door.

Harry Coogle ran the show, explaining that I would be handcuffed and transported in his car to the detention center.

I was anxious to go.

As we headed south on A1A then crossed over the JFK Causeway, a sick feeling gnawed at my stomach as I mindfully absorbed every detail about the beautiful Intracoastal Waterway—not wanting to forget its blue water and sea-washed docks, the fishermen, the pelicans and seagulls, and the picturesque homes tucked among the mangroves.

As we merged onto Highway 1 heading south, I watched the people—all kinds of people, all colors—walking freely about the city sidewalks. *Will I ever do that again?* It was an unfathomable question, a question I couldn't believe I was faced with asking myself.

Soon, it was back to reality as we came to a halt at the curb outside the Miami-Dade detention center, which was blanketed with cameras, reporters, TV trucks, and onlookers. Three helicopters hovered low overhead. A cameraman from one of the choppers actually stood on the landing skid of his helicopter, as colleagues held him aboard.

Once we entered the detention center, the fanfare ceased. In fact, the second I passed through the vestibule doors, it was as if I was suddenly transformed from heroic superstar to Joe Criminal.

I was told to turn over my wallet and personal items, which consisted of some change, a tube of ChapStick, and what remained of a roll of peppermint Lifesavers. I was then guided through a metal detector and led to a locker room, where I was instructed to undress, submit to a full-body search, and put on the bright orange jumpsuit and tennis shoes provided by the county.

Next, I was escorted along a dark hallway of offices, down some steps, and through two more metal detectors before coming into the large, open atrium of the detention center.

"Ground level for you, rock star," said a black guard with the name Rockwell embroidered on his uniform shirt. Rockwell guided me to my cell with one strong hand on my shoulder.

The loud cracks of his billy club striking the bars startled me. Then the door to my cell clanked, jerked, and lurched forward, clinking its way to a close. As the bars locked shut, I came to the full realization that the first-degree murder case of *The State of Florida v. Everett Timothy Lester* was about to begin.

★ ★ ★

Karen stood in the third row of courtroom B-3, wearing a light brown business suit, white blouse, and black square-toed boots. She looked stunning. Her hands were pressed against her mouth and nose in the prayer position as Judge Sprockett fought to quiet the uproar caused by the testimony of former DeathStroke publicist Pamela McCracken.

Karen was flanked by her mom and dad on one side and Mary and Jerry on the other. Donald and Della were seated nearby. We were all overwhelmed by the new revelations that caused an adrenaline rush to pulsate through the courtroom.

There was hope.

Judge Sprockett successfully convinced everyone to take their seats as Pamela explained that once Endora seemingly hypnotized me in the lounge at The Groove recording studio, she began to leave the room through the doorway where Pamela stood. She was forced to flee and returned to her makeshift publicity office.

Ten minutes later there was a ruckus in the lounge. Pamela ran to see what had happened along with other DeathStroke staffers. That was when they discovered the demolished rock water sculpture, the smashed Les Paul guitar, and me in a rage—getting pinned to the ground by Gray and Ricky.

My head dropped to my chest, and I breathed a sigh of thankfulness for Pamela and her testimony, probably the most helpful in my defense thus far.

But there was little time to relish the victory; Frank Dooley wasted no time getting on his feet to cross-examine.

"Good day, Miss McCracken." He hustled around his table—all business—and approached the witness. "I'm certain Mr. Boone and Mr. Lester are grateful you've come forward to help in their defense."

Dooley moved with a smoothness and confidence that made me uncomfortable.

"Tell the court if you will, Miss McCracken, which illegal drugs you have used in the past?"

I could practically see the air leave Pamela's chest as the shock set in on her face.

She stammered but couldn't speak.

The audience was breathless.

Dooley left her to sink or swim.

"I..." She faced Judge Sprockett. All I could see were his frozen eyes, staring at her from above his thin, clasped hands, which covered most of his solemn face. She turned to Brian, who closed his eyes slowly and nodded as if to say, *Take it easy; take is easy.*

"I do not take drugs on a...a regular basis," Pamela managed.

"But when you *do* imbibe, what do you use?"

The expressions on people's faces agreed: Dooley was cold-blooded.

This was not good.

"I've used marijuana before. And I have *tried* cocaine..."

"Okay, let's not list them all, instead let me—"

"Sir! If I may," Pamela interrupted, "there is no *list!*"

"Okay, Miss McCracken. We've established the fact that you use drugs. Let's just move forward."

Pamela was left speechless.

"Let's focus in on that day at The Groove, shall we?" Dooley turned to approach the jury. Pamela shifted in her seat, and a tinge of pink seeped into her face.

"The day you say Endora Crystal supposedly hypnotized Everett Lester." Dooley smiled at the jury. "Let's talk about the drugs you used on *that* day. What were you using, Miss McCracken?"

"That was a totally unusual day for me!"

"Answer the question, Miss McCracken."

Again, she looked to the judge then Boone for an escape, but found zero.

"Let me finish," she insisted. "We were slow that day. I had just wrapped up a whole week of writing press releases and contacting record labels. I was relaxed and didn't have any big responsibilities. I walked into a conference room where people were smoking a...marijuana cigarette. They asked me to join them."

Dooley smiled coldly, turned his back on Pamela, and strolled away from her. "Funny isn't it, how in a court of law it becomes a 'marijuana cigarette' instead of a joint?" Some in the audience laughed. Several jurors even snickered.

"You had no big responsibilities that day. So you got high, figuring you didn't need to be at your best or in top form."

There was a brief silence, as Dooley examined the eyes of each juror down the line. "But in the end, it turns out you *did* need to be in top form after all, didn't you, Miss McCracken? Because here you are, months later, a key witness in the murder case of the decade, possibly of the century."

Pamela opened her mouth but said nothing. Her eyes darted around the room for guidance, but again, she came up empty.

"Can you tell this court today—before the nation and the world—that you were totally straight and sober when you saw and heard this *supposed* altercation between Endora Crystal and Everett Lester?"

"I told you," she said, trembling, "I had used a little marijuana that day. It was unusual for me to do that during work hours, but I was by no means unstable or incoherent."

"Didn't inhale, is that it?" Dooley smirked.

"*Objection*," Boone yelled from his seat. "Harassing!"

"Sustained," shot Sprockett.

"All right, Miss McCracken, I wasn't going to get into this, but you force my hand. You won't come out and admit that you were stoned that day—"

Boone stood but couldn't get a word in edgewise.

"You keep saying marijuana use was *unusual* for you. Would it behoove us to call Mr. Charlie LaRoche back to the witness stand to tell this court just how often you *were* involved in drug usage and drug transactions during the DeathStroke heyday?"

Pamela closed her eyes, raised her chin, and took in a deep breath. She then looked at Dooley and blinked repeatedly, holding back tears.

"You know what I think, Miss McCracken? I think you got *very* high that day at The Groove. And since then, I think you have gotten so caught up in the hype of this trial that you *created* this hypnotism story!"

"Your Honor, you can't allow this!" Boone was finally heard. "Mr. Dooley is badgering the witness with his own cockeyed theories. He's filling the jurors' minds with his own words, not Miss McCracken's."

"Sustained!" Sprockett boomed. "Mr. Dooley, you *will* refrain from presenting your own hypothetical ideas."

Dooley coughed into a fist to cover what may have been a smirk and tweaked each gold cuff link. "Miss McCracken, is it possible that the argument you saw and heard between Endora and Everett was a lover's quarrel?" Dooley glared at Pamela.

Hushed verbal feedback rolled through the audience. "I don't think it was. No. I never envisioned Everett and Endora…like that."

"Never mind what you envisioned, we've heard enough

about people's visions at this trial. What I asked is, *is it possible* this was a lover's quarrel you saw?"

Pamela pursed her lips, shook her head, and threw her hands up. "I guess there's a very slight chance that's what it was, but I truly doubt it."

The black juror who stared at me earlier now focused on Dooley. I hoped and prayed to God we hadn't lost him.

Today had been a roller coaster.

I was wiped out.

It was 7:44 P.M. I jotted down my memoirs while watching TV during leisure time. There were ten or twelve other inmates surrounding me, munching snacks, reading magazines, and watching the tube.

Brian was due to show up anytime to discuss how we proceeded from here. It appeared we'd called our final witness, unless I testified. In any case, once we called our last witness, then Dooley would give his closing argument, followed by Boone's. Dooley then had one last shot at a final closing before the jury deliberated.

I'd been praying about whether or not I should testify but couldn't seem to come to a definitive conclusion. A while back I was certain I should take the stand, but when I saw what Dooley did to Pamela today, I just wasn't sure. Boone knew what he was doing, and he was still vehemently opposed to having me testify.

The TV screen turned bright red. *"Breaking news."*

A handsome, dark-haired anchorman, graying slightly at the temples and wearing a somber expression, sat upright at the Channel 2 news center in Miami.

"Good evening. The girlfriend of accused murderer Everett Lester is missing tonight…"

I stood.

"Karen Bayliss of Topeka, Kansas, who has been a fixture by Everett Lester's side throughout the rocker's sensational murder trial, has been reported missing by the twenty-eight-year-old's parents, Jacob and Sarah Bayliss, also of Topeka."

My mind seared white.

"Sources say Miss Bayliss may have been abducted from the premises of a posh home in Bal Harbour, Florida, which is being leased for her and family and friends during the trial by Everett Lester himself."

"Quiet!" I ordered from my place beneath the elevated TV.

Their pictures were on the screen—Karen, Jacob, Sarah. Pictures from the trial, from today or yesterday. *That's her. She can't be missing. She's right there!*

"The kidnapping comes on the eve of what may well be closing arguments in the case of The State of Florida v. Everett Timothy Lester, *in which Lester has been accused of murdering LA psychic Madam Endora Crystal."*

Zaney. It's Zaney!

My head spun around in search of Donald Chambers—not there.

"Miss Bayliss, a graduate of Sterling College in central Kansas, is said to have been instrumental in leading Everett Lester to his newfound religious faith."

Out of here. I've got to get out, now!

Chambers.

"Chambers!"

He ran toward me.

"You've seen?" He held my arms.

"Just now." I looked back up at the evil screen.

"It's going to be okay, Everett. It's—"

"You've got to get me out, Donald. It's Zaney. *He has her!"*

"I know, Everett. I know." Chambers practically held me up. "Try to be calm. Boone phoned. He's almost here. He has more information. Let's take it a step at a time, brother. Just breathe deep. Breathe deep now, and come with me."

His arm was around me. He was leading me. He was starting to pray...

I felt flushed and weak as Donald swung open the heavy door. Brian was pacing in what little space there was within the cramped metal-and-glass visitor's box.

Boone saw my distress. "Sit down, Everett."

"What's happening, Brian?" I ignored his command. "It's Zaney, you know. Do the cops know it's him? Have you told them?"

"I'm going to talk you through this. Just, please, sit down and let me catch you up on things, okay?" Boone was breathing heavy, trying to keep me calm. "I'm going to tell you all I know."

"Do it."

"Your houseguests all left the trial together today: Karen, her parents, Mary, and Jerry." Boone reviewed some notes he'd scribbled on a white pad. "They headed straight from the Justice and Administration Center back to the house in Bal Harbour. Gray arranged transportation in a rented SUV."

My fists were clenched, pressing into the engraved metal desk. My body rocked. I had the shivers.

"When they got there, everyone went upstairs to change. They had decided to go out to Bella's for Italian. Jerry drove everyone in the SUV, and they made it to the restaurant. They knew where it was, because—"

"I took them."

"Right," Boone said. "Near the end of the meal, Karen

excused herself to go to the restroom...but she never came back."

I shook my head. "That's a small restaurant, Boone!" I slammed my fist on the table. "How could he abduct her from there?"

"Well, listen." Boone urged me to cool down with his hands. "Jacob caught on. He thought he heard a muffled scream. No one else at the table heard it, but he did. So he excused himself, called into the ladies' room, went in, but Karen wasn't there. Then he ran outside and saw some kind of a pickup truck with a camper burning its tires out of the driveway."

"Zaney?"

"Not positive yet, but Jacob got the tag number. It's from out of state."

I fell onto the plastic chair. "Thank God." Then I sat up straight. "Can I get out, Boone? For this? Can you get me a leave or something?"

"Everett, no. I'm sorry. I knew you'd ask. There's no way. I've checked. But I promise you, Jacob and Jerry are all over this; Gray and I are here for you. Mary and Sarah are praying... I know this is going to be tough, but you'll just have to sit this one out."

My neck hurt. I was nauseous.

No one to touch me or hold me.

"I'm so sorry, Everett," came my friend's voice through the glass.

I rose, touched the metal door, and pressed my hands against the cinder block walls closing in on me.

Trapped.

Karen needs me...and I'm trapped.

33

Against prison regulations, Donald arranged for Karen's father and Jerry Princeton to meet with me in the visitor's box. It was 9:50 P.M.

Jerry looked pretty good. Cool and steady, as usual.

Jacob, on the other hand, was frazzled—like I felt. His eyes were slightly bloodshot, and I noticed creases I'd never seen before. His face had lost much of its color, his hair was disheveled.

They brought new information: A copy of a note from the kidnapper found in the sink of the lady's restroom at the restaurant. Jerry held it up for me to read as Jacob paced in the background. The handwriting was immediately familiar.

Lester,
    If you're found innocent, you will never see Karen again. Better pray—preacher boy.
    Z

"Zaney," I whispered, falling onto the chair.

"The Miami-Dade PD are all over this thing, Everett," Jerry assured me. "Zaney's in a stolen vehicle. It's a green 2002 Arctic Fox; basically, a pickup truck with a camper on back."

"Stay here." I rushed out of the hot, confining room.

Staggering ten or twelve steps, I bent over, hands on my knees. *Deep breaths.* Sweat running into my eyes and down the back of my neck, I swallowed back the bile. Breathing in, deep, I saw white stars.

Deep breaths. Take deep breaths.

Oh God—be with Karen. Save her, Lord. Please, please, please…save her.

"The camper was stolen from a Georgia couple at a rest area near Kendall along Highway 1," Jerry said, now that I'd cooled and returned to the visitor's tank with Jacob and him. "It was reported missing two days after Zaney escaped from here."

"Do the cops know how serious this is?"

"Everybody knows, Everett." Jacob stepped toward the glass between us. "I've laid out the whole thing for them: the roses, the fire, the night at Shawnee Lake. The cops here are supposed to get together with the Topeka PD."

"The bottom line is, we've got to find the *camper*," I insisted.

"The Miami-Dade PD is familiar with your trial, obviously, and they know the world's eyes are on them," said Jerry. "They want to find Karen. They're searching all the local campsites, rest areas. There's an APB out for Zaney. He can't get far."

Jacob looked at me, eyebrows raised. He held his big right

hand up to the glass. I pressed my hand against his, with only the cool glass between us. Seeing this, Jerry raised his left hand and pressed it against the petition. I held my other hand up to his.

"Father, we're speechless," Jacob said. "All tapped out. Totally reliant on You. Totally surrendered. Watching You. Waiting. Counting on You to bring our girl home…safe." He broke up, ever so quietly.

"Jesus," Jerry intervened, "bring an end to this nightmare. Turn Zaney's evil plans inward…on himself. Set Karen free, Father. Blanket her in peace. Let her be wise and strong. Recite Your Word to her right now as we speak. Let Your words fill her ears and mind and thoughts. Protect her from injury. Put Your angels all around her. In Jesus' most powerful name we pray, amen."

"Stay here, Everett." Rockwell opened the metal door after Jerry and Jacob left. "Boone needs to see you one more time. He'll be right in. Hang in there, man."

With my hands clasped at my mouth and my elbows resting on the blue metal table in front of me, I saw something carved in the left-hand corner of the table, near the glass, that I'd never seen before.

The words read: Only Believe.

Those same words jumped out at me only this morning. The Bible said the daughter of a man named Jairus was sick. Jesus was on the way to help her. But along the way, some men informed Jesus and Jairus that the daughter had died. Jesus knew Jairus was frantic. And His words to the man felt like they were meant for me: "Do not be afraid any longer, *only believe.*"

That is what I must do.

The papers and folders under Boone's arm blew as he swung the door open. "Okay, Everett. Someone else spotted the camper."

"Where?" I shot to my feet, grabbing the edge of the table.

"Small town called Sandpiper Cove, near Homestead. He's gone now, but police are combing the area."

My eyes shut and my head fell back.

"Everett, I'm sorry, but I need to talk to you about taking the stand."

I snapped out of it. "I'm not testifying."

"Since when?"

"Since Karen disappeared. I want to get this thing over with and get out of here."

"There's no guarantee you're going anywhere."

"I'll take my chances."

"We could still file for a mistrial."

"Brian, they may never find Zaney, or he may be dead when they do—and then where would we be?"

We searched each other for a moment through the glass.

"You haven't changed your mind, have you?" I asked. "You don't want me to testify, do you?"

"No, my best advice is still no."

"And we're not copping a guilty plea."

"We've really passed that window," he said. "It looks like it's going to the jury."

"What's next? Dooley's closing argument?"

"Tomorrow."

I clenched a fist at Brian and gave him a thumbs-up.

"Bring it."

I'd never seen anything like this. They said more than ten thousand people flooded the Miami-Dade Justice and

Administration Center. They were inside the building, covering every square inch of the concrete and cobblestone outside the facility, and flowing down the streets in every direction.

News teams were having a difficult time maneuvering amid all the spectators.

The traffic, the people pressing against me, the questions firing from every direction, the signs with Karen's picture on them—it was like a dream.

As I was escorted into courtroom B-3 by three officers, I searched out Mary and Jerry, Jacob and Sarah, Donald and Della. They were all seated together—close together. I made eye contact and smiled, glad to know they were there.

Brian shook my hand and gave me a sheet of white paper with black type on it. "This came via e-mail. Thought you would like to read it."

Dear Mr. Lester,

Thank you for all your concern for Olivia. She is resting beside me here now as we watch the news of your loved one's disappearance. Please know, during this difficult time, we are praying for you. God bless you. I hope you go free so you can come visit Olivia soon. We'll pick a day when her father isn't home!

Sincerely,

Claudia Gilbert

P.S. Your faith in God has been an inspiration to me. Thank you again.

Frank Dooley saved his finest suit for today, knowing he would be the focal point of the world's wide-eyed gaze. It was a navy Armani with eye-popping red pinstripes and a matching red tie.

Dooley began his closing argument by plainly and powerfully explaining to the jury why the Miami-Dade district attorney's office pursued murder in the first degree. "We believe that we can and *have* proven, without any doubt, that Everett Timothy Lester not only murdered Endora Crystal, but did so in premeditated fashion—purposefully, precisely, and with every intention of ending her life.

"You'll hear Brian Boone go on and on, I'm certain, about 'criminal hypnotherapy' and the defense's stance that Everett Lester was somehow—*without knowing it*—hypnotized before he shot Endora Crystal," Dooley said, relaxed, practically laughing.

"Ladies and gentlemen, don't you buy into that sham for one minute! Are you kidding me? *Hypnotism?* You talk about grasping at straws. And while we're on the subject, why in heaven's name would Endora Crystal want to hypnotize her very own boyfriend so he could, in turn, shoot her at close range? It makes no sense, even in Everett Lester's mixed-up world. This defense is almost as weird as the hooligan who's convinced his legal counsel to peddle it. I don't even like to lower myself to address it, but I throw it out there to let you, the jurors, know that I find it sheer lunacy!"

Dooley acted as if he'd gotten the unimportant small talk out of the way. "People of the jury." He folded his arms, walking directly in front of my table. "Everett Lester's life is typical—typical, I tell you—of the bad boy turned religious zealot. Everything this man has ever done has been to the extreme, always extremes. He grew up a rebellious, hell-raising teen—outdoing all of his friends with his violence, his guns, his drugs, and his music."

I didn't even really care what this guy said. All I cared about was Karen—*living*.

"His rock group, DeathStroke, reverted to extremes as well, becoming one of the rowdiest, most belligerent, vicious, antagonistic groups of its time. That's this man's life story, ladies and gentlemen. Do you understand? Extremes. Always extremes. When you think about it, it's difficult to believe Everett Lester hasn't landed himself in prison long before now."

Boone wrote furiously, as did his assistants. The one juror, the black man, was staring me down again. But today he looked at a different person than he did yesterday. Part of me was missing today. He knew it. He could see it, and so could the other jurors. Yes, they had been sequestered. But both Frank Dooley and Brian Boone appeared to be playing their cards as though the jury had somehow heard the news of Karen's disappearance.

"Everett Lester took divination to the extreme, hiring his own personal psychic—Madam Endora Crystal—to travel with him. He took guns to the extreme, collecting them, taking lessons, building his own shooting range. Do you see the pattern? Extremes. Always extremes."

Jacob just exited the courtroom. He had his phone in his hand. Perhaps it was about Karen...

"Then came religion in this man's life," Dooley said with a smirk. "And the same thing happened. Extremes. Always extremes. We've heard it throughout this trial from many of his own character witnesses. Immediately he separated himself from close friends. Words like *Satan* and *gospel* started peppering his vocabulary. And here's where we come to what really happened in this man's life, people." Dooley pulled his long, stiff cuffs toward the palm of each hand.

"*Overnight* Everett Lester becomes a fundamentalist, right-wing, born-again Christian—and you know what? To him, his old life was evil. To him, his old friends were bad influences. To him, his old psychic—Endora Crystal—was *Satan!* It's true; that's what he thought. We've heard it implied in many ways throughout this trial."

Jacob walked through the double doors at the back of the room and shook his head slightly at me as he returned to his seat.

"Extremes. Always extremes," Dooley said, with his thumbs latched inside his suspender straps, standing directly in front of Judge Sprockett. "Doesn't it strike you as odd that Everett had a romantic relationship with Endora Crystal—a woman some fifteen years his senior? One witness told us Endora said Everett was, and I quote, 'jealous and domineering.'

"What happened that day, last November 11, folks, is that Everett Lester had had enough. Enough of Endora as a psychic, enough of Endora as a secret lover, enough of Endora as a Satanist out to torment him and destroy his newfound religious life!"

This was like a major motion picture. The crowd was mesmerized.

"It was a combination of many things that drove Everett to get the .45 caliber Glock from his dresser drawer and gun down Endora Crystal in cold blood."

Dooley made a gun with his hand and pointed it at me. "But the one thing that you *must* consider, above all else, is that Everett Lester acted consistently that day in November. He acted in the extreme, ladies and gentlemen, always in the extreme. Pulling the trigger to solve a problem. Extreme? *Yes!* Consistent with the rest of his life? *Yes, by all means!*"

Dooley's hand, shaped like a gun, was still pointed at me.

"People of the jury—" he pivoted toward the jury box and pointed his make-believe gun at each juror—"it now becomes *your* duty and *your* obligation to punish Everett Lester for his extreme behavior, for the cold-blooded, premeditated murder he committed last November. As you act, each one of you, I implore you...give him the *extreme* sentence he deserves. Give Everett Lester a murder one guilty verdict."

Anyone who knew me, knew what I was thinking right then. My blank face. The vacancy behind my eyes.

All I care about is Karen.

This trial doesn't matter anymore.

Say what you want, I'm in God's hands now...and so is my wife-to-be.

34

Donald Chambers had a small pad in his hands and a pencil behind his ear. Several guards and police officers surrounded us. We stood in a small, white holding area adjacent to courtroom B-3. The trial had recessed for lunch, but I wasn't hungry. My family and friends were not permitted back here.

Chambers gave me a review of what he learned from his friends at Miami-Dade PD. "A green Arctic Fox camper with no license plates, but matching the description of the one stolen from the Georgia couple, was spotted at a rest area off Highway 1 near Kendall, then again at Sandpiper Cove."

"By whom?" I asked. "Who spotted it?"

"The first time it was reported by a family on vacation," Chambers said. "Two teens who had been following your case closely on TV spotted the camper and had their dad call

911. The next time, a retired gentleman saw it at a Winn-Dixie."

"Did they see Karen?"

"No one reported seeing her," Chambers said. "But listen to this—the camper was spotted again *today* at a gas station in a little town called Leisure City. This time, the convenience store owner says he saw Zane Bender, even talked with him a minute. They're looking at store surveillance tapes now to get a positive ID."

"No one saw anything else? In the camper? Why didn't these people look in the camper? They know Karen is missing, right? Everyone knows…"

"Everett." Chambers raised his chin and peered at me out the bottom of his eyes. "Calm down. He's on the run, okay? They're going to find him."

"It's not him I'm worried about. Will they find Karen?" He put a hand on my shoulder. "Friend, I pray they do. But I can't make any promises. I don't want to mislead you. All I can say is, we're praying. Everyone's trying their best. And I'm here for you."

He started to leave.

"Donald," I grasped his arm, "will you update Karen's parents on this, and Mary and Jerry?"

"That's where I'm headed."

He turned to go, but I caught his shoulder. "You've been a true friend," I said, as he squeezed my arm, pushed open the wooden door, and headed back into the courtroom.

Brian Boone was a fighter.

I didn't have much energy left. My mind was waning. I felt weak and sick and angry. Helpless. Yet even in this fog, even in this weariness, I recognized the fire that burned in

Brian. He was fighting for my life.

Boone had already set up the framework for his closing argument, and now it was getting interesting. Wearing a charcoal gray suit, he had everyone's attention as he slid his tortoiseshell reading glasses across the table. It was so quiet in courtroom B-3, you could actually hear the glasses scratch across the surface of the tabletop and bump to a stop at one of his notebooks.

He walked slowly toward Judge Sprockett. "Have you ever heard it said, ladies and gentlemen, that you should never ask a question you do not know the answer to?"

His shiny black loafers clicked and slid across the wood floor.

"Frank Dooley asked such a question in his closing remarks this morning. The question he asked was: Why would Endora Crystal want to hypnotize Everett Lester so he could, in turn, shoot her?"

Boone continued to walk, using the silence to his advantage.

"Now, the answer I'm going to pose to this question is a bit deep and highly unusual—just like this entire case has been. Remember, Judge Sprockett himself told us early on, this case was going to take us places we really didn't want to go."

He shook his head. "Ladies and gentlemen, Endora Crystal developed a mounting hatred for Everett Lester in the last days, weeks, and months of her life. We've proven that. Endora was into the New Age and the occult; we've proven that. She used various behavior-altering drugs to help her hypnotize people—we've proven that. She was a woman who read palms and tarot cards, who claimed to know the past, predict the future, and communicate with the dead—we've proven that.

"No matter what religious background you and I come from—if any—this case forces us to examine Endora's beliefs. People have testified that she tried to convince Everett to promote her 'gospel' to his many fans. What was her gospel? Well, for example, it was a message vehemently opposed to the Bible's portrait of heaven and hell.

"Endora hated the Bible and organized religion, detested it. Instead, she promoted a different afterlife, one in which every person would 'live again' in some mysterious dream world she labeled the 'Other Side.' Now hear this, Endora cared *so deeply* for this message that it alone, I believe, is what drove her to remain so close to Everett Lester.

"Endora *used* Everett, ladies and gentlemen, to spread her gospel. And yes, for a long time, he was so strung out on drugs and alcohol that he did just that. We don't deny that for a minute. But what Endora did not plan on in those early days was the total transformation Everett Lester would undergo when he became a Christian. And *that*, folks, is when Endora began to turn on Everett.

"Remember Pamela McCracken's words? She overheard Endora warn Everett not to turn on her. 'You do not want me against you!' were Endora's words."

Dooley's arms crossed, and I could hear him groan from twenty feet away.

Boone allowed time for his words to soak in. "We've heard it testified clearly in this courtroom that Endora feared and cursed the day when Everett would become a Christian. Why? Because she had supposedly learned through her psychic powers that he would lead thousands upon thousands of his DeathStroke fans to faith in God. Twila Yonder herself told you that Endora became angry when she was led to believe that Everett would become, in her words, a 'religious zealot.'"

Boone turned and walked slowly toward me, playing the silence.

"Let me ask you a question, a question, unlike Frank Dooley's, to which I do have an answer. Why do you think Endora hypnotized Everett in the middle of a conversation at The Groove recording studio? Why would she do that? Why did she want to try to *impose* her will over him and *make* him smash that rock waterfall? The answer is, she was *testing* her powers. She was seeing if she really could hypnotize my client and make him do things he had no intention of doing in his right mind!"

Dooley shook his head in disgust.

"Folks," Boone said, "this is a lady—a witch of sorts—who made a gun fly into the ocean. That's a fact. She hypnotized Ricky Crazee, and he kicked a powerful drug habit. She made drinking glasses shatter and the hands on clocks spin from across rooms. This is no average case. We've got to get into this woman's mind and think like she did."

Boone was animated now.

"Why did she make up a story to her close friend Twila Yonder about having a romantic affair with Everett? You know as well as I do that this was only a story. Why? Why did she make that up?" He eyed each juror. "Because Endora Crystal was *planning* her own death and the framing of my client for it!"

Chills swept over my body as the crowd erupted.

Dooley's assistants gathered around him like an offensive huddle.

Boone raised his voice and prodded forward. "Endora's goal in life was to make sure Everett Lester never became a Christian; that's the bottom line. And when he did, she made the stark decision that she would give her very life to put him away—in prison or off to the electric chair. She was out to *ruin* his Christian name, to yoke him with a murder rap he did not deserve.

"Ladies and gentlemen, Endora Crystal was evil to the core. And if you're going to make the right decision in this case, you *must* get into her wicked mind and see her death for what it really was: *suicide* with the assistance of an *innocent* man!"

Boone glared at Dooley and took a deep breath as if to pace himself. "Do you understand what she did? Under her bewitching influence, she loaded Everett up with mind-altering, psychotropic drugs—proven to be in his bloodstream at the time of her death. Once Everett was under the influence, Endora used her psychic powers to hypnotize him. Then she sacrificed herself in order to squelch, silence, and ruin Everett Lester's Christian conversion. But it backfired, didn't it? What Endora intended for evil, God is using for good!

"Make it clear." Boone stood next to me, resting a hand on my shoulder. "If you are going to convict this man of murder in the first degree—which is altogether different from second-degree murder, manslaughter, or aggravated assault—you must do so *knowing* without *any* doubt that he is guilty of premeditated—that is, planned...deliberate...set-out-to-do-it...cold-blooded—murder. Ladies and gentlemen, if you can do that, then by all means go ahead and do it. But I doubt there is one person in this courtroom, besides Frank Dooley, who truly believes that."

Judge Sprockett told the court that his goal was to get my case to the jury for deliberation by close of business today.

There was nothing new on Karen. It would be dark soon. I chewed one of the Tums Mary gave me at the break, but it didn't touch the constant burning sensation in my chest.

Frank Dooley had the floor for the last time.

I was surprised to hear him rehash much of his closing argument from this morning. That sat okay with me. Although he had attacked portions of Boone's afternoon argument, he couldn't seem to get around the fact that we'd basically admitted that I killed Endora but had no intention or knowledge of doing so. Boone told me during the break that Dooley must be hating himself for not pursing second-degree murder instead of first.

"People of the jury, circumstances have arisen that you may or may not know about, which may cause you to sympathize with Everett Lester." He looked down, shaking his head and feigning sorrow. "I sympathize as well, believe me. But listen, your remorse and my remorse *cannot* and *must not* have any influence on the decision you make here today. Do you understand?"

He raised both hands toward the jury, drawing the attention of every eye.

"What I want you to do is remember this…" He walked toward me, again pointing his hand at me in the shape of a gun. "Everett Lester is a man of extremes. *Always extremes.* We've been told by more than one witness that Mr. Lester threatened to kill Madam Endora Crystal. He invited her to his Miami high-rise for a séance. *He* was the initiator. *He* was the one who walked to his bedroom dresser to retrieve his loaded .45 caliber Glock. *He* was the one who went back in and pulled the trigger from less than five feet away, killing his innocent lover, Endora Crystal. Oh, yes…extreme!"

Dooley walked directly toward the TV camera. "I don't care what Endora was into; she didn't deserve to die November 11. Listen to me, Everett Lester walked back into the bedroom after shooting Endora, returned the gun to the dresser drawer, and now sits here today thinking he's going to get the same special treatment he's gotten his entire life!

"Let it stop today, people of the jury. It's up to you to draw the line. You twelve are the ones who can tell Everett Lester today—" he turned and pointed his make-believe gun at me—"'You have seen the end of your stardom and your special treatment, Mr. Rock Star.' Get this sick individual off the streets, ladies and gentlemen. Do the extreme. Put this animal where he belongs. *Put him to sleep.*"

Turning to the jury box at 6:40 P.M., Judge Henry Sprockett pounded his gavel. "The case of *The State of Florida v. Everett Timothy Lester* is now in your capable hands." After giving them instructions, he sent the twelve-member jury toward a deliberation room forty feet down the hall from courtroom B-3.

As reporters shouted questions, the dark-skinned juror from the far right side of the jury box walked erectly out of the courtroom, not losing eye contact with me the entire way.

10:55 P.M.

I sat at a large white table beneath fluorescent lights in a midsize conference room two floors up from the jury. Mary and Jerry, Brian and Gray, Karen's parents, and a few other friends and attorneys surrounded me at the table. This would be our headquarters as long as the jury deliberated.

Brian explained that Judge Sprockett ran a tight ship and would likely work the jury long and hard to get a verdict as soon as possible. However, Boone also pointed out that the jury might choose to review and evaluate much of the evidence in the case, which included the testimony of seventy-two witnesses and more than three hundred exhibits, including forensic reports and the infamous .45 caliber Glock semi-automatic pistol.

While talking on his cell phone, Donald entered the room with Della. He punched the phone off and cleared his throat. "They got the surveillance tapes back from the convenience store in Leisure City," he announced, as Jacob and I scrambled to our feet. "It was definitely Zane Bender."

"Was Karen with him?" Jacob asked.

"The store owner didn't see Karen."

Sarah sighed. Mary's hands covered her mouth.

"What did Zaney say…to the owner?" I asked.

Chambers frowned. "Said what a beautiful day it was to be free."

"That's it?" I asked. "What was he buying?"

"Chewing tobacco and gas for the camper. He was in and out in about seven minutes."

"Any more sightings?" Jacob asked.

"Police are looking into what may be several more solid tips. But they're getting a lot of calls—hundreds. Many are either pranks or mistaken identities. They've got a lot to sort through."

"Is there anything else we can do?" Gray asked.

"No," said Chambers. "You can trust me, though, when I tell you Miami PD is going all out on this thing."

"What about the campsites?" Sarah asked sheepishly through red eyes.

"They're busy checking those now, ma'am."

"I've never felt so helpless." Mary put an arm around Sarah.

I walked back and forth behind Mary and Sarah.

Back and forth.

"Can we do something?" Jerry said, with his elbows on the table. "Can we hold hands and pray? Because, I feel like…that's all we can do right now."

★ ★ ★

11:35 P.M.

A tall, gray-haired bailiff with thick glasses pushed the conference room door open and ducked his head in. "Judge Sprockett told the jury to retreat to their quarters for the night. They've been asked to continue deliberating at eight sharp tomorrow morning. Mr. Lester, you will be escorted back to the detention center now. Officers are out here waiting for you."

3:22 A.M.

Sleep wouldn't come.

An occasional wicked laugh rang out from the dark.

I floundered, wide-eyed.

Every now and then, a frightening scream pierced the darkness.

The pending verdict…Karen's kidnapping—they've left me beaten. Alone. Utterly overwhelmed.

It's hot…stifling in here.

And no way out.

I was suffocating in the same desperation Donald Chambers had found me in days ago.

The floor was cold and hard on my knees.

All I could do—literally all I had the strength or presence of mind to do—was scan the small brown Bible that I clutched just inches from my eyes.

Troubles surround me—too many to count!
    They pile up so high I can't see my way out.
    They are more numerous than the hairs on my head.

I have lost all my courage.
Please, LORD, rescue me!
Come quickly, LORD, and help...

Periodically, words poured out of me: *Dear God, this is all in Your hands. Comfort Karen now. Protect her. Please...bring her home. Give us the chance to live together for You. Stop this evil, Lord. Stop it!*

Then I found my way back to the page...

May those who try to destroy me be humiliated and put to shame. May those who take delight in my trouble be turned back in disgrace. Do not delay, O my God...

We had two pots of coffee brewing in the conference room, both caffeinated. The jury had been back in session for an hour and a half. In order to waste some time, I got the idea that Jerry should call his sister, Claudia, in Xenia to find out how Olivia was doing. Jerry talked for a while, then handed the phone to me.

Claudia hesitantly asked my feelings about the upcoming verdict. It was awkward.

"I have no idea." I paced. "There's all kinds of speculation, but I won't play that game. I don't know how it's going to come out... How's Olivia?"

"We've moved her hospital bed to her bedroom. Her condition hasn't changed," Claudia said. "She is fed through a clear plastic tube that attaches to her navel. She stares at the TV most of the day or at the seashell mobile you got her. Sometimes she gazes at the greeting cards taped to her wall or at the birds that come to feast on the bird feeder that's suction-cupped to the outside of her window."

"Do you care for her alone?"

"No. We have a nurse on duty twelve hours a day. She helps change her, feed her, turn her, and hoist her onto her exercise board for physical therapy. Occasionally Olivia laughs or cries for no apparent reason."

Claudia seemed relieved to tell me all of this.

Her husband was at work. Claudia said he now worked overtime almost every day at the fiberglass factory near their home. He was struggling with depression.

Claudia was adjusting to life with a comatose daughter. But remarkably, she had forgiven me. And she began going to a local church, where she was finding friends and newfound peace.

"We've watched every bit of the trial, Everett. Olivia seems fascinated by it. We'll be keeping our fingers crossed."

Police spotted the dark green Arctic Fox camper again two hours ago. It was leaving a campground in Florida City, a small town near Homestead, adjacent to the enormous Everglades National Park.

Karen's dad found out that Miami-Dade police pursued the camper for three miles but lost it when a drawbridge went up and blocked them off. Whether Karen was in the camper or not was unknown.

I was dying inside. I mean, really, my insides, my organs, felt like they were weakening—almost like they were becoming infected or shutting down.

Karen was the one thing in this life I'd ever truly loved...*my rose.*

The thought crossed my mind to just run. To try and sneak away, steal a car, find her... Ridiculous.

The large clock on the wall read 3:42 P.M. The jury had been behind closed doors all day. Sandwiches were delivered to them at 1:30.

This could last weeks.

Various newspapers, pads, wrappers, folders, magazines, napkins, Bibles, coffee cups, and books were scattered across the top of our conference room table. We were all emotionally spent. Gray was asleep on the floor. Although I wasn't allowed to leave the room, Jacob, Jerry, and Donald were constantly in and out, checking with police on what was going on with the search for Karen.

I thought of the black man who stared at me so often throughout the trial. *What did he see? What was he thinking?* Perhaps he'd be the one juror who was vigilant for my acquittal. Or maybe he'd pound that last nail in my coffin.

As I sat here, I passed the time by scribbling some new lyrics. Here's a song called *Release* I envisioned doing as a rock number. I could hear the tune in my head...

There's a place I know oh so well, where I am in control.
It's a cozy place I never want to leave, but then You say,
"LET'S GO!"

Release yourself to the One in charge,
Release yourself tonight.
Release yourself, don't look back,
Everything's gonna be all right!

Do you know the place I'm talkin' about, where you call all the shots?
Well, it seems pretty good from where you sit, but from where He sits, it's not!

Release yourself, He's waiting now,
Release yourself today.
Release yourself, He'll carry you,
Along life's rugged way.

There'll come a day, there'll come a time, when you got
nowhere left to turn.
You'll be all tapped out, all used up, you'll have nothin'
left to burn.

Release yourself,
Release yourself,
He alone can set you free!
Release yourself,
Release yourself,
You were blind, but now you see!

35

Twenty-five thousand people waved their arms back and forth, singing along. Matches, lighters, and cell phones were lit like a zillion stars around the glowing arena. We did one final encore. They loved us. Fireworks exploded. The place went black. Roadies saw us offstage by flashlight.

In the wings, Endora waited. She handed me a bottle of Jack Daniels, put a lit cigarette in my mouth, and we headed toward the dressing room.

"They worship you, Everett," she yelled, laughing. "You are their god."

My body jerked against the carpeted floor.

I opened my eyes and wiped the drool from the corner of my mouth.

Sarah lay on her side near me on the floor of the conference room. She saw me wake up and smiled softly. "Dreaming?"

"Yeah."

"Was Karen in it?"

"No...I wish she had been. It was a bad dream."

"What about?"

"The old days."

"Ah."

"Any word?"

"No. Jacob and Jerry left for a few minutes. I don't know what they're doing." She laughed. "Driving around, maybe. They were going stir-crazy."

"Tell me about it. What time is it?"

"Almost seven-thirty," Sarah said, still lying on the floor. "Boone thinks Sprockett will keep the jury here as long as they'll stay without committing mutiny. They could go till eleven-thirty again."

She sat up, leaned against the wall, and motioned toward the table. "There's a sandwich and chips for you. Gray had it brought in."

"Thanks, Sarah. Where's Mary?"

"Sleeping...over there." She pointed to the other side of the long table.

"I'm not asleep," Mary said from across the room. "Just meditating... That's what my dad always used to say. Remember, Everett? He would take these long, deep naps—snoring and all—and when someone asked him how he slept he would say, 'Oh, I didn't sleep...I was just meditating.'"

We all cracked up.

The hoagie tasted good. I'd barely eaten in days, just had no appetite.

Jacob and Jerry barged in, followed by Donald.

"A family spotted Zaney's camper at a campground near the Everglades." Jerry hugged Mary.

Jacob approached Sarah. "No sign of Karen."

"The cops didn't make it in time," Chambers announced. "He was gone when they got there."

"Bender's either got her in the back of that camper or...I just don't know," Jacob said, as Sarah hugged him and buried her face in his chest.

"Well, it's not going to last," Jerry said. "This thing is all over the networks. The whole state of Florida is watching for them."

The door swung open again.

It was Boone. His posture was straight as a board as he walked into the room, not making eye contact with anyone and taking an enormous breath. "Don't mark my words, but I think we may have a verdict." He crossed to the far side of the room, turned around, and focused on the door.

"Already?" Sarah questioned.

"Just wait a minute." Boone nodded, watching the door.

"What's going on, Brian?" I asked.

Voices...approaching the door. Closer...louder.

The door crept open several inches, and a conversation could be heard. Someone stood just outside. The door opened about two feet, and we saw the gray-haired bailiff there, surrounded by loud noise and turmoil in the hallway. He talked with officers, answering questions and barking instructions.

"Time-out!" he finally yelled to the people outside the door. "Time-out. I'll be back with you in a minute."

He stepped inside our conference room and closed the door behind him. His white, bushy eyebrows raised above his thick glasses. "Ladies and gentlemen, we have a verdict."

Once the bailiff explained what would happen next and cleared out, we quietly and nervously straightened each other's collars and hair and ties. Then we stopped at the door just before leaving, and we prayed.

Even though courtroom B-3 had no windows, it took on a whole new aura toward evening. Somehow the lighting seemed different, almost yellow.

I couldn't recall the courtroom ever being this packed. The usual press boundaries had all but disappeared beneath the sea of bodies, recorders, mikes, and equipment.

Side by side, arm in arm, my "family" sat along the first row, just behind me: Jacob and Sarah, Jerry and Mary, Donald and Della, and Gray Harris.

But someone was missing, and her absence burned at the base of my throat.

Boone's hand clasped mine tightly, and he looked up into my eyes. "Everett, I'm not much of a praying man, but I've been praying for this moment. Good luck."

"Thank you, Brian." I squeezed tighter. "Thanks for everything."

Judge Sprockett glided into the courtroom, black robe wafting behind him.

We were seated.

Just a few formalities.

Judge Sprockett called the bailiff.

The somber gray-haired man approached the bench, handing the judge a white index card.

The bailiff looked directly at me, his face stone-cold sober.

After staring at the card for a good forty seconds, Judge

Sprockett's eyes rose above the card and zeroed in on our table, then shifted to Dooley, who was fixing the jagged white hankie in his left breast pocket.

The judge's head slowly turned to the jury box. As he eyed them good and long, his head nodded up and down several times, almost unnoticeably.

"Ladies and gentlemen," his voice echoed off the silent walls, "a verdict has been reached in the case of *The State of Florida v. Everett Timothy Lester.* The verdict will now be read by the jury foreperson."

It was the calm before the storm, as the bailiff retrieved the index card from Judge Sprockett and walked it directly into the hands of…yes, the black man, the one on the far right. The only juror standing. His eyes were, once again, locked on mine like laser beams.

He took the card from the bailiff and looked at Judge Sprockett.

"Jury, what say you?"

With a fist to his mouth, the black man nodded at the judge and cleared his throat. And then I saw it flash in the yellow light—the silver ring on his middle finger…and the black cross engraved in the top.

"On the matter of *The State of Florida v. Everett Timothy Lester,* we the jury find the defendant, Everett Timothy Lester, *not guilty* on the charges of murder in the first degree."

My knees wobbled.

My eyes felt like they rolled back up into my head.

The gavel cracked.

Rushing and shouting and chaos.

Boone's arms were wrapped tightly around my waist. The family engulfed us.

And the tears came like rain.

★ ★ ★

We were mobbed now.

Reporters and camera crews rammed against us due to pressure from behind.

Gray yelled that a car was waiting.

I just wanted to get out...*find Karen.*

Smiles and laughter and yells of congratulations surrounded us.

We were on our way, pressing forward, moving the scores of people along with us.

A hand tapped hard at my shoulder. I didn't look back, but then the hand grabbed my shoulder, trying to pull me back.

I turned.

The jury foreperson was on his toes, four feet away, stretching his arm out to me, the silver cross ring near my face.

He said something to me, maybe five words, but the noise drowned him out.

Again he spoke, mouthing the words in hopes I could read his lips. But still I didn't understand.

I turned back toward the door and pressed forward.

Have to get out.

But the hand pulled my shoulder once more. And the jury foreperson muscled his way up against me.

I squinted at him, not knowing what he wanted, not really caring.

Then he hoisted himself up to my ear. "I saw Christ in you."

I pulled back and stared at him ever so briefly.

Then I bent down to his ear. "Thank you."

"Go find Karen. *Godspeed!*"

I squeezed his outstretched hand, and he fell away from the pack.

A few feet farther and, finally, a burst of cool air, as we hit the exit and hurried down its white stone steps.

I kept hearing the question, "Everett, how do you feel?" I tried to concentrate on forging ahead. "I just thank God." I looked at the ground, trying to keep my feet moving toward the car. "Now, we're going to find Karen and finish the rest of this story."

More questions pelted me from every direction.

"That's all." I kept a hand on Mary and Sarah as we reached the white SUV.

The sound of the crowd outside was muffled as we shut the doors. Everyone held on to whoever ended up next to them, and most of us had tears on our faces. We smiled and sniffled, but no one said much of anything.

Cameras flashed like crazy outside, and the SUV rocked slightly to the sway of the mob. Then Gray eased away from the Miami-Dade Justice and Administration building. As we were able to accelerate more, it felt freeing to leave courtroom B-3 farther and farther behind.

Gray glanced back at us. "I thought we'd go back to the house and plan our strategy from there.

"Sounds good." I nodded. "Thanks for the car, Gray."

Mary sat next to me in the middle seat, her arm locked in mine. She tried to say something, but instead, could only manage a smile, a shake of her head, and more tears.

From the backseat, Sarah and Jacob reached forward, each with a hand on my shoulders.

It was quiet for a long stretch. The streetlights zoomed past. The trial was behind us. Miles behind us now.

I reached to the front seat and gently rested my hand on Boone's shoulder. He looked back at all of us, with a big grin. "The prayer worked...apparently."

The glass exploded just to the right of my temple.

Screams and cool air filled the car.

In slow motion, I noticed the splintered window next to my head.

"*Get down!*" Boone yelled.

We all collapsed to the floor while Gray crouched at the wheel, raising a bent right arm to protect his head.

"It's a green pickup—a camper!" Boone shouted from low in the front.

I lifted my head just enough to look in the lane to my right.

Crack, crack, cr...cr...crack.

Splinters of glass pelted us, as more of the windows on the right side of the SUV exploded and crumbled in our laps.

"It's him, Gray!" I ducked down again. "It's Zaney."

Everyone was silent as the car rolled on. The girls weren't screaming anymore.

We wanted this monster.

"Is Karen with him?" Gray crouched so low he was barely able to see over the dash.

"She's not in front," I shouted.

"Is anyone shot?" Jacob called out.

A brief silence. We checked each other. "No," I said. "No one's hit. Just cuts from the glass."

"He's dropped back," Gray warned.

"Someone call 911!" Sarah yelled.

"I am." Boone covered his free ear and pressed the cell phone to his head.

"Here he comes again," Gray said as the dark camper picked up speed on the right.

I crouched low, hearing it coming, then peeked... His windows were down. A gun was in his right hand, at the top of the steering wheel.

"Next time he shoots, jam on the brakes and get behind him!" I yelled over the wind.

"I'll try," Gray mumbled, getting down low again.

Now Zaney drove right alongside us. I stuck my hand up in the air to draw fire.

The second Zaney peeled a shot, I slammed into the seat in front of me as Gray nailed the brakes, swerving right. Sarah squealed from the back as the SUV fought to stay on all fours.

"We're behind him." Gray slapped the steering wheel.

"Good! Follow close," Jacob said. "Don't let him get behind us. We'll follow him as long as we have to."

"Did you get the cops, Brian?" I asked.

"Got 'em. They're coming."

"I'm calling Chambers." I pulled my phone from my rear pocket. "Where are we?"

"We got turned around leaving the courthouse," Gray yelled.

"We're now southbound on Route 1," Boone announced.

As I spoke frantically to Chambers, I felt our car slowing, slowing.

"He's up to something," Gray said, as I looked up to see Zaney's brake lights.

Gradually, the camper came to a dead stop, just off the side of the road.

Gray cautiously pulled over to the berm but stayed some fifty feet back.

"He's getting out!" Sarah screamed. "Where are the police?"

No one said anything as Zaney rocked out of the driver's

seat, squinted back at us, slammed his door, and sauntered our way. His long arms hung low at his sides. The gun seemed small in his large right hand.

"Is she in back?" Jacob asked angrily.

"What do we do?" Mary asked.

The silence assured us there was no clear answer.

"If he starts firing, I'm going to mow him down." Gray stared straight ahead.

"We need him alive," I said.

Zaney stopped just past the taillights of the camper. As if he were about to take target practice, he casually spread his legs at shoulder's width, raised his arms in the air, then lowered and locked them out in front of him with the gun at eye level—pointed directly at us.

"Everybody down!" I commanded.

"What do you want me to do?" Gray peeked his head up. "Get out of here?"

I don't know. I don't know. We're so close…

Boom!

The passenger side windshield blew out.

"Ahh!" Boone covered his head as shards of glass rained down on his crumpled body.

"I'm takin' him out!" Gray sent the SUV in motion, its engine roaring to life.

Zaney remained in firing position as we picked up speed, but who…

"*Stop!*" Jacob yelled.

There's someone else…

"It's Chambers! *Stop!*" My body bashed into the seat in front of me again as our brakes locked up and the tires screeched, sending the SUV skidding to a halt.

Ripping open the door handle, I rolled out of the car into the cinders and sprinted toward Zaney and Chambers. Jacob was running, too, and Jerry. Gray stayed back with the girls.

There were sirens now…and blue lights in the sky.

Chambers had Zaney in a headlock from behind, but Zaney lifted him off the ground, whipping him around like a mannequin.

The gun was no longer in Zaney's hand.

Jacob had the door of the camper open and darted inside.

I followed.

"You ain't gonna find nothin'," Zaney moaned as Jacob and I scanned the filthy confine.

I ripped out of the empty camper in time to see Zaney rear backward and plow Chambers into the back wall of the camper, dropping him to the asphalt.

Screams arose from the SUV.

Jerry lunged for the monster next, but Zaney bashed Jerry's face onto his knee, causing him to crumble to the ground.

Pain knifed through my knuckles and up my wrist as I jacked Zaney in the face, then in the stomach with my other fist. But it barely fazed the goon. He grabbed my arm and twisted it like a twig up behind my back and yanked my hair with his other hand.

Boom, boom, boom.

Jerry fired three shots into the air with Zaney's gun, but it still didn't deter him. Instead, he locked his free arm around my neck, practically lifting me off the ground with the arm that was behind me.

Jerry froze with the weapon still drawn on Zaney.

Jacob was limp on the ground, and Chambers lay behind us.

While choking my neck in the crease of his massive right arm, Zaney positioned me fully between him and the gun Jerry now held.

I could hear the frantic squeals of Mary and Sarah nearby.

"You Boy Scouts didn't think I was gonna let your pretty live, now did ya?" Zaney dragged me back several steps. "She was way too dangerous. Had to be snuffed."

"Just tell us where she is, and we'll be on our way," a desperate Jacob gasped from his knees.

"Daddy, that little thing is long gone by now," he cackled. "And you people are next…you and your *crusade for Jesus*."

Zaney's evil laughter boomed into the night as he ratcheted his grip on my neck and yanked my arm higher behind me. I gasped.

"You were right, rock star," he seethed, strangling me. "Endora was sent to stop you, to *ruin you!* And I'm gonna—"

Bang!

An explosion, a flash, and the smell of gunpowder filled the night.

The monster's arms went limp around me. "Ah!" He dropped to the ground. *"Ahhh!"*

I turned to see Donald Chambers, lying by the camper, gun riveted to his hands, arms braced in front of him, still pointing at Zaney.

Writhing, Zaney cradled his fat, bloody calf in both arms. Cops swarmed in from all directions, weapons drawn within two feet of his face.

"Don't shoot!" I yelled. *"Don't shoot.* He's the only one who knows where Karen is."

Media mayhem.

Helicopters hovered with spotlights, and national TV crews, newspaper and magazine reporters, and photographers by the dozen descended like a cloud of locusts on Jackson Memorial Hospital. They converged to find out what could possibly be happening for an encore in the aftermath of my dramatic acquittal in the murder case of Endora Crystal.

Inside a small, stifling-hot hospital waiting room, I'd been pacing, praying, and watching TV reports for the past two hours with Jacob and Sarah, Mary and Jerry, Gray, and Donald.

Meanwhile, seven police investigators, who'd been working diligently on Karen's kidnapping since it happened, were interrogating the wounded but stable Zane Bender at his bedside in a private room just down the hall.

All we knew was that Karen was still missing and Zaney had repeated to detectives that she was dead; he wouldn't say where.

Although I'd pleaded to speak with Zaney, the lead detective in the case—a short, stocky guy named Hardy—refused my request.

Anger tightened my jaw muscles and warmed my cheeks.

Why?

Karen was so good, so pure and innocent. She didn't deserve to die...alone somewhere.

My whole body was tense, shivering...pacing.

Jacob slipped his big arm around my shoulder. "It's going to be okay, you know." He tilted his head to look at me through bloodshot eyes. "Whatever happens, Karen is going to be all right."

I dropped my head, and the emotion from the past week raced to my eyes and nose and mouth. The others gathered close, settling in around me.

Jerry began to pray once more.

Peace descended again.

Okay. You're here. You're here...

Three knocks sounded at the door.

"Mr. Lester," the all-business lead detective interrupted. "I'm sorry. I didn't mean to break anything up..."

I walked over to him.

"We've decided to give you ten minutes with this creep." His eyes fixed on mine. "I'm gonna warn you, though, he may say some things about Karen...ugly things. You must keep your cool. The whole goal is to get a location from him."

"Thank you," I managed, shaking his hand, looking back at the others. "You guys...pray."

Zaney's injured tree trunk leg was in traction, wrapped thick in white tape and gauze. The fluorescent lights from above reflected off the sweat at the base of his fat neck.

"Ha, ha! This is what I've been waitin' for—the headliner!" he said from his hospital bed, which I could barely see beneath his massive body. "I've been holdin' out for you, rock star!"

The other detectives moved in to surround the two of us.

"More than enough time has passed by now, sweet Everett, more than enough." He smirked and made that familiar raspy squeal. "Pretty Karen is certainly no more..."

I sensed Detective Hardy's eyes shift to me, waiting, watching for my reaction.

"Where'd you leave her?" My temper boiled to a rage, yet I fought back tears at the same time.

"Let's see how much faith you have now, you religious fool...now that your *almighty* has allowed sweet Karen to be eaten alive by one of His very own creations."

"Where is she?" Hardy demanded. "In the Glades?"

Zaney glanced at Hardy and turned back to peer at me.

"If you're so sure she's dead, cough up the location," Hardy insisted. "Then we'll leave you alone, let you get some beauty sleep."

"Come over here, choir boy." Zaney sneered at me. "Closer."

I stepped toward him, my legs touching the side of his bed.

Lord, please…lead us to Karen. Make him spill it…

"I wanted to tell you in person," he whispered with a hideous look on his face. "I left your sweet saint—who I became very cozy with—*for the gators.*"

Hardy's hand fell soft on my shoulder as the rage from my entire life was somehow harnessed by an invisible dam.

Instead of borrowing one of the investigators' guns and unloading its magazine somewhere I shouldn't, I attempted to make whatever face Zaney wanted to see in order to keep him talking.

Just keep talking!

"You'll find what's left of her corpse at Everglades National Park. Near Bear Creek campground. In the swamp, tied to a post near a dock."

The investigators guided me out the door, clamor and motion all around me…

"But I can promise you, you're only gonna find table scraps!"

We headed due west, straight into Everglades National Park.

I had never seen such sheer darkness, and the roads were poorly marked.

I was with Jacob, Jerry, and Donald in a dark green Camry that Gray rented and had parked near the ambulance entrance an hour ago. After much pleading, Detective Hardy agreed to let us follow his team's caravan of unmarked cars.

Jacob drove and I sat next to him, with Jerry and Chambers in back. Our windows were down and the noise of the everglades' wildlife sounded almost prehistoric.

Jacob could barely sit still, as we flew through the night.

Lord, don't let it be too late. Please, Father. Please. Let her live.

I looked straight ahead at the marshes, swamps, and wilderness, coming and going in the path of the headlights.

She must have been so scared...

We passed parking areas, picnic spots, and wilderness—deeper and deeper into the marsh we went.

Hurry, hurry...please...lead us.

Stretches of sand-washed road narrowed to one lane and became so dark I felt as if we were in the middle of a jungle. Our task seemed impossible.

Please, God, protect her.

Jacob quietly prayed as he maneuvered the Camry into the eerie depths of this watery nightmare. Jerry nodded in agreement with his prayer as he searched the night outside his window.

"There!" Jacob pointed to a short brown sign. "Bear Creek Campground."

We followed the lead cars another hundred feet and turned right down a slope and into the campground.

As the investigators' cars crept forward, slowly branching out, Jerry pointed way to the right, to a small opening in the trees. "There, Jacob. Pull in there. You see that path?"

"There's barely any road," Jacob said. "Let's stay with the cops."

"I have a feeling," Jerry insisted. "We're close. I know it."

"Go, Jacob. Try it." I pounded the seat. "We can always come back."

Jacob made a hard right away from the pack. Forging through twenty feet of brush, we came upon a sandy path—just two tire tracks of packed-down mud. We rocked and bumped. Branches scraped the Camry, which suddenly dropped a half a foot into the swampy marsh.

The helplessness wanted to overcome me.

"I hope this is right," Jacob cried, shaking his head, peering over the green dashboard light.

"Straight now, Jacob," said Jerry. "Go straight a little farther."

Jacob gunned the engine as the brush that had been scraping the sides of the Camry disappeared.

We pulled into a huge, open expanse where the crescent moon cast a faint glow over a small island of picnic benches—and acres of river grass.

"I'm goin' back." Jacob turned the wheel sharply and punched the gas.

Just as the Camry swung left, my eye caught something in the path of the sweeping headlights.

"Wait!" I strained my head out the window. "*Stop!* It's a dock!"

Most of it was submerged. Only a ten-foot stretch could be seen some one hundred yards in front of us. It was as low as the water and led nowhere, with water at both ends.

We jerked to a stop, and I broke loose out of the car.

When my feet hit the bathlike water, I heard gators slither into the night, at least three or four. The sound of their presence brought tears to my eyes, as I felt myself panicking…crying…bolting through the eight-inch-deep water.

"Karen! *Karen!*"

The headlights behind me projected a huge, eerie shadow ahead. It was me. Racing like a madman through the swamp toward the dock.

Oh God, please, please, please…

I took a wet leap and landed on what was left of the dock. It swayed and almost gave way.

No Karen.

I saw movement in the water: the eyes of alligators sticking up out of the saw grass, illuminated by the headlights.

The car was way back there. I heard Jacob and the others coming.

Quiet.

The water swirled again, but that's not what I heard.

My hands froze in the air, and my head was down, concentrating—trying desperately to separate the sounds of the wildlife from the...singing.

My head spun.

"Heaven's gates to open wide..."

I splashed through the warm water, running as I had never run before, spattering through the prairielike wetlands...to the voice. To the post. To the rope.

To my Karen.

As I knocked on Karen's bedroom door late the next morning, the room was dark, but I could see the bright Miami light gleaming behind the shades.

"Come in," she whispered, rolling over to face me.

"This isn't a dream." I smiled, carrying two cups of coffee. "How are you?"

She smiled slightly and patted the bed, making room for me to sit. I put our coffee on the nightstand.

"What can I do for you, Karen?"

She shook her head and wrapped her arms around my waist.

"Are you okay, baby?" I held her, not knowing what she'd been through, afraid of long-term scars.

She began to cry softly, not wanting to make eye contact.

"I know. Everything's going to be okay now. I'm here."

She sniffed and wiped her nose on the sleeve of her sweat-shirt.

"I was so scared," she whispered. "He meant to kill me."

I tried to calm her with soft strokes through her hair.

"He honestly thought he was doing good…by getting rid of me—*and you*. You were next."

"Don't talk about it now, sweetheart."

"He said if he didn't get you, someone else would." She stared off. "There are thousands like him, he said. They may not know him or Endora, or even resemble them, but they're family. All of them. They're out there. Antichrists. Vessels of dishonor. Out to stop the gospel; that's why they exist, he said."

"He's sick, Karen. But that's behind us. It's over. We're safe now."

"He was…*possessed*." She looked up at me now. "I really believe that, Ev. And your conversion was just devastating to his dark world—and Endora's. I mean, they *lived* to stop you. Zaney was ready to sacrifice himself to do it. He believed that's why he was born! I prayed so hard, the whole time. It's all I could do."

Her arms gripped tight around my waist. "He would talk to himself all the time, laughing and muttering," she cried. "Then in the night, oh, it was so bad. He would toss and turn, moaning and crying and sweating—like he was being tormented."

"I'm so sorry, baby." I hugged her tight. "But now we can start over."

She squeezed me again. "You won." She smiled, revealing the first glimpse of the old Karen. "I knew you would. I just kept praying."

"I was so worried about you, Karen Bayliss."

"I know, and I'm here now, Everett Lester. And you're a free man."

We kissed and held each other for a long time.

The quiet was good. We closed our eyes and prayed our thanks mixed with tears.

Both of us lifted our heads in response to Mary's soft knocks.

She tiptoed in, wearing a pink and purple flowered nightgown. Her eyes and cheeks were red, and she held a Kleenex in one hand, but she was smiling. Smiling gloriously.

"This is for you." She sniffed, wide-eyed, handing me the phone and shooting a teary glance at Karen.

"Hello…Mr. Lester?" came the young lady's voice. "This is Olivia Gilbert calling…from Xenia, Ohio. I wanted you to know…my mother said I should call…"

I fell to my knees, face to the floor.

No words would come. No words.

"I'm okay now. I woke up out of the coma, not long after your verdict was read on TV." She laughed. "My mother almost died. And my father, well, he's a happy man, to say the least. He wants me to tell you—he's sorry…"

EPILOGUE

Dear Reader,

God has been so good to me, a very undeserving man. Karen Bayliss modeled Christ's unconditional love for me, and through her, I was able to learn that I am an accepted, blessed, forgiven child of God! There is contentment in my life now, and security, and acceptance—just like Karen said there would be if I gave my life to Christ.

In order to bring these memoirs to a close and to catch you up on the very latest happenings, allow me to reprint this latest interview I did with *Rolling Stone* feature reporter Steve Meek. The story ran six months after my acquittal.

With warm regards,
Everett Lester
Matthew 11:28–30

Steve Meek (*Rolling Stone*): It's good to see you again.

Everett Lester (formerly of DeathStroke): Thanks for coming. It's good to be with you, Steve.

SM: So much has changed since we last talked. Where do we begin?

EL: How about with my new wife?

SM: Yes, please. Tell…

EL: Karen and I were married in the spring. We had a double wedding with my sister, Mary, and her new husband, Jerry. It was beautiful. The ceremonies were held at a church in Topeka, Kansas, with magnificent stained glass—and Karen's dad officiating.

SM: Karen is a lovely lady. I will note here for the story that we are at one of your homes, this one in suburban New York, where Karen greeted me first today. Now Karen was the young lady who wrote to you throughout the DeathStroke years, correct?

EL: She wrote; she sent gifts; she sent roses. She sent my first Bible.

SM: Is that how your life began to change?

EL: Yeah. I thought she was crazy. But what she did, slowly but steadily, was model the love of Jesus Christ for me. Now understand, her love was not romantic. She hated my music. She was just a girl doing what she thought God was prompting her to do, and that was to write to me—reach out to show me God's love.

SM: Why did she choose you?

EL: *(laughing)* She knew how messed up I was! She has a whole scrapbook of my Siren and DeathStroke days. It's like, she picked the darkest, most demented star she could find and set out on a mission.

SM: Why did you listen? Why did you accept what she had to say, with all the other voices calling out to you?

EL: And there were a lot of other voices! *(laughing)* No, but seriously, Steve. I didn't listen at first. However, I wasn't content. I was miserable. Addicted. Angry. Suicidal even. I needed something money couldn't buy. I needed to be accepted and loved. And the only One who could do that was Jesus Christ… Karen's letters and the Bible helped me realize that.

SM: I must say that, sitting with you here today is remarkable. You have certainly changed. It's dramatic.

EL: That's only because I've accepted the gift of Christ's love and forgiveness, just like you and every person reading your story has the opportunity to do. He's come inside me to live, you see.

SM: I see something.

EL: *He's* who you see, Steve. I promise. It's not me!

SM: Everyone knows you were acquitted of Endora Crystal's murder, but many people do not know what became of the incident in Dayton, Ohio, in which the young girl was injured during a DeathStroke concert.

EL: Olivia Gilbert is the young lady's name, and I'm thankful to say she's doing very well. It's a miracle, really, an answer to much prayer. She's swimming again. Our families have become dear friends. They ended up dropping the charges against me.

SM: There was an aggravated assault charge filed by the Dayton police.

EL: We paid a fine for that, and fortunately, I didn't have to do any time, just community service.

SM: Tell us what your plans are, musically.

EL: Karen and I believe God has plans for us. Part of those plans may involve my music. I've been writing a lot of songs that have to do with this new life I've found. I'm also interested in explaining to people what Christ has done for me—and what He's done for them.

SM: Are you talking about a concert tour?

EL: In some form or fashion, probably.

SM: Let me play devil's advocate here. *(laughing)* Sorry about that.

EL: *(laughing)*

SM: Do you expect your old DeathStroke fans to come out to that tour? I mean, hasn't there been a lot of animosity?

EL: There's definitely been a backlash. Some of the crazy, hard-core DeathStroke fans miss the old Everett Lester and company. But there are thousands of people we've heard from who are intrigued by what's happened in my life. We want to meet those people and share more with them.

SM: Allow me, if you will, to touch on the accident your nephew David was in last year. This seventeen-year-old boy was killed in a head-on car crash. I know he idolized you. How has his death impacted your life?

EL: *(pauses for some time)* A culmination of events led me to Christ. The trauma I caused Olivia Gilbert and her family was one; David's death was another. I am still hurting from that, because I let him and his older brother down. They did love me and my music, and I stood them up time and again… *(pauses)* It's a debt I hope to repay in the days ahead—very soon.

SM: We've talked before about your childhood. I know it was rough. How has your newfound faith helped you cope with that?

EL: When we've talked in the past, Steve, I believed I was destined to be like my father all my life. He struggled with alcoholism, anger, adultery, depression… He actually drank himself to death. And I guess I always just assumed his sins would automatically be passed down to me, and I would have to bear them all my life. But I've got to tell you, dude, Christ changed all that. The lines of those habitual sins have been severed. I'm not saying I don't sin, but I am free, I walk in the power of Christ, and I am forgiven. And that will be the lifeline I hope to pass down to my children.

SM: Are children in the picture?

EL: Karen wouldn't have it any other way!

SM: We've interviewed rock stars on the pages of this magazine who've said they were "born again," said they had been converted to Christianity. Some really mega rock stars. I won't name names. But my point is, they've fallen away. They've gone back to being the people they were before their religious conversions. What about you? Is this going to last?

EL: All I can tell you is that since I surrendered my life to God one day when I was at the end of my rope in a high-rise down in Miami, I became a new person. The old Everett Lester is gone. I'm new—and I've never felt better, never felt like this before. It's better than any drug I ever tried, which is what Karen promised me one time. But to answer your question, yes—it will last, simply because it's not of me. If it was my doing, then it could easily be undone. You get me?

SM: And your desire is to share your new faith with the world.

EL: The problem is, Steve, you say that like it's some heavy burden. But the thing is—it's not! I've been made right with God thanks to Christ. I have new life! Now the Bible says, I should implore others to do the same! That's what Karen did for me! Christ saved her. She became free and found the meaning of life. Then she pleaded with me to do the same, so I could enjoy the same peace and freedom and promise of eternal life she found. She didn't do it out of obligation, but out of love for God…out of the joy that overflowed from her.

SM: If you keep talking like this, you may convince me to be saved.

EL: In that case, how would you like to stay for lunch?

The End…for Now

**Don't miss *Dark Star's*
exciting sequel
Coming May 2006!**

AUTHOR'S NOTE

Dear friend,

What a thrill it is that you chose *Dark Star*. Thank you. I hope you enjoyed reading it as much as I did writing it. There will be more to come in the life of Everett Lester and company, so I hope you'll stay tuned.

Since 1983, I have been writing for a living. First as a newspaper reporter, then a creative director, and for about the past fifteen years, free-lancing as a marketing specialist and magazine feature writer. Several years ago, my work came to a halt. Instead of pounding the pavement to find more, I felt God leading me to write fiction. His words came alive to me at that time: *"What I tell you in the darkness, speak in the light; and what you hear whispered in your ear, proclaim upon the housetops"* (Matthew 10:27).

I had no publisher, agent, promise, or pay—only a burning desire to share the unconditional love of Christ through gritty, contemporary, riveting stories. When you hold *Dark Star* in your hands, realize that between that moment and this, there have been many trials, doubts, fears, rejections, and testings. At times I wondered if the "burning desire" was really put there by God or by me. But the day has come. God is faithful. He wanted this story told.

There are thousands of people like Everett Lester, who are longing for acceptance, because the love of their family, their friends, and this world has let them down; it's been conditional, based on their performance. There are thousands more who are searching for contentment in drugs, alcohol, careers, relationships, material possessions, and even other gods. I know; I've been there myself. Most of us have.

But after all those avenues have been tried, Jesus is still standing at the door, arms outstretched, speaking the warm words He spoke so clearly to Everett Lester: *"Come to Me, all who are weary and heavy-laden, and I will give you rest"* (Mathew 11:28).

My hope is that *Dark Star* made your heart pound with excitement, made you laugh and perhaps cry, carried you away from the cares of this world for a while, and most important, drew you—and those you love—into a deeper understanding of God's grace and unconditional love. If so, to Him goes all the credit.

I enjoy hearing from my readers. You may e-mail me at creston@ crestonmapes.com or write me at: Creston Mapes, c/o Multnomah Publishers, P.O. Box 1720, Sisters, Oregon, 97759. My website is www.crestonmapes.com. Thanks for telling your friends about *Dark Star*.

Fondly,
Creston Mapes

READER'S GUIDE

1. One reason Everett had such a strained relationship with his father was because Vince's love for Everett was based on how well he did, how good he was, et cetera. Have you ever felt like Everett did— trying to perform to earn a parent's or a friend's love? How did that make you feel and why?

2. The "conditional" love Vince had for Everett is the opposite of the "unconditional" love God has for His people—so clearly expressed when Christ voluntarily went to the cross, saying: *"Forgive them; for they know not what they do"* (Luke 23:34). Explain the difference between the conditional love of people and the unconditional love of Christ. Then discuss the personal result of the latter, which Everett felt by the end of the novel.

3. Did you have compassion for Everett at the beginning of *Dark Star*? Why or why not? How did your feelings toward Everett change as the story progressed?

4. Karen's letters to Everett were bold, compassionate, and Spirit-filled. Has God ever led you to step out in such a way to share the gospel with someone? Did you do it? If so, explain what happened. If not, explain what hindered you.

5. Endora despised the thought of one God being the way to eternal life in heaven. How do you explain this concept to others in a way that is kind, patient, and compassionate? Which Bible verses can you share in such instances?

6. Everett admitted that, at one time, he needed to be validated by other people. He said, "The approval of people met a need deep inside me." Can you relate to Everett in this? Or, how have you conquered the inward desire to be a man-pleaser? Discuss.

7. One of the reasons there was great hope for Everett's salvation was because he admitted that he wasn't a good person. Karen helped him understand that he wasn't alone—all people are sinners, and no one can be good enough to earn God's favor. Continuing this train of thought, what other important things did she convey to him about becoming a Christian that he hadn't understood before?

8. What key role did Mary and Jerry play in Everett's journey to salvation? Are you playing that role in anyone's life right now? Explain.

9. Everett eventually realized that if he was going to follow Christ, he must cut the cord with Endora. Letting go of destructive relationships is often a necessary step in the lives of new believers. Has this happened to you? Perhaps it's happening now. Discuss.

10. Karen told Everett, "We're not saved by our own works or cleanness. We're saved only by believing in Him. That's it. End of story." Have you been trying to lead someone to Christ by a more difficult path—one filled with works and burdens? Perhaps you need to confess your error and encourage that person to simply accept Christ's gift of forgiveness and "believe!" Discuss.

11. When Endora tempted Everett to commit suicide—to jump off the building in New York city—what stopped him? Similarly, what stopped Jesus from falling for Satan's temptations when He was in the wilderness? (Read Matthew 4:1–11 or Luke 4:1–13.) How can that same weapon keep you safe in times of temptation?

12. How did Olivia Gilbert's brain injury and David Lester's death eventually help lead Everett to God? What circumstances led you to God? Or, what circumstances in your life now may be drawing you closer to Him?

13. For a while it appeared that Everett would continue to follow in the path of his alcoholic father. What does *Dark Star* show us about the power of God to change the course of our lives—and the lives of our children?

14. In Everett's mind, what was subconsciously so appealing about Karen's letters and conversations? What was it that she conveyed—in word and/or in manner—that helped lead him into a personal relationship with Jesus?

15. Karen wrote to Everett that Satan's goal was to "kill, steal, and destroy." The Bible tells us to be on the alert, because *"your adversary, the devil, prowls around like a roaring lion, seeking someone to devour"* (1 Peter 5:8). What areas of your life are potential "strike zones" for Satan? It's good to know these areas, to discuss them, and to be on the alert.